Maggie Ford was born in the East End of London but at the age of six she moved to Essex, where she has lived ever since. After the death of her first husband, when she was only twenty-six, she went to work as a legal secretary until she remarried in 1968. She has a son and two daughters, all married; her second husband died in 1984.

She has been writing short stories since the early 1970s.

Also by Maggie Ford

*The Soldier's Bride*

# Maggie
# FORD

# A Mother's Love

EBURY
PRESS

1

First published as *The Angry Heart* in 1995 by
Judy Piatkus (Publishers) Ltd

This edition published in 2014 by Ebury Press, an imprint of Ebury Publishing
A Random House Group Company

Copyright © 1995 Maggie Ford

The Random House Group Limited Reg. No. 954009

Addresses for companies within the Random House Group can be found at:
www.randomhouse.co.uk

A CIP catalogue record for this book is
available from the British Library

The Random House Group Limited supports The Forest Stewardship
Council® (FSC®), the leading international forest-certification organisation.
Our books carrying the FSC label are printed on FSC®-certified paper.
FSC is the only forest-certification scheme supported by the leading
environmental organisations, including Greenpeace. Our
paper procurement policy can be found at
www.randomhouse.co.uk/environment

Printed and bound in Great Britain by Clays Ltd, St Ives plc

ISBN 9781785032172

To buy books by your favourite authors and register for offers visit:
www.randomhouse.co.uk

# Part One

## 1894

# Chapter One

Beyond the lace curtains a wet April Saturday was drawing in early. Hackney Road was a clog of traffic from end to end, horse droppings churned to mud by rain, hooves and wheels. People crossing the road dodged erratically between hackney carriages and buses, everyone bent on getting home to make the most of one day of rest before Monday and the start of another working week.

The rumble of traffic and the shouts of paper boys intruded insistently into the quiet room. Mary Wilson drew in a shuddering breath, fingers to her lips to compose their trembling, and turned from the window to her daughter huddled in the high-backed leather armchair. The girl had hardly moved since being led there after her husband's awful accident several hours ago. And them married hardly a year.

Mary compressed her lips and said yet again, 'Harriet, I think you must come home with me and your father.' Harriet Porter didn't reply but Mary went on as though she had. 'You can't stay here after what's happened. In your condition too.' There was no response. If anything, the girl crouched lower into herself, slim, delicate fingers worrying at her beige serge skirt, crumpling it into tight folds, creasing them with small convulsive movements, the auburn head bent to the task as if that and nothing else was her sole intent in life.

She hadn't lifted her head once, not even to sip the tea that was now cold in its cup, the milk a thin pallid film on the surface, as pallid as that small and pretty young face.

Mary Wilson went and plucked a taper off the mantel-piece, merely for the want of something more positive to do, and stooped to light it from the low fire in the grate. Reaching up over the brown chenille-covered parlour table, she drew down the fine chain dangling from the gas lamp above, her small stature only just allowing her to reach it with fore and middle fingers, and applied the taper. The mantle gave a tiny plop and hissed into greenish life, growing quickly white and brilliant beneath its cream glass shade.

The dusk chased back to the windows, Mary swished the heavy drapes together and came to sit opposite Harriet. Her small face, unusually smooth for a woman of forty-eight, threatened to pucker a little as she felt her daughter's grief. The girl looked so wan . . . so completely dazed. She hadn't even cried. It would have released so much of the pain there inside her if she had, but she just sat numbed and dazed. Grief could be so cruel.

'They'll be bringing Will back on Tuesday morning. Till then, I think you ought to stay with us.'

Still nothing. Not even a twitch. A small bubble of annoyance rose up inside Mary, unexpected and unbidden. It was there in her tone before she could check herself.

'Harriet, are you listening?'

The unaccustomed sharpness in her mother's voice

penetrated Harriet's numbed brain. She gave a violent start, and became abruptly conscious of her surroundings as if seeing them for the first time. The prints and photos tilting from their long cords on the walls looked unfamiliar. The clock under its glass dome on the mantelpiece, the ornaments also under glass – wedding presents to her and Will last July – those on the whatnot too: none held any meaning for a moment. The aspidistra fanning out of its blue glazed pot, another wedding gift, on the tall oval table in front of the drawn curtains, looked like a distant forest. The fire, lit for her sake despite this first week in April being warm . . . she couldn't remember it being lit or who had lit it. And in front of her was her mother's small face, sorrow-pinched but demanding an answer from her. She had to say something. But it was hard to make any sound come.

'I'll be all right here,' she managed finally, her voice quavering.

She saw her mother go disapprovingly giraffe-necked under the high collar of her black dress. Already in mourning, she must have changed the moment Mr Hardy from the oil and candle shop next door brought the news of Will's death. The thought, entirely detached from what had happened, of her mother hurrying to dress in the appropriate colour of mourning despite the intensity of the shock she had received, brought a ghost of a smile to Harriet's small oval face, though the grey eyes remained blank. Trust Mum to have everything in its place no matter what.

'Don't be silly. Of course you won't be all right.'

It was the tone her mother had used on her when she was a child. But she wasn't a child now. She was twenty years old and married – or had been until . . . how long ago? Minutes? Hours? Harriet's smile faded.

'I want to stay here.' Part of her wanted desperately to go with her mother, to be as far away from this house as she could and never return. But at her parents' home, with her mind still confused, still shaky from shock, who knew what she might say to incriminate herself?

It was all coming back, leaping into perspective, stark yet still unreal: the crack Will's head had made as it struck the newel post at the foot of the stairs; his body sprawled below her in the narrow hall, head jammed against the door to his printer's shop, feet under the cane table against the opposite wall. It had happened so quickly. He'd been gripping her arm, pushing her ahead of him up the stairs to the bedroom. She could still hear herself, pleading.

'No, Will, please – not like I am. I can't!'

His voice had been harsh. 'Bugger you can't!'

He had let go of her to swing an arm across. Shielding her face from the backhander, her hand on his chest to fend him off, she had heard him cry out, seen his arms reach out for a hold that wasn't there. His large handsome face had been so amazed, his blue eyes fixed on her in surprise, in horror.

But she couldn't have pushed him, a big strong man like him, her a slip of a thing and eight months pregnant at that. His foot must have slipped off the top step. She couldn't have pushed him. But if she had . . . If she had, then she had killed him. If she blurted it out then God alone knew what would happen to her.

She'd said nothing to the police about Will forcing her upstairs to satisfy his lust after an extended lunchtime drink with colleagues over at the Queen's Arms; she'd merely told them that she'd been getting his tea. A smell of bloaters had borne that out. They had accepted her suggestion that he must have lost his footing – drunk, of course; the reek of port and brandy was still in the air – had even commiserated with her, a tragic young widow, heavily pregnant, with no man now. Were they to know . . .

'I want to stay here.' Fear made her tone sharp and Mary gave a shuddering sigh of exasperation.

'I can't force you. If that's what you want, I'll stay with you.'

'No.'

'I can't leave you here alone.'

'I'll take the tincture the doctor left, the laudanum. I'll sleep.' Her voice sounded flat, lifeless. She passed a hand across her forehead. 'I'm tired. You go now, Mum. Come back first thing. I can't think now. I don't want to think . . .'

Mary leaned forward and took her daughter's icy hands between her own. 'Your father will see to all the arrangements. Mrs Hardy next door said she'll make sandwiches for everyone to come back to after the . . .' She broke off, tears glistening in her grey eyes. 'It's going to be an awful ordeal for you, Harriet, like you are. If only I could take this burden off you. To think he'll never see his child, poor Will.'

Her grip on Harriet's hand tightening convulsively, Mary was about to draw her poor grieving daughter to her small bosom when voices and the heavy creak of her husband's tread on the stairs stopped her.

The burly figure of Jack Wilson came into the room, with Mrs Hardy close behind. He already wore a black band on his arm, the conventional badge of mourning, but his manner was as bluff and forthright as always as he looked at his daughter and correctly interpreted her set expression.

'Not changed her mind then? Mrs Hardy has kindly offered to stay if she needs someone with her. Don't like to say it, but I'll have to go soon. My men are still waiting for their week's wages. The boys can wait till they get home.'

A cabinet maker with a small but thriving business, he employed both his sons as well as one French polisher and one joiner. His thick greying brows drew together as he eyed his daughter. His voice grew forceful in a final effort to persuade.

'Look here, Harriet, do as your mother says. It's not as if there's no room for you. Your sisters are married with homes of their own, and only John and George are at home now – the house is big enough.'

The house in Approach Road to Victoria Park was three-storied with a basement for servants. In fact the Wilsons employed two servants: a cook and a maid of all work. Despite being in London's East End, the area had boasted a grander aspect only a few years previously. Its fine terraced houses had been built for the upper middle class who had factories and businesses conveniently near to the London docks, but as the poorer classes had spread further east, the rich had moved out, leaving their large houses to slightly lesser beings: the lower middle class of shopkeepers, smaller businessmen and bank clerks. Now Harriet's and both her sisters' rooms at the top of the house stood vacant.

'You know you're welcome . . .'

'I'm sorry, Dad!' She stopped him in desperation. 'I want to stay here. I want . . .' How could she tell them what she wanted and why?

'I'll keep an eye on 'er,' Mrs Hardy said quickly, her Cockney accent earnest. 'I'll stay with 'er till it's bedtime. I'm only next door. She can give me a key an' all she 'as ter do is bang on the wall an' I'll be in like a shot.'

It was settled. Harriet knew only relief as her cold cheek – it felt icy even to her – was finally kissed, tearfully by her mother, awkwardly by her father, before they both departed with obvious misgivings about leaving her virtually on her own.

Left alone with her, Mrs Hardy became attentive. The girl was her charge now. She was determined to comfort.

'A nice cup of tea, luv,' she decided. The girl was so young. And having a baby after losing a husband hardly bore thinking about.

Emma Hardy had eight children – all living, all married, except for the youngest. She had a good husband, enough money coming in from the shop over which they lived. Nothing in life to regret. But for the grace of Gawd . . . she thought, then shivered superstitiously. Even thinking about it might direct some of this poor thing's plight on to her.

'Yes, a nice cup of tea,' she repeated, collected the cold

pot and used cups and hurried off downstairs with them. Amazing how much tea's needed when trouble's around, she thought as she put the still warm kettle back on the kitchen range. In no time at all she was back upstairs bearing a tray with clean cups and saucers and the refilled teapot.

Harriet hadn't moved. Emma had to put the cup between the girl's cold hands before Harriet looked up, startled. Sitting in the chair vacated by Mrs Wilson, Emma studied her as she sipped her own tea. The cheek bore a faint yellow bruise, an earlier wallop from that pig of a husband. Such a fresh young cheek. A sigh filled Emma's skinny chest. Fifty-five years of East End smoke having sallowed and wrinkled her own skin like a kipper, she regarded the younger face with envy.

The girl still looked numbed and white, but beneath the pallor the healthy glow of growing up in the cleaner air around Victoria Park still showed. Quite well off. The father employed several men in a small furniture factory in Old Ford Road, she'd been told. It was beyond Emma Hardy's comprehension what it must be like living by the park, which was every bit as long as Hyde Park and nearly as wide. People went there for picnics. She'd taken her own kids in her time. All that greenery away from the soot and the grime – it was as near to being in the country as you could get without having to take a train. Hackney Road was a bit of a comedown for Harriet Porter after growing up by the park, lucky girl. Not lucky now, though. Emma frowned.

'Drink yer tea, luv.'

Such a pretty young thing. Porter hadn't appreciated what he'd had. He'd been well off enough with his printing business, but he had no breeding. *She* had breeding. You could see it in those fine cheekbones, the well-spaced eyes, the composed lips – well, usually. Nice-spoken, too: vowels flattened like most East Enders, none of your plum in the mouth accent, but she didn't drop her aitches and t's, nor did her people. That in itself put her a cut above others.

A crying shame to see that shy smile vanish in the short time she had been married to Porter. Incredible how a man so charming outside his home could be a beast inside it. It wasn't just the drink – he'd had a nasty streak somewhere in him. Well, she was free of him now, poor soul. But left on her own with a baby on the way, it was a crying shame, that was what it was.

She saw the fingers tighten convulsively around the cup. The lips quivered. Harriet bent her head hastily. A lock of auburn hair had come loose from the thick bun on top of her head. It fell forward, hiding her face. As the shoulders heaved, Emma came to sit on the hard arm of the chair, drawing the girl to her.

The woman's bones digging into her young cheek, Harriet buried her face in that narrow shoulder and wept as she couldn't have done on her mother's shoulder. A neighbour, an outsider, Mrs Hardy heard only the sound of distress, but Harriet's mother would have sensed little grief in that thin, high weeping. While grief racks the body to its very depths, tearing the bereaved to shreds, fear carries a different sound. She had aided Will's death and, dead as he was, he'd reap retribution. How, she didn't know, but she felt instinctively that he would, and it was fear, not grief, that brought the tears.

Holding her, Mrs Hardy began to talk. Talking, she maintained, was always good for grief.

'There there, luv. I know 'e 'ad his faults. I've 'eard you two going it. And what man don't raise 'is fists now and again? Their answer to everythink if you ask me. My Bert now, 'e tried it once. Blacked me eye for me. But I put 'im right, I did. When 'e got into bed, into the bedroom I went. With a broom. I gave 'im such a walloping with the hard end, I did. Up against the wall, 'e was, 'e couldn't get out of bed. Bashed 'im black and blue I did. I said, "You touch me again and I'll make you so scared to go to sleep you'll mess yer blinking nightshirt." Couldn't do it now, of course. Too old for that. But 'e never did touch me again, not from that day on. A good 'usband ter me.'

What was she thinking of? What the girl needed was something nice said about her husband, not her rattling on about hers.

'But your Will was good in other ways,' she hastened. 'You didn't want for anything. Nice clothes on yer back and 'e never let you go 'ungry. Liked 'is drink, of course, but not like some as drink every penny of it away. No, 'e was a decent enough bloke that way, even if 'e was a bit quick with his 'ands. But you loved 'im fer all that, I know, and ter lose 'im . . . 'E certainly didn't deserve an accident like that – a big fine strong man like 'im, in 'is prime. A wicked shame, that's what it is.'

Wicked shame? Mrs Hardy's reedy voice going on

– what did she know of wicked shame? Harriet wanted to laugh amid her tears, except that it would have become hysterical. What she'd done would go with her to her grave; she was condemned to life imprisonment with no hope of release. The thought beat inside her head in silent rebellion: 'You don't know, you silly old fool. I killed him. He drove me to it, that's how decent William Porter was. I'm glad he's dead.'

Her throat hurt from crying, and her nose was blocked up. Pushing Mrs Hardy away, she fished a hanky from her cuff and blew into it, then with a drier spot dabbed her eyes. The action stabilised her and she felt a little better. She gazed mutely ahead, her mind wandering along a path of its own.

She'd first met Will when he'd come to their home with some circulars her father had ordered. She'd been bowled over by Will's stature and handsome looks, and a little in awe of him, for at twenty-eight he was much older than her. He'd spoken of having no time to think of marrying since inheriting his father's business, and she had thought that commendable. She'd been flattered when he'd asked to see her again, and sorry for him when she learned that his mother was also dead.

When he finally went to her father and asked for her hand, she was already in love and the quick temper that occasionally darkened his wonderful blue eyes only made her love deeper. A man shouldn't be timid or irresolute if he was to be the protector of his future wife and children. But as their wedding day drew nearer that temper was very often directed at her. Vague doubts began creeping in that

Will wasn't quite as admirable as he had first made himself
out to be.

Everyone dismissed her doubts as pre-wedding nerves.
Family and friends had been invited, a carriage and pair
hired to convey her to St John's Church in Cambridge
Road, her beribboned wedding dress of cream satin completed, the reception arranged – how could she bow out
on the basis of some vague premonition? It was silly, even
she had to admit. Despite his hot temper, Will was a good
catch. As Mrs Hardy said, every man had his faults. If only
she had known then just how deep Will's faults went.

Then again, had it been her fault? Had her inability to
cope with her marriage provoked him? Unused to rows
or violence in her own family, her instinct had been to
cringe before those rages of his. Had the cringing made
him angrier, more violent than he might have been? Had
she stood up for herself, like Mrs Hardy, might things have
been different? But then what about the intimate side of
marriage? The shock of that? She knew little of men but
she was sure they couldn't all be so endowed with the
insatiable sexual drive Will had possessed. Every night,
drunk or sober, often during the day too, he expected her
to be the receptacle of his overriding lust, even well into
her pregnancy, and woe betide her if she complained or
tried to resist. That day she had resisted, with horrifying
consequences.

Tears clouded Harriet's vision. She had never told her
parents what he was really like. It would have upset them
dreadfully. She would explain a cut lip or bruised cheek
as accidents, or would keep away from her parents until

her injuries had healed. For eight months she had suffered alone. Now he was dead and there was no one she could tell what had happened to ease the burden that swamped her.

All she had gone through, all she had still to go through – the agony of having Will's baby, the child she could only hate because it was his, conceived in fear and pain – engulfed her like a wall of water breaking over her head.

Mrs Hardy, totally misconstruing the renewed spasm of weeping, broke off talking to pat the heaving shoulders.

'There, there, luv. You have a good cry. Do you good. And look, yer tea's gone all cold. I'll pour out some more and put in lots of sugar for yer. It 'elps soothe away all that shock and grief you must be feeling. To tell the truth, I could do with another cup meself.' She lifted the cosy and felt the smooth brown surface beneath. 'Yes, pot's still nice and 'ot.'

She took the cup from Harriet and refilled both, ladling three spoons of sugar into each. Then, sitting herself down, she continued her homily, convinced that what that poor girl needed was a bit of comfort and advice.

To Harriet, sitting benumbed, Mrs Hardy's voice sounded strangely distant, and the words blurred until they became a continuous, meaningless stream.

# Chapter Two

The funeral was set for eleven in the morning at the City of London Cemetery. Harriet was dreading it.

Will had been brought home the day before, and she'd had a dreadful night. This morning she totally lacked direction. Everything needing to be done had been done. The woman who took in her washing on Wednesdays had sent her son round for it on Monday instead, mindful of the tragic situation. Her mother had tidied round the day before, while her father had dealt with all the funeral arrangements. Mrs Hardy was organising ham and tongue sandwiches – refreshments for the mourners on their return from the cemetery.

Until the mourners arrived then, there was nothing for Harriet to do but to sit and wait, Saturday's events churning over and over in her head until she was sure she'd go mad. Upstairs Will's body lay in its coffin on trestles in the silent chilly parlour, the fire unlit for obvious reasons. The thought of it there – stiff in Sunday best for relatives and friends to pay their respects – terrified Harriet.

Some had already visited the day before – 'Looks like he's asleep, don't he?' The remarks had been meant to console, and she had nodded, letting them think she would

spend her last night with him, at his side as a grieving widow.
But nothing would have induced her to go near him. Rigid
in the bed she'd shared with him in life, she'd had fearful
nightmares, dreaming that he got up and stood over her, his
blue eyes staring down at her. She'd woken up to her own
cry, bathed in sweat, terrified to go back to sleep. On the
Saturday she had slept like a log, drugged by the laudanum.
But this last night, it was as if her mind had suddenly been
revived. And what of the following night and all the nights
to come? Would he always come back to haunt her?

She was up by five, glad of the dawn chorus of rumbling
traffic as London prepared itself for a new day. Putting on
a black blouse and skirt let out to accommodate her bulge,
she twisted her hair up in a bun, then washed at the sink.
By the time she had made some tea and was sitting with it
at the kitchen table, the clock on the mantelshelf still only
registered a quarter to six. Hours before anyone arrived.
Hours on her own. She had to find something to occupy
herself with.

Six o'clock found her filling saucepans from the water
tap then emptying them into the seldom used copper in
the stone scullery, an unaccustomed task with her laundry
normally sent out. She knew enough to add soda and
parings from a bar of yellow soap. Having got the fire
alight, after a fashion, she pushed in the shirts Will would
never wear again, a few towels and some bed linen that
was still clean. It would probably be an hour and a half
before they began bubbling beneath the wooden lid, but
that would be an hour and a half more gone by. Well before
then she was restive again.

Plunging a copper stick into the suds, she hooked up a sheet and began feeding it through the mangle. Waterlogged, the weight tugged on her stomach muscles. Steam rose in clouds, condensing on the cream painted brick walls as she threw her weight against the wrought iron wheel of the mangle, its wet handle slipping in her grasp.

A heavy sensation deep in her stomach made her pause. Leaving the sheet half strangled between the wooden rollers, she made her way to the closet at the end of the yard. For several minutes she sat but the sensation faded, leaving only vague discomfort.

Back in the scullery, she contemplated the mangle. She shouldn't be straining herself with the baby due in three weeks. Not that the baby mattered. If it was stillborn, there would be nothing of Will to haunt her, would there? But she didn't want to harm herself.

'I need another cup of tea.' Spoken aloud, the words accentuated the silence in the house, reminding Harriet of the corpse upstairs. She shuddered and went into the kitchen, hands on her back to ease the odd feeling that still lingered.

'Mornin', Mrs Porter. You there?' A gravelly voice from the door of the passage leading to the yard made her jump violently.

She collected herself and called, 'In here,' thanking God for another presence in this silent house. The round face of Will's journeyman, Bert Higgins, appeared at the kitchen door, the rest of him hidden but for one hand worrying his chin in a gesture of uncertainty.

'I thought I'd just toddle round, pay me respects to Mr Porter, if that's orright?'

'Yes, of course.' She was feeling human again. She filled the kettle, put it on the range. 'I'm sorry about all this, Mr Higgins. You losing three days' pay this week.'

'Oh, that's all right, Mrs Porter. I ain't got no grumble. After what you said on Monday, puttin' me full time instead of the part time Mr Porter allowed when he was ali . . . was me employer.'

'I need extra help now.' She tried to sound grief-stricken.

'It's bin a real godsend . . .' He stopped abruptly. 'Oh, not your poor 'usband goin', Mrs Porter. I mean the extra money . . .'

'How many children do you have, Bert?' she changed the subject.

'Eight. One married, seven still at 'ome. But what I meant . . .'

'You do understand, Bert, about losing three days' pay?'

'Understood, Mrs Porter.' Emerging fully from behind the door, his clothes wafted a musty smell towards her. 'Mr Porter was good ter me. But with 'im working as well, I only ever expected part time and . . .'

'As I said,' she cut in again. The kettle was starting to steam gently. She didn't want to offer him tea. Employers didn't do that sort of thing and she was now an employer. It felt daunting. 'I need the help now, knowing nothing about printing. If you want to go up . . .' She fished out a hanky, held it to her nose. 'I'd go with you, but for the stairs.'

'Of course.' He took in her condition with honest

agreement. 'I won't stay but a minute, Mrs Porter.' The door closed quietly.

'Coo-ee! Harriet dear? Her mother's voice, quiet yet forceful, came at the back door almost immediately after Bert had disappeared upstairs.

Harriet stood up as her mother came into the kitchen, hurrying forward to take her daughter to a bosom too neat to meet the current notion of what constituted a fine figure. Buckram and frilling sewn on to undergarments did their best, and larger than usual leg-of-mutton sleeves helped the chest's proportions, if not her small height.

'Your father's paying off the cabbie,' Mary said, releasing her hold. She regarded Harriet with mingled severity and concern.

'You know, you should have come home with us. Not to even to let us stay here with you . . . Grieving's one thing, Harriet, but you mustn't wallow in it. Not with the little one on the way. How did you sleep?'

'Not bad,' Harriet lied. The worst thing she could think of was to have had her parents sighing over her, her having to force the tears for their benefit. Even now, knowing what she had done made her go all shaky.

Hat and coat hung on the cane hallstand, Mary took it on herself to reach down cups and saucers from the shelves beside the kitchen range. Emptying the teapot, she lifted the boiling kettle with a padded woollen holder around its iron handle and warmed the pot, casting Harriet a sad look as she measured fresh tea into the pot.

'I couldn't stop thinking about you all night, with your poor Will there in the next room, and how you must be

feeling with him so near yet so far. I still can't believe
what happened. One year. Lord knows he'll be as far away
tomorrow as he'll ever be, my poor love.'

Thank God. Harriet smothered a sigh of relief.

Mary paused, teapot half filled, listening. 'What's that
sound?'

'Dad,' Harriet said absently. Jack Wilson's heavy tread
made the passage floorboards creak like creatures in pain.

'No.' Mary Cocked an ear. 'Someone's moving about
upstairs.'

'Oh, our journeyman.' Automatically Harriet used the
plural pronoun.

Under the high jet-beaded collar of her mourning black,
her mother had gone turkey-necked with disapproval. 'You
mean your journeyman's up there – alone? Harriet, he's a
common employee! Will is there for friends and family.
Not common *employees*. How long's he been there?'

'Only a few minutes.' Harriet poured the tea, her hands
shaking so that it slopped into the saucers. She felt ill
envisaging the next three hours, trying to feign grief before
her mother's pitying gaze.

Mary seated herself at the kitchen table while Jack
came in and stood with his back to the range. He frowned,
like Mary, faintly annoyed.

'I'll give him another half minute then I'm up there to
turf him down,' he muttered, stirring his spoon round in
his cup noisily and with purpose. 'Improper. I take it he
realises he won't be needed the rest of the week, with you
in mourning? After that, we'll see.'

Harriet wasn't sure whether to be glad or annoyed that

her father was virtually taking over. 'There's an order,' she said hastily. 'Posters wanted by Friday. I said he could come in Thursday and Friday and I've put him on full time at thirty-two shillings a week from now on.'

'You what?' Jack choked on his tea.

'I do need him. He's a good worker and he was very grateful.'

Jack's business sense flipped over in disbelief. Beneath his mourning black coat, his corpulent stomach trembled as he paced the linoleum between the kitchen table and the range.

'I bet he was! And you must be tuppence short of a shilling. Why'n't you speak to me before committing yourself like that? Cut it by five bob before it goes too far.'

'I can't,' she said, awkward and inadequate in this new role of a woman alone in a man's world. 'I can't go back on my word.'

Mary allowed her neck another disparaging stretch. 'You should remain closed the whole week – a time like this. And you shouldn't be worrying about business matters in your condition either. Women aren't meant for that sort of thing.'

'What sort of thing?' Defiance made Harriet's tone sharp, evoking corresponding terseness from her mother.

'A woman's place is in the home with her husband and children.'

'I haven't got a husband, have I?'

'More reason to've asked my advice, Harriet.' Jack's heavy brows drew together in bluff sympathy. 'Paying employees more than they're worth – typical female approach. Will wouldn't've had it.'

Harriet's defiance hadn't diminished. 'Will's not here now to have anything. Or have you forgotten?' She heard her mother gasp but Jack retained his composure, concerned only for his daughter's wellbeing.

'Your mother's right, Harriet. You shouldn't be worrying about business matters. You can't say Will hasn't left you comfortably off. My advice is to put the business into the hands of a firm of auctioneers who'll get you the best price for it. With you living on upstairs with just rent to pay, if the money's invested properly, it'll last you years.'

'Or until you marry again, eventually.' Her differences with her daughter shelved, hope glowed in Mary's grey eyes. Harriet was still young and so very pretty. There was every likelihood:

Harriet's eyes began to brim over at all she'd had to put up with from Will. 'If keeping house, having children and being under a man's thumb is all there is to marriage, I never want to marry again. As for having babies—'

She broke off, choked by tears. Conceived in pain, the baby would be born with even more pain. She knew how near she was to spilling out a confession of Will's callous indifference to her tender virgin state on their wedding night, how she had cried out in pain as he had viciously entered her for his own satisfaction. She wanted to shout at them, 'I don't want his brat! I hope it's born dead.' But she didn't.

Her mother had given another gasp at what she'd already said, her teacup clinking sharply on to its saucer.

Harriet was being quite impossible. It was grief, of course. She could be forgiven.

Mr Higgins came down and, seeing his new employer's parents there, beat a hasty retreat. After he'd gone, Harriet sat by the kitchen range while Mary went to rescue the washing from the cooling suds. The ache in her lower back had become heavier. The warmth from the range penetrating the heavy black skirt helped to soothe it, but the weight within her distended stomach was an inexorable reminder of what lay ahead. Even though Will was dead, the pain and the degradation he had brought her would live on – the existence of his child would ensure that.

No one understood. Clara and Annie's marriages were happy. Fully occupied with tending their children, they could count on their husbands to support them. They had no fear of the future. Even her brothers, not yet married, employed by their father, had no need to fear it. His business would be theirs one day. How could she, a young widow with a baby, keep a business running, even if she wanted to? Better take her father's advice. Sell it.

Her mother returned, drying her hands. Harriet got up and took the cups to the sink. She was still dwelling on her dismal future when a raw twinge, expanding outward like a twisted knife wound, stabbed out all other thoughts, exploding panic inside her. She clutched the sink.

'Mum!' Her voice was a high squeak. 'I've got such a pain . . .'

For a second her mother's expression was as alarmed as her own, the unspoken question arcing between them, but Mary managed to smile.

'It's not that, dear, there's three weeks to go yet.'

'But it hurts!' The saying that a woman carried her own coffin with her during pregnancy came unbidden to Harriet's mind, and she remembered all the stories of women dying in premature childbirth. An aunt, her mother's youngest sister, had died that way. She didn't want to die. Didn't want to join Will in hell. She'd had dreams . . .

'It must be the shock of losing Will, that's all.' Mary sat her down, soothing her, while Jack, who had gone very white, looked on with some embarrassment.

Mary chewed her lip, thinking hard. 'It can't be, not on the day of the funeral! Someone must go for the doctor. I can't. And you, Jack, you have to be here when everyone arrives. Go and ask that Mrs Hardy if she can go. *Now*, Jack!' as Harriet gave another squeal. He jumped as though scalded, hurrying off swiftly for a man of his size.

Mrs Hardy was in within seconds, clutching a thin roll of oiled cloth, the sort used for kitchen tables and shelves.

'Something to pop on 'er bed so's it won't get stained,' she said. 'Pity we can't let 'er go upstairs in the parlour. Not with 'er poor husband lying up there. Terrible thing, never to see 'is little'un. I'll get my May to run for Doctor Rubin and Mrs Mason. Good midwife, that one. Yer daughter'll benefit from 'er.'

Mrs Hardy was talking as though Harriet wasn't there, but Harriet was in no mood to care, being more concerned by the thought of May as a messenger. Mrs Hardy's youngest was eighteen but definitely lacking. May was usually to be seen sitting behind the counter smiling at nothing in particular while her mother served customers with candles or kerosine or gas mantles. Harriet didn't give much for her chances of getting a message to anyone, least of all a midwife and a doctor.

Mr Wilson beat a hasty retreat to wait for the mourners, and the two women went upstairs. Left alone, Harriet listened to their footsteps going back and forth above her in the bedroom, willing them to come down to be with her before the next pain came. When it did come, her shriek brought them to her side in seconds. Mrs Hardy took her hand.

'There, there, luv. We're getting you upstairs and into bed. See, it's not so bad. Up you come.'

Hoisted to her feet, with Mrs Hardy's arm around her waist and her mother holding her hand, Harriet was guided up the narrow stairs. As they went, she was dimly aware of her father opening the front door to Aunt Sarah, the first of the mourners.

The midwife took her time, arriving seconds behind the hearse to find the hall and kitchen full of people talking louder than normal so as not to hear the bereaved widow in labour above them.

Since the bearers were handing the coffin downstairs with their customary reverence despite the howls from the bedroom, Mrs Mason's large bulk had to wait for it to pass before going on up. Already put out by the unsavoury experience of a coffin passing within inches of her nose, she entered the bedroom as Harriet let out another yowl.

'What's all this noise then?' The black straw hat was coming off, hat pins being thrust back into it, then it was dropped on the chair along with the midwife's coat. Rolling up the sleeves of her brown linen blouse, she glared at the girl.

'What a blessed lot of fuss! You're scaring them all out of their very wits downstairs. It ain't as bad as all that.'

'I can't help it,' Harriet wailed at her.

'Yes you can,' came the unsympathetic reply. 'It ain't hardly begun yet.'

The rest of the day promised to be composed not of time but of one vast swamp of agony as far as Harriet was concerned. Mrs Mason took a brief peek at her underparts then announced that she had ages to go yet.

Next to arrive was the doctor, squeezing in at the door as the mourners were filing out. He made an even briefer examination, his fingers cold. He smiled encouragement at Harriet as she winced. 'All going splendidly,' he said brightly and left, almost part of the funeral cortege, so quickly had he come and gone.

'What if I have complications?' she implored weakly. 'I could die and no one seems to care.'

'You won't die, strong gel like you,' said the midwife, while Mary smoothed her daughter's hand gently.

'You mustn't worry. The doctor would have stayed if there'd been any complications.'

'I'd better get on with the sandwiches,' Mrs Hardy said, 'or they won't be ready for when everyone comes back.' She hurried off.

Jack had gone with the others to represent his bereaved daughter and her mother and to make sure the cause of their absence didn't escape those who hadn't been to the house.

Harriet would have the sympathy of everyone around the graveside today. Thus alerted, there was none of the bright gush of conversation that usually concluded the return from a funeral with the worst part done with. Mrs Hardy's tasty ham and tongue sandwiches were hardly touched. After drinking a warming cup of tea and expressing heartfelt hopes of the grieving widow's safe delivery, all the guests beat a hasty retreat. No one lingered except for Harriet's godmother, Aunt Sarah, her mother's sister. Even she kept strictly out of the way, and Harriet was not even aware of her presence downstairs.

Towards evening, the pains grew closer together. Harriet reacted with gasps, back arching, face contorted with a need to strain. Mrs Mason got up to assess her charge, then quickly twisted a bedsheet into a rope and tied each end to the bottom rails.

'Right, deary,' she commanded. 'Hold on to this. Pull hard on it and push down only when I say. Right – push, now!'

Her face twisted with the pain, Harriet stared uncomprehendingly. Mrs Mason tutted at such ignorance.

'As if you was doing Number Twos, but harder . . . Harder than that!' Harriet pushed, gripping the sheet rope for dear life. 'Come on, girl! With all your might and main. That's it. And once more! No – don't give in. Come on – once more – another nice push. Then you can rest.'

It took so very many pushes, the sheet rope straining under the pressure, Harriet felt she would burst at the seams, or force the footboard clear off the bed. It seemed to go on for hours – her awful, grunting scream with each contraction, not like her own voice at all but like an animal, and Mrs Mason bellowing, 'Push, woman, Push!'

She lost count of the times she collapsed, begging to be left in peace, her body slowly losing all power to respond, her bloated abdomen like a great dead bladder of lard refusing to shift its load. Then, when there seemed no more breath or ounce of energy left in her, something wet slithered from between her thighs in a great gush.

Pain vanished like magic, leaving her numb. The midwife's sharply satisfied 'Yes!', mingled with Mrs Hardy's protracted sigh, 'Bless it, the dear little thing!' only just reached her exhausted mind.

'Girl,' stated Mrs Mason in succinct triumph. Boy, girl, it didn't matter to her so long as she brought it live into the world. She had been bringing babies into the world – or at least the East End – for nigh on twenty-five years and nothing frustrated her more than a stillborn after all her hard work.

'A luvly little girl,' Mrs Hardy enlarged, to ensure Harriet had comprehended. 'I've never seen one born so easy – not a first one anyway. Twelve hours ain't bad, y'know, for a first. And not even a doctor's 'elp needed. What're yer going ter call 'er, Mrs Porter?'

When there was no response from Harriet, she turned to the new grandmother. 'How many grandchildren does that give you, Mrs Williams?'

There were tears in Mary Wilson's eyes as she smiled over at her, ignoring the misnomer. 'Five. My other daughters have two each.'

Mrs Hardy was washing the child free of blood and

mucus while the midwife busied herself relieving Harriet of the afterbirth with a fierce pressure on her abdomen that made Harriet cry out and Mrs Mason click her tongue in exasperation at such silly nonsense from the mother.

'There, all nice and clean,' Emma Hardy announced, surveying the child wrapped in a soft linen sheet and woollen shawl. The sweat still damp on Harriet's forehead, her body limp from exhaustion, the swathed bundle was laid in her arms for her to view her achievement.

A purely reflex action made her glance at it. There, framed by the satin frill of the shawl, was a diminutive version of Will. Creased from its entry into the world though the tiny face was, there was no mistaking the likeness.

Harriet felt the whole of her insides flinch.

'No!' She heard the shriek of her own voice. 'Take it away!'

Three pairs of eyes stared at her in disbelief. The tiny bundle was taken up almost on the rebound by her astounded mother as, twisting her head from Mrs Wilson's mystified gaze, Harriet burst into gulping spasms of uncontrollable sobs.

# Chapter Three

'What about Catherine?' One hand gently rocking the cradle, Mary gazed down at the scrap within. 'Or Emily? Or Sarah? That's a nice name. After your Aunt Sarah. You've always been fond of your Aunt Sarah.'

Harriet shrugged. Her aunt lived in Cadogan Square on the far side of Victoria Park. Widowed when Harriet had been small, and fiercely independent, she earned her living doing beadwork and embroidery at home, making tassels and braiding for dresses and furnishings. The silk skeins were delivered each week in parcels from some employer in Regent Street. As a child, Harriet had been fascinated by all the beautiful colours, the sheen of silk strands pinned to boards to be deftly woven into amazingly intricate designs.

'Sarah then?' Her mother's voice cut across her thoughts.

'If you like,' Harriet murmured without interest. Her mother gazed at her in astonishment.

'Don't you care what you call her?'

No, she didn't care. The baby was one day old, and she was still tired. They said it had been an easy birth. They hadn't had to go through it. Twelve hours. Twelve terrible hours. It was a wonder it hadn't been born dead. Trust it to be awkward and come into the world lively as a cricket, strong as a lion. A weakling might have slipped away, left her free to forget Will and carry on her life. But there it was, the image of Will. Through its lusty crying, she seemed to hear Will's voice: 'I'll make you pay, you'll see.' The lace-trimmed cradle her parents had bought shuddered to each frantic kick – the child was alive and well, there was no denying it.

Each time she looked at it, she felt Will's hands on her, groping, his lips wet against hers, his tongue forcing its way into her mouth, his breath hot, gasping his lust, his weight pounding her into the mattress. She was glad to feel dislike for his child. It was a measure of getting back at him – though he couldn't know that. Or perhaps he did, from where he'd gone. Harriet hoped with all her being that it was Hell.

She shuddered, thinking of the dream that had begun the second night after she had pushed . . . no, after Will's accident, her thoughts quickly corrected. But the dream, recurring three times now, denied that it was an accident, condemned her out of hand.

She would be in her nightdress. His hand on her elbow, he would be pushing her up the stairs, his hand trembling with lust for her. Suddenly she would find herself naked, filled with terror of the pain she would suffer when he took his fill of her. Pushing him away in dread of what was to come, she would see him receding, becoming smaller and smaller, his broad handsome face surprised, his arms outstretched as if he were flying. Her arms, too, would be stretched in front of her. He would no longer

be there but she would still feel her palms on his chest
and the sensation would fill her with a sense of evil. That
was when she would awake to her own muffled cry, the
sensation still on the palms of her hands.

As Harriet drifted off to sleep again, she would dream
that her mother had come running to her cry, was holding
her, soothing and rocking her. Then her mother would ask
her what she had dreamed. Harriet would be afraid to tell
her in case her mother guessed the truth, but her silence
would proclaim her guilt and her mother would recoil, her
face full of horror. In a quandary as to what she should
do about it, her mother would tell others – others eager to
share the awful secret. The police would hear and Harriet
would be taken away and held in a cell, then led down
a cold stone corridor to where the hangman and his rope
waited.

It didn't end there. Dropping down, down on an
endless rope, she would see the Devil's face below her,
shining orange with fire, grinning up at her – except that
it was Will's face, his handsome smile demonic. 'I've
got you!' The words would echo as though in a cavern,
and she knew that his unending use of her was to be her
everlasting punishment for what she'd done. She would
push him from her as she had pushed him to his death;
would try to claw her way upwards, but the downward
descent would become more rapid as he reached up to
catch her. It was the sensation of falling that always jerked
her back, drenched in sweat, to the reality of morning that
in itself felt unreal.

Sometimes the dream seemed to carry on into her

waking hours; hung upon her all day like a shroud, as it hung upon her even now.

'Are you feeling faint, Harriet?' Her mother's hand on hers jerked her back to reality. 'My poor dear, you've gone a ghastly colour. A drop of water . . . Shall I get you a drop of water?'

'No.' Harriet winced, then gazed around the solidly furnished bedroom, avoiding her mother's anxious eyes. 'I was thinking of Will, that's all,' she conceded, which was better than saying nothing.

'That's all?' Mary's face shadowed with sadness and self-reproach that she should overlook her daughter's pain of grief in her own hastiness to watch over her health. She almost moved forward to cuddle her, but she had tried that several times. Each time Harriet had pushed her away as though her closeness alarmed or annoyed her. Instead she touched the arm briefly beneath the sleeve of the silk nightdress, surprised to find how cold it was, and hurried over to the small washstand on the pretext of tidying up.

Will's shaving mug, brush and razor still sat on the narrow shelf above the basin; his strop still hung on its hook, the leather black and shiny at each end, the well-used centre scuffed to a dull buff of raw leather. Quickly, Mary gathered up the things, unhooked the strop and thrust them all into the side drawer. Harriet mustn't be reminded of Will's absence any more than need be. Nothing must be allowed to cause her to fret with the baby to feed. Any more grief could stop her milk and perhaps bring on milk fever. Harriet had to live now for the baby's sake. Will would have wanted that.

The baby began to mew. Mary turned resolutely and took the mite up from its crib. Now wasn't the time to pester Harriet about names.

'Ready for a feed, I think,' she announced. 'She sounds hungry.'

She was having a task getting Harriet to feed the child properly. When Harriet made no move to assist, she herself plucked at the neck ribbons of the nightdress and with clinical detachment, so as not to cause Harriet embarrassment, began folding back the material from the girl's right breast, the harder of the two. Even so, she sensed a drawing back, one hand hovering as though Harriet wished to shield herself. Mary tutted, irritated by her daughter's unnecessary coyness.

'Harriet, this is a natural thing, you have to feed her.' Harriet relaxed reluctantly and let her hand fall away.

There was plenty of milk. The small breasts were tight and shiny, laced with mauve veins, the nipples already oozing opaque droplets of bluish liquid, tiny opal beads. Harriet eyed them with distaste.

When she didn't attempt to take the baby from her mother, Mary tutted again and laid the baby in the unwilling arms, gently pressing the small, screwed-up face against Harriet's nipple, guiding it. Responding to the warmth of its mother's breast on its cheek, the smell of milk, the tiny head bobbed, puckered mouth instinctively searching for the source of the smell that meant nourishment. The protrusion found, the mouth nuzzled briefly then greedily began to suck.

Harriet winced. 'It's hurting.'

'It'll hurt more if she doesn't take from you. It's bound to feel peculiar the first few times, but you'll soon discover it's the most wonderful feeling in the world.'

Harriet thought not, but didn't say so. She endured the noisy guzzling in silence. This was what Will had reduced her to, a feeding machine for a brat she already loathed because it was his.

As the nipple came free, Mary moved to transfer the child to the other side. 'Do we call her Sarah, then?'

It was more confirmation than question, but she expected a reply. She drew in her breath when none came. Harriet was being too apathetic for Mary's peace of mind. It was unnatural. Her lips tightened, but only momentarily. The whole situation was unnatural: a man's child born on the very day of his burial, who wouldn't be apathetic? What Harriet needed was to have her mind made up for her.

The baby had fallen asleep, already full. Mary lifted the sleeping scrap. 'Sarah it is then,' she said firmly as she placed the child back in the crib in a sort of baptismal gesture.

Emerging from the cool dimness of St Leonard's, Matthew Craig briefly narrowed his eyes against the brilliant May sunshine. Behind him, the church with its park of neat walkways and its graveyard of gothic tombstones was a haven amid the chimneypots and narrow side streets of Shoreditch. Before him the intersection of Old Street, Hackney Road, Kingsland Road and Shoreditch High Street gave a sense of space in a clutter of poverty. Matthew felt suddenly pleased with the world.

On weekdays these streets would be alive with traffic. Today, although the odour of horse dung, powder-dry from a rainless week, hung warmly pungent on the air, peace reigned. If any trams or buses ran on Sundays, there was none in sight, but a cab stood at the kerb, nosebag slung between the wheels, the nag ready to move off with a flick of the reins and the driver alert for any fare coming his way.

Matthew decided against hailing him. He needed to stretch his legs. A stroll towards Liverpool Street station, something less than half a mile further on, would do him good. He would get a cab from there to Waterloo Junction, and then a train to Winchester. He had all day to get home.

He had never been in the East End before. He had stayed the night with an old friend from his Oxford days, David Symonds, and had been kept awake half that time by the drunken commotion below his window, gusts of laughter, singing, colourful curses in ripe Cockney slang – and the discomfort of a strange bed. Only after midnight had peace descended, though even that had been broken by a hollow yowling of cats echoing through the alleys.

The following morning the sight of churchgoers dressed in their Sunday best had revived his confidence enough to venture into an unfamiliar church. Sunday morning service was very much part of Matthew's family life. David was not one for church, so Matthew had made his farewells as early as decently possible, hoping to find a church somewhere on the way home and enjoy a quiet hour or two.

It had been good to see David again. When they had

come down three years before, David had gone into his father's firm of solicitors, Peeker, Stymes & Symonds, whose offices were in Kingsland Road. His parents' home was in Highgate, but David had a flat near the office, needing to be independent, but for all that, was a credit to his father. Matthew had been more a disappointment to his.

'A waste of good money,' he had complained. 'All you seem to have gained is a bit of knowledge at the expense of a lot of wisdom.'

Matthew's brown eyes, which contrasted starkly with his fair hair, took on a musing look as he remembered this conversation. It would have been wisdom to have let his father have his way and to have gone into law, but wisdom hadn't come into it. A love of words – not legal words but beautiful, flowing, magic words; words to make readers shiver with pleasure – dominated Matthew. Except that he was burdened by an inability to set them down magically. So he had found others who could, and got them to do it for him. He'd started up a monthly journal; a very modest monthly journal which a small inherited trust just about managed to finance – because he was also burdened by a sympathy with those woman who for years had been demanding a right to a political voice. This sympathy having transmitted itself to his journal, that was what it became – a political women's journal, *Freewoman*, which the general public weren't overly inclined to subscribe to.

A woman's romantic paper would have been better, but having nailed his colours to the mast he could hardly tear them down now without looking a failure, especially to a father who saw his son as a complete fool and a mother who considered his venture totally misguided and was appalled by women who went about preaching female suffrage, whatever that was.

'All I know,' she dismissed, always trying to forget she was the daughter of a common ironmonger, 'is that it makes such persons very masculine and injures the self-respect of decent women.'

Matthew quickened his pace unconsciously as his thoughts turned to his plans for the future. The office he rented to turn out his few hundred copies a month was too close to home and parental influence. He needed new premises, in London. It was this that had brought him to visit David. David had been sceptical: London wasn't Hampshire.

'They'll scalp you as soon as they look at you, fresh up from the country, old man. Though I suppose I might find you something around here: it's cheaper than the City.'

Deep in thought, Matthew had walked past an estate agent's board before its message registered. Backtracking a few paces, he scanned the wording:

BEREAVEMENT COMPELS SALE OF A PRINT-ING BUSINESS AND STOCK. AN AUCTION TO BE HELD AT THE PREMISES OF PORTER'S PRINTERS, HACKNEY ROAD, SHOREDITCH AT 10.30 AM ON 24TH MAY, 1894

Matthew's mind was calculating. There'd be plenty to draw on in the East End: the poverty, the lowly status of women, their constant fight for survival. The thought brought a surge of excitement.

The twenty-fourth was the next day. Ten-thirty – just time enough to check his bank account. Funds had been a bit slim of late, but if he sent a telegram to his father as to what he had in mind, with a promise to drop the journal's political bias, he might see that his son was serious about publishing. Some of its flavour could be retained a little more subtly, and his father, he trusted, would be none the wiser.

Coming to a decision, he signalled a cab, a four-wheeled growler, so called because most of the drivers were considered to be miserable growlers themselves, rarely given to smiling. This one, however, was nothing but smiles as he lifted the reins, glad of a fare.

'Where to, guv'nor?'

Matthew gave David's address in Queensbridge Road. David wouldn't object to his spending another night under his roof. An enthusiast for dubious ventures, he wasn't at all Matthew's idea of a solicitor. A few years of examining conveyancing contracts would probably buff off the restive edges and excitable corners and mould him into a more acceptable pillar of the legal profession. But for now he might give some advice on acquiring new premises – without charge, Matthew dared to hope.

In the shadowy hallway, where she would be less noticeable, Harriet sat with her eldest sister, both of them in deepest mourning. It was such a relief to be up from her six-week lying-in period, with her mother pottering around bemoaning the inconvenience of her unreasonable refusal to stay with her, Mrs Hardy forever popping in and chattering nonstop, and the baby's unrelenting demands. Between them she had been stifled. She felt stifled now by her widow's weeds. Like the Queen, Harriet thought, who had hidden herself under hers for years, and who still dressed in black. Defiantly, she lifted her veil back over her tiny black hat.

'I thought there'd be more people here than this.'

'It's still early.' Clara's effort to comfort didn't help.

The shop door opened to admit the only prospective bidder in ten minutes, together with a noisy rumble of outside traffic and a glimpse of the weather, which wasn't heartening, the pavement looking as glossy as sugar icing from a heavy downpour. The rain had now abated a bit, and people were emerging from doorways and scurrying by – men with their necks down into collars, cloth caps pulled low; ladies with umbrellas fending off the lingering drizzle, skirts held clear of the wet. Inside the shop, gas jets lit against the dismal morning cast a stark white glow over the faces of the few men gathered there.

Clara pressed Harriet's hand. 'Look, someone else coming in.'

'That makes eleven.' Nothing was going to lift her despondency. 'Most of them have only come in out of the rain. More than likely it's kept away anyone who would have come to buy.'

Clara leaned nearer. She wrinkled her small nose encouragingly. 'It'll pick up in a minute.'

Harriet wasn't so sure. The screen between the printing

area and the counter had been removed to accommodate the crowd she had so confidently expected. She eyed those who had wandered in to look at the items for auction with only moderate interest. As soon as the rain ceased, they would wander out again, she felt sure of it.

She found herself looking at the items for sale through their eyes, imagining how unimpressive they must seem. The largest item was the dilapidated platen press Will had used for years. Even the new one he had bought only five months ago wasn't drawing the interest she had thought it would. She watched reams of paper being inspected, type moulds, printing blocks, composing frames, inking rollers, guttering – all those things she couldn't have put a name to until the auctioneer, Mr Jones, had told her – being fingered; took dismal note of the speculative downturned lips.

'We'll soon shift this lot,' Mr Jones had said, full of cheerful confidence, but she had lost faith in anything he said. Even the latest arrival, a tall, thin young man in a damp ulster, remained hovering by the door as if ready to slip out again. She would be lucky to make anything from this auction – might as well have kept the business.

Will had left about three hundred pounds in cash. Clara and Annie's eyes had gleamed, but she was going to have to live on that, and the rate money was going out . . . The christening had set her back a tidy penny. The funeral had cost even more: an oak coffin – five pounds; hearse, black horses, black plumes, black harness – eight pounds all of fifteen shillings; pallbearers' fees – fifteen shillings; not to mention the carriages for the mourners, and the undertaker to settle up. In all, she'd spent over twenty pounds to bury a man who had used her so badly that she had grown to hate him.

The meagre attendance this morning after the numbers who had seen him off seemed like a retribution, God's punishment for her part in sending Will to his grave. Harriet gave a visible shiver, then smiled hastily as Clara cast her an enquiring glance.

'The auctioneer's looking impatient,' Clara whispered.

'It's all a bit of a farce anyway,' Harriet whispered back.

Everything had been a farce. The christening, thanking God for her deliverance more than for the baby's; her smile so false that her face ached. Holding the baby as a fond mother until, professing weakness, she had given it to her mother to hold. Clara, Annie and Annie's husband as godparents cooing at it all through the ceremony. Aunt Sarah remarking, 'She's the image of Will. She'll be a beauty.' Her father's two sisters, bosoms shuddering over the tragedy of it all as they planted moist kisses on her frigid cheeks. Her father himself being bluff and hearty.

She had been glad when, christening over, she'd dropped the baby back into its crib. Sarah Mary Porter – to her the baby was still an it. The passing of time had dulled her initial loathing, leaving her now with no feeling at all. She wouldn't neglect the child, but there was no motherly love for it in her, and that was how it was.

She didn't relish living above the business on her own with it, but what else was there to do? Braced to decline another invitation to live with her parents, she still felt deeply hurt that they'd not pressed again.

In defiance she had even considered keeping the business going, but as a woman she was handicapped. Those unaware of her circumstance would ask for the proprietor, and then be disconcerted to find that they were already talking to the proprietor, this woman with the small, wan face, dressed in her mourning crepe. An older woman with arms like hams and coarse features beneath a man's cloth cap would have fared well, but not her. And so she had finally agreed to the auction, and to dispensing with Bert Higgins's services, since the shop would probably be used for something other than printing.

'What's wanted is a grocer's,' said Mrs Hardy. 'Ain't none till you get nearly to Cambridge Road. Tobacconists, drapers and things, but no grocers.' She was hoping that she would not have to traipse so far to put in her weekly order for groceries.

Mrs Hardy slipped in now with a cup of tea for Harriet and Clara. 'Need something to cheer you up, sad day like this,' she whispered to Harriet and went quickly back to the kitchen, where she was cooking a small meal for the poor unfortunate to eat later.

'Don't worry, Harriet.' Clara's blue-grey eyes peered thoughtfully over the rim of her teacup at the poor attendance. 'Once things get going . . .'

Harriet gave her a small tremulous smile. 'I'm glad you're here.'

Clara was small and pretty, plumper than Harriet and their sister Annie. She blamed this fact on her age – twenty-six – and on having had two children, for all Annie also had two children. Clara took after their father, but without his height; she had been plump even as a child. Had she been taller, she would have been a fine figure of a woman.

'That young man over by the door.' She pointed with her cup. 'At least he looks interested.'

Harriet followed her direction, and studied the young man more carefully. Tallish and quite thin, he had a refined, rather gentle face, angular enough to prevent him being what one might call handsome. He had removed his bowler to reveal wavy hair, sandy-coloured under the gas light, and his luxurious moustache was also fair. He had also divested himself of his damp ulster, but his high-buttoned jacket in a buff check gave him an appearance of overall warmth on this miserable day. He did indeed seem interested, except that anyone serious would be inspecting the items for sale instead of staring over towards where she sat. It was very rude of him, Harriet thought, looking quickly away. The fact that she was in mourning and the wording of the auction announcement must surely have told him of her situation.

Two more people had arrived, The rain had finally ceased and the sky had brightened a little, so their arrival was heartening. That no one was leaving was even more heartening.

The auctioneer consulted his pocket watch, and tilted a significant eye towards Harriet. She took a deep breath, then inclined her head. He acknowledged her gesture with a sharp rap of the gavel on the table behind which he stood.

'Gent'men, your 'tention please.'

After a short preamble he began: 'Set of oak stools – excellent condition. Shall we start at four shillings?'

Start! It was no start at all. 'Come, now, gent'men, suitable for office or domestic use. A present for the wife? What am I bid?'

'Free bob!' came a reluctant response from the body of the crowd.

'Three shillings. Do I hear four?'

'Four.' There were no more takers. The gavel came down smartly. Harriet glanced towards the thin young man. He had not bid at all.

Two more men came in, a purposeful look to them as though they had been hurrying. Delayed by the rain perhaps. Harriet's eyes turned again to the man near the door. She started as his glance flicked towards her as if by some unspoken signal, then brought her gaze sharply back to Mr Jones and tried to concentrate on the proceedings. It was going more briskly now, but nothing was going for what she had hoped. She said as much to Clara.

'There's your printing presses yet,' Clara hissed. Harriet looked sideways at her. Had there been a faint sting in the remark?

'Money always goes to money.' Annie wanted so much to buy that beige blouse she'd seen in Regent Street but Robert had said it was too expensive. 'Not content with the three hundred pounds Will left, she's selling his business too. She must be looking at – at least five hundred. My Robert earns forty-six bob a week and has to work hard for that in his job at the bank. And we've two kids.'

Lucky Robert, Clara recalled thinking sourly. An office clerk, her Fred got several shillings less. Admittedly it kept them and their own two comfortably in their nice house in Ruth Road by the park, around the corner from Annie. But three hundred pounds, in one lump, made even her mouth water. She remembered thinking that what she couldn't do with three hundred pounds wasn't worth talking about.

The same thought had occurred to Annie, to judge by the way she was speaking. 'Providential accident, Will's – for Harriet.'

Clara thought it best at the time not to query that rather unkind remark. After all, to lose your husband and have a baby all at the same time was a terrible blow for any woman to bear. But some of Annie's poison had rubbed off and she couldn't help the envious tinge to what she had intended to be a consoling remark about the printing presses.

'And now, gent'men,' announced the auctioneer. 'A platen printing press. Top of the range – "Arab" Crown Folio – bought brand-new by the late Mr Porter just weeks before his unfortunate demise. Who'll start the bidding at fifty pounds?'

'Forty!' This from one of the two newest arrivals.

Mr Jones looked affronted. 'Come now, a quality machine, brand-new in perfect working order. Let's be charitable to the widow!'

'Fifty-five!' Harriet's eyes turned in the direction of the staccato offer. It came from the young man by the door. Her heart flowed out towards him on wings of gratitude.

There was a small hiatus as those around drank in the

bid. Then, unwilling to be outdone, the first man called out again.

'Fifty-six.'

'Sixty!' The young man had become very alert and upright.

'Sixty . . . two!' There was uncertainty in the tone.

'Eighty!'

Harriet was staggered. A low hiss of astonishment swept through the room.

Mr Jones's voice rang out, pitched high with exaltation at such an exorbitant – one might say silly – bid. 'Eighty pounds I'm bid.'

The bidder obviously had no idea what he was about. There were no more bids. Mr Jones didn't expect any, but he was well pleased, given that he had previously calculated that the commission he'd get out of the auction would hardly justify the work involved.

'Eighty pounds then?' Mr Jones declared on a falling note. His gavel rose. 'Going – for the first time . . .'

'Eighty-one.' The newcomer stretched an antagonistic neck towards his rival. His look spoke for him. *Goad the fool one more time.* It was taking a chance, but worth the risk to see the fool go in deep.

'Hundred!'

Even Harriet, knowing nothing about prices, was staggered. At her side, Clara gasped. 'That must be twice what it's worth brand-new.'

This time the silence drew itself out in defeat, with no counterbid coming. The auctioneer challenged for the third time, then brought his gavel down with a triumphant thud, revealing unprofessional elation at this mad offer. 'Sold to the gent'man by the door! Name please?'

But from the hallway, Harriet didn't catch the name.

The sale of the second, older press was even more surprising. The young man's opening bid for a well-used 'Model' printer worth thirty-six pounds new was a staggering fifty pounds. There was no one else silly enough to bid but the auctioneer was beaming. The man was a raving lunatic – more money than sense – but who was he to tell him his business? His commission was now up far beyond his expectations.

The young man seemed bent on buying up the whole shop. The auction closed finally to ragged clapping. Those who had managed to buy something moved to the table, while the rest filed out, their conversation animated in appreciation of a good morning's entertainment. Harriet watched the young man speaking to Mr Jones. She felt quite giddy.

'With what's been sold and the money Will left, I've got nearly five hundred pounds. I can live on that for years.'

She realised she'd said 'I', the child forgotten for the moment. It would have to be brought up, fed, clothed. Some of her joy waned. For some reason she recalled her nightmare and pushed it away in a small wave of fear, concentrating hard on what was going on around her.

Clara was clutching her arm, as excited as if she was the one who had made all this money. Harriet's legs felt shaky as she moved towards where Mr Jones was still talking with the young man, now the owner of her late husband's printing equipment. She had to thank him. Had he given it more thought he could have got it at a fraction of what he'd paid. Her eyes wide with gratitude and shyness as she came up, she saw that his were deep velvety brown, contrasting oddly with the sandy hair.

'This is Mrs Porter,' Mr Jones began. 'Widow of the late owner. Mr Craig has arranged to take over the lease of your late husband's shop premises for a publishing business.'

'Matthew Craig,' the young man filled in. 'I publish a journal – not very large,' he added with some modesty. 'I've been looking for premises in London but I hope you will forgive me if I seem to have traded in on your misfortune. May I offer my condolences on your bereavement, Mrs Porter, if that isn't too audacious of me?'

Taking the offered hand, she felt the warmth of his grip pass from his fingers into hers. She looked up at him, startled, to find his gaze riveted on her so intensely that she blushed and lowered her eyes hastily in utter confusion.

Of course he'd paid out far too much. Of course he was a fool. That fact showed in the expression of the auctioneer. But it was seeing the wan face of the girl in the shadows, her expression full of dismay as she viewed the paltry gathering, that had galvanised him. The one with her was much more self-assured. He'd guessed immediately which of them was the widow and his heart was unexpectedly moved to pity, compelling him to bid as he did. He had been foolhardy, but having now looked more closely into her eyes, such clear grey pupils, arrestingly dark-edged, before they were lowered in acute embarrassment, the girl's pale cheeks turning fiery, he was glad he had been.

# Chapter Four

Sarah Morris surveyed her table laid for tea: scones, damson jam in its opaque blue glass dish, seed cake, a plate of cold ham. There was just the bread to be sliced and buttered. Her best china, decorated with pink roses, positively sparkled in the sunshine through the window facing the park. Sarah chewed on her lower lip, her mind wandering from the generous spread.

Would Harriet be bringing the baby? She hadn't last Tuesday; had left her instead with that neighbour of hers, that Mrs Hardy woman. Too soon after the birth, she'd said; she was not strong enough yet to cope with bringing a baby all this way. Good Lord, six weeks since the birth – of course she was strong enough!

Sarah's lips grew thin. Turning up in a hackney . . . spending poor Will's money when more modest transport would have done . . . It didn't require that much strength to bring little Sara! That was another thing, dropping the 'h' like that. She'd never heard such nonsense. Sara – what sort of name was that for a baby?

Her parchment cheeks sucked themselves into hollows as she sawed wafer-thin slices, the loaf clasped in her hand in a determined embrace. Her brows drew together beneath her scraped-back greying hair at the prospect of reminding Harriet of her maternal duties.

In the kitchen the kettle lid began rattling at the same moment as a rap came on the front door. At least her niece was prompt.

Sarah hurried to answer it only to have her cheeks sink again into hollows as she noted Harriet standing before her, empty-armed.

'I know, Aunt,' Harriet began hastily, seeing the disapproval on her face. 'I was going to bring her but I still don't feel up to it, and then when Mrs Hardy offered . . . I will next time, I promise. In a few more weeks I'll feel a lot more confident, I'm sure.'

By Sunday Sarah had a pressing need of her sister Mary's advice. It had been a stressful Tuesday afternoon. It had worried her ever since.

She hadn't said any of the things she'd intended to say, somehow lacking the courage – she who seldom let anything or anyone stop her speaking her mind when there was reason to.

Something in Harriet's eyes – haunted would be the word – when she mentioned the baby made it quite impossible to instruct her on her motherly duties. In fact the girl's expression had given her the shivers. Was she hiding something? But what? She felt she dared not enquire. She was almost glad when Harriet left.

'There's something I should discuss with you, Mary,' she said as they took the air in Victoria Park after Sunday morning service at St John's Church in Cambridge Road.

Mary favoured St John's. 'Far nicer than those nearby,' she maintained. After the service it was Sarah's custom to have Sunday dinner with her sister and brother-in-law. If the weather was fine, Jack saw her home across the park to Cadogan Square afterwards. If it wasn't, he would put her into a hired cab. This Sunday, however, it was warm and fine enough for her and Mary to enjoy a brief stroll in the park before returning for dinner.

'It's about your Harriet,' Sarah continued.

'Harriet?' Her sister's smile was innocently enquiring.

Sarah took a firmer grip on the slender stem of the cream umbrella protecting her cheeks from strong sunlight. She had hardly heard any of the service for wondering whether to confide to Mary the suspicion she had formed.

She'd have to tread carefully. As the girl's mother, Mary might not care to hear hints of something not being quite right – something concerning her daughter and that young man downstairs perhaps. It could only be that. What else *could* it be?

'You know she visited me on Tuesday,' Sarah began as they passed between the wrought-iron park gates with their ornamental stanchions. 'I'm worried about her. She seems to be acting very oddly to my mind.'

Mary nodded understandingly as they crossed the low bridge over Regent's Canal. Tears gathered in her eyes for her daughter. 'Poor child. She's had such a terrible time. I feel helpless for her. I don't think she'll ever get over the shock.'

'I mean, there's her attitude towards Sara – she doesn't appear to have any interest in the child, and . . .'

'Oh, I think she does. She's still terribly shocked by the sudden turn of fate. Who wouldn't be? I just thank the Lord she has Sara. That baby will keep her sane. Looking after it for poor Will's sake, it'll keep her mind off what's happened to her – at least, I hope so.'

*I beg to differ . . .* The protest sprang into Sarah's mind, but she stopped herself voicing it, feeling again the weight of her uncertainty where normally she never had qualms about voicing her opinions. What if she was wrong? There . . . uncertainty again. This wasn't like her.

No one could call Sarah Morris a fine figure of womanhood, yet what she lacked in height and a well-rounded bosom was more than compensated by a bearing that intimidated even the most forceful. And as she grew older – she would be fifty that August, two years older than Mary – she became more potent. Will, a fine, sturdy, forceful young man, had been very wary of her, to the point of diffidence, and had been most caring of Harriet in her presence. Which struck an odd note – for it had often seemed to her that the girl was in some way frightened of him, even though she had always made such a point of saying how content and happy she was. Sarah still retained a strong intuition that there had been something more in that need to stress a happy and contented marriage than met the eye. She was even more suspicious since Harriet's visit the previous Tuesday.

'She mentioned that person who took over Will's shop – several times,' she added pointedly.

'Mr Craig,' Mary supplied, taking in deep breaths of the fresh tang of the recently mown grass bordering the pathway.

Sarah nodded. 'What's your opinion of him?'

Under her fawn umbrella, Mary tilted her head towards her sister in surprise. 'I've not met him. Clara said he seemed a personable enough young man.'

'First impressions!' snorted Sarah.

Mary's brow wrinkled beneath her greying, tong-curled fringe. 'You sound disapproving. This isn't one of your odd insights, is it? You're very prone to them.'

'That's what I want to talk about – the way she speaks of him more than I'd have said was necessary. Has she mentioned him to you?'

'No. Is it important?'

'You don't know if he's married? Or engaged to be?'

'I really wouldn't know.'

The short, somewhat irritable laugh that accompanied Mary's frown put Sarah at odds. She walked on in silence for a while, using the time to gaze at the other people in the park strolling under trees or sitting on benches; at children playing, and families picnicking on the grass by the fountain a little distance away that looked like a small version of the Albert Memorial.

For a while they both stood watching, then on an unspoken decision turned back towards the park gates.

Sarah still needed to speak her mind. She took a deep breath and began on another tack.

'Perhaps it isn't my place to say so, Mary, but I never hear her mention Will's name. Nor have I once seen her cry.'

Mary's back stiffened. 'Grief does strange things to some people. Sometimes they can't cry.'

'When my Edmund died, I couldn't stop tears filling my eyes, not for years. Seeing him fighting for breath from pneumonia, even now, if I think about it, some familiar smell or a certain sound, I feel choked. But Harriet . . . Then there's another thing: little Sara. When I asked why she hadn't brought her to see me, she became so . . . guarded. You know me, Mary, I'm not one to let anything daunt me. But there was something about her that made me almost frightened to ask. I felt I would hear something I wouldn't wish to hear.'

'Now why do you say that?' Mary stopped in her tracks, her tone sharp enough to make passers-by look in their direction.

'It bothers me, that's all.' Sarah stood her ground before her sister's darkened expression. 'Something odd's going on . . .' She stopped short of expressing what was really in her mind. 'As I said, she doesn't cry . . .'

'Because she can't. Grief takes us all sorts of ways.' Mary's umbrella snapping shut put an end to the subject. There was no more to be said. Mary moved on ahead of her sister as they passed back through the gates, Bonner Hall on their left, golden in the sunshine, and on into Approach Road, with its fine terraced houses.

Sarah was compelled to put on a little spurt to catch up with Mary. She had intended to mention the doorway between Mr Craig's printing shop and the rest of the house not yet being boarded up, but the snapping umbrella had put paid to that for the while, though it was a subject that couldn't be left too long, for everyone's peace of mind.

She had questioned Harriet about it on the Tuesday.

Harriet had replied that Mr Craig already had it in hand, but Sarah had felt far from reassured.

'People gossip,' she told her. 'A young woman so recently widowed can't afford gossip. Make sure that door's sealed off properly.'

'Of course, Aunt,' Harriet had said, but the eyes swivelled away too quickly for comfort as the girl sought another scone, which Sarah knew full well she didn't want. She had felt irritated. Did her niece take her for a fool? Did she think that because she was old, had no children, she knew nothing of the world's ways?

'You mustn't let it worry you, my dear,' Matthew said when she told him of the perceptive way her aunt had regarded her.

She stood watching him work on the next month's journal. He called her 'my dear' now. Of late, she'd given him every reason to do so.

'But I don't want her to think badly of me. She's very close to me. When I was little, she'd give me sweets and cakes, tell me stories.'

There had been so many stories. Like the one about her brother, Neil, who as a young man had come home drunk after seeing *Faust*. Scared by the play, he had walked into their mother's washing line in the dark yard of the cottage in Three Colts Lane in Bethnal Green. In a frenzy of fear he had torn down the line of washing, and had dared not confess to it next morning when his mother had ranted about urchins dragging her clean linen in the mud. Grandmother had been a formidable woman in her day, by all accounts.

Harriet never knew her, and such stories made her laugh as a child. But today she wasn't laughing. Aunt Sarah's formidable perception loomed large in her mind.

'I'm sure she knows what's going on – deep down,' she said, biting her lip. 'She seemed so suspicious when she asked me about this door.'

'What if she does?' Matthew stopped what he was doing and came over to her. 'Neither of us have anything of which to be ashamed.'

'Except that I've only been a widow two months. It does look bad, Matthew. I have to hide the key every time my parents come to see me and shoot the bolts you put on. It's so underhand, so furtive. I wish we didn't have to keep it secret, but I know we do have to – for months yet, at least long enough until everything looks respectable. What would people say if they knew? What would Aunt Sarah think?'

He wiped his hands clean of ink and took hers. 'It'll remain our secret, I promise.'

'Except that she's so uncanny at winkling out the truth. I'm sure she's clairvoyant enough to read a crystal ball.'

She hadn't meant it as a joke but he threw back his head in an explosive laugh, tugging her towards him in amusement. She remained rigid in his embrace, her mind racing over these past two months.

From the way Matthew Craig had looked at her that day of the auction, she had realised that she was still a catch, even saddled with a baby. Of course, the door connecting the two parts of the building would have to be permanently sealed, for decency's sake, and she had had every intention of boarding it up. For the time being it was left locked, and the key hung on a hook at the top of the stairs in case of an emergency. A woman on her own – who could say when she might need help quickly?

There had been no emergency the day after Matthew Craig took over the shop. The baby had been crying most of the day, driving her to distraction. More to escape its incessant noise than anything, she'd lifted the key from its hook and popped her head round the door to apologise for the noise.

He seemed surprised to see her there, but very understanding, his smile wide and warm.

'I hardly noticed. Far too wrapped up sorting out the interviews I'm trying to arrange with some of those poor women around here.'

Boyishly enthusiastic, he told her of a far different band of women striving to end the oppression suffered by their lesser sisters.

'I hope my journal helps their cause. They need as many voices as they can get.'

Harriet smiled grimly, remembering Will. Matthew gave her a look that hinted he'd read in her smile some shadow of a past fear still lurking inside her. He said nothing, but she felt him to be an ally, even though he knew so little about her and she about him.

As he closed up for the day, intending to go home to the flat he'd found in Teale Street, she offered him a cup of tea. By the end of the week she was adding a sandwich for midday. The following week he asked if she might help with a bit of filing now and again. She said yes, and again yes when he suggested she take a breath of fresh air with him that Saturday evening.

'It will do you good, cooped up in those rooms of yours,' he said so quietly that it brought tears to her eyes.

To escape if only for a short while the claustrophobia of being cloistered with the baby day in, day out, she had flung herself at the offer, begging half an hour of Mrs Hardy's time to keep an eye on the child on the pretext of having to post a letter.

She prayed as she walked beside him that he wouldn't misconstrue her ready acceptance, and see her as common as a picked-up woman of the streets. But he was a perfect gentleman. Keeping a foot of space between them, he told her something of himself, his life at Oxford, his ambitions for his journal, pleasant everyday things.

He told her his father was in property: 'A sort of estate agent. He's always yearned to be on a par with the professional people he touches elbows with, but I think he thinks they still regard him as a common tradesman, even now. That's why he wanted me to take up a profession. Law, he had in mind; It might have made him feel on the same footing as them. But I'm afraid I've been a disappointment to him, becoming a tuppenny publisher instead. That's what he calls it.'

Matthew chuckled with mild self-deprecation, a full, deep-sounding chuckle. He had a deep voice for a thin person and was so well spoken that at first she had felt obliged to put on what she termed her best voice, but as they swapped life stories and she grew more at ease, the flattened vowels crept in again. He didn't seem to notice at all. In fact he confessed with a tinge of amusement that his mother had spent her entire married life living down the fact that she was the daughter of an ironmonger.

'No one dare risk life and limb mentioning it. Mother is very much part of Winchester society, well up in her Lit. App. Society . . . Literary Appreciation,' he expanded to Harriet's puzzled look. 'She would like to see me marry well. Last year she played matchmaker with a certain Victoria Elliot-Cobbdon, but I shied well away from that.'

It was good to laugh with him. With Will truly laid to rest, and the baby forgotten for the while, Harriet thought she had never felt so free.

The following Sunday he had asked if she'd care to go with him to watch the official opening of the new Tower Bridge. It was such a wonderful day, watching it from the river, sharing the excitement of the occasion, mingling with other people and no baby to drag on her, for she had once again left Sara with a surprisingly willing Mrs Hardy.

But it made the rest of the week all the more dreary. Trying to cope with Sara, she counted the days to the next Sunday, when Matthew had offered to take her to see Crystal Palace, her first ever visit. They watched the Brock's firework display afterwards and on the tram coming home he gently threaded her arm through his, saying he hoped she didn't object. Object? How could she when she was overcome with gratitude?

That night, for the first time, she didn't dream of Will trying to drag her down to only he knew where. They still hovered, the dreams, like bats in the dark ready to flap at her at any moment when shallow or disturbed sleep made her vulnerable. But Matthew was becoming her saviour. None of this did Aunt Sarah know. As far as anyone in the family was concerned, she was still the grieving widow – and it was just as well for her and Matthew that it stayed that way for the time being.

Matthew watched Harriet at the compositor's bench, the tall stool half-hidden by the folds of her black skirt. Head bent on its slender high-collared neck, auburn hair smoothly coiled but for a curl of fringe, she was totally absorbed inserting type from the wooden case into the narrow metal sticks and then into a galley. Her fingertips stained by ink of previous printings, she tied the lines of type together into a block, to be proved for errors.

Matthew smiled tenderly. 'You do that very well, my love.'

The previous night, strolling arm in arm through the October dusk, he had kissed her on the cheek. Her hand touching the place, she had smiled up at him, grey eyes reflecting the light of the street lamp.

He could still feel the cool smoothness of her cheek. It made his heart pump like a steam hammer. He had never been in love before. During his Oxford days, he had thought he was on a couple of occasions, but he had never before experienced such tenderness of feeling, such longing to protect as he felt now.

Harriet's lips thinned with concentration. 'I'm getting better and better. I bet I could get proper work doing this – if I was a man.'

'You could,' he agreed, smiling at her Queen's

English. He could even smile at the many errors she made typesetting it.

Two months before, she had found him sitting at the compositing bench, setting up the next month's issue. Realising he was being watched, an unusual stab of embarrassment had made him assume a note of flippancy.

'I know. I need a compositor. But I can't afford to pay a man for a while yet. I did hope my father might finance me a little, but he has no faith in me. So until the journal pays its way, I have to do this myself.'

Moving forward, standing on tiptoe to peer over his shoulder, she had touched his arm to steady herself, the warm, womanly smell of her making his heart race. 'Can I try?'

'It's not that simple.' Near choked by that pounding heart, his voice was hoarse. 'You must be able to spell . . .' Confusion made him fumble the words badly but she didn't seem put out.

'I can do that. I went to school just like my brothers. I learnt all they did – or nearly all.'

'There's more to it than that. It's a skilled job.'

'It doesn't look that difficult. You could teach me.'

He'd turned to see her face tight with determination. Until then, he had seen her as helpless, a delicate creature thrown out into the world, in need of support. This new enthusiasm to do a job meant for men – he nearly laughed, but those set lips stopped him. Thin lips were said to denote a hard core, a cold heart. Thin hers might be; but at rest, softly moulded along the closure, they contradicted hardness, betrayed an inner insecurity. No cold heart there.

Nonetheless, he realised there was a certain concealed stubbornness in her.

He conceded. In a week or two she would give up in frustration and hand it all back to him. Eventually he would engage a typesetter but until he could afford one, he would give Harriet tuition, and reset the errors she had made after she retired to her rooms. She had learned after a style and he remained happy to correct the errors she still made.

'Women don't get this sort of job, anyway,' she now said ruefully. 'I wish I was a man and not stuck with looking after a . . .'

She stopped, her eyes filled with a haunted look he'd seen before.

'I'll shove the kettle on for some tea,' she said abruptly and after struggling down from the stool, nearly slipping, made for the kitchen.

Matthew began slowly stacking the new copies of *Freewoman*. 'Not stuck with looking after . . .' His mind completed the sentence she had left unfinished. Harriet hardly ever spoke of her daughter. He could understand her avoiding mentioning her late husband; it was natural for her to be guarded on the subject. But her own daughter?

Harriet had not yet allowed him up to her rooms and that was as it should be. But now he wondered whether it was not so much from a need to be discreet as to keep the baby out of sight. Why? She was a perfectly normal child – six months old now, a pretty little thing from what he'd seen of her, although he rarely saw her except when Mrs Hardy took her or brought her back, seemingly more in charge of her than the child's own mother. Something should be said. After all, he could be Sara's stepfather one day.

He took the opportunity after taking Harriet to see Little Titch, the comedian, at the recently refurbished New Lyric in Cambridge Road. Emerging from the cloying odour of close-packed bodies and the tang of orange peel into the freshness of a rainy night, he hailed a hansom and helped Harriet in. As the cab moved smoothly off, he confronted her gently.

'Sara seems happy with Mrs Hardy,' he said casually.

It was a bad start. He felt her stiffen immediately and knew this wasn't going to be simple. The more he was getting to know Harriet the more he realised how easily she could change from being coyly happy to becoming almost defensively hostile.

'I was thinking of Mr Hardy,' he hedged hastily. He had a fleeting image of the small man with bent legs and amiable features. 'Does he mind her being there so often?'

'Why should he? He's never said he does.'

'No, I mean . . .' He wasn't saying what he meant at all.

Harriet was gazing out of the cab window, intently interested in passing carriages, pedestrians hurrying home through the rain, vendors on the kerb braving the downpour.

Matthew made another attempt at saying what he meant. 'Why do you refer to Sara as "her" or "the baby"? You never mention her by name.'

'I do.'

'Hardly ever.'

'I do.'

'I don't think so, Harriet.'

'Matthew, I do!'

The exchange was threatening to degenerate into a farce. Harriet began playing with the corner of her lace handkerchief, head bent.

'You never talk about her, Harriet,' he persisted more forcefully.

With sudden venom, she turned on him. 'What's so special talking about her? I thought you were interested in me, Matthew, not her.'

'I *am* interested in her. She's your child and I hope I shall see more of her – if all goes well.' He didn't elaborate any further, but Harriet suddenly snuggled close to him.

'Don't let's talk about her. Let's talk about us.'

His arm tightened significantly around her. 'And the future.'

She was silent for a while. Then she said, 'I didn't have a very good start in my marriage, did I? One year.'

'I know, my sweet. But you might think to start again, some day.'

He heard her sigh. 'Sometimes it's so lonely up there in my rooms, just me and the . . . and Sara. I'd like to think there was more than just that. But not yet. Not so soon after . . . You know how people talk.'

Matthew held her close, wanting so much to propose properly, but it was still too soon. As she said, people talked.

In the hallway his kiss lingered. She didn't push him away.

'May I come upstairs, Harriet?'

'Mrs Hardy'll be bringing the baby back.'

'She needn't know I'm here. I'll wait in the shop till she goes.'

They spoke in whispers. It sounded so clandestine, he turned it into a small joke. 'I could make friends with Sara.'

'I don't think so.'

'I'm sure we'd get along very well.'

Harriet's laugh was low and meaningful. 'One day you might have to.'

'That's an odd thing to say, might *have* to.' But he was encouraged. 'May I?'

'What?'

'Come upstairs.'

She tilted her head, listening to the growing patter of rain on the stained glass of the hall door. 'I think you'd best go on home before it gets any heavier, Matthew.'

He gave up. He would have to learn to be patient, that was all.

In a cab jogging through the steady downpour, he listened to the light rhythmic clop of hooves on the wet cobble blocks. He wished he hadn't suggested going upstairs. He was almost glad that she had refused. Christmas, he would ask her then. He was certain she would say yes. They would marry a year from then, a decent enough interval, he thought.

Umbrella held firm against the slanting rain, he alighted from the cab outside his lodgings, paid the man and hurried on inside.

# Chapter Five

Matthew was to spend Christmas and New Year at Winchester with his family. It was only right he should, but Harriet was already feeling the tug of separation, especially as a week before he was due to go she felt a cold coming on and needed him with her.

'Why can't I come with you?' she sniffled.

'Your family will expect you to be with them,' he told her gently. 'Christmas is a time for families. You know that!'

She did, but it made no difference. 'Your parents will have to meet me eventually. I thought this would be a good time.'

He drew her close as they sat together on her sofa, safe from the promise of snow hovering on a stiff December wind outside.

'I'd rather tell them about you before they meet you. Parents need a while to adjust to the idea of an offspring's intention to wed. I'm sure mine will. I know yours will also.'

She had to agree, loving him for his decisive command of things. As it was, she hadn't yet found the courage to drop any hint to her own family, and still made sure that the door to the printing shop was conspicuously bolted on her side when they came visiting. She could imagine their reaction when she eventually told them. She knew exactly what they would say – Will was only eight months in his grave. How could she cast his memory aside so soon? How would he feel? (As if by some strange supernatural quirk he was still alive and capable of having injured feelings.) She would explain, of course, that a baby needed a father. And dear God, how true that was.

No one knew what it cost: scooping slops from those lips every time she fed her; steeping dirty napkins in salt water, gagging as she rinsed the bits of towelling free of revolting poop; her sleep broken at night by its crying; having to beg Mrs Hardy to keep an eye on her so she could spend a secret hour or two with Matthew, praying the woman was still unaware of their relationship – though it was only a matter of time before she found out.

What a godsend it was that Matthew had begun to spend more of his time with Sara. Yes, the baby needed a father.

'And you'd better not spoil things for me,' she upbraided the mite when Matthew left that evening, her emerging cold making her peevish.

From her cot, the child stared back, deep blue eyes below a mass of dark curls so like her father, she could have been his reincarnation.

Harriet shuddered.

'Yes, you!' she spat as though it was Will she addressed. The eight-month-old had no idea what she was saying, but it did no harm and it helped relieve the strain of coping with her. She had no thought of hurting the child intentionally

– no more than she'd intended to hurt Will the day she'd pushed him . . .

Harriet shied automatically from that memory. She wasn't vicious by nature. She would never see her child go cold or hungry; it was just that she could feel nothing for her, going through the motions of administering to her needs as she might a stray puppy. Sometimes it was almost as though this infant wasn't hers at all – had been foisted on her when she hadn't been looking.

'You don't even know, do you, how I feel about you?' She found her baleful gaze being met with one of sweet innocence. 'You've no idea what I'm saying, you ugly lump.'

Even as she railed, she knew how untrue that was. Will had been breathtakingly handsome. She hadn't realised when he'd captured her heart, how black was his beneath those good looks. It must surely follow that, having inherited his looks, the child had also inherited the heart of the man who had sired her with such swinish self-indulgence.

'You!' she sneered, giving vent to her hatred of a man dead but living on in his daughter. 'If I could give you away, I would.'

It wasn't so bad when Matthew was there. He'd grown fond of Sara, and would pet and coddle her while Harriet looked on, glad to be rid of the burden.

It was when he wasn't there, when Sara cried nonstop, compelling Harriet to hold her, rock her, that she would feel herself becoming unhinged, wanting to stuff a rag between those red lips to shut her up. She never did, of course. Shaking Sara in total frustration, throwing her back into her cot and fleeing to her bed to cover her ears with a pillow, she would be filled with a sense of helplessness. The punishment Will had inflicted on her would never end.

Yelling made things worse. The day before had become so bad that she had smacked Sara – really hard – on her arm and her legs. It was as though she couldn't stop. She was only expressing her frustration, she told herself; she was fully justified. Except that Matthew's concern when he noticed the angry pink stains of her handprints on Sara's plump little limbs made her cringe in remorse.

'You should be careful,' he warned. 'She's still a tiny mite.'

'A tap,' she brazened. 'What harm does a tap now and again do? I remember being strapped many a time when I was little. I only used my hands. Children have to be taught when they're naughty.'

'She's not old enough to be naughty, Harriet.'

'You don't know what it's like,' she had wailed defensively. 'Here on my own. If you had her all day, all night, no one to help . . .'

He had put his arms around her, comforting her, kissing her gently.

'You won't be on your own for much longer. Soon I'll be here all the time to help take care of her, my sweet.'

Oh, how she longed for the day, But meanwhile . . .

A tingling in her nose made her tilt back her head. The exploding sneeze rocked her small frame. There was a thickening in her head. She would have been better off in bed, but the baby, tiring of its spoon and starting to whimper, put paid to that luxury.

Being with her parents over the festive season meant that Sara was taken off her hands, doted on, cooed over by the whole family gathered at her parents' home, allowing her to nurse the remnant of her cold in peace.

'Will would've been so proud,' Clara said, sitting beside her on the sofa in the parlour. Everyone had made a beeline for the cosy room after Christmas dinner had been cleared away, and out came the port and cigars and nuts.

Clara was jogging Sara on her lap, enjoying her giggles while her own three-year-old Henry, and eighteen-month-old Alice played with empty cobnut shells on the rug in front of the bright hearth.

Annie, sitting nearby, her own youngest on her lap – six-month-old Robert George – was taking little notice of Sara; had done so all day, and Harriet felt galled, puzzled and a bit hurt by her offhand behaviour.

'If only Will was here,' Clara's voice was heavy with pity. 'Poor fatherless little mite.'

Harriet's attention was averted from Annie for the moment, and she grabbed at the chance Clara presented. 'There's something I've got to tell you,' she began, but Clara wasn't listening.

'What a lovely smile – just like her poor father's. And those pearly teeth – how many has she got now? She's really going to be a beauty, Harriet. What did you say you've got to tell me?' she asked at last, her eyes still on the baby.

Harriet swallowed. 'The matter of Sara not having

a father . . . I was going to say I don't think she'll be fatherless much longer.'

There, she had said it. 'You see . . .'

'Shall I take her awhile?' Aunt Sarah stood before them, small and commanding.

'Of course, Aunt.' Clara gladly handed over the mite. She was tiring of holding the baby anyway. And her eyes were now on her own two, who were dropping roasted chestnut shells all over the rug far too freely.

'Don't make a mess, Henry! Your grandma can't keep on clearing it all up. Sorry, Harriet, what were you saying?'

Harriet took a second gulp, almost tempted to abandon her confession. But she'd already embarked upon it, and if Matthew could tell his family, she must tell hers. The words tumbled out in a gabble.

'I said . . . Sara might not be fatherless for much longer.'

Clara was suddenly all ears. 'What *do* you mean?'

'Someone . . . more or less offered . . . to marry me.'

Clara's disbelieving laugh tailed off. 'You mean, take you *and* the baby? Who? Do we know him?'

'Matthew Craig.'

'Not your landlord . . . Not him!'

'Why not him?' A sense of protective love caught at her heart, surprising her, and she returned her sister's incredulous gaze in an unfaltering challenge. Clara blinked, yielded.

'Well, I'm amazed. You *are* a dark horse, Harriet. So how long's that been going on?'

'Nothing's been *going on.*'

'But . . .' Clara had grown cautious. She dropped her voice. 'You haven't *been* with him, have you?'

'No, I haven't *been* with him. Mr Craig's a perfect gentleman. He wouldn't dream of . . . that.'

'What about Will?' Clara's voice dropped even lower, leaving a chill to run through Harriet's veins. Again, it was as though the man lived. Why did he persist in haunting her? She forced herself to speak his name.

'What about Will?'

'He's hardly been gone eight months.'

'I'm not marrying tomorrow. There'll be a respectful period before anything like that happens. Just that Matthew – Mr Craig – offered to take me in marriage. For the sake of the baby.'

'Well, if he means it, that's really generous.'

'Of course he means it. He had to ask me several times before I said I would.'

'So you said yes? My goodness! You're a quick worker, Harriet, and no mistake. Hey – listen, everyone! Harriet's got some news!'

Clara was on her feet before Harriet could stop her, clapping her hands above the buzz of happy conversation. Slowly the babble died as the handclap continued to demand their attention. Clara stood like an orator before a mass meeting. 'Guess what – our Harriet's had a proposal of marriage.'

There was a brief, startled silence as the family took in the news, uncertain how to react, followed by a sigh of indrawn breath like a wind soughing through tree tops. 'Oh my . . .'

This was from most of the aunts and uncles, significant looks passing from one to another, fingers held to mouths in some sort of deference – to the dead was Harriet's interpretation. Her own family reacted rather more frankly – a gasp from her parents, knowing snorts from both her brothers, a clearing of the throat from her brothers-in-law. Annie's sniff was audible, to say the least.

Harriet sat very still, not knowing quite how to cope with this reception. Some sort of explanation was obviously called for.

'I wasn't sure . . .'

Her voice, small and wary and still croaky from her recent cold, died away, but then grew in strength as she realised there was nothing for it but to brazen out this awkward moment.

'The proposal came from Mr Craig, who took over the printer's shop downstairs. He asked me about two months ago, but I refused. It was too soon after . . . Well, he's asked me again. And I began to think that Sara did need . . . does need . . . someone . . .' This was getting far too complicated for comfort.

As her faltering voice broke and tears began to cloud her eyes, her mother, galvanised into action, came across the room to catch her to her small bosom.

'Oh, my dear, it's been a terrible time for you. I'm so happy for you, Harriet.'

Tension eased. Suddenly everyone was crowding round congratulating her, expressing amazement, pleasure, saying how large-hearted this Mr Craig must be.

Annie, she noticed in all this, hadn't moved.

Only when her husband, Robert, touched her arm, prompting her, did she get up and bother to join the cluster of relatives, although even then didn't seem eager to offer her congratulations.

Even as Harriet smiled appreciation of all the good wishes, having half expected condemnation instead, she felt the hurt of Annie's odd behaviour. True, she hadn't seen much of her since Will's death – as if Annie had made a point of avoiding her.

Aunt Sarah, too, was being somewhat withholding of her good wishes, standing near the fireplace, still clutching her little namesake to her, although she at least was looking relatively relieved. But then Aunt Sarah had always been a little bit difficult to understand, whereas Annie might have been expected to show a little more warmth.

Questions were assailing Harriet from all sides, giving her no chance to dwell on Annie's strange behaviour. What was this Matthew Craig like? How old was he? Had he any family – children, that was? He too was bereaved, perhaps?

It was obvious that those who had never met him guessed him to be some aging, probably balding, widower, possibly in need of a housekeeper, a mother for his children – even the nurse that a second marriage would provide in his dotage, while affording the young widow security.

'You must thank your lucky stars,' Uncle Albert, her father's brother, boomed, echoed by his wife Tilly.

Harriet smiled graciously. If they only knew how handsome, how single, how eligible Matthew was, and how she felt her own worth in having caught him. She answered them all, of course, but wasn't sure they believed her.

In their old bedroom at the top of the house, as Clara and Annie put their children down to sleep in the beds they themselves had once used, Annie remarked acidly, 'Lucky for some.'

Clara was taken aback by the caustic tone. She stared across at her sister's thin face. 'What d'you mean, lucky for some? Who?'

'Who d'you think? Knows what side her bread's buttered, all right, doesn't she? Money left by one husband. Now she's after the next, and well off by the sound of things. No flies on her, is there?'

'I don't suppose she planned it that way.'

'Huh!' was all Annie said, tucking the counterpane in around her babies and sailing out of the room before Clara had time to make any comment.

Clara followed at a distance, knowing that Annie had voiced the words that had been at the back of her own mind – words that she had refused to acknowledge, until now. But Annie had sown seeds on fertile ground, and it was Clara's turn to assume Harriet's luck had been more engineered than springing from sheer providence.

Annie managed to buttonhole her brothers, but they were not as suggestible as Clara, shrugging off her sour remarks. Who cared? Unmarried, secure in the knowledge that their father's business would be theirs one day: what Harriet did didn't concern them.

Harriet, blissfully unaware of her sister's venom,

continued to revel in the attention her news had brought,
enjoying this New Year's Eve spent with her family. The
beer and port were flowing as on the stroke of twelve the
bells rang in all the churches around; and neighbours
leaned from windows to call a Happy New Year to each
other. Friends flooded in as the last chime struck, making
sure that at least one had dark hair and a lump of coal for
luck, and was the first in at the door. Despite her happiness,
Harriet found herself wishing that Matthew could be here
to share it with her.

Matthew's home, Mullions, was a rambling Georgian
edifice set in an acre of ground just outside Winchester.
Occupied only by his parents, a staff of six, and a weight
of furniture, dusted and polished daily but seldom used in
most of its twelve rooms, it had a withdrawn air, which
even New Year's Eve couldn't abolish. It hadn't been a
lively Christmas, and would be an even worse last day of
the year: Mrs Craig, Matthew's mother, was having one
of her heads. In consequence, the servants – butler, lady's
maid, footman, cook, housemaid, skivvy – were creeping
around on tiptoe.

Matthew sat in the sitting room, the previous day's copy
of the *Manchester Guardian* lying across his lap. He'd
scanned it but hadn't read a word so far. He thought of
Harriet, wondered how she was, what she was doing. He
was deeply in love and missing her.

He had planned to say nothing about his news until
this evening, his last before going back to London. That
way he would avoid days of strained silence and painful

postmortems, especially with only himself and his parents here. Richard and Evelyn had been with their own little families this year, his brother's wife expecting her first in February and his sister's first only four months old.

He had planned to wait until after dinner, due in twenty minutes, but his stomach was already in turmoil as well as being empty. Coming to a decision, he thrust the *Manchester Guardian* aside and strode out of the sitting room. It was better perhaps to have Father pave the way, his way, rather than spring a surprise on Mother with one of her heads.

He found his father in the library. Accepting the offer of a brandy, he took a fortifying sip, then came out with it: 'I suppose you should be the first to know, Father. I've decided to get married.'

Henry Craig regarded him at length, his square face registering relief as well as surprise.

'Anyone I know?' he asked finally, his tone even, and Matthew took heart.

'I shouldn't think so. She's a London girl.'

London, that metropolis of varied areas from the fashionable West End to the poverty-stricken East End – all sorts of odd people lived in London. Henry Craig's expression became a touch more severe.

'What part of London?'

Matthew found himself hedging, dreading the moment of truth. 'I thought it best to tell you and Mother before approaching her father.'

'I see,' Henry said slowly. With deliberation he swirled his brandy around in the bulbous glass, then lifted it to contemplate its pure amber colour against the light of the chandelier, apparently fascinated by the way the candle-light reflected off the facets of festooned crystal drops on to the smooth crystal bowl he held.

Matthew waited, taking mental stock of his father. A tall man, but broader than Matthew could ever hope to be, at fifty-one he was beginning to stoop, and his blue eyes were less bright than formerly. His round nose always looked at odds with lips thinned by years of property dealing. His hair was receding now, and taking on that yellowish grey that fair people acquire in middle age, but it had once been as Matthew's now was. However, Matthew favoured his mother more, having inherited her dark eyes and her slim figure. She had been a handsome woman, still was, for all her enjoyment of poor health, with her face lined from needless fretting over insignificant matters.

Henry continued to study his brandy. 'You've given me no name as yet, Matthew.'

Matthew almost jumped. 'Harriet Porter.' He found himself facing a frown of distaste. 'Her maiden name was Wilson,' he added hastily. That sounded better. But it was a mistake.

'Wilson? Porter? You mean she has been married at some time?'

'Widowed, tragically, some time ago.'

'I see. How old is this . . . Mrs Porter?'

'Twenty – her husband was killed in an unfortunate accident.'

'And her parents – what does her father do?'

This was turning into an inquisition. Matthew braced

himself. As he expected, the inquisition began stringing itself out, stopped only by the hollow buzz of the dinner gong. By that time he'd confessed to Harriet's home being unforgivably east of St Paul's. Even Winchester folk had heard of London's East End, a notorious sprawl. The capital had its pockets of poor even in the finer West End: casual labour, washerwomen, chimney sweeps, crossing sweepers, hauliers, cartiers – people who made some sort of living off the wealthy. But the East End was vastly more congested by poor people and Henry Craig could imagine no respectable middle-class family voluntarily remaining at such an undesirable address unless there was something odd about them.

'How anyone can live among all those buildings and streets,' he said with ill humour that boded no good, 'and remain unsullied by the squalor and dissolution, is beyond me. How our dear Queen manages to reside there is a marvel.'

Partially recovered from what he had heard so far about Harriet and her people – moderately wealthy or not – Henry Craig had reached the conclusion that this widow, already with issue from her previous marriage, was not for Matthew.

'Your mother's not going to like this one bit. She's a woman of standards, and to know how you've been conducting yourself while in London . . . She is not a well woman, Matthew. A shock like this isn't going to do her any good. I daren't imagine what she will say.'

Matthew put down his glass and stood facing his father, his hands curled determinedly into fists at his side. But he knew better than to give way to anger and lose control.

'With respect, I think there's little she can say. I intend to marry Harriet, and there's an end to it.'

'Is that what you think, eh? I might remind you, Matthew, that I am presently helping you fund that ridiculous journal of yours. Your promise to curtail the political stuff you churn out appears to be as brittle as pie crust. Yes, I've been keeping an eye on it, sir, and it's not changed – not one iota. No wonder you can't sell the damned thing except to a handful of idiotic women with inflated ideas of their role in life. You'd be better advised to come home and turn it into a decent, respectable publication, if you must be a journalist or a publisher or whatever you think you are. There's no hope, of course, of your taking up law, but at least you can learn to run a decent journal down here. As for this woman you've been hanging around with – best forgotten, my boy.'

His outburst spent, Henry Craig finished the rest of his brandy in one gulp.

'No need to bother your mother with all this,' he advised over his shoulder with bluff confidence as he led the way into dinner. 'Between us, eh? In time you'll see the wisdom of what I've been saying.'

Matthew had different ideas, but he said nothing.

Eleanor Craig's face paled. 'I can't believe what I am hearing.'

With her tight-laced corset threatening to cut off her air supply, she was verging on a swoon. Her hand reached feebly for the chair behind her. Recognising the signs, Henry helped her sink into it. But there was still enough strength left for her to glare up at her son.

'Do you imagine your father has spent money sending you to Oxford to have you marry a common . . . a common . . .' Her heart had begun to palpitate. 'And second-hand at that? How can you treat us so? How can you bring such disgrace upon your father, and upon me?'

If Matthew had felt like laughing, he would have. This was high melodrama – just like those Harriet herself adored so much. But they were talking about his future – his and hers.

'Disgrace, Mother? Harriet comes of a respectable family. Her father is a man of means, in business. That he chooses to live where he does is because his business is there, and it's convenient.'

Eleanor held a hand to her forehead. 'You are besotted, trapped by this . . . person. I forbid you to associate with her any longer. There are perfectly respectable girls here, of good families. You could have your pick of any one of them, with your fine looks, Matthew. Such a waste. Henry, I feel most unwell. Help me up, dear.'

She held out a flaccid hand to her husband, fingers protruding from bulbous leg-of-mutton sleeves like sticks of petrified wood.

'I need to go to my room. Matthew, ring for Lizzie – I must lie down. See what you've done, Matthew, with your irresponsible ways.'

Watching the melodrama being played out, all Matthew wanted to do was to get away, be with Harriet. But how could he tell her all that had transpired here?

*

Breakfast the next morning was eaten in huffy silence. Too much had already been said. Without the usual pleasantries, they served themselves from the dishes on the sideboard, but ate little of what small portions they'd chosen.

Matthew finally touched his moustache with his napkin as the butler, Honeyford, signalled to a thin, subdued girl named Rogers to clear away the used plates, and laid the cloth down on the table.

'About yesterday,' he began, paused as his parents looked up, then ploughed on. 'I'm deeply sorry if I upset you both. But I must make it clear. I intend to marry Harriet Porter. I love her and she loves me.' How trite it sounded. But he was merely expressing his true feelings.

Eleanor pushed her plate from her with a gesture as though the food lying untouched on it would choke her if she attempted to eat.

'I don't wish to hear any more, Matthew. Not another word.'

'It makes no difference, Mother.'

His father's fist came down on the table. Not heavily – this was a breakfast table, not a company board meeting – but forcefully enough to convey his profound displeasure.

'I'll thank you, Matthew, to address your mother with more courtesy. She isn't a servant to be spoken to as you please. She is your mother. Kindly speak to her as such.'

'For God's sake!' Matthew hissed under his breath, Aloud, he said, 'I'm sorry. I was merely stating a fact. The fact is, whether either of you listen to me or not, whether either of you approve or not, it will make no difference. I told you I wished to marry Harriet, not to ask your permission, but so that you know what I intend to do.'

Henry Craig got to his feet. 'And I remember telling you, Matthew, that if you go ahead with this idiotic notion, there'll be no more support from me for your journal. You'll have to make do with what's in your trust – which I should imagine is a little slimmer than it once was. You'll find it a pinch trying to support yourself, a wife and . . .'

'If you'd just meet her.'

'I think not.'

'You can't prevent me bringing her down here.'

'I can prevent the both of you crossing my threshold.'

Matthew couldn't believe what he had just heard. 'You mean you'd disown me?'

'I would. And I will, if you persist in this charade.'

'Henry, dearest!' Eleanor had her hands to her mouth.

He looked down the table to her, his square face grim but concerned for her. 'It has to be done, Lean.' He only ever called her Lean in moments of stress. 'He needs to be brought to his senses. If he can't find a decent girl around here, if he prefers to let this family down and to upset you, then he'd best not come here to upset you further.'

'But he can't be left penniless. He'll need money.'

'Let him learn to earn it. As I did.'

Matthew was seething. 'As you did?' he burst out. 'You inherited from Grandfather. The business, the house, everything. And Mother wasted no time snapping you up. It didn't bother you then that her father was no more than an ironmonger . . . To use her own words, a common . . .'

'That's enough!' The words exploded from his father's

lips. He slammed down his table napkin, knocking over his long-stemmed wineglass in the process, and spilling its contents like thin blood across the polished rosewood.

From the corner of his eye, Matthew saw Honeyford ushering young Rogers before him towards the door, discreetly guiding her out and following close behind, his long standing as a butler affording him the ability to appear not to hurry at all.

'I feel faint.' His mother had risen to her feet, was swaying.

Quickly, Henry strode to the door, bellowing, 'Honeyford – send Lizzie to Mrs Craig's room. Immediately.'

Immediately, sir,' came the stentorian voice, muffled by distance.

Matthew had hurried forward instinctively to offer support to his mother, but Henry was there before him and thrust him aside.

'I'll attend to her. I think you'd better go. If and when you come to your senses, I shall welcome you. But I warn you, Matthew – if you bring this . . . this widow with you, Honeyford will have orders to refuse you entry. Is that clear?'

Matthew gave no reply, but his father did not wait for one, engaged in conducting his distraught wife from the room.

He stood for a long time staring at the door. Only Honeyford and Rogers coming to clear away prompted him to shift himself. Slowly he climbed the wide central staircase. Passing his parents' room on the left in the upper passage he could hear weeping, but he hesitated only fractionally. What point was there in making any further issue out of this?

Slowly he packed, then went back the way he'd come. He paused at his mother's door, listening to her distressed sobbing. His father was with her, he could hear his deep voice droning comfort. Matthew tapped gently, calling a cautious goodbye. There was no answer; only the uninterrupted sobbing.

# Chapter Six

As Matthew anticipated, the wedding, planned for early
June, promised to see none of his own people attending.
On the other hand, Harriet's relations looked set to flock
en masse to see their widowed relative marry her intended,
restored to wifely status, her daughter no longer orphaned.

By April he was already keenly feeling the absence
of his family. He tried to cloak it by suggesting that the
wedding be a quiet one. 'No need for anything too grand.
Just your immediate family perhaps.'

They were sitting together on the sofa. Sara had been
laid down for the night in her cot in the bedroom, and they
had the evening to themselves. Curtains undrawn, the gas
as yet unlit, a smoke-laden sunset fading behind London's
brooding rooftops, the parlour was bathed by its soft
madder glow. Below them, the muffled rumble of Hackney
Road's traffic continued unabated. Harriet had been
snuggled in his arms, at peace with the world. Now she sat
up, regarding him as though he had slid down several pegs
in her estimation. Her eyes swam with bewilderment.

'I can't ask one without asking the other. You can't start
picking and choosing. Someone'll always be offended.
How can I turn round and say, we don't want you because

it'll be *a quiet one*?' The last three words, mimicking his Oxford accent, making him feel foolish, were spat out.

He was irked but didn't show it. 'I thought you'd prefer it quiet.'

'Well, I don't! Unless you're frightened it'll cost too much.'

'It's not that, Harriet, Just . . . I'd rather it not be too grand.'

To some extent she had hit the nail on the head, though she didn't know it. His financial situation was indeed shaky. His father, true to his word, had withheld the support he had previously given, leaving the journal only just bumping along the ground. But Matthew knew he couldn't explain the one without having to explain the other.

Hopeful of reconciliation, he had written to his father. There had been no reply and he felt hurt beyond measure, and angered. How dare they treat Harriet so! So what if she didn't match up to their idea of polished manners, or if the breathless way words tumbled from her mouth outpaced their precisely measured tones? She was as respectable as any of them, certainly more sincere than a lot of his mother's church-going associates with their backbiting, sanctimonious self-righteousness. The more he thought about it, the more it brought him out in a sweat of rage and made his heart pound until he felt quite sick. How could he tell Harriet any of this?

He vowed never to stoop to bothering them again. To hell with them! His father was right in one respect, though: the journal was too specialised; suffered poor circulation because of it. But pride would not let him alter its political

voice now, even if he had wanted to. Trying to explain all
that to Harriet was out of the question. She'd be so hurt.
She was hurt enough now.

'They're my *family*, Matthew. I can't offend them. I
wouldn't want to.'

'I know, my love. But this being your second
marriage . . .'

It was entirely the wrong thing to say. He knew it as
soon as he said it, stopped short, but the tears had really
started to flow now. She threw herself away from him.

'What you really mean is that God doesn't approve of
brides who've had . . . who've been . . . soiled?' The word
dragged itself out. 'I thought you loved me. How can you
be so . . . so hypocri—hypocrit—'

'I *do* love you.' Moved to sympathy by her inability in
her hurt pride to get round the word, he made an attempt
to catch her to him, but she resisted and held herself away
from him, her body rigid.

'I didn't mean it that way.' He tried reasoning in
desperation now. 'How can He see you as anything but
pure? As I see you. Oh, Harriet, my love, you're good and
wonderful and you deserve the best I can give you – my
heart, my soul, every last thing I possess, my very life if
you want it.'

She had relaxed only fractionally, unwilling to be won
over. He tried to make a little joke. 'But if I gave you my
life, I'd not have the joy of you, would I?' It fell flat. 'It's
that I am not given to ostentation,' he fought to explain.
'I'd much prefer . . .'

'That my family aren't there,' she finished, pouting. 'Not

good enough to meet the likes of yours from Winchester.'

'It's not that at all. I'm not considering inviting my own family either, Harriet.' But she wasn't to be mollified.

'So I'm not to invite mine. Well, that's just dandy, that is.' Vehemence crept back into her voice, tears flowing afresh from the melodrama she was creating for herself. 'I tell you what – let's not bother about any of it! Let's cancel everything. Go and find some genteel rich heiress in Winchester you'll feel more comfortable with. I'm no good to you . . . not clever enough for you. I just get on your nerves. Why don't you . . . Why don't you just leave me and go . . . and . . . and . . .' He put his hand firmly over her lips, stopping the hiccupping flow.

'Now that's enough. No more, my dearest.' Removing the hand, he kissed her swiftly, then, as it melted some of her peevishness, let the kiss linger, a little surprised that she didn't resist.

It was rare for her to allow him this much licence. The merest hint of anything more suggestive than a cuddle usually had an instant effect of frightening her off. This time it seemed that she was more terrified of the pictures she had created for herself of his taking her at her word and leaving her than of the reality of his ardour.

He felt his urge rising. His hand automatically sought the close row of tiny buttons on her blouse. Fingertips slipped the first, then the second. A third. Two more and there was room enough to slip his hand between the silky blouse and the cotton bodice. He could feel the firmness of her small breast beneath the harsh material, its warmth penetrating through the cloth and beckoning him to seek the smooth flesh itself. His breath was choking him. 'Oh, my darling . . . my precious darling . . .'

It was his undoing to give a voice to this special moment: it seemed to freeze her. 'Matthew – what are you doing?'

He felt her hands against his chest, pushing him away. He could feel her beginning to tremble. That unreasonable fear again.

'I love you so much, my sweet . . .'

'No, Matthew. Not before marriage. I mustn't. Let me go!' Her voice had risen to a shriek. From the bedroom came a thin cry. She leapt up. 'That's Sara – I must go to her.'

But no more sound came from the bedroom. Matthew sat trying to contain the disappointment of his shattered desire, but lost the struggle. 'She must have been having a dream,' he said defeatedly.

Harriet sat down in the armchair, out of reach, busying herself refastening the buttons. She didn't speak, but looked so pathetically embarrassed that he could only say, 'Forgive me, Harriet?'

Nodding, she continued fiddling with the buttons as though she feared they would come undone again. Matthew just sat bleakly watching her. After a while she got up and lit the gas jets on either side of the mantelpiece. This time, to his profound relief, she did not return to her seat but came and sat down again beside him with a look that intimated he must behave himself. Of course he would behave himself, his brief moment of passion flown.

After a moment she said in a small, shaky voice, 'We

can invite our families, can't we, Matthew?' *Not mine*, he thought, but said nothing about that. Soon he would have to explain to her.

'We can, can't we?' she urged again innocently.

He capitulated. It wasn't much to ask, giving her what she seemed most to desire. A reception wasn't going to break him. Especially as he had been secretly robbing the *Freewoman*'s tiny profits each week, putting aside a regular sum. It was a special secret – it was to take her to Paris for their honeymoon. He visualised, with hardly contained pleasure, her overwhelming joy when he finally revealed his secret. Harriet would, should, have the best he could afford. What if funds were a bit tight at the moment? He wasn't exactly poverty-stricken. He would manage, somehow.

A few weeks before the wedding the journal received a lift: out of the blue its circulation went up. The reason was that Dr Pankhurst, whose wife was the radical Emmeline Pankhurst, became the Independent Labour Party candidate for Gorton, Manchester. Four months earlier Mrs Pankhurst herself had been elected as ILP candidate to the Chorlton Board of Poor Law Guardians. The ILP being the only political party to encourage women to play a central role in its affairs, this was something of a fillip to the type of woman who bought journals like the *Freewoman*.

Matthew felt he could breathe again. If his journal continued its upward swing, he wouldn't need his father's handouts. It did indeed continue. His dream of taking

Harriet to Paris became a reality and he told her of his plan just two weeks before the wedding. He thought he'd never seen her so overwhelmed, weeping and laughing both at the same time, throwing her arms about his neck, covering her face with her fingers in sheer excitement and disbelief, dancing like an elf around the room despite the impediment of her skirts.

He watched her antics with amusement and a good deal of relief. For some weeks he'd had to face her bewilderment and frustration at his reluctance to take her to meet his family. Hedging for a long time, he had finally come out with the truth – or part of the truth: that, like his brother and sister, he had been brought up by a nanny, had been packed off to boarding school at the age of seven, then to public school and, finally, Oxford.

'So I've never been that close to them,' he explained happily while she gaped in disbelief that children could be so carelessly sent away, herself having known no other school than the one round the corner from her home. Indeed, until her first marriage, she had never been away from home. 'I had a wretched time at boarding school,' he told her. 'I'd never subject my children to that sort of upbringing.'

The remark prompted a speculative frown, but he gave it no thought as he went on to point out that as it was a long way to go to visit his parents, and as his mother was not a strong woman – which was why she wouldn't be attending the wedding – it was best to leave it for a while.

She had seemed satisfied though concerned, imagining his mother hovering at death's door. But he made light of it, saying that his mother was *given* to ailing, in fact had made an art of it over the years, which appeared to put Harriet's mind at rest.

'I'll write to your mother,' she said sombrely. 'She'd like that.'

'It's not necessary,' he'd hastened, cuddling her to him. 'But I love you, darling, for your thoughtfulness, with all my heart.'

Love? That was far too mild a word for how he felt about Harriet. Adored was more the truth. Little Sara he loved. Harriet he adored.

Sara, very forward, had begun to walk amazingly early. She had taken her first step on her birthday and had progressed this last month until she could totter unaided across her mother's parlour. A month from now she would be off like a steam train. He loved spending time with her. She was so charming, the blue eyes in the little round face so alert, she had quite taken his heart. How Harriet could be so unaffected by her winning ways, he couldn't understand. She never doted on or praised her as some mothers would their first child. He did mention it once and had been taken aback by her reaction. The sweet Harriet he knew had been transformed into a virago, ending in floods of tears, accusing him of being unreasonable – him, unreasonable!

'I do believe you think more of her than you do of me,' she railed at him and he hadn't dared to trespass again into that side of her nature, mostly because he couldn't bear being the cause of her tears.

\*

The church ceremony was brief. The reception would have done his own family credit; hearty though it was, it was conducted soberly and with propriety.

Each taking a turn, songs were sung – more the gusty music-hall type than the warbled gentility of so-called well-bred circles – poems and ballads recited, a story or two told. But no one got roaring drunk, no one stomped a raucous knees-up, no one started an argument or hit anyone – it was all a far cry from what his family had possibly imagined it would be; from what he himself had expected. Harriet's people had that flat East London edge to their voices when they spoke, most certainly, but they were not raucous or loudly garrulous.

He'd grown used to the loud Cockney accent. Daily it was bellowed outside his printer's shop, below the window of his now vacated digs in Teale Street; wherever he turned in the East End, there it was jarring his ear. Mrs Hardy's voice was certainly loud enough, any conversation yelled as though her listener were fifty yards down Hackney Road. Mr Hardy, too: his expletives were ripe, to say the least, and delivered in a voice like a rusty nail. Yet hearing the conversations around him, Matthew had come to recognise a depth of fellow feeling that seemed to be shared by all who lived here, a brash, quick wit that helped a man face the grinding poverty that constantly threatened and often overwhelmed; not so much resigned as a head-on meeting, fists clenched, chin out. Life here was harsh, vibrant, aggressive, but always confronted with a grim smirk – from the drunk carted off to the clink in a police wheelbarrow to the woman cleaning her doorstep, her eyes dry, the day after the birth of her stillborn sixth or seventh, or the untimely death of a child or a sickly husband, or the knowledge that her days too were numbered.

Here was a pride Matthew felt would have done his family a power of good to have seen. He had once been like them, thought himself above the denizens of the East End. Today, he often felt humbled by their fierce self-esteem; had come to feel some of that pride even within himself.

Perhaps the wedding reception would heat up later to something more raucous, more typical of what he'd learned to expect of this area, but he wouldn't know, with him and Harriet leaving within the hour to catch the boat train.

Harriet could hardly contain her excitement. Paris. She felt utterly opulent. No one she could think of had ever been abroad.

'Lucky devil, that's all I can say,' her brother John laughed as he toasted the happy couple with a glass of pale ale, allowed him now he'd turned eighteen. 'Might go meself one day.'

'One day? Next year, me, I 'ope.' His brother George nudged him, slopping the liquid over his wrist. John scowled and lifted the glass clear, wiping off the splashes with his free hand.

'Watch it! An' what makes you fink Dad'd let you go at seventeen, you 'alf-baked 'Arry!'

A look from their doughty Aunt Sarah shut them up. She didn't abide arguing boys, even though both were grown nearly as big and thickset as their father; nor did she approve of the way they spoke. They might mix with their father's employees – they did not have to talk like them.

Harriet laughed happily, thanking them both for their good wishes, but Annie and Clara reacted exactly as she had expected them to, bidding her farewell with ill-concealed jealousy.

'I don't think I'd care for all that foreign food,' Annie said, making a point of sounding unenthusiastic, which her husband Robert seconded in all innocence.

'I agree. Give me good plain English food any time.'

'The people there aren't like us,' Clara imparted as though wild horses wouldn't have dragged her there. 'However will you get on if you can't be understood? It's not as if you can speak the language.'

'Matthew does. He speaks very good French.'

'He would.'

'He learnt at Oxford. German too. And Latin . . .'

'Yes, we know. We all know he's been to Oxford.'

Mary was full of fear at the thought of her daughter crossing that stretch of water between Dover and Calais – as though it were the Atlantic. 'I do hope it's not rough, dear. You don't want to be seasick on your wedding day. And don't worry about Sara. She'll be as good as gold with us. I expect she'll miss you, but it's only a week. And you will be careful, won't you? For Sara's sake – for all our sakes.'

Her father added his own warning as the guests assembled to wave the happy pair on their way and she kissed everyone goodbye. 'Don't drink the water unless it's boiled,' he shouted over the calls of bon voyage. 'Don't want to get yourself dysentry. That's what killed a lot of our boys fighting out in the Sudan and in South Africa, as much as any bullets did.'

'I'm not going to South Africa, Dad,' she laughed as Matthew helped her up into the cab. 'I'm going to Paris. They're as civilised in Paris as we are.'

Though looking at some parts of the area where she lived, she wondered about civilised. Paris had to be cleaner.

At Victoria they gave their trunks and bags into the charge of the porters and boarded the train. They settled in a first-class compartment with only one other occupant, a middle-aged man in a dark morning suit and top hat who spent much of the journey rustling through the *Manchester Guardian*.

Shy and awkward, Harriet sat opposite Matthew, hardly speaking, lest their fellow passenger guess their newly wed state. But he already had, occasionally looking up as he turned a page to glance briefly from Matthew to her, and she was sure she saw his lips twitch now and again beneath that well-trimmed grey moustache as though privately amused before returning his gaze to a new page. If Matthew felt awkward, he carried it off well. But even he said very little.

The carriage grew hot as the afternoon sun moved round. It shone into her eyes and she wished she could change sides to be out of its glare, but she felt too self-conscious to move.

'It's hot,' she whispered to Matthew, who immediately leapt up with a forthright 'Do you object?' to the man, who graciously shook his head – again, Harriet thought, with a quirk of the moustached lips.

With the window down, the air was a relief, but the soot smell from the engine and the black smuts landing on her new green outfit and her trim-matching hat made her wish she hadn't complained. Yet she dared not reverse her request, and sat trying not to inhale the reek of smoke passing by the open window. She felt thirsty, too, and uncomfortable, her new corset, still needing to mould to her figure, biting into her ribs. She was glad when they reached Dover.

Amid the rumble of trolleys trundling trunks on to the quayside for loading and the chatter of passengers and those seeing them off, they mounted the gangway to the boat. Harriet walked up it cautiously.

'I hope the sea's smooth,' she whispered to Matthew, and felt his hand tighten reassuringly upon hers as he helped her climb.

The Channel, however, was as calm as a duckpond. But for the heavy thud of engines that seemed to pound right through her chest, they fairly glided. They must have gone faster than it appeared, for the boat ploughing through the oil-flat water stirred up a breeze Harriet hadn't expected as she walked with Matthew around the deck, obliging women to hold on to their hats. But the tang of the sea had got into her blood and in a fit of abandonment she discarded her own hat and held it in her hand. Her glowing auburn hair, neatly coiled, exposed to the elements, she felt gloriously free in her married state.

Under a celestial blue sky of amazing dimension to her unaccustomed eyes, which took her breath away, she leaned over the rail to take in its even deeper reflection in the sea, fascinated by the white purity of foam hissing serenely below her from the bows cutting through the tranquil water. The breeze ruffling her hair was wonderfully warm.

Luxuriating in its sensuous caress, she longed to reach Calais, where Matthew had pre-booked an hotel for the night before they went on to Paris. In the privacy of their room, she saw herself revelling in his kisses, responding to his caresses, and she shivered deliciously as the sea breeze fondled her hair, her skin. She hardly ate any of her dinner, served in the boat's ornate pink and blue restaurant, for thinking about their first night together.

When in the dusk they disembarked, she was speechless with wonder, unable to believe they were on French soil, foreign soil, no longer England. It was all so strange, so different, the voices around her alien to her ears, loud, garbled, angry almost. She grew anxious.

'Why're they all quarrelling?'

Matthew laughed out loud, as though he too saw no reason to keep his own voice down, English reserve cast off like an old hat.

'It sounds that way because you don't understand their language.' He squeezed her arm. 'I shall teach you, my love, so that next year when we come again, you'll speak as fluently as any of them. I shall teach you much more than that, my darling,' he added slowly, lowering his voice, and Harriet shivered pleasurably at the double meaning. Suddenly she felt very French, very liberated, could hardly wait to reach the hotel, where she would become in every essential Matthew's wife.

*

But once they were in their hotel room, the sensuality of sea breezes, the exotic allurement of being in France, the undertone of Matthew's promises, all faded from her mind. It was all so different from what she had expected.

The tension of undressing in a cavernous bathroom; having to pass Matthew standing gazing out of the open window so as not to look at her and embarrass her; the very act of slipping into the narrow bed that promised to bring them purposely closer together; the way the bed yielded even to her light weight with a faint groan – it all began to feel sordid. She drew the covers up to her chin but still felt so terribly exposed.

Then, as Matthew, still without looking at her, moved in turn to the huge bathroom to get ready for bed, came the waiting, unnerving her. Long before he lifted the covers and slipped in beside her, she was already rigid, her teeth clenched against his first preliminary caress.

And there, in the darkness, Will's intense blue eyes surveyed her, his virile body floating in her head, the memory vivid of his hands forceful with brutish need for satisfaction. 'Men,' he whispered in her ear, 'we're all the same, fobbin' you off with lovin' words when it's your sex we need, and this new one's no different from me, you'll see.'

It didn't help that Matthew was obviously as nervous as she, that he was being so gentle, so thoughtful of her. She found herself fighting against him. 'Matthew! I can't! I'm sorry. I can't . . .'

'It's all right, dearest.'

He tried to be even more gentle, but the mere touch of

his hands on her flesh set Will laughing, and her cringing.

'Oh, Matthew . . . please . . . I'm sorry . . .' He was already moving away from her, trying to pull his nightshirt back down over himself without making the movement too obvious to her.

They lay side by side, both of them rigid now.

'I don't know what to say,' she whimpered. 'I don't know . . .' There was no way of explaining. But he turned his face towards her and kissed her cheek gently, whispering, 'I understand. Goodnight, my sweet.' He turned carefully on his side.

After a while she heard his breathing become regular, but she lay awake, ashamed of her stupidity now that Will had faded away, wanting to reach out to Matthew, to say she was sorry; needing to snuggle close to him. But fear of his natural reaction to any such move kept her where she was, lying still and very alone.

# Chapter Seven

In Paris, Matthew proved himself the most attentive of husbands, if no longer an ardent lover. 'I understand, dearest,' he said tenderly, a little perplexed on the second night of her distraught pleading and abject apology. 'Whenever you are ready, my sweet.'

He was so wonderful, so understanding, that she felt all the more guilty. But however much she vowed to herself that she would behave like a proper wife, there would come this overwhelming fear, this tensing, the moment he touched her. As the week progressed he became even more perplexed and, she was sure, more impatient with her. Though he insisted that he understood.

'I know, it takes time. Don't blame yourself. It's quite natural. I'm sure it must be,' – the last echoing a certain doubt.

The days were so different. Hand in hand they hurried off each morning on a tour of discovery. There was so much to see, not enough time to see it all. The new wrought-iron wonder of the Eiffel Tower, the highest structure in the world, amazed Harriet though she could not bring herself to climb it despite Matthew's cajoling. Roaming the bohemian quarter of Montmartre, watching artists there in the streets painting pictures, perhaps one day to become as famous as those whose pictures they viewed at the Louvre, her eyes popped.

'We've got to buy some of their paintings, Matthew!' And pointing to one market stall after another, 'Oh, that vase Matthew! And, ooh, look! That statue! Oh, Matthew – can we have it? Can we?'

'How can we carry them all back home?' he laughed, but nevertheless indulged her, arranging for what they purchased to be sent on.

Leaning over bridges they gazed down at their reflections in the quietly flowing Seine; felt very much in love. Lost in each other they ate out in the warm June sunshine. Sitting at pavement tables in full view of passers-by who did not so much as glance at them was an experience that delighted Harriet. So did the ever-present aroma of percolating coffee and freshly baked breads. They often dined out too – after a theatre or merely strolling around.

It was all so enthralling. At the theatre she was dazzled by the lights; the hubbub of conversation all around; the men in their evening dress of silk-lined cloaks and silk top hats; the ladies in fashionable gowns of all colours, feather and lace fans flapping, gloved hands brandishing them like weapons with every word uttered, jewellery glittering under a myriad of gas chandeliers as they were handed down from their coaches. The coaches drew up one behind the other in a seemingly endless queue; as one at the head drew away empty, another would join the rear. It was obvious that many people owned their own vehicles, their own livery.

'Everyone's so elegant,' she whispered as Matthew helped her down from the carriage he'd hired to convey them to the Paris Opera, very aware of her own ordinary gown of blue crepon. Until that moment it had seemed the height of fashion, flounced and beribboned, bishop sleeves ballooning – as part of her trousseau it had cost her a pretty penny – but now she shrank against Matthew, himself as well dressed as any man there as they moved forward with the crush towards the glittering golden foyer.

'I really must look for something more suitable while we're here, Matthew. I feel dowdy in this thing.'

Matthew only laughed, brown eyes lovingly taking her in. 'You look ravishing enough to eat. And very expensive.'

Nevertheless, the next day she had to drag him to the Rue de Rivoli for a dress she'd seen earlier: fawn shot silk, with a lace-trimmed basque waist, a cape of frilled lace, and bouffant sleeves to the elbow then tight to the wrist, the skirt fluted and edged with yet more lace. She would have loved something exclusive, for evening only, but even she realised that at Paris prices such luxuries were beyond Matthew's pocket. The dress would easily double for day and evening. There were gloves to match, and a lace-trimmed hat, but Matthew also picked out for her a tiny hat with lace and roses for evening wear.

'You're so good to me,' she whispered, barely able to wait to get back to the hotel to don her new outfit before going out yet again to discover more of this wonderful place.

Her arm threaded through Matthew's, she giggled coyly beneath the gaze of the hotel's proprietor, Monsieur Petit.

They had not, of course, confessed to being newlyweds, but he beamed at them just the same, from long experience recognising all the signs.

'Enjoy your fine day, *monsieur*, *madame*. It goes slow, *oui*? But then . . .' Bunched fingers exploding a kiss into the air, he raised his large bulbous eyes ceilingward, which could have indicated heaven or the nuptial pleasure apparently to be re-enacted above him, his broad smile familiar with secrets as old as time yet as new as today.

They returned the smile, polite but embarrassed, and hurried on.

'Annie and Clara'll be green with envy when I tell them about all this,' Harriet gloated, embarrassment forgotten as they ate a simple but beautifully served cold lunch at a pavement table beside the quietly flowing Seine, washing it down with an inexpensive wine now that funds were getting a bit low. 'I bet they'll be badgering their husbands to take them here when I tell them all we've seen.'

Public gardens, parks, palaces, boulevards, the breathtaking Arc de Triomphe, the lovely tree-lined Champs Elysees, the awe-inspiring Notre Dame – and still they had seen only half of what Matthew had planned to show her, even though they took a fiacre to get around more easily. He was already trying to teach her some French, making her repeat after him, *fiacre* – cab, but she failed miserably, making him chuckle, fiddling with his moustache, as he always did when amused. He was growing it longer, and twiddled the ends to make them stand out more stiffly. The habit made him look debonair, and she loved him so much. Yet when the day ended and they crept into bed, always the ghost of Will came between them – at least, so it seemed to her; Matthew's attempts to make love becoming Will's groping hands.

Their last night was the culmination. She was acutely aware of his trying to be patient with her, his touch upon her bosom so light, so gently coaxing, as one might coax a wild bird to the hand. And she tried so hard, telling herself angrily that there was nothing to fear: Matthew would behave properly, would treat her with care. In marriage, this had to be done.

She steeled herself as his hand, gaining confidence from her continuing non-rejection, moved cautiously down towards her lower parts. This time she wouldn't shrink. Matthew's kisses on her cheek remained like the flutter of bird wings, so gentle were they. She could hardly feel his hand as it moved, but knew it did move, ever closer to the moment when she knew she must respond to him.

She felt the soft brush of her nightdress against her legs, the warmth of his hand on her bared flesh, and gritted her teeth. She loved him so much, yet this . . . this . . . She felt her breath suck into her lungs, held it there until she felt she would burst. His hand went no further, but now he moved so that his body lay lightly on hers. No, she would not flinch. She would try to be a good wife. Try . . .

Something touched her between the thighs, sent a sensation through her. Before she could stop herself, she gave a short, sharp scream of fear and doubled up beneath his lightly held weight.

'Oh, Matthew! Oh, Matthew – I'm sorry!'

The weight was no longer there. He was sitting up

beside her, his dark brown eyes, visible in the moonlight pouring through the gauzy curtains at the window, like deep, angry hollows.

'My God!'

'I know,' she sobbed, shamed at her behaviour. 'We can try again.'

'No we will not try again! I've had enough, Harriet. This is becoming quite idiotic. I'm beginning to believe you've no love for me at all.'

She was mortified. 'I have, Matthew. I have. Don't say that.'

'Then what is wrong with you?'

'There's nothing wrong.'

He flung back the bedclothes, got up and roamed about the room. The moonlight through the gauze curtains revealed his long narrow frame beneath his nightshirt. But she could see only anger in his stance. She had never known him so angry and she was afraid.

'I don't know what's the matter with me,' she tried to excuse, her voice trembling. 'It's jut that . . . it's all strange to me . . .'

'Strange?' he threw at her, his voice hollow with frustration. 'How in God's name can it be strange after a week together? Every time I breathe on you, you cringe. I couldn't have behaved more gently with you then I have. If you really loved me . . . Harriet, you make me feel I'm an animal.'

She was crying now, her hands to her lips. Matthew ignored the weeping, the first time she'd ever known him do so.

'I think I've been more than patient, Harriet.'

'I know.'

'Then tell me what's the matter with you?'

'I don't know.' How could she tell him?

'You must know. We can't go on like this. How long am I expected to put up with this? I'm flesh and blood, Harriet, not some . . .'

'Don't shout at me.' She was out of bed, clasped hands raised in front of her, beseeching the forbearance that was no longer forthcoming.

'I shall – so long as you behave as if I'm about to rape you.'

That was it. She broke down completely. 'You're being horrible to me. You're being horrible.'

Weeping copiously, she fled to the cavernous bathroom. Locking herself in, she threw herself down on to the tiled floor. Its chill struck like a knife through the fine lawn of her nightdress, but she welcomed its discomfort as a flagellant would the whip. Rather than calm her, it impelled her to a greater need to hurt herself, to be hurt. Then, when she finally emerged, shivering with shock from the cold pain Matthew had indirectly inflicted on her, he would be sorry.

Her racking sobs echoed pathetically from the white tiled walls, until near exhaustion finally made them cease and she got herself up off the chilly floor and sat on the soft fluffy towel draped over the huge iron bath, glad of its warmth. In a while she must let herself out, face Matthew. But how could she? Warmer now, she felt ashamed of her outburst. She'd have to let herself out, beg his forgiveness.

He would forgive her, that she knew, when he saw how abject she was feeling.

She heard his gentle tap on the door.

'Harriet?' His tone was soft, questioning, concerned. 'Are you all right?'

The words only prompted hiccupping sobs. 'I – I don't – Oh . . . Matthew. I'm – so – so – unhappy!'

'Don't cry, darling. Come out. Let me cuddle you better.'

He spoke as though he were talking to a child. Indeed she felt like a child, wanting his arms about her. Swallowing her pride, she made herself get up from the edge of the bath. She was about to let herself out when suddenly the image flashed into her mind of his hands around her, his grasp becoming intense. He would grip and sigh and bring her to him, and take her, use her.

'I'm not coming out!' she cried in terror. 'I'm staying in here!'

For a moment he didn't reply. When he did, she couldn't believe it was Matthew speaking, his voice was so harsh and sibilant. 'Then stay there!'

Listening intently, she heard him moving about the room. It sounded as though he was getting dressed. But it was almost the middle of the night. How could he be dressing? She heard the bedroom door open, then close gently. She felt suddenly frightened. Where was he going in the middle of the night?

'Matthew?' she called. Then, more loudly, 'Matthew!'

After unlocking the bathroom door, her fingers hasty and fumbling, she flung it open and ran into the room. It was quiet and empty, only the moonlight shafting on to the bed. Propped against his crumpled pillow was a roughly scribbled note.

'Gone down to the bar for a drink. Go to bed.'

Nothing more, no loving word, no tender message, no scribbled goodnight. She had a vague thought of getting dressed and going after him, but that would have looked improper.

Her pretty face creased with anguish, she could only do as he had ordered. She got into bed, her eyes stinging from all that weeping. When he came back, this time she really would behave as a proper wife should. He wouldn't hurt her – not as Will had. Matthew was far too gentle a person. With all this in mind, she lay waiting, ready for what lay ahead.

But he didn't come up for a long time. When finally he did, she, worn out by weeping and waiting and the normal need of the body to sleep, was unaware of it.

# Chapter Eight

Sunday afternoon tea had been enjoyed and cleared away in the Wilson household. The two boys had gone out – George with several mates to ogle the girls in the park, John to the same place but to gaze at one special girl he had seen walking with her parents the previous week, in the hopes that she might favour him with a glance or two of her own.

Mary and her sister retired upstairs to the front parlour to allow the housemaid, Violet, to clear the tea table downstairs before having the rest of the day to herself. Jack had taken himself down into the yard to smoke a quiet cigar and to glance in at his factory.

Situated at the rear, its entrance opening on to Old Ford Road and taking up the rear of several other yards, it was quite a tidy-sized place, accessible to main roads for bringing in wood and taking out the finished product: well-made sideboards, fine tables, well-turned chairs. Today being August Bank Holiday, it was, naturally, deserted. Jack loved the smell of his factory when it lay silent – the raw tang of sawn wood and sawdust, the heavy lingering odour of glue, the acrid invasion of French polish. And of course his cigar. He particularly enjoyed the aroma of his cigar in this quiet place. It was one of his keenest pleasures to stand here at ease, puffing away. And it got him away from the chatter of Mary and her sister.

In the front parlour, Sarah sat near the window for extra light, keeping her hand in embroidering some new handkerchiefs with her initials, SM, in pink silk entwined by deep green vine leaves. Her brow was furrowed into a frown, but not over her work.

'I'm beginning to wonder about Harriet and Matthew,' she said with her usual blunt approach to any matter about which she felt strongly.

Mary was gazing down at the street below, enjoying her usual Sunday afternoon pastime of watching families drifting in droves towards the park to take a breather from the soot and smoke that, even in August sunshine, hovered over London roofs. Now she turned enquiring eyes to her sister. 'Wonder about them? What's there to wonder about?'

'Something's not quite right.'

'They seem all right to me. Matthew's journal's doing quite well, I think, and Harriet's fine. They're forever out and about, though I wish Harriet would give more time to Sara. The child always seems to be with that Mrs Hardy. By the time she starts to talk she'll have picked up their way of talking. Lord knows, I did my best to bring my children up to speak as correct as it's possible around here. I think I made a decent enough job of it, considering. Jack's never felt the need to move away, but sometimes I wish . . .'

Shrugging off the unspoken wish, she returned her gaze to the scene below. She'd probably have been bored somewhere else anyway. No one could say Approach Road wasn't an interesting place to live. There was always something to watch, especially in summer with the comings and goings of people. She could spend whole afternoons taking stock of the world passing by below this window. Like today.

As always there was a sprinkling of silk toppers mingling with the cloth caps, and smart feathered toques were noticeable among the cheap straw boaters. At intervals a hired hackney cab would be held up by a trundling old barrow, the driver with no time to spare and in need of his next fare yelling abuse at the barrowman to get out of his way. But more often the droves passing below were the products of grubby poverty. Some obviously strove to bring themselves above the normal hand-to-mouth existence, being tidily but cheaply dressed, and trying to keep their kids clean. But there were others who either couldn't care less or had been submerged by circumstances, not bothering or unable to dress any better, taking their ragged kids for a blow, escaping some sunless basement flat reeking of damp and dustbins; a couple of chamberpots their only convenience, a communal pump in the yard their only means of washing so that they seldom bothered to wash properly. Children with lice and scabby mouths; bedbugs and cockroaches lurking behind wallpaper while sick babies huddled beneath ragged blankets – Mary often thought of it from the comfort of her parlour and felt guilty that her life *was* comfortable while others were so wretched.

But this late afternoon, her mind was more on her

granddaughter's upbringing than on what was going on outside.

'It's the Hardys that worry me – that child picking up that aht-an'abaht way they talk. I'm sure Matthew wouldn't want that for her. He dotes on Sara. It's wonderful for a stepfather to be like that. She really is fortunate to have a father like him. Harriet is, too, finding a good man like Matthew. And he does talk so nicely. Sara could pick it up, so long as Mr and Mrs Hardy don't influence her too much.'

Sarah drew in a deep breath, indicating an intention of not being sidetracked from her original purpose.

'Yes, Mary, that's all very well, but what I'm worried about is how her parents have been behaving.' She breathed an even deeper intake of park air, then came to the point: 'I've got to say it, that marriage has never been consummated – I'm almost certain of it.'

Mary turned again, this time with a look of amazement, horror and downright effrontery.

'Has never . . . What an awful thing to say.'

Sarah ploughed on determinedly. 'You only have to look at her. Surely you've noticed. She came back from that honeymoon looking as if she'd been flung in prison rather than the glow you usually see on a bride's face. You saw her. You must have noticed *something* wasn't right.'

'It didn't even dawn on me to look.' Mary's small back was up, or, rather, stiff as a ramrod, as it always was whenever she was put out. She sat on her chair like a small pouter pigeon. 'I think that's being very out of order, Sarah, saying things like that.'

'You think so?'

'I do. Where's your proof for saying such an awful thing?'

'You wouldn't exactly say Harriet was in raptures as you would've expected when they came back. As for him, he looked positively . . .' She searched desperately for a word to fit Matthew's thunderous face when she, Mary and Jack had met them off the boat train at Victoria station, and failed. She finally ended: ' . . . and still does.'

'It *was* a long journey,' Mary excused hotly. 'And they *were* tired.'

'And still tired two months later, I suppose. Even you must have noticed that – or something like it. Perhaps nothing did come off during their week away, but it should have by now. The thing is, I'd be willing to stake my last farthing that nothing's happened – not on their honeymoon, and not since.'

Mary smothered her natural urge to defend her daughter and laughed disparagingly if a little apprehensively.

'That's ridiculous! You do think up some funny things, Sarah! Whatever makes you imagine . . . ? Anyway, that sort of thing's private. It's nothing to do with anyone but them.'

But the truth was, she *had* noticed something peculiar about her daughter and son-in-law that until now she hadn't been able to put a finger on; even now she didn't want to admit something was wrong. Harriet wasn't happy, nor was her husband, anyone could see it, though until now she wouldn't have dreamed mentioning it. 'What do you imagine's the cause? If it is that, of course. Which I don't think it is.'

'You ask me!'

The offhand shrug immediately nettled Mary. 'I *am* asking you, Sarah. You're the one who's supposed to have all the intuitions – or so you say. You should know.'

'I don't know. I'm just saying what's in my mind – what I . . . *feel* in my mind. And I'm saying, I don't think that marriage has clicked. I don't think he can produce the business, if you want it bluntly.'

'Sarah!'

'Well, what other word would you use? Either he has or he hasn't. Either he can or he can't.'

'Can't?'

'Perhaps he's not . . . well, capable. You know. You can hardly call him . . . manly looking. Not like Will was. Mind you, that one was a bit too much. Howsoever, that's another matter,' she added hurriedly. 'Nevertheless, there's men and *men*, if you take my meaning. Far be it from me, Mary, to put a down on a person, but, surely, a wife as pretty as Harriet . . . She hasn't exactly got a face like the back end of a dustcart. Though sometimes, with that down-in-the-mouth expression she's been adopting lately . . . No, I'm sure there's something not quite right with them two. Something that we don't know about.'

Mary's back was still rod straight. 'It sounds as if you've already made up your mind something's not right. Anyway, it's early days yet, and all I can say is we'll find out in time if everything's all right in that department when Harriet tells us she's expecting.'

'Let's hope,' Sarah concluded, undaunted, 'it won't be too long.'

*

Autumn moved into winter, and by the time Christmas was upon them, Sarah found that hope becoming ever more empty.

'Doesn't look too good, does it?' she said darkly to Mary, who gave a sniff and changed the subject, saying she had enough on her mind worrying about having the family for Christmas as usual. Not that there were many this year: it was Annie and Clara's turn to spend it with their husbands' people. But it seemed that Matthew and his own people, whom none of the Wilsons, including Harriet herself, had yet met, weren't the sort to honour Christmas with family gatherings. So he and Harriet and little Sara spent Christmas with Mary and Jack.

And again, as 1896 began leaving '95 well behind, Sarah commented with monotonous regularity: 'Still no signs yet.'

Again and again Mary chose to shrug it off, but others too were taking note of Harriet's continuing lack of fruitfulness.

Mrs Hardy was one such, relaying her concern to Mr Hardy one Saturday evening in April as she joggled the now two-year-old Sara on her lap.

'Odd, ain't it? Ain't no signs of any little additions to that family yet. And she ain't pregnant yet – I can stake me life on that.'

Bert Hardy humphed awkwardly and rustled his *Evening Star*. Talk of women's conditions always bored and embarrassed him.

'Poor little mite,' Emma went on, gazing down at her

charge. 'She don't 'ardly ever see them two. Always orf somewhere togever, they are. Even went owt on 'er little birfday last week, poor little mite. I know they bought 'er some nice presents, but it ain't the same. Pity they don't get tergever at nights an' sort owt a little bruvver or sister for this poor little'un.'

Bert turned noisily to the sporting page to see if the horse he'd laid out on had come in. It hadn't. He girded himself for more regalement on the Craigs' problem, as Emma termed it, but Emma had realised it was time to get tea and, having popped the Craig child into the old cot she kept for that purpose, was making her way downstairs to the kitchen.

'I did say, didn't I?' said Annie to her husband. 'I always said that marriage wasn't a love match. Marriage of convenience, I said, didn't I? She only married Matthew for his money. Now didn't I say that?'

'I believe you did,' Robert murmured absently, his thoughts on one of his underlings at the bank. The man had been late on two occasions that week and absent on Tuesday the week before, blaming a heavy cold. But the branch manager was sure the man had skived off for the day and had charged Robert, promoted the year before to assistant under-manager, with the task of conveying a severe warning on his behalf to the man that the next time it would be the Manager's Office itself and possibly his being handed his notice. Robert liked the man and wasn't relishing the prospect one bit.

'So I'm being proved right, aren't I?' Annie hurried on.

'Yes, dear, I think you are.'

\*

Annie tackled Clara over tea and cakes in a teashop on one of their weekly shopping trips up Oxford Street. 'I did say, didn't I?'

'She might not be the sort to fall easily,' Clara excused as she stirred her tea thoughtfully, but Annie's tongue clicked impatiently.

'She fell easy enough with Sara.'

'Perhaps it's Matthew. Perhaps he's . . . sort of barren?'

'Don't be silly. Men can't be barren. And Harriet's certainly proved she can bear children. No, it was a marriage of convenience. She knew where her bread was buttered, that one did.'

'That's cruel, Annie. Whatever she got from marrying Matthew, don't you think she deserved it, after losing Will so tragically?'

'Yes, she got what she deserved all right,' Annie said primly and took a vicious bite of her cream bun.

Mary discussed the matter with Jack, worried now at the passing of time and nothing yet to show for it. In his down-to-earth way, Jack said it was best to let time sort itself out.

'But they've been married a year, or almost, and there's no sign of her being anything near . . . having something interesting to tell us. It's not Harriet, obviously, so it must be Matthew.'

Young Violet came into the room at that moment, bringing tea and scones on a tray. She couldn't help hearing what her employers were saying and immediately put two and two together, particularly since their conversation suddenly went dead – until she absented herself. She couldn't wait to get down to the basement to tell Mrs Cullen what she suspected.

The woman kept her fleshy face directed at the suet pastry she was rolling. The master loved his meat puddings, even though it was May and such fare was better reserved for winter meals. Sleeves rolled up, her thick arms wielded the rolling pin back and forth with unusual vigour.

'You've got big ears for a small girl, Vi. Too big.'

'No one couldn't 'elp over'earing when it comes out in front of them. I can't put a cloth over me ears when I goes into the parlour, can I?'

Mrs Cullen stopped her rolling to regard Violet with steady blue eyes. 'Don't be saucy! What you heard'd better not go outside these four walls, that's what I say. Can't have half the street knowing our employer's business.'

'I wouldn't dream of breathin' a word.'

'And you'd better not. If it was to get back, you'd be the first to be suspected and lose your position. And so would I lose mine for listening to your gossip. That's what it is, Vi. Gossip. Remember that and keep your lips shut tight about what's said in this 'ouse.'

'Yes, Mrs Cullen,' said Violet, chastened by the sharpness of her superior's warning. But from then on she looked upon her employer's son-in-law with great disillusionment. Hitherto she had been wont to dream herself to sleep in her bed under the roof with the handsome Mr Matthew Craig as her bedfellow, his gentle way of speaking translated into the whispering of sweet nothings into her ears. Now she had second thoughts about that gentleness. What if . . . It didn't bear thinking about. Poor Mrs Craig.

Matthew felt he could not handle this situation much longer. He felt alone, isolated, with not a soul to turn to for advice. What a confession for a man to have to make: that after twelve months his marriage was still no marriage at all, that in all that time he had not once made proper love to his own wife, with her still behaving in bed like some coy maiden who'd never in her life seen a man half-naked, much less had one in bed beside her. At a loss to understand her, he could almost hear the echo of disbelief were he to confide in someone, imagine the sidelong glance that would speak volumes on a fellow so lily-livered as to let a wife dictate to him in the conjugal bed. There were times he himself began to wonder.

He needed advice, but whom could he trust? Doctors? He had considered them – impartial men who wouldn't bat an eyelid – but their imperious regard would make him feel a fool. His friend David Symonds, who had also acted as groomsman at his wedding? But he hadn't seen him in months, although he still resided in Queensbridge Road, now a junior partner of Peeker, Stymes & Symonds, solicitors.

Solicitors were hardly the people to consult in matters of this sort. But it was desperation that finally led Matthew to seek out David, going to his flat one Sunday morning rather than formally to his office on a weekday with other clients hovering for attention.

David welcomed him in, still bleary from sleep, but

delighted to see him. Helping Matthew out of his wet ulster, David vigorously shook off the raindrops before hanging it on the hallstand.

Chatting amiably as though it were only yesterday that he'd seen Matthew, he led the way to the tiny sitting room that overlooked Haggerston Park. Only in the brighter light from the window did he become aware of Matthew's tense expression.

'God, man, you look as though you've done a murder. What's up?'

Indicating a leather easy chair to one side of the empty grate, he poured Matthew a fortifying whisky, and came to sit opposite him.

'I take it that the look on your face is the reason for your call.'

Matthew nodded. With no idea how on earth to begin this delicate and personal subject, he found himself idiotically bursting out: 'If I don't confide in someone, I shall end up throwing myself under a brewer's dray.'

David's lips quirked to one side, giving his rounded features the appearance of a music hall comedian. 'A bit drastic, old man. I shall do my utmost to prevent that ultimate happening. Now settle yourself and tell me the problem – it's deep-rooted by the look of it.'

In the three years since entering his father's profession he had begun to show a tendency to rotundity, although the restive joviality Matthew remembered from their Oxford days was in no way diminished; if anything it served to instil confidence – certainly enough to prompt Matthew into a halting account of his marriage so far.

'You possibly deem me a weak thing,' he ended ineffectually.

David had remained professionally friendly during the story, leaning forward in his easy chair to take in every word. He had twice refilled Matthew's glass from the decanter on the small table at his elbow while he listened, but had taken only one himself. Now he leaned back, the chair leather creaking, to regard Matthew as he debated his own thoughts.

The hiatus drew itself out. From Haggerston Park Matthew could hear the distant squeals of some children playing. From somewhere nearby pigeons were cooing to one another, a hollow, haunting warble.

His thoughts snapped to attention as David spoke, his tone taking on a legal ring.

'You do realise, your Harriet is a woman who has a natural need to be dominated, and, as with such women, when she senses a weakness in the master of the house, she'll take advantage of that.'

'That's not Harriet,' Matthew broke in, but David gestured his interruption away with a chubby hand.

'She obviously doesn't realise it. I've seen it many a time in this business – the little woman, subservient to husband or employer, if given the chance, becomes herself a tyrant at the first opportunity.'

'Harriet's not like that,' Matthew defended heatedly. 'She's one of the mildest . . .' But he remembered Harriet's occasional outbursts and changed the word hastily to '. . . meekest of people. Nor do I see why women must be browbeaten into submission by their husbands.'

David's round face grew sombre, the perfect legal man. 'The trait isn't confined only to women. Men too will take advantage the second they are let off their employer's tight leash, turning on them or on weaker beings. Little fish eat smaller fish, to coin a phrase.'

He ended with a chuckle – at himself rather than Matthew, but Matthew didn't share his amusement.

'She isn't like that, David.' He put his glass down on the small oval table beside him, a signal that this interview was going nowhere, and half rose to go. But David was ahead of him. He leaped up and placed a hand on his shoulder, bearing him sternly back into his chair.

'Now listen to me, Matthew. You're a gentle person, and obviously a most caring husband. But a little dominance wouldn't do any harm. That's all I have to say. Now, how about a cigar, old man?'

Matthew put down his pen and read what he had written. A page of the usual: how was his father faring? Was Mother in reasonable good health? That his own health was fine; the journal doing well and picking up satisfactorily; all else fine . . . He stopped short of mentioning Harriet by name. He wished them continuing good health, closed with *God bless you both*, and then sealed the letter into an envelope.

Two months had passed since his last letter to them – unanswered, of course – and over two years since he had set eyes on them. One day there had to be an answer. He was their son. One day they must surely come round to wanting to see him again. He only hoped it would not be bad news that prompted them to write. But his worst fear was that even with, God forbid, dire news, a sudden death, neither of them would see fit to tell him, their minds wiped utterly clean of his existence.

'The morning post, sir.'

At the breakfast table Henry took the four letters from the salver Honeyford held and sifted through them.

'One here for you, Eleanor.' He laid the letter aside for Honeyford to take to her for opening. 'Two for me.' The remaining letter he placed back on the waiting salver. 'This one you can get rid of, Honeyford.'

Eleanor was gazing towards him, her narrow features oddly stiff. He looked down at his plate while Honeyford moved towards her with her letter placed carefully to the front for her to take.

Laying her fork down beside her plate of kedgeree, Eleanor took the letter, and as she did so, recognised the handwriting on the other.

'Henry?'

'No, my dear,' he growled without looking up.

But there was something about today. She couldn't have said what, but it was a day for disobeying her husband's most express command. Prompted by this inexplicable something, Eleanor plucked the second envelope up and, before he could bellow out a warning, had torn the flap open with her thumbnail.

'I'm sorry, Henry,' she said to his as yet unspoken reprimand though she saw anger brighten that square face; saw the broad hands ball into fists on each side of his plate. 'It's gone on long enough. It's making me ill.'

'*You* are making you ill!' he thundered, finding his voice. 'Can't you get it into your head, Lean, that it's *all finished with*?'

The letter unfolded, the single sheet fluttered in her trembling fingers, so that the writing wavered in front of her. 'It's *this* that makes me ill, Henry. Wondering, worrying. Two years! I can't let it go on. I have to . . .'

He was at her side, gentle now, controlling his temper with an effort. 'Give it to me, my dear. It'll only upset you more to read it. Things are best left as they are.'

Her hands palsied now, he took the sheet with ease and, as she watched, gnawing her lip with a weak and trembling bite, he screwed it up and laid it back upon the waiting salver.

'That'll be all, Honeyford,' he said abruptly. The butler bowed briefly and moved from the room, while Henry took his wife gently into his arms for her to have her little weep. Weeping did women a power of good. In a while she would feel better and forget all about it.

In her room Eleanor sat at the little walnut escritoire writing to her son. She could hardly see her words for the tears misting her eyes from memories:

Matthew as a baby being brought to her by Nanny Edwards to be kissed goodnight; Matthew playing with his brother, Richard, and his little sister, Evelyn; going off to preparatory school, then away to public school, then, a young man, to university.

When had she lost him? Not that awful New Year's Day when he had stalked out of the room, out of the house without saying goodbye, but before then. Perhaps when they had first employed a nanny for the children, puffed up with their own new opulence, Henry going from strength to strength with his estate business. Yes, she must have lost Matthew then – all that time ago.

But she hadn't lost her other two. Happily married, they visited regularly. Not often, but regularly enough. So why had Matthew been the one to sever himself from all family ties without a fight? But then, he'd never been the type to fight with any strength of will. He had always been the one who had never caused her a moment's anger, the one who was the gentlest, the most loving, the most thoughtful . . . Until that day, that dreadful New Year's Day. Eleanor's shudder shook her whole frame visibly, and a pain shot through her head, making her groan aloud.

Slowly, she laid down her pen, took the half-finished letter upon which the words were becoming more and more laboured, and, folding it carefully, laid it between other old letters in a small drawer of her escritoire.

# Chapter Nine

The shop, as Matthew called his two printing presses and the rest of the paraphernalia downstairs, was becoming cramped. The journal was selling well, thanks to national news coverage of the Independent Labour Party's Sunday meetings at a park called Boggart Hole Clough, near Manchester. The meetings had never made news before, until this May, in 1896, when the city's parks committee had suddenly taken exception to them. The police warned the speakers, Mrs Pankhurst among them, that they would be booked if they persisted. The warnings were ignored, and in fact prompted even bigger crowds to attend, numbering thousands, until finally Mrs Pankhurst and several others were summonsed for, went the excuse, occasioning an annoyance.

Eagerly, Matthew contacted a news agency in Manchester, asking them to forward him all they had on the events. It cost him quite a bit, but he was delighted by the information flowing in on how Mrs Pankhurst had courageously dared the magistrate to put her in prison, causing the summons to be adjourned for fear of public indignation. To Matthew's joy, further news came in that, rather than people being deterred, even more had crowded into the park on the following Sundays, eager to hear Mrs Pankhurst and Keir Hardie speak.

On the strength of it, Matthew kissed Harriet goodbye in July at the height of the controversy, and took a train up to Manchester to get the news first-hand. There on that first Sunday of the month he was in time to witness a crowd of nearly forty thousand, Dr and Mrs Pankhurst arriving in an open barouche to roars of applause.

It was a sight to behold. The Clough, as the park was known, was sited between two hills, the slopes forming a perfect amphitheatre for the enormous throng. Positioned near to the speakers' platform with the ready group of news reporters, though still jostled by the crowd all around, he had a good view of Mrs Pankhurst and her young fourteen- and fifteen-year-old daughters, Sylvia and Christabel; Dr Pankhurst and James Keir Hardie, Labour MP, as they mounted the stage.

'I've never seen anything like this,' Matthew yelled excitedly to no one in particular as anticipation built up through the crowd like some giant intake of breath.

'Yes, and to think it is in aid of women's freedom to choose,' came a smooth female voice beside him.

Glancing in the direction of the voice, he saw at eye level a mass of frizzy fair hair beneath a black toque, and a longish pale face above a severe black coat. He smiled, and the handsome face with its high cheekbones and long straight nose smiled back.

'Are you for women's enfranchisement?' The tone was somewhat demanding.

'Rather!' His chuckle sounded stupidly boyish. 'I'm

here to get something for my journal. It's called the
*Freewoman*. It's a London journal. Not very big yet. But
one day . . .'

'Good for you.' The face looked away. Keir Hardie
had his arms raised for the crowd's attention. The hush,
beginning at the front, flowed back in waves up the hillsides.
A few moments of silence followed, and then Keir Hardie,
a small but imposing figure with a full beard and deep-set
commanding eyes beneath low heavy eyebrows, began to
speak.

Matthew took in every word, glad that he possessed a
good memory, as he tried desperately to write it all down
in the notebook he held ready.

After Keir Hardie, Dr Pankhurst said a word or two,
then came Mrs Emmeline Pankhurst, her voice ringing
strong and clear, while her two daughters threaded through
the crowd collecting money.

It was over so soon. The hovering ring of policemen
containing the assembly remained well behaved as, amid
deafening applause, the speakers moved off and departed.
In his enjoyment of the proceedings, Matthew had
forgotten the woman who had spoken to him, but as he put
his notebook away, well satisfied with his morning's work,
her voice commanded his attention again.

'Are you going back to London now?'

'No. I rather thought I'd stay for a few days, see what
else develops.'

'Oh, a lot will develop,' she said emphatically. They
were walking together now, moving with the dispersing
crowds. 'Mr Leonard Hall is to be released next week

from Strangeways Prison. He was given one month's imprisonment for refusing to pay a fine for "occasioning an annoyance".' She spoke the words with a sneer. 'Mrs Pankhurst would have been proud to share that honour with him, but the magistrate had not the courage to sentence her.'

She paused suddenly to look him full in the eyes and he noticed that hers were green, a true green that quite took his breath away.

'I say, would you care to come along and see him emerge? I guarantee there'll be a thousand or more people there to welcome him. If you want something to put in your journal, that's where you'll get it.'

'I'd like that very much.' He smiled.

'Then I'll meet you on Saturday. That's the eleventh. Go early to the near gate and I'll find you. In the meantime, would you care for a spot of tea?'

Matthew stared wordlessly at her. He'd never met a woman with such self-assertiveness before, except for his mother, who mainly used it to emphasise her ill health.

'There's a teashop not far from here,' she went on as if he had already agreed, or, more precisely, accepted. He nodded.

'Good.' She held out a hand in such a way as to compel him to crook his arm for her to thread her waiting hand through. Together they moved off out of The Clough and along a narrow street. At the far end they turned into the designated teashop. 'I shall pay my own share, by the way,' she whispered as they entered and were shown to a small table at the bow window by a thin, pinch-faced but smiling waitress. 'You pay and I'll settle up afterwards.'

Again Matthew nodded, a little awed by his companion's manner. But as tea and the plate of cakes he had ordered arrived, he found himself becoming more at ease. He told her his name, where he lived, again what he did. He didn't mention Harriet. 'I haven't discovered your name yet,' he broke off to ask.

'Constance Milne-Pitford,' she offered. Matthew felt her first name suited the person very well and the hyphenated surname certainly spoke of someone of at least middle-upper-class upbringing. But as she offered no more than what he had requested, he felt he dared not intrude further to prompt any more information from her.

The conversation turned to the day's events and he detected the animation mounting in her tone as she spoke of the release of Mr Leonard Hall. 'We expect thousands,' she said confidently. 'Not during the day, of course, because people have to work. But we are holding a meeting near to the prison in the evening and then we expect a multitude to turn up. And they will.'

Matthew noticed she referred to 'we' most of the time and asked if she was a prominent member of the ILP.

'Not a *prominent* member,' she corrected, staring down at her tea. He noticed she hadn't touched the plate of cakes he had ordered. 'One day I hope to be.'

'I bet you will,' he agreed enthusiastically. 'I'm certain that one day you'll be up there with the Pankhursts and Keir Hardie . . .'

She looked at him sharply, cutting short his words. 'I wouldn't presume.'

There was a light in her green eyes that might have

shone in those who once spoke of gods on Mount Olympus. 'I'm sorry,' he said quickly, and she relented sufficiently to wave his apology away with one gloved hand, the gleam now fading.

'What shall we do after finishing our tea?' she asked suddenly.

Matthew was taken aback. 'I don't really know.'

'I would like to go back to my lodgings and rest. I feel quite exhausted now from this morning.'

'You live in lodgings?' He was surprised.

'Of course. You don't think my family would abide me, with my so-called outrageous ideas on women's franchise, to reside with them? Nor do I want to. I need air to breathe, space to fling wide my arms, a room to write my journal, a place to be myself, to be with those who speak out against the tyranny over women.'

'You're writing a journal?'

'I hope one day to turn it into a book and have it published for everyone to read. I shall not use my own name, of course. My family would consider that as bringing disgrace upon them.'

Her handsome lips curled in contempt, but she did not mention who her family were or where they lived. Again, Matthew considered this to be none of his business and that should he attempt to make it so, he would be rebuffed in no uncertain terms.

'What will you do?' she enquired.

'Go back to my hotel, I suppose.'

'You could come back to my lodgings to share my rest for the afternoon. There's really not much else to do.'

'I couldn't do that,' he exclaimed, shocked.

'Why not? Are you married?'

'I . . . No . . .' The word came out of its own accord before he could stop it. Good God! He felt stunned, frightened that he could deny his marriage by that one word. Marriage – that was a laugh. Harriet, as cold as ice, said she loved him yet she could still deny him. And he loved her, he had always told her he loved her. But three days away from her, he hadn't once thought of her. Was that love? Was he married in God's eyes? A contract unsigned after eighteen months was no contract at all, was it? Harriet had herself to blame if . . .

Constance gave a low, ringing laugh. 'I'm not asking you to be naughty, Matthew, if that's what you're thinking. Heavens, I am not a woman of frail virtue, you know.'

'I wasn't thinking that at all,' he blurted out, and she laughed again.

'The look on your face!'

He was silent, and drained his cup to cover his embarrassment. His cake, a rather dry little thing with very few currants visible, was only half-eaten, but he couldn't have touched it now to save his life.

'It's not right – you shouldn't risk your reputation . . .'

'My reputation! I'm not even known around here.' Again that low, ringing laugh, then she leaned towards him as though confiding in a child. 'I do have a lady who shares my rooms. She is very proper, and will see to it that nothing untoward occurs. We can have Sunday dinner together, the three of us, and afterwards play a game of cards if you wish. Then you can go back to your hotel.

It will help while away a drear Sunday afternoon. As for what people think who see me enter my lodgings with a man – to you-know-what with them! Do say you'll come, Matthew.' She reached out and laid a hand upon his. He felt a thrill run along his arm, upwards to his heart, and cursed himself for the sensation.

'Will you?' she pressed. 'I would dearly love to hear more about your journal and how women fare in London.'

Matthew took a deep breath. 'I would be delighted,' he heard himself saying.

There was no harm in it now and he felt annoyed with himself for serving Harriet so by his denial of being a married man. But he could hardly go back on his denial now and make himself look a fool. After all, he'd be going back to London in a week's time and would probably never see this woman again. In the meantime he might learn a lot from her.

They took a horsebus back to the centre of Manchester, her arm through his in a most familiar way, so that they could easily have been mistaken for husband and wife. They walked the short way to where she was living, where she unhooked herself from him to fish in her small black reticule for the door key. Inside, he followed her up the dark narrow stairs, feeling a little unusual now, at any moment expecting to be leapt out on by some landlord's wife and asked where he thought he was going. He was glad there would be someone in her rooms to lighten the sense of unease creeping upon him.

With a second key, Constance opened the door to her own rooms and went in, obviously expecting him to

follow. He did so, rather cautiously, then heard her give
a little cry of annoyance as she hurried to the fireplace to
pluck a small square of white notepaper propped against
an ornate glass-domed clock on the mantelpiece.

'Oh, bother! Now that's tiresome of her.'

'What is?'

'Alice – she says she has decided to visit her mother.
She left just half an hour ago. She could have warned me.'

'Will she be gone long?'

'Returning tomorrow, it says here. Her mother lives in
Stretford, and it is a long way for a woman to travel on her
own during the evening.'

In the midst of his dismay, Matthew gave her a quizzical
look. It was an odd thing for a woman of her expressed
opinions to say, he thought, and saw through the chink she
had unwittingly opened for him. She was clearly a woman
to whom the old values still clung, who still felt vulnerable
before the ruling of men, despite all she had said.

'I'll go,' he said inadequately. He didn't want to now,
but knew he must.

She turned to him, a resolute look on her face as though
she too realised the chink she had revealed in her armour
and was ashamed of it, 'No, now you're here, you might
as well stay. There are two lamb chops in the larder. Alice
will not want one now. I'll cook them for us. Sit down.
There's the Sunday paper for you to read while I'm busy.'
It was an order: Constance was once more in control of
herself.

He did as he was told, watching her bustling about in
the tiny kitchen off the main room. He took note of the

room itself: age-darkened square-patterned wallpaper; a few photographs – her parents, perhaps – on an oak chest of drawers; two leatherette easy chairs that had seen better days; a luxurious potted fern in a tall green and slightly chipped jardiniere – at least the fern was well looked after; a small drop-leafed table; three upright chairs with badly worn and sunken leatherette seats; a thin rug with most of its pattern worn away by the shoes of a succession of previous tenants.

She came in, lifted a leaf of the table so that it would be large enough for the two of them and spread a cloth, disdaining his offer of help. After setting table mats, a condiment set and knives and forks on the table, she hurried out, then came in again with two steaming plates, each hand protected by a tea cloth.

They ate in silence – chops, mashed potatoes, cabbage that Matthew suspected had been warmed up from a previous meal, but covered with Simpson's gravy – it all proved surprisingly appetising. It was the silence that was not enjoyable – oddly strained, not like the ease he had felt in the teashop. He was almost glad when he had finished, almost wished he hadn't accepted her invitation.

'I'll make some tea,' she said abruptly as he laid his knife and fork down on his empty plate. 'I'm sorry there's no pudding.'

She stood up and leaned over to take his plate. On impulse, he reached out and took a gentle hold of her wrist. It felt unexpectedly fragile.

'There's no need to hurry.'

It was all far too nervously hurried, and he wanted not

to feel nervous, for her to feel at ease as she had been in
the teashop. He wanted to say, 'Let's just sit and talk for a
while,' but she had already sat down again, his hand still
on her wrist preventing her from moving any further back
from him. And what he had said hadn't come out as he had
meant it; it sounded vaguely suggestive.

She was still so near – so near that if he leaned forward
just a fraction their lips would have met. Something told
him that if they did, she would not draw away. The green
of her eyes was the colour of the ocean, seemed to be
drowning him like an ocean. But he would swim . . . swim
in her . . . He felt suddenly excited, reckless, his heart
going like a steam hammer. He felt stifled by the sensation,
but inside he was trembling.

Suddenly that fraction of space between them was no
longer there. And she didn't draw away. Her lips were
warm, much softer than he'd imagined. He felt their
warmth drive through his whole being, settle in his lower
regions, and he knew she was as hungry for comfort as
he was. The perfume from her fair frizzy hair was driving
him almost beyond the edge of reason. He couldn't think
any more.

Together they rose and moved from the table, gripped
by the embrace, the breath from her nostrils hot on his
cheeks. He could hear it rasping in and out, and in between
kisses, her hungry whispers: 'I've never . . . Matthew . . .
I've never . . .'

It didn't matter. He wanted her. If this was her first time,
it would be his too. He was a virgin. Nearly two years
married and still a virgin. A kind of anger gripped him

as he took her with him to the door he assumed was her bedroom. He had to have her, and to prove himself. And he knew she needed to prove herself too, that life was passing her by, and she needed to have something to make her human for a while.

If he was brutal in taking her, careless of her first cry of pain, she accepted it with voracious sighs, panting cries that mounted ever higher, until he wondered how they could both live through it to the end. Never had he known such ecstasy, such sensations. Then it was over.

Lying spent and breathless beside her, he heard her sigh, then her breathing began to slow down. He thought she slept as he too drifted into his exhausted sleep. When he awoke it was in the small hours to realise where he was, instantly ashamed of what he had done. He'd have to creep away from this iniquity. He began easing away, but his moving disturbed her.

'Oh, Matthew,' she sighed. 'Oh, Matthew, my dearest.'

In an instant she was in his arms, her lips on his, her naked body pressed against his. Her breasts were so hard, brushing his chest with a life of their own. And he, may he burn in hell, felt himself again rising to her, was pressing himself into her, taking her with as much urgency as before, hearing her joyous cries – of pain and pleasure. And when it was over, they slept again, utterly spent.

The eleventh of July outside Strangeways Prison saw a huge gathering, which Matthew was later able to report numbered ten thousand, cramming the streets to welcome the release of Mr Hall. It ought to have been the most exhilarating moment Matthew would remember: the cheering, the thousands of women and not a few men booing authority, the pack, the swaying squash of the crowd, the released man being congratulated on his stance against authority, the knowledge that Mrs Pankhurst herself had been prepared to go to prison but that authority would have had its nose put out of joint imprisoning a woman of her middle-class calibre.

But it was not the most exhilarating of moments, for he'd already experienced that, and, God forgive him, now wished he hadn't. He thought of Harriet. He had betrayed her and he could never tell her.

Constance had had plans. They would buy an engage-ment ring, make plans for their wedding day. This was on the day after her friend Alice had gone to visit her mother. They had eaten breakfast that morning, Constance with all the contentment of a woman assured of her future, he with a heart so sick he couldn't touch a thing. She had been with him the whole of the next two days, but there was no more lovemaking now that Alice had returned, and he wouldn't allow her to demean herself, he told her, by coming to his hotel room like a common kept woman.

He caught a train home without telling her, and all the way back to London he squirmed at what he had done to a woman professing to be so hardened, championing the rights of women to be equal to men, yet in a moment willing to give herself with such servility, no matter that she thought she'd been on the same footing as he in her decision. But she had still imagined it leading to marriage, to security, and he now felt a criminal to have treated her so. What would she do now? Worse, would she try to trace him? She knew the name of his journal. Harriet would find out. All for an irresponsible moment of desire. He had felt like a god; now he merely felt scared, juggling with questions and half-formed answers. What proof did she have? But then, what if he had got her with child? She would seek him out with that proof. He could deny it as his. But as the saying went, there is never smoke without fire. God, what a fool he had been! Why had he done it? But he knew why. Harriet, cold Harriet, had pushed him to it. Harriet . . . not cold, he hastily changed the thought, just not ready. He realised that he did love her, wondered how he'd cope if she found out. How could he have hurt her so?

He fought to dismiss it, tried to think instead of all the ideas he had gathered in Manchester for his journal before he had met Constance Milne-Pitford. The journal was obviously about to grow in stature. For the rest of the journey he frantically trained his thoughts on making plans for expanding it. There was a lot to do. By the time he reached home, he had begun to feel just a little better. Manchester was a long way from London. He'd been on the train four hours already with still a good couple of hours to go. Would a woman travel so far on her own? He remembered again the chink in Miss Milne-Pitford's armour and began to feel a little safer. Manchester was behind him.

He'd make it up to Harriet. Perhaps one day she might overcome her fears, melt into his arms as Constance had done. There, at the very least, he had proved himself a man.

# Chapter Ten

He wasn't disappointed about the journal. For the rest of the year his office buzzed with burgeoning numbers of subscribers clamouring for copies that gave them far more information than any newspaper would. His two printing presses were working overtime, and he and Harriet hardly had time to stop for meals. Up at five-thirty each morning, paying Mrs Hardy overtime to look after Sara, they worked until late at night, Harriet at the compositor's bench, her fingers permanently black, he working the presses, his arms aching and at times feeling ready to drop off; she collating, he stapling, stacking, arranging the distribution – and still the orders poured in.

To a large publisher, it would have been small beer, but to a one-man business, it was overwhelming. Harriet was his right hand, a tower of strength. He couldn't ask more of her.

'I must look for an assistant,' he announced in October. 'At least until the excitement subsides.' That would not be for a long while yet, he hoped.

He found a young man named Leonard Hallet, spindly, bespectacled and fresh out of university, but with dreams of one day having his own journal or newspaper – he hadn't decided yet, he said grandly. In the meantime he was happy to knuckle down with a will that spoke of a huge and abiding ambition.

The small shop area had a job to accommodate the three of them and the piles of journals awaiting despatch which lay stacked against the walls in the hallway. Harriet had to pick her way around them to get upstairs, and even the parlour housed parcels of paper for printing.

Matthew began to harbour thoughts of moving to larger premises – for the journal's sake, he told himself – but in truth he was tired of the narrow streets, the boxlike room above the cramped printer's shop, the smells of the East End: a mixture of soot, beer, stale cabbage water and sewage. It hung on one's clothes, was carried about everywhere one went.

He was restless. Where he'd once revelled in seeking out the downtrodden wives of the East End, now the same old stories were becoming tedious; he had grown inured to it, like an experienced old soldier to dead and mutilated bodies. The family starving whilst its man drank away his wages; the pregnant young wife lifting a weight of scalding water in a tub, her baby due the next day; the hollow-eyed mother trying to protect her young from the nailing fists of her drunken husband; the girl forced on to the streets to keep herself alive; the elderly widow taken into the workhouse – all seemed commonplace. It had, he was ashamed to say, become boring.

He needed not only to expand but to seek new fields, to interview the women who really mattered: the middle-class champions of women's enfranchisement who railed

Parliament for non-action, made speeches to crowds in parks and wrote pamphlets on it all. He thought about Constance Milne-Pitford. He tried not to, but that was the sort of woman he admired, one with a latent strength of character within her. He had not fallen in love with Constance, but he certainly admired her greatly.

'This place is too small for all this,' he said as he relaxed one evening by the parlour fire lit early this year, October having come in quite chilly. 'I'm wasting my time here.' As Harriet's grey eyes widened with fear, he laughed. 'I mean, my sweet, *we* are wasting our time here. Sara's two and a half. We will soon need a larger place anyway.'

'But she's in the other bedroom now, next to ours. It's small, I know, but there's still plenty of room. If we moved away, Mrs Hardy wouldn't be around to keep an eye on her. I couldn't help you.'

'And what if the family grows larger?' he queried. He still hoped that one day Harriet might overcome her incredible fear of the sexual side of marriage. One day they would – must – have more children. He yearned for that as much as anything. 'I'd like to have a son or daughter of my own, for all I dearly love little Sara as if she were mine.'

He leaned forward in his chair to fondle the dark curly head bent over the doll in a crib that he'd bought her that week. Sara lifted her head and smiled in response, but lost her grip on the little doll so that it fell on to the rug. In a huff she turned and swept it up, then shook it with mock annoyance, glaring at it.

'Oh, doddit! Dod-oo, naughty gel!'

Matthew smiled indulgently. He loved hearing her talk, stringing whole sentences together now. It was no longer Gan-gan for Grandma or Gan-gar for Grandpa, but the whole word, though she still had some trouble pronouncing 's', which lent a certain appeal to her efforts.

'Nec' time me 'mack you 'ard!' She threatened the doll, holding it close to her face to emphasise the scolding. 'In dere, dilly cah!' With this, she plonked the doll down into its crib.

Matthew's amused smile turned to a frown. He'd heard her say this sort of thing before. A language of her own, he'd thought. Now the truth began to dawn on him.

'Did you hear that, Harriet?'

She looked up from darning socks. Now that the business was doing well, a woman came in to clean and cook, but mending was still left to her to fit in when she could. 'Hear what?'

'What this child is saying.'

'I take no notice of what she says. It's just prattle.'

'It's not prattle – she's swearing.' He leaned forward and took a gentle hold of Sara's shoulder, compelling her to turn to look at him. Picking the doll out of its crib, he held it up. 'Sara, what is she?'

'Naughty,' said Sara, round eyes innocent. 'Fall on der floor.'

'And what do you say to her when she's naughty, Sara?'

Sara executed a harassed-mother frown and pursed her rosebud lips the way Harriet was wont to do at times; for a moment she looked exactly like her. Then the illusion was gone.

'Dilly cow,' she repeated. The pretend frown deepened dramatically. 'Awd dod!'

Matthew sat back, staring down at the child. 'She's saying silly cow, old sod.' He'd heard it said many times by the Hardys, careless of who heard them – usually as a term of endearment between them: You silly old sod, you silly old cow . . .

He looked up at Harriet's impassive face. 'She doesn't pick up that language from us. It comes from the Hardys. Even the accent.'

'She picks anything up, that one,' Harriet shrugged.

'But we can't have this! It's bad enough bringing up a child in this place without her learning such things from the people who have charge of her. I think it's about time we paid off Mrs Hardy. I don't think I care to have that woman taking charge of her any more.'

Harriet's stare had become alarmed. 'But that's the only way we're able to go out together on our own.'

'Then we'll employ a children's nurse. Or take her with us.'

'Do you know how much that would cost? I know you were brought up with a nurse, but we can't do that on what you're bringing in. And she'd have to live in. We don't have the room.'

'We'll have to find a larger place. Sooner or later.'

Harriet's laugh had a hollow sound. 'And if this good patch we're going through turns out to be a flash in the pan – what then? Do we come back here? You can't afford to pay a nurse and move to bigger premises.'

She got up suddenly, threw her darning on to the chair

seat, and went to poke the fire, wielding the poker with vicious stabs at the glowing coals.

'I thought we'd have money. But everything that journal makes you plough back to buy even more paper. I can't see any profit yet, not to go renting bigger places and hiring nurses. Emma costs us hardly anything. And Sara doesn't talk that badly.'

'And those swear words?'

'She'll grow out of it. Kids do.'

He looked steadily at her, a stab of irritation catching him. 'Not that you even notice what she says!'

'What's that supposed to mean?'

'That you hardly ever notice her. Sometimes, Harriet, I just do not understand you, this coolness of yours, this fear of showing your feelings. You must have feelings – towards Sara, towards me. But you act as though . . . Night after night we go to bed and even after two years, you still shrink back when I go to kiss you goodnight. I don't know why. I suppose I've come to accept it, but you're the same with Sara. You never cuddle her – not as a mother would.'

He paused, remembering his own childhood. Did his own mother ever cuddle him? He couldn't recall. He remembered being led by the hand by Nanny Edwards, into the dining room, to have his cheek pecked by his mother, his head patted by his father, then being led out and up the stairs to the nursery and bed. He had a picture of the nursery where he and Richard and Evelyn used to play for hours on end: warm, cosy and golden, and of the rooms downstairs: cold, formal, unfriendly. He had loved his nursery, but had felt only awe of his parents . . .

Harriet's voice, sharp and accusing, wrenched him back to the present. 'Are you saying I neglect her?'

'Of course not,' he said hastily. 'You've never let her want for anything. Except . . . Harriet, can't you hold her close to you once in a while? I know you love her, but you seem frightened of giving love, of being loved. You only ever pick her up to take her to bed. It's I who tuck her in, tell her stories, play little games with her before she goes to sleep.'

'That doesn't hurt you, does it?'

'I've never seen you kiss her. Can you be that cold, Harriet? I know you're cold with me and I understand. I know how it must be for you. But with Sara . . . Don't you feel any warmth for anyone?'

Harriet's eyes had begun to blaze and to moisten. 'I'm sorry if I can't oblige in bed. Yes, Matthew, fling that in my face, but you're nothing but an animal. You said once that you weren't. But you are . . . All you think of is trying to use me. Like . . . Like he . . .'

Breaking off, she flung the poker into the hearth. Startled by the loud clang, Sara began to cry.

'And you can shut up!' her mother yelled and like a small hunted creature dashed from the room.

Matthew heard the bedroom door slam behind her. No – this was too much. This time, he wasn't having it. Months ago David Symonds had told him a stronger hand was needed with her. After the shock of hearing this had passed, he had thought more carefully about the advice; but always that apparently innate fear, the way she would stiffen in readiness for his onslaught, would override David's advice. But after all his gentle understanding of her condition, to then be called an animal when he'd done nothing to merit it – his anger boiled.

Briskly he picked Sara up off the floor and brushed away her tears. Hurriedly he undressed her before the warm fire, then took her to her tiny bedroom. With a flannel dipped in the water from the washbasin and wrung out, he wiped her hands and face. She had already had her warm milk, so he laid her gently in bed.

'No story tonight, little one. Papa's busy,' he said as he tucked her doll beside her under the covers and lit the tiny nightlight in its shallow saucer. He kissed her goodnight and crept out. After closing the door, he made for their room. The door was locked, but he had expected that. He kept his voice low.

'Harriet, let me in.'

'Go and sleep on the couch,' came the choked retort. 'You're not coming in here to molest me.'

God, it was a nightmare. He wasn't going to reply to that sort of attitude. Instead, he lifted a foot and crashed his heel against the door. The thin wood gave at the first blow, burst open. He stood at the foot of the bed, panting from his exertion.

'Molest?' he enquired of the terrified face peeping out above the cover. He forced his voice to gentleness. She needed to be soothed. 'When have I ever molested you, Harriet? Come on, my dear, when?'

She snivelled plaintively. 'Never. But you know what I mean.'

'Then I shall not molest you, if you promise not to molest me.'

What sort of joke that was intended to be, he wasn't
sure; he only knew that it was the first thing that came into
his head. He was surprised when she laughed suddenly,
a nervous high-pitched sound, not a giggle, but the sort
of titter that escapes involuntarily from one deathly
afraid. Even so, it heartened him. Aggression, even gentle
aggression, did work; it had taken him two years to realise
it. Quickly he undressed.

Yet as he slipped in beside her and reached out, there
came the old reaction, the flinch, the tensing. Again he was
to be rejected. Unable to take her against her will, it was he
who found himself breaking down, the accruing misery of
too many rejections welling up inside him.

He heard himself saying he could no longer go on; she
was driving him from her; and did she know how close
she had come to losing him? In Manchester he had almost
allowed himself to be seduced by a designing woman.
Only the thought of Harriet had stopped him.

He was only vaguely aware of this untruth. Had he been
stronger minded then, it would now have been truth. But to
admit the lie now would lose him her love, if indeed there
was love, had ever been love.

He was stunned to find her throwing herself into his
arms, her words tumbling out, filled with fear. 'Matthew!
Don't go away! Don't leave me – I'm so sorry – I don't
know what I'd do if you went away.'

Ashamed of himself, he tried to calm her, smoothing
his hands along her neck, wanting only to ease the pain
he'd caused her. In tears, she seemed not to notice the
caress or how his arms embraced her, how close they

lay together, that his hands had forsaken her neck to find her body, her thigh. Clinging desperately, sobbing as she mouthed frantic words of love, she was crying still as he found her, seemed not to know that he had entered her. She must tense now, pull away, he was sure of it. But she didn't. Her lips were eating him, smothering his face, her body had arched towards him. Her clasp had become even more urgent, her breath almost pain-racked in her need not to lose him. When they finally both lay still and spent, she was still crying quietly like a child. 'Don't leave me.'

'How could I ever leave you?' he whispered, drawing her close.

Never had he felt so wondrously protective, so joyously happy, so content. Here was his marriage, his wife, truly his wife. Here lay his future, his life, his all. Nothing else mattered . . .

He awoke to a cold, clear dawn filled with the rumble of passing traffic, noting that neither of them had moved one inch in the night, sleeping the sleep of the content.

Harriet rose as shy as a young bride, cheeks glowing, eyes full of her new role. Matthew felt new and strong as he washed and shaved, trimmed his moustache, dressed, and carefully combed his hair while she prepared breakfast and got Sara up. Nothing now could ever tear this marriage apart. Then came the image of Constance Milne-Pitford and the joy vanished out of him as though a hand had smashed against a blown-up paper bag. Could fate be so cruel as to bring his past mistake back to haunt him? Oh God, he prayed, don't let it come to spoil this.

\*

She felt completely drained, having only just reached the outside privy in time to be sick. Leaning against the jamb for support, she stood in the doorway of the kitchen, gazing towards him.

'Matthew, I think I'm expecting,' she said waveringly.

He was enjoying a leisurely breakfast over the morning papers. His assistant was already in the shop preparing the day's printing, having let himself in at eight. There was no urgency. No urgency indeed. The Manchester episode last summer had long ago subsided. Since the City Council had been compelled to permit public meetings to be held in its parks, the ILP's newsworthiness had died a natural death as attendance at its meetings diminished to just a few hundred.

At first Matthew had been concerned, but luckily, although the subscriptions to the journal no longer burgeoned, the *Freewoman* didn't actually decline. It was now February and they were still living comfortably from its profits. Even so, Harriet felt she'd been right about cautioning him against seeking grander premises. Had they done so they might easily have been having problems by now.

He looked up at her, only half hearing. Then, as her statement sunk in, he swallowed the piece of bread he'd been chewing in one lump – she almost visualised it going down – and dropped his spoon beside his half-consumed boiled egg.

'My God – are you certain?'

She nodded. 'I've been sick a lot and my curse is over-due. You are pleased, aren't you, Matthew?' she added tremulously when he continued to stare as though stunned.

'Oh, my precious darling!' Ignoring her grey cheeks, he leapt up to hug her to him. 'Pleased? I'm ecstatic!'

Dancing her around the tiny kitchen, he held her so tightly that she could hardly breathe. 'It's the most wonderful news you could ever give me. A baby. Our baby!'

He stopped dancing her to hold her away from him, gaze at her, his brown eyes glowing.

'When?'

'I must be two months.' She was laughing now. 'It should be born in . . .' She made a quick calculation, feeling suddenly coy. 'September?'

She could see that it didn't matter a hoot to him when it would be born, just that it would be, and at this very moment knew herself to be the happiest woman alive. It was still difficult accommodating him in bed, but now she was reaping the reward.

He had grown serious. 'Now we must definitely look for somewhere bigger to live. We can't bring up my baby in this cramped space.'

She hadn't thought of that, so happy had she been with her news.

'But we can't afford it!'

She immediately had visions of being dumped some-where in the wilds with a new baby and Sara – especially with Sara – to cope with; no Emma Hardy to turn to any more. How would she cope?

Matthew was chuckling at her. 'Yes, we can. I know the journal has levelled out. But it's still paying its way. I know we can manage. And we'll not be going out so often with two children in the family, so we'll save money on that.'

Glumly she nodded. She wanted so desperately to give Matthew a child, to prove herself a good wife and mother. She had been a good enough mother to Sara, for whom she had no feelings – so how much more a good mother she would be to this coming baby, which she would love because it was Matthew's, her gentle, thoughtful Matthew. Now he was asking her to sacrifice herself even further to prove her love, as if what she'd already done for him still wasn't enough.

'I don't want to move away,' she said plaintively. 'I feel settled here.'

'We can't stay in this place forever.' He smiled. 'And should the family grow even larger, or the journal becomes more successful . . .'

'But we don't have to go miles away though, do we?' she pleaded.

He drew her close once more. 'My darling, we'll move to wherever you wish. I only ask that it be some better locality than here.'

'If we moved nearer to my parents?' she suggested hopefully into his shoulder. With Emma Hardy no longer near to look after Sara, maybe her parents would oblige on those odd occasions when she and Matthew went out together. Harriet felt herself brighten again at the thought. Perhaps it wouldn't be so bad after all.

'There are some nice parts around Victoria Park,' she continued hurriedly. 'And you can move the journal into somewhere more spacious nearby. We could do that, couldn't we, Matthew – if we had to move?'

She felt his arms tighten confidently. 'Of course we can. In time we might get ourselves a fine house, with staff, lots of staff. And you will want for nothing, and be able to give orders. In time, my sweetest . . . in time you and I and our little family will be just as comfortably off as my parents.'

*And it will be without any help from them,* he thought with a small stab of bitterness as he continued to clasp Harriet's small frame to his breast.

# Chapter Eleven

It wasn't proving an easy pregnancy. She'd never been sick with Sara, not that she could remember that time with any clarity. Emma Hardy prophesied a boy, rightly or wrongly, saying that morning sickness always happened when you carried a boy. Harriet hoped it would be, although she didn't care for this part of it. Even when the sickness finally abated, she felt no easier, with persistent heartburn and the increasing weight of the growing child dragging on her, even at five months.

'It's going to be big,' she confided to Emma. 'I'm carrying it all in front this time. I feel a proper barge.'

'It 'as ter be a boy then,' Emma commented, her coarse round face certain. 'That'll be nice for Sara. She looks proper lonely sometimes. It'll be luv'ly fer 'er to 'ave a bruvver ter play wiv. That's what she wants, y'know, a bruvver ter play wiv.'

'Mmm, I s'pose so,' Harriet sighed, her speech slipping as always in her neighbour's presence so she wouldn't be accused of putting on airs. Sometimes Harriet felt she was two people – one for those like Emma, another for Matthew. But, like him, she too was concerned by the way Sara was talking. She'd tried to correct her, especially the words she ought not be learning; had even resorted to a sharp slap now and again, but beyond reducing Sara to tears, it hadn't cured her. The child was perverse like her father; didn't care about upsetting her at every turn; drove her to distraction. Perhaps once they had moved away, things would be easier, and Sara would be less spoiled.

'I think it cannot be too soon,' Matthew had said, and he was probably right.

'It's in Victoria Park Road – ever so nice. And Matthew's found shop premises just around the corner. Really spacious.'

Nursing her bump, Harriet sat in the front parlour of her parents' house. Her mother was still sipping tea. Aunt Sarah had finished hers, and was now embroidering a runner with the rapid application of the skilled.

Jack and Matthew had gone down to the yard, the former to smoke one of his beloved cigars, Matthew to enjoy a cigarette while they discussed the making of furniture for the spare room to be occupied by the baby when it was old enough. It was a bit early to think of furnishing the room, but Harriet hadn't wanted it to lie empty.

'We're moving in next week.' Inside her the baby gave her ribs a small kick of approval. 'It's just the sort of house I wanted.'

'About time.' Her aunt didn't lift her gaze from her embroidery. 'Looking at this one, looking at that one – I wondered if you'd ever find anything to suit.'

'You have to be careful what you're looking for,' Harriet said a little tartly, causing her aunt to glance up at her.

'Well, it's not like buying a loaf of bread. We'll be living in it for a long time, I expect. You have to be careful.'

'Yes, one can't be too careful,' Mary put in. 'If you don't like a new place, it causes such a lot of worry having to move out again, or putting up with it. And what with the baby due soon . . . Two months to go, isn't it, Harriet?'

'Ten weeks,' Harriet supplied. She had seen her doctor, who had asked lots of questions and come to that conclusion. 'But I only wish I felt a little more well carrying it. It's this heartburn; it still keeps me up at night. I can't sleep at all. I have to keep walking backwards and forwards – it's the only way to disperse it. And I keep Matthew awake too. But he's so kind. So concerned. No one could be more concerned.'

*Not like Will*, she added mentally. He hadn't given her condition with Sara a moment's thought; rather, he had complained incessantly about being kept awake if she had to go down more than once to the privy because the baby was sitting on her bladder. He would swear at her and once had even got up and taken a swipe at her, telling her to get herself back into that bloody bed and not make so much bloody fuss so he could get some bloody sleep. Many a night with Sara she had lain beside him not knowing what to do with herself, too frightened to move in case she angered him.

'Matthew often has to get up and go downstairs to fill stone hot water bottles,' she said with pride. 'To put against my back to ease it. It's such an awful feeling, like it's suffocating me. He'll get me a glass of water so I won't have to hobble downstairs, and he often has to rub my back to ease it. He's been so wonderful.'

'He's a good man,' remarked her mother. She reached for the teapot to refill her cup, and tutted. 'Oh, bother, it's gone lukewarm.'

Getting up, she took a small brass bell from the sideboard and opened the door, then rang the bell urgently. Harriet heard Violet's voice drift up from downstairs and then her mother asking for another pot to be made.

Aunt Sarah fastened off a green leaf with a flourish and searched among her other colours for pink silk for a rosebud. 'You should've waited for this one to be born before moving. All this upheaval at so late a stage isn't good for you. You should be taking things easy.'

'I don't think I could face it afterwards, Aunt – having the baby and Sara as well as all the confloption of moving.' Confloption was a family word, always used for something difficult to overcome.

She paused as Violet came in, grabbed the teatray with its remains of their afternoon tea and bore it away.

'Once we're settled in,' Harriet went on as the door closed with a noisy click, 'I can concentrate on this baby. Though what we're going to do about Sara when I'm having it, I don't know, now that I won't have Mrs Hardy to turn to.'

'Your mother and me will take care of her without too much fuss,' Sarah offered briskly. Her sister nodded her ready consent.

But Sarah Morris noted eager relief on her niece's face as she accepted the offer. Too eager. The girl definitely displayed some strange sort of aversion to that child, though how she could towards such a pretty little thing as Sara she couldn't imagine. Perhaps that was all it was – imagination. She was too imaginative by far. Mary had always said so. But she felt it so strongly, in her bones so to speak. And she always trusted what she felt in her bones, no matter what Mary said.

Matthew went and picked up the mail from inside the shop door, his last duty before leaving this hole forever. He realised now just how much he had hated the place, the squalor all around, the closeness of the traffic going by, the noise – almost as if he were operating his business on the pavement. He was heartily sick of Mrs Hardy forever popping in, of Mr Hardy's hearty conversation, his rusty voice uttering ripe epithets every other word he spoke. There would be plenty of passing traffic where they were going, but the pavements were wider, fending off the nearness of it. One thing he'd noticed about the new premises was the feeling of space. And to close up every evening and walk the five minutes to a nice orderly home would be heaven.

The move was going more smoothly than he had hoped. He had found shop premises in Cambridge Road, just by where it became Mare Street – quite large and very promising, with a decent yard at the rear. The house was just five minutes away in Victoria Park Road, not as large as the house he had always dreamed of having – just a kitchen, scullery, parlour, dining room, study, four bedrooms upstairs, basement and two rooms in the attic.

It was not exactly the mansion he would have liked – his money didn't stretch to mansions – but he could still dream that one day . . .

Harriet had been delighted with it. She had gone with him to find the wallpaper for the new nursery, taking ages to choose the right colour. Her father had made the furniture for the room, and Harriet had spent hours deliberating over the drapes. In fact she had been so intent on the new baby's room, she had left little time to think about Sara's new room at the top of the house. He himself had to find things suitable for it, and as far as he could see he had done her proud: pink flowered wallpaper with fawn curtains and a fawn bedspread. At nearly three and a half, Sara was now old enough to show appreciation of a room that wasn't a box. She had squealed delightedly as she climbed on to the newly painted attic windowseat to gaze out over the park across the road.

'Twees!' she squealed, pointing happily to the plane trees in full leaf along the park's perimeter. And listening intently at the open sash window, she laughed. 'A didcky-bird singin', daddy. A didcky bird singin'.'

'Yes, darling.' He had knelt beside her, gazing at the foliage opposite as he put an arm about her little body. 'Singing, darling. Sing-ing. Sing-ing.'

'Sing . . . ing,' she repeated faithfully. 'Me like the didcky-bird sing-ing.'

At least it was a start. Lovingly, he had squeezed her diminutive torso, so delicate in his clasp. One day, if he had anything to say about it, she would be a fine lady, tall and elegant and with nothing in this world to be ashamed of as the young men crowded around her hoping for her favours. And he would choose her a fine husband with wealth and, who knew, a title. And she would be so happy, for the young man would be her choice too. But if he wasn't, there would always be another of equal standing for her to claim.

He smiled at the thought as he bent to gather up the letters. Sara was quite the loveliest, most charming child. He sifted briefly through the different-sized envelopes: a few bills, but also a decent amount of subscriptions as far as he could see. The journal was more than holding its own. One day it would be a substantial publication distributed countrywide. He and Harriet would have their mansion.

He could hear her coming down the stairs, taking her time, her tread lumbering and heavy. Mrs Hardy was helping her. It sounded like a regiment of elephants coming down.

'Now yer'll be orright, won't yer, luv? You take it steady now. And don't ferget yer ole friend, will yer? Pop in whenever yer like, luv. Bring the baby ter see me when it's born. I'd like that. I'm proper sad ter see yer go, 'Arriet. I'll miss yer.'

'I'll miss you too, Emma. You've been a real friend to me.'

'I 'ope I always will be.'

Matthew smiled, listening to them. Emma Hardy was like an old hen, fussing, ever fussing. But he'd be glad to be rid of that incessant rough voice of hers. Still, she had helped Harriet such a lot. He nodded to himself on that thought. Still grinning, he went on sorting through the envelopes, opening one or two at random, then with an effort spreading out the bill or the letter he drew out. He should really wait until he had a flat surface to do this on, but just one more, then he'd put the rest away.

Awkwardly, he spread out a single sheet from one envelope on top of the mound of correspondence. Another letter, obviously from a satisfied subscriber.

He began casually to scan it, his mind still half on Harriet and Emma Hardy's parting conversation. Suddenly he realised what he was reading and his smile froze.

Dear Mr Craig,

I have been meaning to write to you for simply ages. You do realise how very cross and upset I was to have you leave in such haste. Surely, dear Mr Craig, you must have realised the fact that I was very angry and very, very hurt – deeply hurt. Wounded. I so believed that you loved me. But I fear I may have frightened you off, my dear, with talk of our future. I thought you true. I gave myself to you in my bed in the belief that you were indeed true, that your intentions were wholly honourable, and that what happened between us was a token of that honour. But I saw in your frantic haste to depart how dismally mistaken I was; that you had no intention at all of honouring anything and took me into bed solely for your own lamentable desires.

I was so humiliated. I saw myself unclean, deflowered, defiled by your ill use of me, and had every intention of seeking you out and confronting

you to avenge myself of your night of rapture that
so beguiled me into thinking you honest and loving.

And now, Mr Craig, I am writing to tell you . . .

'I'm ready to go, dear.'

Harriet's voice at the door behind him sent a shock
searing through him. He swung round, trying to stuff the
letter back into its envelope, in his haste dropping the rest
of the mail, which scattered itself around his feet.

He would have dearly loved to devour it, do anything to
destroy it, but could only hide it among the rest of the post
as he bent hastily to gather everything up.

What was Constance writing to tell him? That she had
been made pregnant by him? That she'd be coming here to
confront him with the evidence of his adultery? He made
a rapid calculation – the baby would be two months old,
old enough for her to travel. His blood felt as though it
ran cold in his veins, yet his brow had grown damp with
sweat. Harriet, herself seven months pregnant, to be faced
with . . . this.

There was no time, nowhere to hide to read the rest of
it. He had to concentrate on the move, and with Harriet
constantly beside him directing this, organising that, the
hours passed, and still he had not read the letter. Harriet
seemed exasperatingly tireless; everything was apparently
designed to thwart him in his purpose.

'You must be tired, sweetest. Our room's ready, you
know. Why not go and lie down awhile? I'll finish the rest
of the unpacking.'

'I'm not the least bit tired.' She laughed. Even after

all the moving, the following four hours unpacking and sorting and setting up, she still looked as bright and chirpy as ever as she prinked the new curtains of the baby's room he'd put up for her – flowery cream-coloured chintz, suitable for boy or girl, though she had now got as far as insisting it would definitely be a boy.

'You'll tire yourself out completely doing that,' he warned in desperation. 'That can wait. It's not as though the baby will be going in here this very afternoon,' he attempted to joke.

She laughed in response. 'If I lie down,' she said, still busy, 'I'll only get heartburn again. I'm much better on my feet. But for that, I feel so well these days.' Her pride in her condition rang out in her voice.

There was nothing he could do but hold on to the hope that when she did finally tire towards evening, he'd have a chance to read the rest of the letter.

But she didn't tire. As the evening approached, with everything at last neat and tidy, she was eager to enjoy the novelty of sitting in their new parlour overlooking the park, the late sunshine slanting in through the large bay window, insisting he sit opposite her after Sara had been put to bed in her new bedroom upstairs.

'Your silly old work can wait,' she retorted when he mentioned unread letters. 'I want you to myself for a little while. Later we'll have supper and then go off to bed. Worry about work in the morning, my love. Tomorrow's a new day.'

But even then she was unable to relax, all sorts of ideas tumbling through her head.

'We really ought to see about getting someone for the housework. No one too expensive – I can still do the cooking – but cleaning will get hard for me. We could afford that, couldn't we? And another thing: I think it's about time we went to see your parents, Matthew. With our first baby soon to be born, we ought to visit before it gets too late for me to travel. For the sake of properness.'

Unable to stay still, she got up to potter about, straightening up the silk embroidered antimacassars on the sofa, patting the matching cushions. All Aunt Sarah's work, they were exquisite. She was very proud of them, of her aunt's talent.

'After all, they'll be our baby's grandparents, and they'll being to wonder why you persist in staying away. It was different when you had no reason to see them, but they must be getting curious about me by now. I know you aren't a close family like mine are.' He never failed to emphasise that point whenever she mentioned meeting them. 'But this is different.'

At first she had been quite happy not to meet them. Before Matthew came on the scene, she had always felt herself to be part of the elite of the area. After all, her family were in business; she had been educated to an extent while most girls in these parts had hardly seen the inside of a classroom; and she always had nice clothes, even if some were handed down from her sisters – although she always had her own shoes.

She knew of children who never had any shoes to wear, who lived in cast-off rags, running alive with vermin. Her mother would warn her never to play with such children

– and that wasn't just snobbishness.

Her cheeks, rosy from good if plain food, had compared startlingly with the under-nourished pasty faces, runny noses and scabby mouths she would see in the street, and she had heard how they slept four or five to a bed. She had only shared a bed with Annie until Clara had got married, and then she'd had a room of her own.

So by comparison, she had always felt a cut above the lower denizens of London's East End; had often pined that her father felt it not necessary to move his family to nicer surroundings. Then Matthew had come along, well spoken, well bred, startling the wits out of her by choosing her to wed. She was still amazed, even to this day, bearing his child, that her upbringing, falling so far short of his, should have been no barrier to him.

Until then, it hadn't concerned her to wonder how the upper classes lived. She had never been allowed to go up West to gawp at carriage folk as some poorer-class girls did, so there had been nothing in her insular world to destroy her own sense of her family's standing. Matthew had spoken a lot about his family at first, but as their wedding approached, he'd mentioned them less and less and had even baulked at any idea of taking her to meet them.

Growing acutely conscious of her own upbringing, she had in some ways been relieved. She would have felt awkward and stupid, introduced to his stuck-up parents. But by now her years with him had made a difference. She had gained confidence knowing that when the need arose, she could speak as well as him . . . he . . . him . . . She'd have to ask him about that one. Grammar was her downfall. She would have to watch that, but she felt confident she could hold up her head with the best of them where speaking proper was concerned.

'It might be nice if you could write to your parents and say we're thinking of going to see them,' she suggested after they had eaten supper: cold boiled bacon, tomatoes, mashed potato and lots of bread followed by rice pudding, making up for the few sandwiches they'd had during the move.

The day was beginning to tell on her at last. Matthew helped her with the dishes then guided her back to the parlour afterwards with the suggestion that she take herself immediately off to bed.

'You'll be fit for nothing tomorrow, my dear.'

'At least it's Sunday tomorrow.'

'Yes, but you still shouldn't overdo things, my love.' He might at last have the opportunity he'd been looking for all day to read the rest of that letter. He ached with dread of what else Constance might have to say. He had gone through the day like a man in a dream, forcing himself to act naturally, but all the while his innards had been churning relentlessly.

'Your parents'll be so happy to know we're expecting our first child,' Harriet murmured as she stood gazing around the now complete and comfortable room.

The sofa was against the wall opposite the fireplace, the footstool just where her feet could reach it. The rug in front of the grate would store the warmth from the fire in winter, transferring it to slippered feet. The baby would play on it, safe behind the brass fender which, like the

brass fire-irons, now shone from polishing with Glitto.
Matthew's leather upholstered armchair to one side of the
grate looked as though it had been there since the house
had been built, so naturally did it fit the room.

She covered a pleasurable yawn with her hand and did
not notice the quick look the last three words of her remark
drew from him as she went on happily: 'I am about ready
for bed. Just think, Matthew, our new room. All that space.
I never thought I'd ever have a house like this . . . Are you
coming up now, Matthew?'

Matthew dismissed from his mind the fact that Harriet
had somehow overlooked Sara as being her firstborn. But
then, she was correct if it came to splitting hairs. And
anyway, he had something else on his mind.

'I'd better write the letter to my parents first,' he said
quickly and she smiled.

'You can do that in the morning.'

'I should go to the shop in the morning,' he excused.
'Things to be sorted out for Monday. The quicker that
letter is written . . .'

She nodded from the doorway. 'Well, don't be too long,
my love.'

Her eyes were bright with love for him. He got up,
walked across the room and kissed her lightly on the
brow. From the wide hallway, he stood watching her climb
the broad flight of stairs, smiling her on her way, but the
moment she disappeared from view, he hurried into the
dining room, where the pile of untouched morning post
still lay on the sideboard.

Searching, he found the envelope, dragged out the

crumpled letter, smoothed it and began to read from the third paragraph:

> . . . I am writing to tell you that my intention to seek you out and avenge myself of the wrong you did me was very real indeed. I went so far as to buy the train ticket for London, except that in my haste I fell headlong in the ticket hall, spraining my ankle so badly I could not walk . . .

A stab of relief penetrated the fear in Matthew's heart. She had fallen and lost the baby, surely. If that was so, the fates had truly exonerated him. She would have no claim . . .

He read on hastily.

> I was helped to my feet by a gentleman so considerate that he bade me rest on a seat while he bought me a cup of strong sweet tea to revive me. I have since that day been walking out with him and we are now become engaged to be married.
>
> But do not labour under any misapprehension, Mr Craig, that I write to you out of any sense of forgiveness or to relieve your conscience, but rather that you will not flatter yourself as a gallant and I your sad victim. Although I shall never forgive you your caddishness, I merely wish to prick that bubble and to assure you that despite your abysmal behaviour, I am now very happy, and in case you did think to gloat, that I no longer even care to trouble myself enough to wish you ill.

I will not say yours truly but merely sign this letter:

C. Milne-Pitford (Miss)

Gloat, she said. Matthew could not have felt less like gloating as he put a match to the letter, then dropped it into the grate to watch it burn. He felt very near to tears of relief as he slowly stirred the blackened remains into oblivion until not a sign of it remained.

Wiping the end of the brass poker clean with his hands, he hurried to the kitchen to rinse them clean under the cold tap. He'd learned his lesson. Never again. Never again.

# Chapter Twelve

In her bright south-facing parlour Harriet sat with her sisters sipping afternoon tea and munching biscuits. She felt pleased and proud, seeing her new home afresh through the admiring eyes of Clara, and Annie's too, whose hardly veiled envy was as rewarding as any praise.

She had positively relished showing them over the house, and had revelled in the reactions of each. Both sisters' homes were just as nice as hers, but it was as good as a tonic no longer to have to endure the looks of pity they had cast in her direction when they visited those cramped rooms over the shop in Hackney Road.

It was a noisy afternoon with Clara's seven-year-old Henry, his five-year-old sister Alice, and Annie's two boys, Robert and Albert, playing on the rug, but she didn't mind. It was nice to know she had the room for them to play. Sara was playing with another addition to the family: Annie's little girl, now eighteen months old. The latest addition, Clara's William, who had come along after two miscarriages, was asleep, despite the noise of play around him, being rocked protectively on his mother's lap.

'When do you think you'll be visiting them?' asked Annie in between sipping tea. Harriet shrugged.

'It's a bit late now.' She patted the bulge beneath her loose-fitting lounge dress that helped to hide it. She'd be heartily glad when she could get back into something nice and tight-fitting instead of this shapeless thing dangling from her shoulders by straps and bows.

'I couldn't very well travel with only a month to go. I'd be so uncomfortable, and it's dangerous. I'll wait now, till the baby's a few months old, then Matthew will take us by train.'

'Took his parents long enough to ask to see you,' Annie said pointedly. 'A baby on the way before they ever bothered. I'd have felt almost as though they didn't much approve of me, if I'd have been you.'

Harriet hid the prick of indignation. She was sure there had never been anything like that. It was just that . . .

'They're not a close family,' she explained huffily, because she'd explained this before when Annie had said much the same thing. Annie could be so annoying at times. 'I have told you before that Matthew spent more of his young days away at public school and at Oxford than with them.'

'Ah yes,' echoed Annie, whose husband, Robert, had had to pull himself up by the bootstraps to get where he had got, in line for promotion very soon to under-manager of the bank where he was employed. 'Public school and Oxford. Yes, you have told me.'

'Well, I'm glad I'm not you,' Clara said, putting her empty cup back on the little round table beside her. 'Having to go and meet your in-laws after all this time – especially grand ones. Doesn't it make you feel just a bit frightened?'

She had meant it to be sympathetic, but sounded to Harriet almost as spiteful as Annie.

'Why should I?' she snapped. The happy afternoon was turning sour. 'I'm as good as them. Mrs Craig's letter was very nice.'

She recalled Matthew's almost painful joy as he opened the letter. He had once told her that he took after his mother in looks, and as he read aloud, she could almost envisage the woman who had written the words he relayed. They were words of regret for the time elapsed since she last saw him, how much she missed him, how she longed to see him again.

He hadn't read everything out. At one point he had fallen silent, his gaze moving down the page, his face growing serious. Then, realising she was waiting to hear more, he had brightened and resumed reading aloud: his mother, eager to see the new baby when it was born, was proud of him, soon to become a father. But she knew he had left out a part of the letter, and had prompted 'Does she mention me?' He had looked startled for a second, but had nodded briefly and hurried on to convey that his family sent their love and were looking forward to seeing him . . . 'Us,' he altered almost with the same breath. He had stuffed the letter into his pocket, so she had not read it herself. But it was his letter, his prerogative not to show it to her if he didn't wish to.

'She sounds a nice woman,' she added, mellowing towards Clara.

Sara's cheeks glowed rosy from the warm sunshine and the stiff warm breeze in Victoria Park. Her father had come home the previous evening with a mysterious but intriguing flat parcel for her. Her mother had not been pleased.

'You spoil that child far too much,' she said sourly as Sara tore open the wrapping with delighted squeaks. As a flat surface of blue and red tissue paper began to show, Sara frowned.

'It's a kite,' Matthew told her, and as her frown deepened he knelt beside her. 'You've seen the children in the park flying kites in the sky on the end of strings?'

Sara's face cleared, her frown replaced by a look of excitement. 'Can me fly it, Daddy? Up in the sky! Can me fly it up in the sky?'

'Tomorrow,' he promised. 'It's getting dark now. We'll fly it tomorrow morning. It's Sunday tomorrow.'

It had been a wonderful afternoon. Daddy was always ready to play with her. Mummy never was. The kite became a symbol of his love as she watched its triangular shape rise up under his firm hand, going up and up, whipping and diving, getting smaller and smaller until it looked like such a tiny thing – a tiny dot. Then he had given her the string to hold and she felt the tug on her fingers – so strong for something so small – and she squealed with delight. The afternoon flew by. She was sorry when he took the string from her to wind the lovely kite in, back to the ground in readiness to go home.

'Make it go up again. Can it, Daddy?' she pleaded, but he was looking a little concerned as he gathered up the kite.

'We should have been home half an hour ago, my pet.

Mummy will have had dinner ready and we're not there. She'll be cross.'

The thought of Mummy being cross quietened Sara's pleas. She didn't like it when her mother scolded her, didn't like the sting of the smack on her arm or leg. But worse was the way her daddy looked when she did it. It made a great hole come inside her chest that she didn't understand, and that was as bad to bear as the stinging smack Mummy would give her.

At home, Harriet had been standing at the window for fifteen minutes. Before that she had been pacing the floor, fretting, for the past half hour. Where were they?

'Oi'm sorry, mum, but Oi don't know what ter do with it, but it's getting orl burnt up. Please, mum, would you come an' look at it, please?'

She turned as Carrie, the little fifteen-year-old maid-of-all-work, came into the room.

'What's the trouble now?'

'Loik Oi said, it's orl gettin' burnt. Please, mum, come an' look.'

'Oh . . .' Harriet gave a deep, exasperated sigh and followed Carrie along to the kitchen.

Matthew had engaged the girl some weeks before. Fresh up from the country, she'd had to be shown how to cook and iron, though she was good at cleaning, making beds, washing and sewing. But the minute anything went wrong she was totally lost and needed help to set her right again. It was rather like having a dog and barking yourself. But she had come cheap – which was all Matthew could afford at the moment with the journal just ticking along after that peak last year. She hoped his fortunes would increase before long and they could afford at least two domestics of better quality than this one – a proper maid and a decent cook at least.

'See, mum,' Carrie opened the oven door for Harriet to inspect the waiting Sunday roast. The beef was beginning to dry around the edges, and the potatoes were becoming far too baked. The sprouts simmering in the pot were growing softer and sloppier by the second.

'Take it all out!' Harriet ordered sharply. 'Set the table . . .'

'It's orlready set, mum.'

'I know. But get the meat out and put it on a dish and take it into the dining room, with the potatoes. Strain the sprouts in a colander, put them in a tureen and take them in too.'

'They'll get orl cold, mum, waitin'.'

'I don't care! Do as I say. If everything's cold, it's their fault.'

'Whose fault, mum?

'Nothing to do with you!'

It wasn't fair. How dare they be so late! Her in her condition, with only three weeks to go, standing on her feet half the morning supervising this fool of a girl when she might have been up in her room taking things easy in readiness for the birth!

She heard Matthew's key turn in the lock. With difficulty she lumbered into the hallway. They were glowing, the pair of them, glowing from the fresh air they had enjoyed while she had been confined to a stuffy parlour – no matter that the sash window was up – and a steam-filled kitchen. Matthew had asked her to go with them, but how could she have stood for hours in her condition while they played silly fools with a stupid kite? She had told him so. He had looked apologetic, but had gone off with Sara anyway. And now they were laughing.

'Lovely!' she burst out. 'Nice, I must say. I hope you've enjoyed yourselves?'

Matthew's laughter died. He looked crestfallen. 'I'm sorry, we are a bit latish. We . . .'

'A bit latish! Nearly an hour latish! There's me stewing where you've got to, not knowing. The Sunday dinner's got spoilt. Carrie flustering all over the place not knowing what to do. I honestly don't know what use she is to me – it's money down the drain. I have to do nearly everything myself. For a couple more pounds a year you could've got someone with more idea what they're doing.'

'I'll dismiss her, my dear. Look for someone better.' But she wasn't interested. That wasn't her immediate complaint.

'I told her to put the dinner out, and if it's got cold, then it's just too bad. I don't care!'

She shrugged away from the arm he curled about her waist in compensation for his thoughtlessness. 'It's got me really wound up, wondering what might have happened to you. How would I know if there'd been an accident? Standing at that window, stewing.'

He stood, lost and ineffectual, looking at her, forbidden to touch her. 'I really am sorry, my dear . . .'

'Don't *my dear* me!' She put a hand to her stomach and

then to her head. 'If you want to eat, it's all there in the dining room. I'm going upstairs to lie down.'

'What about your dinner?'

'I feel too wound up to eat. I'd be sick. I have to lie down.'

'I'll come up and sit with you.'

'You stay down here. With her. You seem to prefer her company to mine anyway.'

She turned as sharply as her heavy stomach would allow. Something on the floor impeded her movement, caught her foot. Sara, worried by her mother's attitude, had laid her kite prudently down against the wall of the hallway, but it had fallen over and now lay on the floor. It was this that Harriet's foot caught.

'Oh . . . damn the thing! Everything you do,' she blazed at her. 'Everything . . .'

In blind rage, she stamped on the offending kite, tearing the red and blue tissue paper in all directions, and snapping the slender cane supports. The sight of destruction only drove her to greater need to destroy as she savagely kicked and buffeted it before the horrified gaze of her husband and daughter until all that remained was a shapeless mass; all the time screeching hatred of them both for their insensitivity to her feelings.

It was unreasonable. She knew it was unreasonable. But she felt she had no power to control herself. Had Matthew come near her, she would have hit him. Had Sara come within hitting distance, she felt she would have gladly killed her. Instead she centred every vestige of her pent-up emotions on the thing at her feet.

Tears were pouring down her cheeks, and her screeching had become foreign to her ears, as though it were someone else's voice she heard. Now, suddenly, Matthew was holding her tightly to him and she was weeping on his shoulder, utterly without strength. She had a blurred vision of her daughter standing there, her face puckered, clenched little fists grubbing at her eyes as she too wept.

'And you, you little wretch,' she found strength enough to blurt out over Matthew's shoulder. 'You can get out of my sight! I don't want to look at you. I hate you!'

'No, Harriet! You don't mean that. Take a hold of yourself.' He held her from him to stare into her face. His own was tight, his eyes like caves in his head. 'You're becoming hysterical. Now calm yourself. Breathe deeply.'

With an effort she tried to comply, did to some extent, but she couldn't help weeping. 'I'm sorry, Matthew. It's just that . . . I didn't mean to . . . You paid out for that thing. I'm so sorry . . .'

'It's not the kite,' he said slowly. 'It doesn't matter. It's Sara. It was her you stamped on, don't you see?'

The child paused in her crying to look from one to the other, bewildered. Of course it was the kite her mother had stamped on, not her. It had been such a lovely thing, swooping up so high in the sky. She had wished she could hold on to it and fly up there with it, had been sure she could in time. But now it was all broken. It would never fly again.

Something inside her said nor would she. Then something else inside her said no, but one day she would make it her aim to fly far and strong in the face of all adversity. But she was too young to understand its meaning and thought only of her poor kite all broken and useless and she burst into tears again.

It was dark outside. She'd never been up so late before. Nanna Wilson had brought her back a little while ago. She had taken her up to her bedroom and then gone away after giving her a cuddle, saying she must be good until Daddy came to fetch her to see Mummy.

She had stayed with Nanna all yesterday and all today. She loved staying at Nanna's house, where she would hide in all sorts of nooks until Grandad found her. Then he'd chase her, puffing, as she ran squealing with laughter until she let him catch her. She never had as much fun in her own house – Mummy was always cross the moment Daddy tried to play the same sort of games.

She'd had such a lovely time, and now she was home again and it was all quiet in the house, except for a funny sound coming from Mummy's bedroom – a thin, harsh mewling that she couldn't properly make out.

Sara looked up from playing with a doll as her father came in. He stood looking at her for a moment, his eyes gentle and loving. Then he came and crouched beside her.

'You have a little baby brother come to live with us, Sara.'

Comprehending that a baby would be staying with them and that he was a brother, Sara gazed up at the beloved narrow face with its tickly fair moustache and its deep brown eyes.

'His name will be James Matthew,' he went on. 'And you must love him very much.'

Must. A word she knew very well. It meant she had to do as she was told or her mother's eyes would flash at her, often followed by a sharp smack, and her father's eyes would go dark and sad.

'We will all love him very much.' Matthew smiled down at her. Touched by the child's unsmiling face, he attempted to explain. 'We are his mummy and daddy. We are *your* mummy and daddy. And we love you too – very much. As you love me and Mummy.'

'Me love you and Mummy,' she repeated dutifully.

'*I* – love you and Mummy,' Matthew corrected, smiling.

'Me love you and Mummy too,' she stated solemnly.

Matthew's smile broadened and he let the childish error pass. She was so sweet in her efforts to express herself, and Matthew loved her so very much that his heart often ached from it. Time enough for her to correct her babyish way of saying what she meant.

The baby lay in its crib. Its face was very red and all screwed up. Sara thought it very ugly, not at all like the doll she had in its toy crib in her room. She had seen other babies, passing in those wheeled things called perambulators, a word she couldn't say, though she'd heard Mummy talking about having to have one and it now stood in the spare bedroom waiting for this baby. She knew Aunt Clara had a baby she constantly held on her lap whenever she came visiting. Sara wasn't sure she wanted to keep coming for years and years to look at this baby who was to be her brother.

'What do you think of him?' Daddy was asking. His voice had an odd sound to it, like someone near to tears.

She looked up and saw his eyes were indeed glistening. Perhaps it had something to do with the baby, she thought, as she leaned over the crib to get a closer look, which she thought was expected of her. It tilted towards her a little. She reached out a hand to touch the red, crinkled cheeks. She wasn't prepared for the sudden fierce push against her shoulder that nearly took her off her feet.

Harriet watched Will's daughter approach the crib, the small face stiff with jealousy and dislike. She hadn't wanted Sara to come anywhere near the baby, but Matthew had insisted.

'We must not let Sara feel left out, my dearest. I know she'll probably not understand, but once she sees him, it will be much easier for her to accept him. Far better than explaining to her.'

The baby had been born at about six in the evening after two days of unbelievable pain, the excruciating labour of straining and pushing until the sweat poured from her brow, her body trembling with fatigue with nothing achieved until finally the birth of her son took away the pain, leaving only its recollection.

She had been too weak to argue with Matthew and lay already hating Sara's intrusion long before Matthew reappeared holding the child's hand, leading her towards the crib.

Harriet felt herself grow cold as Sara leaned over the flimsy crib, felt a shock of terror rip through her as it tilted, saw the hand reach out towards her tiny newborn son's cheeks, those childish nails ready to scratch the tender flesh. Like some fearsome wraith, Will seemed to hover behind his child, guiding those nails to rip and tear.

She heard herself cry out. 'Don't you dare touch him!'

Automatically she rolled on to her left side towards the child, the hovering demon behind her. Her right arm extended, her hand struck Sara's shoulder, sending her tumbling, but her son was safe.

Matthew had leapt to Sara's aid, was picking her up, his face creased with disbelief, directed towards herself.

'She wasn't going to hurt him, Harriet.'

'She could have done.' Tears of distress clouded Harriet's vision. She fell back, weakened by her sudden movement. There was pain in her stomach where the midwife had unfeelingly kneaded the afterbirth free. 'She could have done,' she wept feebly.

Matthew put Sara aside and came to crouch beside her. 'I know, my darling, my sweet wife. It's all been too much for you. I'll take Sara away now, then come back and sit with you. Try to sleep and I'll be back in a tick.'

He bent and gently kissed her brow, pushing aside the strands of auburn curls stiff from their recent bath of perspiration.

'I love you, Harriet,' he whispered, 'and I'm so proud of you.' He patted her hand, then crept out with his hand around Sara's.

She watched them go, stepfather and stepdaughter, the child with no idea of Matthew's true relationship to her, confident of her hold on him. Dear God, far more than my own hold, Harriet thought with a deep-seated pang as she saw him smile down.

She turned her face away as the door closed and gave herself up to a welter of sobbing, quiet lest he hear and come back with that lost look he had when he wasn't sure how to cope. She felt so lonely, so forsaken, so betrayed. Sara had become Matthew's life, even above his own newborn son, whom she felt, looking back on the last few hours, he hadn't taken all that much note of.

Sara coming first? She'd put a stop to that, as soon as she possibly could. Hatred welled up in her, her sobs growing even more distressed. That child had a demon inside her, Will's demon, which pushed her to ever greater evil. Harriet sniffed wetly, her tears soaking her pillow. As soon as she was strong enough, she would tell Sara of the true relationship between her and Matthew. Show Will he couldn't steal Matthew from her, she mused, her eyelids closing.

She was asleep when Matthew returned. He stood looking down at her for some time, his love pouring out for her, noting the damp pillow, her still wet lashes, her face wan from her labour even in sleep, the strewn auburn hair. Carefully, so as not to disturb her, he hooked a strand of hair from her cheek with his little finger and dropped a light kiss on her forehead.

His son was asleep too, the little red face surrounded by its embroidered linen cap beautiful in repose, tiny red lips petal soft, the mouth small and round as a button.

He would have liked to have lifted his son from the crib, but it would have awoken the pair of them, both needful of their sleep. With a last lingering look at each of his dear ones, he tiptoed out, closing the door quietly behind him.

# Chapter Thirteen

'I especially requested you not to write to him.' Henry Craig fingered the letter from his son, which had arrived with the last post. His heavy features were grim. The wording had so obviously been in the form of a reply that he deduced immediately who had instigated it.

Eleanor did not lift her eyes from the book she was reading, nor did her thin face lose its determined expression. 'I'm sorry, Henry, I felt it was all becoming a little silly.'

'Silly?' Annoyed by her attitude, he rose from his armchair to pace the sitting room. 'You didn't think it silly at the time, Lean. As I remember, you wanted him gone out of your sight, as soon as he could possibly take himself.'

'I didn't dream it would go on so long,' she said stiffly. At the back of her head a tense headache was hovering, threatening to make itself a nuisance at any moment. 'I thought Matthew would see sense and come round to your way of thinking, Henry.'

'But he didn't. And that's the crux of it. He didn't. If you hadn't weakened, he would not be coming here now, bringing that . . . that woman with him.'

'They've had a baby, Henry. Surely that makes a difference.' She was definitely on the verge of a headache.

She could feel it. 'I know I ought not have written to him, but I could stand it no longer. After all, Henry, he is our flesh and blood. He is our eldest son. I am his mother. How could I not . . .'

'Well, the damage is done now,' Henry broke in roughly, coming back to sit down. 'I can hardly countermand your invitation.'

'We must all learn to bury old feuds, Henry.'

'Maybe so. Maybe so – but I don't feel particularly minded to make them welcome.'

'There's the baby. Matthew's baby. A little innocent who has no part to play in this. At least him we will want to welcome, dear. As his grandparents.'

'I suppose so,' he admitted gruffly, and he felt that under his grudging admission, he too was glad and relieved that his son would be visiting.

'But I'm not disposed in having any truck with this wife of his. A money-grabbing, fortune-hunting hussy, to my mind.'

'What fortune, Henry dear? He has his business, of course, but I should hardly think that would bring in a fortune. I am sure she married him for love, not money. You mustn't be too hard on them. You mustn't judge her without even hearing her side of it. After all, you might find you like her.'

'I'm still not disposed to it,' he grumbled, laying the letter aside to pick up his own book. 'And I'm not prepared to like her.'

'We'll see,' she murmured below her breath, too low for him to catch the words as she bent again to her book.

She did not look up again until Honeyford tapped lightly on the sitting-room door to admit their maid carrying a laden tray for afternoon tea. Graciously Eleanor inclined her head as the maid bobbed and retreated; Honeyford closed the door after her. The tension in her head had quite gone. She had won. Her son was coming to see them with Henry's blessing – albeit grudging – and she felt much better. And her headache wasn't going to develop after all.

Harriet stared at the imposing aspect Matthew's house presented as he helped her down from the cab that had brought them from Winchester station. From the far end of the short drive bordered by trees whose fallen leaves were being swept up by a gardener, it loomed, frowning through a November mist at her as the cab entered through the low double iron gates, its frown deepening still more as they drew up outside the churchlike portal.

Mullions. Well named, Harriet thought, as Miss Gilbert, the children's nurse Matthew had recently engaged, alighted holding little James while Matthew helped Sara down. Narrow leaded windows, each divided by a stone mullion, studded the entire frontage, which itself looked ill proportioned, all corners and protrusions. It looked like a castle in miniature. The line of small false battlements edging the steep-sided roof between the three high gables added to the illusion, giving it a brooding, forbidding air, a portent, she imagined, of the people she was about to meet.

Matthew paid the cabby, who tipped his hat and briskly flicked the reins to make the horse start off at a trot, then guided her up the long flight of steps to the front door. A very erect, well-built, dignified-looking butler answered Matthew's tug on the bell pull. His smile was cautious.

'Very nice to see you, Mr Craig,' he greeted in a flat, husky tone, and moved aside with surprising stately grace for one so big to allow Matthew to enter. Matthew's reply was cheery.

'Nice to see you too, Honeyford. Is my mother well?'

'Better for your coming, sir.'

The butler's reply conveyed deep respect, but as Matthew guided Harriet inside, she felt not only dwarfed but cowed by the man's bulk and bearing, feeling that she was in fact creeping by him as though she had no right to be there at all.

All her life she had known only the wiry, mostly small people of the East End. Her father was the only large member of her family, originally coming from Hertfordshire. Matthew's height had never worried her because he was so noticeably thin. But moving past Honeyford, it came to her that she would be like a child amidst these strangers she was about to meet. Matthew's parents would both be as tall as him, but without his familiar sensitivity, she was sure.

'Where are Mother and Father?' Matthew asked as lightly as if he had been absent from the house a day or so instead of years.

'In the sitting room, Mr Craig.'

A maid having taken their outdoor clothing, giving each adult a small, respectful bob as she did so, Matthew made for the sitting room without waiting for Honeyford.

Holding Harriet by the hand, and leaving Miss Gilbert with her two small charges to hold back until bidden to follow, he burst into the room unannounced.

Harriet found herself staring at her in-laws: Matthew's father with both hands on the arms of his chair, leaning back in it, seeming to fill the thing; his mother tall and slender, perched on the edge of a sofa, her back perfectly straight, her head poised and high, hands folded in her lap. Obviously they had seen their son arrive and had sat down in readiness for his entry. It was all so formal Harriet felt herself already shrinking.

Almost dragging her with him, Matthew made for his mother and bent and kissed her startled but automatically offered cheek. He straightened up, still holding Harriet's hand.

'You look well, Mother.'

'I could be more so. My looks belie my health, Matthew.'

Matthew nodded, appropriately solemn for a second or two, then brightened and turned towards his father, who rose in readiness to shake his hand.

'And how are you, Father?'

'Usual fine fettle.' The slightly greying moustache seemed to bristle as Henry Craig turned a pair of heavily bagged, blue eyes to settle on Harriet. Matthew caught the movement and parried.

'Father, this is Harriet, my wife.' Harriet only just stopped herself dropping a curtsey, already feeling awkward and gauche.

'Yes, of course,' came the only response.

Harriet said nothing, but dear Matthew had already

swung back with her to his mother, who was sitting exactly as before, not one inch of her smooth dove-grey dress disturbed. She looked like a statue, her mouth composed or rather set in a thin straight line, her brown eyes pain-ridden, her high brow furrowed, no doubt by the same recurring head pains Matthew had told Harriet she had endured since he could remember. The dress was beautiful, very expensive and superbly made to fit the thin form. And what taste, Harriet noted with envy amid her confusion of being presented to the woman. Not one thing out of place, no excess of jewellery or ornamentation, despite her wealth. Just a simple jet brooch fastening the high, gathered neckband – that was all.

Harriet's hand moved upwards in an attempt to hide the rather heavy ornamental brooch she had chosen to wear on her sage-green outfit. Matthew said it looked very elegant, but now she wasn't at all sure.

'Mother,' Matthew announced. 'My wife, Harriet.'

Eleanor Craig lifted a hand towards her, limp but not weak, in gracious response. Harriet felt for one idiotic second that she was expected to fall on to one knee and kiss the opal ring glowing there. But the bubble of mirth came solely from tension.

With the tips of her fingers, she took the hand lightly, to have it withdrawn immediately, protocol observed, though the cold brown eyes, like Matthew's but without the gentle glow, continued to survey her, a ghost of a smile – was it sympathy? – trembling on that straight line of a mouth.

'Pleased to meet you,' Harriet heard herself blurt. Oh, no, it should have been how do you do, she remembered, too late. But she could only let the pleased-to-meet-you suffice, and fell silent.

Her mother-in-law's gaze switched to the open but vacant door. 'Where is my grandson, Matthew?'

'Oh, yes! Half a tick!' He was like a raw schoolboy. At the door he called into the hall, 'Miss Gilbert – the children. Bring them in.' The high ceiling echoed to his call.

Harriet watched as her son was brought in and handed to his waiting grandmother. She was astonished to see the transformation in the woman. The stiff mien seemed to melt like frost before a risen sun, brown eyes misting, and now she saw in the gentleness she would never have suspected in the woman, her resemblance to Matthew. The hands loosened and fluttered as she received the bundle, lifting aside the frills and lace of James's bonnet. When she looked up, her thin face was lit up with pure delight.

'He's like you, Matthew, as a baby. I could be holding you in my arms. Richard's boy is like his mother, and Evelyn's girl is like her father. It's so refreshing to have at least one in the family who resembles one's own.'

James let out a small fretful cry, sensing alien arms holding him. Immediately, Eleanor was all attention.

'There, there, there. Is it all so strange to him then, little man?' She rocked him gently. The crying died away. She looked up at Matthew in triumph. 'See, my dear, old habits die hard. It *is* as though I were holding you.'

Ignored during all this baby business, Henry Craig got up and came over to stare down at his new grandson. 'Hmm . . . Looks a bit weak.'

'He's only two months old, Henry.'

'Thought he'd be more robust than that.'

'Give him time, Henry. He'll grow stronger. Who d'you think he looks like?'

'Can't tell with babies. All look alike. Bit of you in him though, I suppose.'

'Of course. He's like Matthew, and Matthew takes after me, so of course there's a bit of me in him. There, sweet little boy . . . James, is it?' And as Matthew nodded, 'Sweet little James. We'll have your christening here, in Winchester. Ours is such a lovely church. James . . . what?'

'Matthew,' Matthew said, grinning all over his face.

Eleanor nodded her approval, then frowned. 'It would have been nice to have added his grandfather's name. Though I suppose the christening has long since gone. Its a pity you didn't think to invite your father and me.'

'He hasn't been christened yet,' Matthew broke in. 'Harriet hasn't felt strong enough. It will be very soon, though. In a couple of weeks, at the most.'

Eleanor brightened, even executed a wide smile of relief that made her look quite human. 'Then it's not too late. Oh, you must add it! James Matthew Henry – does it not have a good ring to it? What do you say, Matthew?'

'I can see no objection.' Grinning, he mulled over the name. 'James Matthew Henry. It does have a good ring. It flows.'

'Yes it does, doesn't it?'

Listening to it all, plans being made, the extra name being added, Harriet stood dumb. No one asked whether she agreed or objected. No one had considered that her family would have to come all this way to a christening. No one had enquired if she wanted the christening here or whether she had other ideas. No one even glanced her way. She felt as excluded as Miss Gilbert, standing by the door holding Sara's hand.

Sara too looked lost, but Sara didn't matter. It was a pity she had had to bring her really. Aunt Sarah had taken charge of her after Jamie was born, but now that Miss Gilbert had been engaged, she could hardly ask her aunt to look after Sara while they came here. Sara was still under her feet, even with Miss Gilbert around.

'What do you think, Harriet?' Matthew's arm came lightly about her waist. 'Henry. It'll be nice having the christening here, don't you think?'

Shaken from her reverie, she tried to smile, and instead of voicing an opinion, heard herself saying, 'Yes, nice.'

Confronted by three pairs of eyes demanding her acquiescence, what else could she say? Satisfied, the eyes returned to admire James, leaving her once again on the perimeter, already wishing the day over.

They were staying overnight. 'The children and their nurse will have the old nursery quarters,' Mrs Craig declared as James was deposited back into Miss Gilbert's arms. 'You can have your old room, Matthew. It is a little cramped for two, so I have arranged for the blue guest room to be aired to accommodate your wife – if that's agreeable to you, Matthew? It *is* only for one night.'

Harriet thought he looked a bit surprised, but he nodded passively. She felt she could have shaken him.

Lunch was a cold buffet laid out for her and Matthew at

one end of the highly polished, oblong table in the somewhat chilly dining room. His mother had arranged to have just a little soup brought up to her in her room, saying she felt rather drained and needed to rest. His father had arranged to meet a client and was eating in Winchester. The children were borne off to the nursery for their lunch, providing Harriet with a golden opportunity to tax Matthew on what she saw as his not so submissive concurrence – enthusiastic was more like it – with his mother's suggestions over the baby, but she found it impossible to voice her feelings, even with no one else there.

She ate in brooding silence, and when Matthew asked her what was wrong, she made a headache her excuse, refusing to smile when he said jovially that one in the family was enough, meaning his mother.

'If we were to have the christening here,' she said finally, unable to maintain her sulk any longer, 'what about my parents?'

'I imagine they'd enjoy being here,' he said lightly, reaching for a liberal helping of home-made mayonnaise to drown his final bits of salad in. 'Make a change from London, I should think.'

'They might not want to come all this way.'

'Not to see their own grandchild christened? Of course they will.'

'It's a long way, Matthew.'

'A few hours by train – not all that long.'

'Wouldn't it be easier to have it in London? Dad does have his business to look after. He can't just walk off.'

Matthew munched on the last of his salad like a

contented cow. 'Your brothers would most likely keep an eye on the place.'

'They might like to be at the christening.'

He grinned sagaciously. 'If I know young men, they'd have some other axe to grind. Isn't John keeping company with a young woman these days? And you mentioned George was talking seriously about becoming engaged to that Alice – I don't know her other name – of whom he has been seeing a lot these past eighteen months. Again, when do you ever see them?' He chuckled and pushed away his empty plate. 'I'm sure they'd rather be murmuring sweet nothings into the ears of their young ladies than attend some christening.'

She had no answer to that argument. Matthew reached for an apple from a silver dish of fruit. She watched him regard it, polish the red skin to a fine gloss against his waistcoat, then take an enormous bite.

In spite of herself, Harriet's lips twitched into a smile of amusement. He was more like a boy sometimes, instead of a man of twenty-eight and a father, talking of George and John as though they were mere boys when they too were men. She didn't hold with his mother's decision at all, still felt annoyed for his ready compliance with the woman, but she loved him so very much. How could she hurt him, content with the decision made and believing she was too, by going against him?

The afternoon became pleasant with only themselves to please. But all that changed the moment Eleanor Craig emerged from her room. Harriet immediately crept into herself like a tiny tortoise, wishing she did have a shell to cover herself with. For all her apparently poor health, Eleanor overpowered her with that weight of dignity oozing out of her. It was a wonder she didn't explode from it.

When Henry Craig returned home in the late afternoon, his large frame towering over her, Harriet's misery was total. She longed for the refuge of the room she'd been assigned, even though it wasn't with Matthew. But that was hours away: there was dinner to get through yet.

Dinner on a Saturday didn't warrant such a sumptuous spread, surely. It was a formal affair, with Honeyford standing to one side, and a couple of female servants hovering, ready to serve or clear away under his direction. The meal commenced by Honeyford pouring a liberal measure of deep red wine into each crystal goblet – they had to be crystal, the way they glittered. In her growing uneasiness she drank most of it without thinking and had it immediately refilled. She had not eaten much at lunch, so had come empty-stomached to the dinner table, and the wine went instantly to her head. What made it worse was that although Matthew looked across at her, his parents seemed to go to great pains to ignore the incident.

She wanted to cry, flee from the table, but all she could do was pick at her meal, frightened lest she use the wrong knife or eat too fast or drop something on to the napkin across her lap. The wine had made her dizzy; fear had made her awkward, made her fumble too often. She had no idea what it was she was eating – some sort of soup, some sort of game, some sort of sickly pudding that refused to stay on her spoon.

Once it made a horrible sucking, gurgling sound at her as she made to prise a spoonful away from the serving on her dish. She giggled. It was the wine, of course, but all three stopped talking, while Honeyford delicately cleared his throat. Matthew asking if she was all right made it all the worse. She managed to mumble that she was perfectly all right and went on trying to eat the revolting souffle.

She was glad when dinner was over. But more torture was to follow: the ladies – she and Matthew's mother – retired to the sitting room, as was the custom, while the men – Matthew and his father – lingered on to chat over after-dinner port and a cigar.

Getting through the half-hour cloistered with his mother until the men joined them was something like a nightmare. Still dizzy from the two glasses of wine, and fighting to fill hiatus after hiatus, her attempts at small talk struck even her ears as utter tosh. When they did join them, Matthew's easy conversation at least left her free to sink, relieved, into a corner of the sofa beside him.

The evening was interminable. After Jamie had been brought down to be cooed over prior to going to bed, there seemed to be little to stay up for. Except that Henry Craig deemed it opportune to toast the baby's health with a drop of his best Madeira.

The wine was a good vintage, Harriet imagined, and strong, she was sure, but very nice and wanning, slackening her taut nerves. She had a second glass to help them on their way – and when tentatively offered a third, accepted readily. After that things didn't feel so bad after all. Matthew's mother was really quite nice, she decided, his father more a rough diamond than a hard nut. She was suddenly finding all sorts of things to talk about, most of which came out very wittily to her immense satisfaction. Suddenly it struck her that the journey here this morning was taking its toll. She stifled several yawns, found them funny; fell against Matthew's shoulder giggling.

Vaguely she heard Mrs Craig's voice with a frigid edge to it.

'I think your wife is rather tired, Matthew.' She was being helped up off the sofa, finding the process hilarious, and guided out of the room to the hall, up the stairs that seemed too steep for her feet. As she stumbled, Matthew picked her up bodily and carried her the rest of the way to her room.

Matthew was angry with her as he helped her out of her clothes and into a nightdress; the way he spoke to her as he got her into bed reduced her to maudlin tears but he didn't stay to listen to her explanation about the wine, merely stalked out of the room. The excess of wine sent her to sleep quickly but woke her early, to be plagued by the last night's events. Pre-dawn birdsong spoiled any chance of her going back to sleep and forgetting it all. The sound of the birds was eerie, and she was glad when daylight came.

She mentioned it to the maid who came in to wake her. The girl said, 'Them's robins, madam. Them do sing earlier than most. Coming into song, they are.'

Harriet sat up carefully, wincing against a jolting headache as her morning tea was handed to her. 'But they were so loud.'

'Good Lord, madam, that's nothing. You should 'ear the

dawn chorus in the spring. That wakes you up, that does, and keeps you awake. But it's lovely with the dawn all rosy red and them singing away. Now if you want anything, madam, there's a bellrope just beside you.'

The morning began in frigid silence, but for the odd obligatory exchange of words when need arose, delivered as briefly as possible. Her eyes heavy, Harriet mentally cringed from her mother-in-law's averted gaze, her father-in-law being very obviously absent.

She overheard Matthew and his mother in some sort of heated argument after she had gone upstairs to see Jamie, voices harshly whispering. She knew it was about her. Soon afterwards, Matthew came up to tell her that they had a long journey ahead of them and it was best to start early, meaning straight away.

'You've got your wish,' he said stiffly as they waited for Miss Gilbert to bring her charges downstairs dressed for travel. 'The christening's to be in London after all.'

She was shocked. 'But I didn't mind it being here. What's made the change?'

'Don't tell me you didn't work all evening towards that end, Harriet. You disgraced me. You disgraced yourself. You intended for them to see you in such a bad light they would never want you here again. Do you know what you've done? How you've made me feel with my own parents? How you've divided us? It's taken me years to get them to accept you. Now you do this. I'm ashamed.'

'I didn't intend anything. It was that sherry-stuff. That Madeira. I hadn't eaten much all day because I was so strung up. It made me go peculiar.'

What did he mean, taken him years to get them to accept her? Who cared, anyway? They were just stuck-up, ignorant prigs for all their high and mighty attitude. But to see Matthew behaving like this towards her who had done nothing intentionally wrong – she was angry and hurt and blamed them utterly.

'I didn't do it on purpose, Matthew,' she defended, but at that moment Miss Gilbert came down with the children, stopping any reply he might have made. And perhaps it was just as well.

The journey home was as silent as their leavetaking of his parents. The family brougham, protecting them from a thin morning drizzle, took them to the station. Matthew helped her down from it but it was a mere duty and there was no smile for her. She was too crestfallen by now to attempt to cajole him out of his mood.

It was no better arriving home. The wet afternoon had begun to draw in early, and the four-wheeler conveying them from Waterloo Junction rumbled through almost-deserted, rain-washed London streets, depressing her still further. Their musty smell, however, was infinitely preferable to that dank, woody odour of wet countryside, so full of a lingering loneliness that she still felt as dejected by that as by Matthew's continuing moodiness.

Edgy, she turned on Sara as they came into the house, railing at her for getting under her feet. It was a natural reaction and didn't warrant him saying what he did.

Very well, she had raised her voice in irritation, but Matthew had no need to turn on her, telling her she had little to shout about after the way she'd behaved, with Miss

Gilbert overhearing it all. It was unfair, and she snapped back at him, very close to tears, telling him so in no uncertain terms. Miss Gilbert, James clutched in her arms, hurried Sara before her up the stairs as both parents glared at each other, snapping like small dogs, finally breaking off to sweep separately into different rooms.

In the parlour, dreary in the fading wet light, she lit the central gas lamp and furiously swished together the heavy curtains. She remembered the glow that had stolen over her after those three glasses of madeira and wished she could feel that way now. There was no Madeira but there was some brandy in the corner cabinet. Pouring herself a small glass was satisfyingly like defying Matthew and she found a certain pleasure in that private gesture. She took a tentative sip, grimacing at the taste, but it took away some of the hurt, and she drank a little more.

The second glass tasted much better. It made her feel better, too. When Matthew eventually came into the room to apologise for his conduct, his naturally fair nature enabling him after a while to see both sides, she was quite ready to accept his apology with magnanimous grace, the bottle now safely back in its cabinet, and the glass hidden.

# Chapter Fourteen

Jamie wasn't proving as robust as his start in life had predicted. Those first months produced a crop of baby illnesses: croup, then a persistent ear infection, and one cold after another.

Horder, whom Matthew had engaged as the family practitioner when they'd first moved into Victoria Park Road, was a constant visitor, and a boon to Harriet, whose ever-present fear was of Jamie becoming a sickly child.

'He'll grow out of it – be as strong as a lion by the time he's britched,' he reassured her, his own ample proportions radiating strength, and she was grateful for the comfort his words gave her.

But that Jamie was never going to be a sturdy lad was obvious. He was so like Matthew, fair-haired, but blue-eyed now the baby hue had settled, tall for ten months and thin, his first baby fat already dissipating. It gave an overall impression of a delicate constitution and, consequently, without realising it, Harriet tended to over-mother him. She was still breastfeeding him at ten months, though little milk was left, whenever he turned towards her, which was now from habit more than anything, but she believed it indicated a need for sustenance. And she had become irrationally over-protective, especially where Sara was concerned.'

'Keep away from Jamie! I can see what's in your mind.'

Matthew said her fear of Sara going too near him was unreasonable.

'She can't harm him. She only wants to love him.'

'She's jealous of him. You can see it in her eyes.'

'You're just imagining it, my sweet.'

'Kids do all sorts of things when your back's turned. Say she poked his eye, or pinched him, or bit him? You wouldn't be so cocksure then, would you?'

'I think you're being . . . over-cautious,' he said, himself cautious.

Sara looked on, learning. Babies, even as they grew bigger and sat up almost on their own, were apparently not to be touched except by grown-up people, in case it damaged them. But when her mother wasn't there and Miss Gilbert had Jamie to herself, she was allowed then to hold those soft, podgy little hands, kiss those velvety cheeks.

Once, Miss Gilbert had let her hold him, sitting her on the floor on a cushion and putting him in her arms. He felt unexpectedly heavy, not like her dolls, and she held him tight so he wouldn't fall. She was four now, Miss Gilbert said, and becoming a big girl.

Being four was a wonderful time. She'd had a birthday. Daddy had bought her a doll's house and she had been given a party at her nanna and granddad's, and lots of aunts and uncles had come. There had been a heavy fruit cake, though she didn't like its bitter-sweet taste, but she liked the sugar icing on it; and jelly and cream and pink blancmange, and shrimps and winkles – she liked shrimps but the grown-ups enjoyed the winkles, attacking them with pins and chewing the gritty top ends with relish. But she had preferred the ham and tongue.

Everyone had made a fuss of her, especially Great-Aunt Sarah, who, she was told, was one of her godmothers. Daddy had made more fuss of her than anyone else, but Mummy had gone all sulky and wouldn't talk to him. And as she lay in bed that night she heard them arguing and Mummy crying, but she didn't know why, for it had been such a lovely day.

Matthew had become quite wrapped up in the garden at the rear of the house. It was rather narrow, overshadowed by other houses and a few straggly plane trees, but when they had moved in, he'd seen its potential for recreation purposes. Winters were now something to enjoy as he sat in the long dark evenings studying seed and rose catalogues. Spring found him digging and planting furiously; summer evenings were busy with weeding, tidying, and generally enjoying the fruits of his labours.

This summer Jamie was just about toddling – wobbling and gripping his mother's hand as she came to inspect what Matthew was doing. Sara was his constant help, trying to assist in plucking out weeds, but more usually uprooting a treasured annual on the verge of flowering. He had found one way, however, of preventing that – a tiny plot of her own in one corner of the garden.

He smiled this evening as he covertly watched her

planting sticks, solemnly digging a hole for them with the toy metal fork and spade he'd bought for her on her last birthday, hoping she'd share in his new hobby, which, by the look of things, she was showing every sign of doing.

'Should she be doing that?' Harriet's voice was sharp as she sat Jamie in his wickerwork bassinet at the end of the garden to enjoy the last of the sun's rays over the rooftops.

Matthew looked up and smiled indulgently. 'Keeps her out of the way.'

'And gets dirt all over the path. Look at the mess she's making.'

'I'll sweep it up later.' He surveyed the soil strewn across the narrow flagstones, then returned to his task as Harriet walked back towards the house. He had hardly bent to it when a shriek of pain from the bassinet made him spring upright again. But already Harriet was down the garden and now he saw what the trouble was.

Sara's little spade had caught on something, a stone or a root. But in her effort to free it, the spade had suddenly released itself and soil had flown up in the air, most of it landing in the bassinet. Worse, a small portion had caught Jamie in the face, and he was now furiously rubbing his eyes, getting even more soil in them.

Before Matthew could reach them, Harriet was there, grabbing at Sara rather than her baby. She raised her free hand and struck the girl's face, the dark cringing head, again and again, her shriek demented.

'You wicked, wicked little fiend! You did that on purpose! Always wanting to hurt him, you wicked . . . I hate you. I wish you were dead!'

Before Matthew knew what was happening, she'd grabbed up the small metal spade, raising it in blind fury above the child.

Matthew saw its descend, the small dark head too transfixed with fear to duck out of the way.

Still too far away to stop the downward sweep, Matthew launched himself bodily at Sara and collided with her, pushing her aside with the impetus. The spade landed squarely across the back of his neck and he went down like a felled ox.

Harriet's scream echoed across the gardens.

'Matthew! Oh, dear God, Matthew!' Dropping the spade, she threw herself down beside him and tried to turn him and lift his head. Blood from the nape of his neck streaked her hands, her cream summer blouse. The sight heightened her cries, combining them into one hysterical howl.

In his bassinet Jamie wailed, still trying to dig the smarting out of his eyes. Nearby, Sara lay on the path gasping, too winded to cry, too frightened by what had happened to move.

From the neighbouring house voices called. 'What is it? What's happened? Is someone hurt?' Harriet responded.

'Help! Oh, God, someone, help! I've killed him. Oh, Matthew – not again! Not you!'

Two people were beside her, helping her up. She tried to fight them. 'I've killed him . . . Like I did before. I'm a murderer. Let me go!' But the man held her firm while the woman bent to examine the prone bleeding figure.

It moved. It groaned, lifted itself on its arms, while its

would-be helper started back. Twisting round painfully, it
sat up.

One hand clasped to the back of his neck, Matthew stared
up at his neighbours. He seldom saw them under normal
circumstances. He knew their name to be Billington, but
that was all.

Seeing that he was all right, the woman went to retrieve
Jamie from his bassinet, cuddling him in one arm and
wiping the dirt from his eyes with the aid of a hankie and
a little spittle, it being an emergency. The man had helped
Sara up, who now stood crying feebly. Harriet, released by
her captors, threw herself on Matthew, almost knocking
him back down again.

'You're not dead! Oh, Matthew . . . If I was to've killed
you I . . . I'm glad I killed him, but . . .' She stopped herself,
but Matthew hadn't seemed to hear.

Instead, a brief laugh shook him, apparently seeing the
funny side of it as he moved his head to survey the scene,
but the movement made him wince and he brought his
head up sharply.

Harriet was all repentance. 'Does it hurt? Oh, my love,
I never meant to do anything terrible. I could have killed
you.'

Any amusement he had felt dissipated as the wound
began to throb. He brought his hand away, looked for a
moment at the blood on it, then his sleeve soaked in it.
Switching his gaze up to Harriet, his eyes were now devoid
of all humour.

'If this is what a toy spade could do to me, what might
it have done to a four-year-old? You could have killed her,

Harriet. What got into you? How could you contemplate harming her like that?'

'Is there anything we can do?' Mr Billington was bending over them. Matthew met the anxious regard sharply, then moderating it with an effort, gave an appropriate smile of gratitude.

'No thanks. But it was kind of you to come running so swiftly. It might have been an emergency. Thank heavens it wasn't. Even so, I appreciate it.'

'Well, if you think everything is all right.' He began to retreat, hopeful of not being expected to contribute anything further.

'Yes, perfectly, thank you.'

'Good.' The baby having more or less stopped crying, his wife laid it back in the bassinet and followed him.

With Harriet's help, Matthew got himself to his feet and took a deep breath to steady himself. Feeling more stable, he shrugged off her efforts. Before his harsh, disbelieving stare, Harriet wilted.

'Don't look at me like that, Matthew. Anyone'd think I *meant* to hurt you.'

'You *meant* to hurt her.' He reached out and took the child gently by the arm, drawing her against him in a protective gesture. 'What in God's name got into you? There was hatred in your eyes as you raised that thing. No two ways to say otherwise. Why should . . .'

He stopped, at a loss to explain it. 'Honestly, Harriet, sometimes you frighten me. Most of the time you're the sweetest, most docile, loving person anyone could wish to meet. There are times I think you walk this earth in mortal fear of doing something wrong, you can be so timid. Then suddenly . . .' He raised up both hands. 'Out of a clear blue sky.'

Harriet was already crying. She seemed to collapse as though her bones had turned to jelly, no longer able to hold her upright.

Matthew saw it coming, and let go of Sara to catch Harriet as she swooned. Lifting her up, he bore her into the house, calling for Miss Gilbert; Mrs Downey, their cook; Ellen, their new housemaid – for anyone, to run for the doctor.

All three had been alerted by Mrs Craig's screams, but having let the next-door neighbours in through the side gate to help, had kept themselves discreetly out of the way, knowing that more authoritative assistance was at hand. Now they all came running at the master's call, to do whatever was wanted.

'Oh that *is* a pity.' Mary Wilson nodded, pouring tea for Matthew while he related the sad news to her and Aunt Sarah, who spent more time with her sister than ever these days. 'I know how she must be feeling. I've suffered the same loss in my time. Still . . .'

She brightened as she laid the teapot back on its stand and handed him his cup. 'There'll be other times. Hardly into its seventh week – she'll get over that and start again. But it's disappointing.'

Her sister pursed her lips over her own cup. 'She doesn't strike me as that strong, or stable. She worries me, that girl. Always edgy.'

'There's nothing wrong with Harriet,' Matthew said

quickly. 'She had an upset. If I had known her condition, I would have been far more careful. I don't think she was aware either – at that point.'

'Careful?' Sarah Morris caught on to the word, switching her glance from the window, its panes streaming with a brief summer afternoon thundershower. She cast him a look, her brows beneath her greying frizz of fringe drawing together. 'What on earth did you do to her?'

Defensively, he told them in the briefest terms of the upset two weeks previously, how Harriet had swooned from the fright of some harm to Jamie. He avoided saying just how vicious a turn her temper had taken. It had been pure hysteria, her believing her son could have been blinded. Like a female leopard protecting her cubs, she had struck out – a natural reaction – and he should never have shown his anger as he had. And now he was reaping the bitter harvest of it, his child miscarried. He still hadn't got over blaming himself. He wanted to weep.

'I lost my temper. Over something quite stupid. But it truly did upset her. I shall never forgive myself.'

Mary leaned forward and laid a hand on his. 'You mustn't blame yourself.'

Sarah was made of different stuff. 'Losing your temper's no reason to make her lose a baby. Unless you struck her. Did you?'

'I certainly did not!' Matthew's contrition erupted into instant outrage.

'Only . . .' Sarah stopped, the abrupt way she broke off causing both pairs of eyes to turn towards her.

'Only, what?' Mary prompted.

'Nothing. My silly old mind's wandering.' Sarah took a quick sip of tea, averting her eyes from theirs.

But the way she had glanced towards Matthew, her look full of some veiled knowledge he couldn't define, prompted recollections of his own, fleeting intimations he had submerged at the time as being too outlandish to be taken seriously.

Harriet had done nothing but cry after the doctor had left. She had been wretched, blaming herself for her failure to keep the baby. That night, she had woken up from a nightmare, crying that *he* was punishing her for what she'd done – that *he* said he would.

She had been so inconsolably terrified, clinging on to Matthew, begging him to protect her from 'him', that he altered his first thought of her referring to God and His punishment, to the Devil. But her cry that 'he said he would' had a more earthly ring to it than that, and for no apparent reason Will Porter, her first husband, sprang into his mind as he tried to soothe her.

He had never felt entirely comfortable about that man. It wasn't jealousy – how could it be – a dead man? But there was something that had always nagged: the way Harriet never referred to him; that inexplicable haunted look that came upon her if his name cropped up.

Thinking of it now, he wondered, had she been frightened of Will Porter? A silly thought, but . . . Aunt Sarah had stopped so sharply just now. 'Only . . .' What was so awful that she had made excuses for not continuing? What did she know that no one else knew?

With an effort, Matthew pulled himself together

and drank a large gulp of his tea to subdue these idiotic phantoms. He was entering into the realms of melodrama, and he must stop it.

Yet another sentence, cut short, forced its way into his mind, though at the time it hadn't done so. 'If I was to have killed you – I'm glad I killed *him,* but . . .' She had broken off so suddenly, even in her distress apparently aware of having said too much about something.

Long after he'd left his in-laws, the thoughts still plagued him until he had to push them away forcibly, making his mind turn to more normal things in order to submerge them. Finally they did disappear. It was not until two weeks later that they re-emerged, stronger than before.

Harriet recovered more quickly than expected. For all her small stature she was strong, at least physically. Within days of the miscarriage she was on her feet, but so subdued that Matthew worried for her.

It was the way she looked at Sara that gave him most worry – such a look of hate, as though she blamed her for the loss of the baby. Again he had an impression that there was something more to this than met the eye. Even though Matthew tried to shrug it off, it persisted. Did Sara's own father have something to do with Harriet never displaying the least fondness for her? He kept wondering.

As it got stronger, he decided enough was enough. Four weeks after the miscarriage, he left the journal in the capable hands of his assistant, Leonard Hallet, and went on a visit.

The *Freewoman* was ticking along nicely these days.

If anything, it had expanded. Women's suffrage societies were still making their presence felt in the north of England, if not to the extent of the 1895 gatherings, at least enough to keep women in the south subscribing to the *Freewoman* in substantial numbers. There was now a new and up-to-date printing press, the old printer long since gone. Hallet now took a large part in the journal, sometimes even being sent out on consignments, but mostly making himself useful in the office sorting the advertisements to go in, while Matthew did page layouts. He would also sift through the mounds of subscriptions, handing them to the new apprentice to file away after they'd been listed – a youngster named Bob Pullings who did all the menial tasks while learning his trade.

Confident of Leonard's ability to take care of things for an hour or so, Matthew found himself a cab and gave the destination. Outside the oil and candle shop in Hackney Road he paid the driver and went in.

Behind the counter Mrs Hardy was weighing currants for a customer. At the far end of the shop Mr Hardy was drawing vinegar from a barrel for another, the brown liquid a slow noisy trickle from the tap into a metal jug.

Neither looked up as Matthew came in. He waited quietly. Mrs Hardy was the first to notice him as she closed the till with the customer's departure. She stared for a fraction of a second, then was galvanised into life.

'Good Lawd – it's Mr Craig.' Throwing up the hinged bar of the counter she came round the end at a near sprint, skinny arms, with sleeves rolled up, stretched wide in joyous welcome.

'Well I never! What a sight fer sore eyes! Bert, look oo's 'ere.'

Mr Hardy glanced up and smiled, the metal jug still under the tap to be filled to the brim, preventing him from showing any other welcome. His wife had already grabbed Matthew by the hand and was pulling him through the gap to the other side of the counter and towards the stairs at the far end.

'Come on up, dear. We ain't busy at the moment, as yer can see. We can spare an' 'alf-hour or so. You can tell me and Mr 'Ardy all yer news over a cup a' tea an' a nice bit of cake. Bert, when yer can, come up fer a chat wiv Mr Craig, an' I'll come an' take over down 'ere.' She bustled him on up the stairs and into the front parlour. 'Well, ain't this nice? Sit down then, Mr Craig, an' make yerself nicely at 'ome. I'll go an' stick the kettle on. Won't be a tick.'

She hurried out. He could hear her tripping down the stairs to the kitchen behind the shop, which the two of them obviously used most of the week as a combined sitting and dining room; eating by the warm range, taking their ease in ancient comfortable armchairs until it was time for bed, similar to the way Harriet and her first husband had once lived, the way most people did around here.

He stared around the parlour. As with most parlours in this area, it was chilly from little use, kept only for high days and holidays or for guests. Unused, it was left to capture all the musty blending of odours that rose from the shop below: vinegar, lamp oil, sacking that held a variety of dried foodstuffs – peas, haricot beans, rice and oatmeal and such – and a certain cloying but stale smell of soap, potpourri and household polish.

Matthew grimaced, as he would have liked to have done before the sounds coming from Mrs Hardy's mouth, but that would have been impolite. Harriet had never spoken like that. From the first he had thought how better articulated she was than others around here. She often boasted these days that her speech had become much nicer with him beside her, though if it had, he had no recollection of it ever being anything but nice to his ears. Mrs Hardy's speech merely jarred.

'There you are, Mr Craig, a nice steaming pot fer the three of us. We'll 'ave a nice little chinwag first, and then I'll call Mr 'Ardy up while I take over the shop. Now 'ow's your dear wife? I did 'ear from somewhere as she 'ad a little boy, but that was some while ago. Lost touch wiv you two, proper, I 'ave.'

Talking without hardly drawing breath, she poured tea into what was obviously her best china, added milk from a matching pot-bellied jug and offered him sugar from a similar bowl. He accepted only one small teaspoonful, which she put in for him, stirring mightily on his behalf. She handed him his cup and sat opposite him in one of the hard green leatherette armchairs to sip her own tea.

'I miss your little Sara. I bet she's gettin' a big gel now. An' like I said, if I 'eard rightly, you've got a boy too. Any more on the way?'

The tea was strong. Matthew forced himself to drink, but only as little as was politely necessary until he could eventually put his cup back on the brown chenille-covered table beside the rest of the tea things.

'My wife had a miscarriage a few weeks ago, unfortunately.'

'Oh, that is 'ard. Tell 'er I'm sorry. But she'll 'ave another.'

'I expect so.' He leaned forward a fraction. 'There is something I wanted to ask you, Mrs Hardy. You may be able to enlighten me.'

'If I can, Mr Craig.'

'It concerns the matter of my wife's previous husband, deceased.'

Did he detect a guarded look creeping into the faded eyes? He would have to word this enquiry very carefully if he had rightly gauged what he saw there. He had no wish to alarm her into telling any lies, thinking to shield the man – or Harriet . . . Good God, what was he thinking?

'How did Mrs Craig . . . then Mrs Porter . . . and Mr Porter get along in their marriage? Were they happy?'

'Why d'you ask?'

'I worry for Mrs . . . for my wife. She appears not to recall her previous marriage as a happy one. Not that she says as much, but she has dreams which alarm her severely and which seem to be connected to her previous husband. They seem to terrify her, and I have a strong belief that her husband was . . . unkind to her. That he treated her, physically, not as he should have done.'

Matthew placed his tea on the table, glad to be rid of it. 'I am not prying. I merely wish to help my wife. If you have any means to help her, I shall be most obliged for anything you can tell me.'

'Is she ill, poor dear?'

'Not *ill.* But not at ease. I am most serious about helping ease her mind from . . . what might have occurred in her past.'

Mrs Hardy thought with an great effort. Frowning, she placed her teacup back on the table without looking where she was putting it, fortunately in the right place. She began slowly.

'It ain't fer me to tell tales, Mr Craig. Not after all this long time. But I can safely say your wife found 'er previous marriage not exactly an 'appy one. I've seen 'er that distraught . . .'

She began to hot up to her tale. 'I've seen 'er wiv a black eye an' a swelled lip many a time. She always said it was 'er fallin' and knockin' herself. The day Will Porter died, she 'ad a great yeller bruise on 'er poor cheek, an' 'er such a pretty little thing too. And eight months gone wiv 'er baby. Fell down the stairs 'e did – her 'usband. Mid-afternoon, it was. I remember thinkin' at the time, what was he doin' upstairs that time of day when 'e 'ad a business ter run? I 'eard 'er crying, long before I 'eard 'is tumble. And I know they come from the top of the stairs. These walls, y'know, thin as cardboard. Yer can 'ear everythink. I've 'eard them 'aving many an argy-bargy. At least I've 'eard 'im bellowin'. She never yelled back, poor dear – too refined to yell. I know 'e 'it 'er many a time too. Can 'ear everythink – even mice gnawin' on next door's floorboards. The police came, y'know. Well, they would – someone goin' down the stairs like that, and endin' up dead on the floor below. They asked a few questions, I think. Not many, for they could see 'er condition, and 'er just become a widow a few seconds before. I 'eard she said she was in the kitchen gettin' 'is tea when 'e fell. But I'm sure she was up them stairs when he did fall. I'm certain of it.'

'You mean, you think she . . .' He could hardly bring himself to say the words. 'Pushed him?'

Mrs Hardy waved her hands about. 'Oh no, nothink like that. A tiny little fing like 'er, and eight months gone? No. 'E was a big man, y'know. Ever so 'andsome, though 'is 'eart was black as Newgate's knocker. She wouldn't've had the strength. No – what I'm sayin' is 'e was drunk. Come back from the pub, two – three o'clock, fancied a bit of the other, if yer forgive me sayin'.' She gave a self-conscious titter and continued quickly.

'Bundled 'er upstairs, I reckon. In that condition too. But 'e didn't care, long as 'e got what 'e wanted. Bein' drunk, 'e must've fell down the stairs like a dead log. An' I'll tell yer this fer nothink – a jolly good riddance too. Then you came along, Mr Craig, and 'er life changed. She deserved it to change, bless 'er 'eart.'

It was a thoughtful man who left the Hardys' shop that day.

# Chapter Fifteen

The summer sunshine pouring in at the window from over the park all lovely and warm on her back, Sara sat on the floor of her room, surrounded by her family of dolls while she served them all tea.

She was five now and felt very grown-up. She would soon be going to school, Daddy said, and he had looked so sad it worried her a bit. She didn't like to see him sad. Secretly she was looking forward to meeting lots of other children her age, but she didn't really want to go if it was going to upset him.

Mummy had said thank God – she'd be out from under her feet – and had actually looked quite pleased. Though why she should say she was under her feet confused Sara, because she always tried to keep out of her mother's way. It made it easier to stay out of trouble, especially lately. Mummy had been getting very fat around the middle lately, and the fatter she got, the more upset with Sara she got. So it was always a good idea to keep out of the way up in her room.

She loved her room, staying up there for hours on end. Miss Gilbert would bring her meals up to her and then go and get Jamie, who slept in the little room next to hers, and bring him in too. She was quite content with this, going downstairs only when her father came home, or when the family went to church on Sunday, or he took her over to the park on Sunday afternoons.

There was everything here she wanted: her dolls' house, her dolls, a little chair and table where she served them all tea from a tiny china tea set, some funny toys that moved when you wound them up with a key, all of which her father had bought her at one time or another.

Here there was no need for anything more. Her room was her domain. Her word was law. Just as Mummy's was downstairs. In winter she'd snuggle up and watch the rain outside her window and feel all warm and cosy. In summer, she'd play in the sunlight until Daddy came home and then go down and help him in the garden. So long as she kept out of Mummy's way, life was really nice. She guessed that this was how it was with all children – keeping out of their mothers' way while they waited for their daddies to come home and play with them. She guessed that when Jamie got to her age, it would be the same for him.

Unable to remember what her babyhood was like, this was what she guessed.

A few days later, Miss Gilbert, holding Jamie like a baby as though fearful of letting him go, for all he was nearly two, stopped her abruptly as she laughed out loud at his peevish face at being cuddled like that. Her expression was not so much severe as sad.

'Hush, Sara! You must be quiet and not disturb your

mother. She has been ill all night. She has lost her baby and is very upset.'

Sara had been awoken in the night by someone crying. It was so anguished and went on for so long, she thought it would never stop. There had been footsteps too, and whispering voices – her father's and one that sounded like Dr Horder's, a hoarse sort of voice she remembered from when he had come visiting her when she had been ill with measles the year before. She remembered him saying she'd got over it remarkably well and her mother retorting, 'Trust her,' without any smile on her face, though her father had leaned over and caught her to him, tears of relief running down into his soft fair moustache.

'Mummy's not lost him,' Sara said, confused as she looked towards her brother in Miss Gilbert's arms. Her mother always called Jamie her baby. 'Tell her Jamie's here.'

Miss Gilbert's smile was tremulous. 'This was a baby she was going to add to the family. It was to have been a new little brother or sister for you both. But something happened. No one knows what. It just came into the world too early and the angels thought it best for it not to stay here, because it wasn't well. So they took it back to live with them in heaven where it will have a lovely time.'

'Where Jesus is?' Sara queried. She wondered why, if this new baby was going to have such a lovely time in heaven, Miss Gilbert was looking so miserable.

Tears glistened in the woman's pale blue eyes. 'Yes, Sara. He'll be happy there with Jesus. Now you mustn't speak about it any more. Certainly not to Mummy and

Daddy when you see them. You understand?'

Sara nodded solemnly. There was something mysterious about all this but she remembered in church that the vicar often said they must pray for the souls in heaven, and people must not grieve, because they were only grieving for themselves in their loss, and that they should be rejoicing instead that these souls had been spared the trevails of this world.

She had never bothered to understand what he was saying, his voice ringing through the vast dimensions of the church, but now some of it made sense. If Mummy's new baby had gone to heaven, surely she shouldn't be crying about it, and Miss Gilbert's eyes shouldn't be filling with tears? It certainly didn't tie in with what the vicar said. It was all very mysterious.

Harriet had felt low after that first miscarriage but finding herself pregnant again had brought her out of it. Perhaps she shouldn't have been so excited – Matthew said she had been far too excited for her own good, but she hadn't believed him. It was probably that which had made her miscarry, for there had been no other apparent reason.

Her moods since losing this second one, just when she had thought everything was going so well, worried him. They worried her, too, fluctuating so violently between high spirits and deep depression, especially when Sara came near her and she noted the comparison between her rosy good health and the pale insipidness of Jamie.

She thought of her two babies dead before they'd had a chance to come into the world and felt nothing short of hatred for this robust girl with all the good looks and wellbeing of her loathsome father.

Matthew was no help when she tried to tell him how she felt. He would merely give her a look that mystified her – a sort of puzzled contemplation – but he never said why. He was as loving as ever any man could be, but this non-committal attitude of his blocked all her efforts to share her loss with him. Sometimes it was as though all she had was Jamie to ease the pain it brought. Jamie and occasional expeditions to the corner cabinet where Matthew kept his brandy.

It warmed her as it trickled down her throat, penetrated her whole being and made her feel so much better. She would send Ellen out for an identical bottle, fill Matthew's one to the level it had been before use, then enjoy what was left of her one until compelled to resort again to Matthew's store. Then she could go through the process as before. This way, Ellen wasn't being sent out too often, and nothing need be said; nothing had to be explained to Matthew.

Not that she drank that much, just enough to compose herself to meet the forlorn days ahead, drown the memory of those two poor little lost, half-formed babes, her poor lost self thinking of them.

Matthew was concerned by her plunging state of mind. To bring her out of it, he was taking her out and about more. It was so much easier now that they had money to pay staff – no more having to beg favours of a neighbour and family. With Miss Gilbert to take care of the children, and young Mr Hallet to look after the journal, Matthew would take her occasionally to the theatre in the evening, and many a Saturday afternoon shopping in the West End. He had even spoken of going back to Paris next summer, but that was a long way off yet. This was only October.

It was a lovely afternoon, the sun warm and mellow. Harriet clung to Matthew's arm as they shopped in Knightsbridge. He had brought her up here to buy a new dinner gown before the Christmas season began to send prices soaring. She would choose carefully, wanting the best but knowing she mustn't overdo it. Matthew's pockets weren't bottomless, and she'd had enough of skimping and scraping when the journal hadn't been doing so well not to want to risk punishing their savings too drastically.

Ignoring those jostling past her, deaf to the noisy congestion of traffic behind her, she stood gazing into the window of one of the smaller stores at the most delightful dress she'd seen all day. A tea gown of palest green chiffon and lace, it was expensive, nearly eight pounds – five weeks' wages for Mr Hallet. Yet the more she knew it to be too extravagant, the more the sight of it drew her.

'No, it's far too expensive,' she demurred, hoping it would have the opposite effect and sway him. But he too was studying the price.

'Do you think it's practical, my dear?'

'It's for Christmas. Christmas gowns are never practical. They're for special occasions. They're not meant to be practical.'

'That is true . . .' Her anticipation rose. Even though he was still looking at the price, he was at least melting a little.

She became aware that the sound of military music from Hyde Park, where there seemed to be parade going on, had grown much louder. Forgetting the gown for a moment, she turned with the other shoppers, interested in the now fast-approaching music.

The traffic began drawing to each side of the road, making a space down the centre. A couple of elderly crossing sweepers came smartly to attention. And then she saw it, the head of the column appearing, a glint of brass in the autumn sunshine, a flash of scarlet.

The rolling drumbeats had begun to shiver the air. Bugles and trumpets blared. Through the centre of the halted traffic it came, a wide column of wonderful, well-built men, every man the same height, every face florid with health, expression stern and proud beneath its white, low-peaked pith helmet, every rifle at the same slant on the shoulder as every other, Blanco'd webbing white as the driven snow, boots polished to such a shine as to send the sun's reflection back to blind onlookers. And those boots crunching in step – it was like a single tread, as loud as though a huge giant was shaking the ground.

The blare of bugles and the thrump of drums going right through Harriet's breast made her head ring with its joyous noise. Then came the mounted troops, harnesses jingling, plumes jiggling, the erratic clatter of hooves in stark contrast to the measured crunch of marching feet.

Cheers rose from the pavements as column after column passed by, bound, every onlooker now realised, for South Africa to show the Boers, who had dared to declare war on Britain two weeks earlier, what she was made of.

'Isn't it wonderful?' Harriet cried, her voice drowned out by all the music and cheering. But Matthew saw her lips move and read what she was trying to convey.

'Splendid,' he bellowed back, and she could only just about hear him. 'Makes one proud of one's country.'

The column passed on its way to entrain at Victoria station, she imagined, and thence to the coast to board some great ship. It was all so romantic.

The music fading, the traffic began to move together again to reform into as big a congestion as before: cabs, carriages, carts, omnibuses, their sides advertising Nestles milk, Taylor Bros cocoa and Ogden's cigarettes; mundane after the glory that had passed by just a moment before. Pedestrians resumed their shopping. Harriet dragged Matthew into the shop to buy her gown.

She looked a picture in it, its waistline fitting so tightly that she was forced to purchase a new corset while she was about it to help restrict a waist she was sure had expanded after four pregnancies.

She didn't know then, of course, that the gown would not be used for Christmas after all. By Christmas, her waist would already have begun to thicken another inch or so to make the wearing of the gown virtually impossible, despite all the help her new corset could afford her.

The last Christmas of the century. Because it was such a special occasion, Matthew paid a visit to his parents, going early on Sunday morning, Christmas Eve, so as to return the same evening. He went alone, knowing by now that they wouldn't welcome Harriet. Though it hurt, though he should have felt chagrin over it, blood was after all thicker than water.

He would have liked to take Jamie to see them, but it would have upset Harriet and as two wrongs never did make a right, his parents must settle for him without their grandson.

His mother was writing to him on a regular basis now – once every couple of months, with all the family gossip. His father had mentioned coming up to London in the New Year, and hoped to meet him somewhere – possibly even to be shown over the journal. Matthew thought he might attempt in a circuitous way to bring him back to their home. Who knew, it might break the ice for good.

Christmas at Harriet's parents was as jolly as ever, with every member of the family gathering for dinner. It was made even more pleasurable, not only by their celebrating the last Christmas of the century, but by a special announcement being made by Harriet's eldest brother.

Everyone was leaning back from the table, replete and contented, after Jack Wilson's brother George had toasted the Queen: 'A grand old lady, frail in body now but as strong in will and keen in mind as ever – an example to us all – may she reign over us for many years yet – God Bless Her.' John chose this moment to make his announcement. He stood up, thrust his thumbs importantly into his waist-coat and cleared his throat to attract everyone's attention.

'Right, everyone, while we're all gathered here round the dinner table, and I've got you all captured, so to speak . . .' He laughed. 'I've got something to tell you that's of great joy to me.'

He looked fondly down at the fair-haired, oval-faced young woman sitting beside him. Some of the family had already met her at John's home, but few had been in conversation with her, the pair always being too eager to be on their own for anyone else to see much of her. Her name was Charlotte – John called her Lottie. Her family lived in Dalston. That was all they knew about her, but they'd suspected something had been in the wind for a long time.

'Last week,' John continued, trying hard to contain his joy and making a poor job of it, 'I asked Lottie to be my wife and she has accepted . . . *And* her father has given his blessing,' he shouted above an outbreak of forks being tapped on glasses by all the men and cries of pleasure by the women. 'We plan to become engaged next month. The wedding'll be around July. Everyone's invited, of course.'

Everyone was getting up, coming round the large family table to shake his hand or embrace him, all without exception kissing Charlotte's pretty blushing cheeks, she looking flustered all the while.

'Twenty-four,' bellowed Uncle George, who still lived way out in Hertfordshire. 'That's a nice age for a young man to wed, that is.'

Later, in a corner of the parlour, John was buttonholed by his brother. 'I can't announce anything myself, but you know I've been going out with the most marvellous girl these past three months, though I've not brought her home yet. She only lives in Roman Road but her people are very nice. They took to me straight away, I think. In fact her father treats me as though I'm Irene's last chance.'

'She that plain?' John stifled a chortle.

George looked offended. 'Of course not, but she's so shy, they despair of her. But she's not shy with me. In the New Year I'll bring her here. Then you'll see for yourselves. I hope after that, in a while, to propose to her.'

'You? You're only twenty-two. You've got a life to live before you knuckle down to marriage.'

'I'm old enough.'

'How old is she?'

'Twenty-three.'

'Good Lord! Baby-snatching?' John's voice ringing around the room brought everyone's eyes to George's quickly crimsoning face. Jack Wilson came over, grinning benignly.

'Take no notice of your brother. I don't doubt that she's a very presentable young lady, George, and I'm glad to see you've decided to stop sowing all those wild oats of yours. By the time you do wed, you'll be John's age. So you, young man . . .' he glanced in amusement at his other son, 'have nothing to put on airs and graces for.'

With this, he slapped both sons on the back and went to join his brothers, who were making for the piano for a singsong.

Harriet's announcement was delivered more modestly as, a sherry in her hand, she sat in the hot, crowded parlour with her mother, Annie, Clara and Aunt Sarah while the others gathered around the piano to sing the rest of the evening away.

'I have been to see Dr Horder,' she confided. 'According to him, it'll be around the time John gets married.' And this time she was certain the baby would be full term, healthy, and another boy.

Jamie had been taken downstairs. He was always being taken downstairs, and Sara, approaching six years old, was beginning to sense the oddness of that.

She was hardly ever allowed to go down. Daddy came up quite often, and once he told her that he'd practically lived all of his childhood up in a nursery, and after that had been sent away to school.

'But why can Jamie go downstairs and not me?'

'He's a baby. They are special to their mothers. And he's a boy. One day he'll go away to school, as I did. She'll not have him for a long while and she wants to make the most of him while he's here.'

'When I was a baby I wasn't ever brought down to see her.'

'You didn't have a nurse or a nursery then. We couldn't afford that in those days. We all lived together. Do you remember?'

Yes, she did remember, but even then her mother had been distant – cold. Even when her father played with her, she hadn't joined in or laughed with them.

'If I didn't go to school,' she stated now, 'I'd be bored up here all on my own.'

'You like school, don't you?'

She nodded, staring out of the window across a park that was grey and damp on a cold March Sunday morning. Had it not been for school, she wouldn't have thought her life any different to other people's. But from friends she had made there, she learned that they enjoyed far more of their mothers' attention than she ever had. It made her think: what she had imagined to be jealousy when Jamie seemed to have more of his mother's time than she did, had really been a sense of loss she hadn't understood. Now she did. What she still didn't understand was why. Perhaps mothers did love sons more than daughters. After all, she was coming to understand that men were more important than women, had to be more educated, so perhaps they needed more attention than women.

In a way that new thought made her feel a little better.

# Chapter Sixteen

Harriet's hands unclasped from prayer and moved tentatively down to her stomach. She lifted her head. 'Annie – I think it's started.'

Annie, who wasn't so much praying as watching the couple kneeling together at the altar steps, looked more peeved than concerned. 'It can't have – not here.'

Hearing the hissed exchange, Clara, kneeling further along the pew, looked round her husband at them and mouthed, 'What's the matter?'

Fully attentive now to the situation, Annie mouthed back, 'She's started,' and her finger stabbed at the now cringing figure.

Clara shook her head, her lips forming the words, 'She can't have – not here?'

Annie nodded. To add weight, Harriet moaned.

The sound disturbed Matthew, lost in private prayer while the two at the altar received God's blessing upon their union. He looked up, saw Clara's incredulous expression, then glanced quickly at his wife.

'Harriet, are you . . .?' Wordlessly, she nodded, becoming more distressed by the knowledge of where she was than what was happening.

'She oughtn't to have come,' Annie whispered angrily.

Her husband craned his neck round her. They'd arrived late, Annie having spent far too much time fussing over her sons as pageboys. Trying to create as little disturbance as possible, Robert had sat on the wrong side of her, too late to change places as Lottie, looking like a dream, made her serene way down the aisle on the arm of her father, yards of lace floating behind her, scalloped hem held unsteadily by Sara and her cousin Alice, while two other bridesmaids and Annie's boys in eighteenth-century costume clogged the length of the aisle.

Robert was looking anxious. 'What can we do? Can't she hang on till the end? There's not much more to go.'

'Of course she can't!' Annie's reply was a stage whisper, bringing other heads up to see what the fuss was about. 'She should have known better and not come. She knew how near her time was.'

'We must get her outside.' Matthew had his hand under Harriet's arm. 'Can you get up, my dear?'

'I can't move!' Her voice was a sob. The pain, coming from nowhere, was growing more intense by the second. She had thought herself safe – at least a week to go. Plenty of time. Now she was caught by fear, seeing a repetition of her last pregnancy, which had ended in painful miscarriage. 'Oh, God – I'm frightened.'

Her words, rising on sudden hysteria, echoed around the church, rebounded off bare walls, unabsorbed by pictures, the Stations of the Cross, the painted robes of the Virgin and Child, the eagle-topped lectern, the gold and white pulpit, the gilded Saviour on the great cross above the altar, or the stained-glass windows behind.

Most of the congregation was agog now. Even the bridal couple had turned, Lottie's face a picture of dismay at the most important moment of her life being interrupted. The vicar, towering over the kneeling pair, stood stark and alone, arms frozen in a crucifix-like gesture, in the act of concluding his blessings, his expression of godly joy now transformed into one of human irritation.

Clara was squeezing hastily past her husband, past Matthew, to Harriet's side.

'Quick, Matthew! Help me get her outside. Carefully and quietly as possible now.'

It was amazing how silently it was done. As for unobtrusively – every eye, including the vicar's, followed them on their way, everyone transfixed by the business. Annie, her husband and Clara's Fred in train, Harriet stumbled down the aisle, supported on one side by Matthew, and on the other by Clara. Her parents, in the front pew, were unable to move, torn between concern for their daughter and respect for their son and his future wife.

Once outside, Clara put herself in command of the situation and ordered them to help Harriet to a bench. 'She can rest there. It's only just started. She's got plenty of time. When the pain dies down, we'll get her into one of the carriages and get her home. Fred, you can bring it back when we've done with it. Someone'll want it to get home in. Robert, you take another carriage and go for their doctor. I think she'll need you here, Matthew.'

'Hold on!' Annie was stiff-necked. 'Don't order my

Robert about like that. If anyone's to tell him what to do,
I . . .'

'Oh, blow you, Annie! What does it matter? Fred'll go
– I don't care! S'long as *someone* does.'

'Would you, Robert?' Matthew's quiet, anxious voice
intervened.

Robert shook his head, mainly to dismiss the plea. 'Of
course, old man. You stay with Harriet. That's y'place.'

The pain subsiding, Harriet was helped gently to the
carriage, and half lifted into it. Clara got in beside her with
Matthew. Robert hurried off to procure a spare carriage to
speed off to Dr Horder, while Annie went back into the
church to pass the word about being two carriages short
and to tell her parents what was happening.

As Harriet's vehicle started away at a gentle pace so
as not to cause her more discomfort than necessary, she
heard the joyful peal of bells behind her. John and Lottie
were married. Soon they would be coming out of the
church after signing the register. But she had other things
on her mind. This baby would be born whole and healthy.
Nothing else mattered.

All in all it had been going on for thirty-two hours. Harriet,
feeling remarkably well and brave, had insisted on getting
up and walking about despite the midwife's warnings to
rest in readiness for her labour proper. She had eaten a
good lunch and a small dinner. That night she had even
slept between her bouts of contractions, slight as ever
they'd been through the day. Dr Horder had pronounced
her in fine fettle and told Matthew to call him as the pains

became stronger and more frequent. He had patients to deal with elsewhere, he remarked jovially, and it could be in inestimable number of hours before she needed to call him again.

The next morning, just after she had enjoyed a moderate breakfast, her labour began in earnest. Bundled into bed, her shrieks had Matthew ordering Ellen to hurry for Dr Horder. He was with her now, hadn't left the room at all. The day passed agonisingly slowly, and it was now almost dusk, and still her cries rang from the bedroom – beginning to sound exhausted, Matthew was sure.

Dreadful cries. If he could have left the house, to be out of hearing, he would have, but his place was here, as near as possible to her. Not that a woman in labour wanted her husband anywhere near, but he felt that to leave would be a betrayal. If she had to endure such prolonged pain, then so would he endure hearing it.

As dusk faded, Matthew relaxed his vigil and walked the garden in the warm darkness with Harriet's father, wreathes of smoke from cigarettes drifting up to a star-studded sky on the still air. Her parents had left the wedding reception as soon as they decently could, and Harriet's mother had made herself busy around the house instructing Mrs Downey on the preparation of an evening meal, though Matthew had hardly eaten a thing. How could he, with Harriet suffering so upstairs? But her mother ate well enough. 'No point in starving ourselves to death. Harriet will be fine. I know she will.'

He was back inside the house when the midwife came

puffing down the stairs. From above, Harriet's cries sounded more feebly, already causing some anxiety.

'There are complications.' Her face was grave as she met Matthew's apprehensive one. 'Doctor's doing all he can. But it don't look good.'

Unable to take in the full import of what the woman had said, Matthew felt inexplicably angry. 'Why wasn't I told before? What complications?'

She looked blank, unsure how to explain to a layman the complication of hydrocephalus, which could occur unforeseen often without any known cause. Ordinary people called it water on the brain, and it was known to be incurable.

'Doctor never anticipated this sort of complication,' was all she felt able to confide. 'He'll be coming down to speak to you himself about it as soon as he can safely do so, sir. I must hurry back now.'

'It's a rum do,' Jack Wilson rumbled, as the woman puffed her way back up the stairs to the labour room, the anxiety on his usually benign face belying the shallow statement.

Mary Wilson, coming up from the kitchen, saw the looks on the men's faces and was immediately alarmed. 'What's happened? What's wrong?'

Matthew shook his head, unable to trust himself to speak.

'Complications,' Jack Wilson said for him. 'Midwife just told us.'

'Oh, dear God – what?'

'Maybe not as bad as it seems, my dear,' Jack said

hastily. 'These midwives, they're scaremongers. Horder's coming down anyway to talk to us.'

Matthew looked from one to the other. He could hear Harriet, her cries, though markedly weaker, ironically heartening to his ears. At least she wasn't lost. For one terrifying moment he had thought . . .

'Oh, my poor child!' One hand to her lips, Mary had sunk down on the chair near the door where Matthew was wont to throw his coat when he came home after a day's work at the journal. In tableaux, the three waited, unsure what to do next. They looked up as one as a movement on the stairs alerted them.

Horder came down quite nimbly for a corpulent man. Taking Matthew by the arm, he guided him into the drawing room, closing the door.

'I'll not beat about the bush, Matthew.' Not prepared to waste time explaining the whys and wherefores when he himself was at a loss for a cause, he went straight on. 'The child's head doesn't come through. I've done all I can. Your wife's exhausted. It's become a case of mother or child. If I don't act now, it will be mother *and* child. I needed to warn you.'

William Horder forced himself to meet the husband's bewildered look. The man knew well enough what he was saying but could not believe it. The question, 'Isn't there anything you can do?' was written all over that face.

'I've done everything.' He answered the unspoken question. 'She's been far too weakened for me to perform a caesarian operation. The shock would kill her, and I doubt it would save the baby.'

Of all the potential difficulties in labour, this was the dilemma he hated most. To save the mother he must kill the child. There was no other way when a fetus became a foreign body within its own mother's womb, killing her slowly with its inability to be born. It would die even without his crochets and scissors; would putrify, spread poison through the mother's system – if she didn't die within the next hour from sheer exhaustion.

He must apply his murderous instruments to the living fetus – the most heartbreaking, gory task imaginable. Then the enlarged head, pierced and drained of its fluids, would come through. The mother's life would be saved. Would there come a time in the medical world when such terrible, drastic measures would be rendered unnecessary?

He had come into the profession at the time ether was first being used in surgery. These days no doctor would dream of performing any surgical operation without it. So many great leaps had been made in medicine; if only a man might one day be able to peer into the womb so as to see before a child was born whether it was becoming a threat to the mother. But that was asking too much. No stride in medicine would ever achieve such a thing. It would be too like trying to step into God's shoes, and, no – that wasn't to be countenanced. To his mind, medicine had gone as far as it ever would. There would always be death in childbirth, and though he might pooh-pooh the belief that death was God's will, something inside him said that God must have the last word and the humble doctor and surgeon could learn only so much and no more. It was a great pity.

'I need your answer, Matthew.' Though he knew the

answer; should not have wasted time asking; but as a family doctor – a friend – knew he must.

The husband's expression wrung his heart. 'Save her . . .'

'If I can.' He laid a brief hand on the trembling shoulder and hurried from the room, the stricken gaze following him as he mounted the stairs to his task.

William Horder had washed his hands thoroughly and packed away his bloodied apron so that nothing of his deed could be seen. The tiny, mutilated remains had been wrapped up in sheets, well out of sight. The mother, sleeping the sleep of the exhausted, would know nothing about it until the next day. Then would come her husband's part, helping her as gently as he could to face her loss. She would never know the truth of it, of course – only that her child had been stillborn. Aware of the highly strung nature of Harriet Craig, he felt that would be bad enough. But he had worse news yet. Politely he ushered the husband and her parents into the drawing room.

'Let us sit down.' He felt he should smile to reassure them that it wasn't all dire – though it was dire enough for the smile to be solemn.

Matthew immediately thought the worst. His voice rose. 'She's not . . .'

'She's sleeping.' He waited for him to compose himself. 'I do, however, have something of gravity to tell you. The extent of it, of course, depends on how you view it. But the considerable length of time the head was pressed . . .' He stopped, in danger of becoming too technical for everyone's good. He began again. 'The crux of the matter is that she has been damaged internally – quite considerably, I regret to say. I doubt she'll be able to conceive again. If by some chance she does, it could . . . well . . . imperil her life.'

He directed his gaze straight at the husband. 'It will be up to you – the responsibility of making certain she is never put in that danger. I'm sorry.'

Matthew rose without nodding his understanding. He looked neither at Horder, nor at his wife's parents. 'May I go up and see her?'

'Of course.' Horder also rose, prompting the others to get up too. 'I shall send a nurse to take care of her. She should be here within an hour.'

'I can take care of her,' Mary put in, but he shook his head.

'She will need care for quite some weeks from someone with expert knowledge of nursing, Mrs Wilson. But there's no reason why you may not help look after your daughter if you wish.'

He walked towards the door. His bag stood outside, together with another hastily procured from the basement by the midwife some while back.

'I shall return in the morning to check upon your wife.'

Matthew was still standing in the middle of the room, looking at none of them, his gaze trained sightlessly upon one of the brocade easy chairs. 'What was . . . the baby?'

Horder stood with one hand on the door handle. He had expected this question, knew he must answer it without circumlocution.

'It was a boy.'

Matthew's face creased. He took in a great breath to control himself, then straightened, but still without looking at any of the faces regarding him anxiously. 'May I see him?'

Horder had anticipated this request too. Any father would want to gaze at least once at his dead son. But in this case, it had to be denied, at least for the moment. The sight of the tiny bandaged head, bloodied matter still seeping into the cloth, would only add pain to pain.

'I think it better not to, Matthew. Later, perhaps.'

At last the eyes focused, so filled with knowledge that Horder almost recoiled. Then they fell away.

'Thank you for all you've done, Doctor.' His voice was utterly flat.

'I'll return in the morning.' Horder opened the door, said his goodbyes to the older couple and hurried out, gathering up both bags before the housemaid let him out into the night.

In the mortuary, the tiny body would be cleaned up, made safe to look upon in swathing lace robes and a heavy lace cap over the tight bandages. Matthew could see his son without fear before the little body was laid to rest at the foot of another's coffin, being unbaptised.

While Jamie stayed at home as a comfort to his mother, Sara was sent away to spend the school summer holiday with everyone else in the family but her mother and father. Her father didn't think it a good idea, but her mother's poor health prevented him arguing about it.

So Aunt Annie had her for one week and Aunt Clara

for another, which was quite nice as she could play with
her cousins. Then there were two weeks with Nanna and
Grandad, who treated her like a baby but spoiled her
utterly, which was very enjoyable; and two weeks with her
godmother, Great-Aunt Sarah, who treated her exactly like
a grown-up rather than a six-year-old, which was a very
special feeling.

'As you can expect,' Great-Aunt Sarah said as they
took a walk in Victoria Park in the hot late August sunshine, her papery complexion shielded by a cream sun
umbrella, 'your mother will seem to behave strangely for
quite some time to come. You must expect that. You see,
when a woman has a baby and loses it just as it is being
born – what is usually called stillborn – it leaves her in
great shock. It is in fact bereavement. Do you know what
bereavement is?'

Sara shook her head, walking very upright beside her.
Everyone said she was tall for her age. She believed them;
she was already up to this small woman's armpit. If Great-
Aunt held her arm straight, Sara could only just stand
erect beneath it, and more and more that arm was having
to be raised a fraction to accommodate her. She guessed
that in this family of small people she probably took after
her grandfather, who was large, or her father. His parents
were tall too, she recalled from the only time she'd met
them, though she couldn't think whose colouring she had
– dark hair, blue eyes – no one in the family she could
think of.

'A bereavement,' Great-Aunt was saying, 'is when
someone very dear to you dies. A loved one. It makes

everyone terribly sad, and those nearest to the dead person feel the loss almost like a pain inside. It's called mourning. Not like *this* morning – it's spelt differently. It means you feel miserable and upset and terribly empty.'

'But if the loved one is going to heaven,' Sara argued, feeling very grown-up, talking like an adult with this woman, 'shouldn't their families be pleased that the loved one is happy in heaven?'

Sarah smiled. 'That's what's preached. But people are human. They have feelings. They mourn because they feel empty, and no one should expect them to feel otherwise. Your mother is mourning her dead baby, and it's making her ill. I just wish she wouldn't wear such deep black. People don't go in for that now so much as they did in my day.' Her tone grew absent. 'Why, only ten years ago a woman would wear deepest black for two full years if her husband died. Your mother did. At least she did the first year, when your . . .'

She stopped so abruptly that Sara looked up at her, thinking she had choked on something, the way a person will sometimes choke on their own spittle. But her great-aunt hadn't choked at all. Her face hadn't gone any funny colour, apart from a strange expression as she stared down at her. Sara felt driven to prompt her.

'You said, Great-Aunt, when my . . . Who?'

'Never mind!' The tone was sharp. Hastily averting her eyes from Sara's inquisitive probing, Sarah spotted a kiosk near to one of the park's entrances with something like relief. 'Oh look, Sara, refreshments! Shall we buy ourselves a cool drink or an ice cream?'

The mysterious unfinished sentence was swept instantly
from Sara's mind by such a wonderful idea. She concurred
with cries of delight.

Great-Aunt had been right – her mother *was* strange, not
for weeks but for months. If she had been distant towards
Sara before she had that dead baby, she was more so
now, as though she saw Sara as some sort of slimy insect
that had crept out of a hole to touch her skin. She would
practically recoil if Sara came too near.

There was no reason for it as far as she could see. She
didn't behave badly. She did all she could to be good.
None of it helped. But for friends at school whose mothers
behaved so lovingly towards them, it probably wouldn't
have hurt so much. But at times it *did* hurt, excruciatingly,
like something bitter – she was coming to know what
being bitter felt like. It wasn't like any other feeling she
knew. It was much more horrible.

Her father was strange, too. When her mother wasn't
there, he would sit her on his knee, kiss her tenderly, tell
her how much he loved her and hold her close. But as soon
as her mother came into the room he would put her from
him as though guilty of something. And if he paid attention
to her when Mother was there, she'd snap at him and tell
him to 'leave that child alone'. The awful part about it was
that he would do as he was told; would never argue on
Sara's behalf. It made her feel mean.

Her mother was still not well by the time Christmas
came. It was a miserable time, her mother refusing to
leave the house, moping in her room, wanting only Jamie

with her. The weather was damp and muggy, not at all like Christmas should be. Even though her grandparents came over for the day, nothing cheered up. Sara was glad to go back to school.

'Why does Mummy hang on so much to Jamie?' she asked towards the end of January as she sat with her father at the drawing-room window, watching one of those snow showers that promised to settle in, only to die disappointingly away.

'Does she?'

He seemed preoccupied, his dark eyes intent on following the thick flakes weaving past the window panes. It was Sunday afternoon. Everything outside was silent, the park, hardly visible in the fall of snow, deserted. Indoors it was almost as hushed but for the steady, sonorous tick of the long clock in the hall and an occasional spit of gas from a piece of coal in the firegrate that Ellen had made up until it burned brightly enough to send cosy radiant heat into every corner.

Sara and her father were alone. Mrs Downey and Ellen were in the kitchen, taking their ease before preparing the evening meal. Mother was upstairs resting, as she did most of the time, Jamie beside her.

At two and a half, Jamie was still being treated like a baby, what with Mother cuddling him, dressing him in frills, and talking about how she didn't want the day to come when he'd have to go into knickerbockers. She hardly ever let him out of her sight and he had come to rely on her for everything. He seldom took any notice of his father, and cried after her if she wasn't there to pick him up. At the first whimper she would come hurrying to kiss him better.

Sara thought he was becoming just a spoiled little boy. In fact she didn't like him all that much. Miss Gilbert would never have allowed him to make such a fuss. But Miss Gilbert wasn't with them any more. Mother had dismissed her last September after Sara went back to school.

She remembered the tremendous row her parents had had over it, her father saying she should have kept Miss Gilbert on until Jamie was of school age; that she shouldn't have got rid of her without consulting him. He had accused her of being jealous of her own son, said she was mollycoddling him, and he did understand her grief over the dead baby, but did she realise that he grieved too, but that life must go on?

Her mother's weeping had been dreadful to listen to, but this time he hadn't cuddled her, wouldn't have done so even if she'd let him. They hadn't spoken for days afterwards. Eventually he did cuddle her and she cried all over again. Then they talked together for a long time in low tones, so Sara hadn't heard what they were saying.

After that, however, she was met from school by her grandmother in a hired cab and taken home by her to await her father, who would eventually bring her home. It seemed an odd arrangement. After a quick supper it was up to her room. She missed Miss Gilbert being there, and quite suddenly her happy bedroom didn't seem happy any more.

# Chapter Seventeen

It was a gloomy time. A black wreath hung on the front door; nearly every front door had one as far as Sara could see. People passing in the street all wore some sort of mourning, everyone looking solemn.

All over the country people were displaying deep sadness. Queen Victoria was dead – had died quietly on Friday, 22 January 1901 – and a whole nation was in mourning, so Ellen told her, and would be so for several weeks to come.

It was Sunday. Sara had been put in a black velvet dress, a black velvet ribbon in her hair, which hardly showed amongst the darkness of her curls. She was to wear black during the week, too, but in cheaper material not half so nice to touch. Even Ellen's housemaid pinafores had been hastily edged with cheap black crepe, and Cook looked as funereal as anyone could – her hat and coat, as well as her skirt and blouse, probably worn for every funeral she'd ever attended, had a rusty, greasy look. Even Jamie's petticoats were trimmed with tiny black stitching. As for their parents, already in mourning for their dead baby, they didn't look much different to usual.

Sara wished it was Monday, wished she was at school,

then there would be something to do. She'd been taken to church this morning and it had been a most dreary service, all about the passing of a Great and most Gracious Queen who had Reigned for such a great Length of Time and with such Wisdom that she had become an Incorruptible Institution. Which meant absolutely nothing to Sara, much less the Queen herself.

Mother hadn't gone. Saying that it brought back too many memories, she had retired instead to her room with Jamie, her lunch being taken up to her. Sara overheard her father muttering to himself as he came to the table that it sometimes made him wonder what was going on inside her that she dared not tell of. It sounded so cryptic, so unusually cynical, that Sara turned in surprise. He smiled hastily at her, the way some people will when caught doing something wrong.

After lunch, when Ellen had stoked the fire in the drawing room until the underside of the high mantelpiece and wood panelling of the fireplace glowed like dark toffee, everything warm and cosy chasing away the grey outside, he took her on his knee. Cuddling her, as her mother was probably cuddling Jamie, they played draughts, which she won so easily – three times to his once – that she suspected he had let her win. They stopped only when Ellen came in again to draw the gold-coloured chenille curtains to make the room even cosier.

With the evening descending, he left her to play by herself while he dressed for dinner. He returned looking splendid as usual, his fair, curling hair shiny and nicely parted on one side, his fair moustache soft as he dropped a kiss on her cheek. She told him she loved him, and he smiled and tweaked her nose. It was such a lovely feeling.

But when Mother came down with Jamie, her small, delicate figure elegantly attired in a beautifully shaped black silk velvet dinner gown, the atmosphere grew suddenly cold. Sara was almost glad to be banished to her room soon after, Ellen bringing dinner up to her.

The triple oval mirrors of Harriet's walnut dressing table reflected her face three times, two of the faces looking at each other as though discussing her, the middle one only returning her gaze in lonely isolation.

All three reflections looked haggard. She was twenty-seven, but felt more like seventy, all youth and vivacity drained. Where was the newlywed whom Matthew had escorted down from a carriage outside a Paris theatre in a champagne-coloured evening gown? Had it been a champagne colour? She couldn't remember. But she remembered the glitter of chandeliers. She remembered how she felt them glowing in her eyes as she hung on to Matthew's arm, surveying the scene of rich elegance; remembered how she had felt as fine as any in the lovely dress Matthew had bought her; remembered how she had thought happily about her bright future.

What bright future? A husband who ploughed his life into a journal that never seemed to go anywhere. Two miscarriages. A poor dead baby. A small boy whose health struck her as being so dubious that she feared he might never reach adulthood. And – still the most tenacious – Sara, a daughter who never ceased to remind her of pain and subjection and violence. Would that memory never fade? Would she ever cease to shudder whenever she thought of it?

Harriet forced her mind to blankness, bent towards her reflection to study it, the other two simultaneously bending forward to consult each other.

All three showed Ellen's unsuccessful efforts to brush some life into her hair. Where was the lustrous auburn she had once been so proud of? There were dark rings under her eyes. The corners of her mouth were drawn down, making her look a bit like Annie; Annie, who'd always been sour by nature, taking after, it was said, their mother's mother, who had apparently been a bit of a tartar. Harriet, who had never had those traits, flinched at the shape her mouth now assumed. A smile would remedy it, but somehow a smile wouldn't come.

Despondently, she picked up the cut-glass tumbler beside her and drained its dregs in two small hurried sips. She still couldn't gulp down brandy, but a small sip always made her feel better. The glass needed refilling – only a little, enough to fortify her. She wouldn't ring for Ellen to bring up the decanter. It made it all too obvious. No, she'd go down herself.

She felt a fraction unsteady getting up from the dressing chair. It was often like this. The grief made her weak. Would she ever get over the grief? Ten months had passed, but the pain of it had hardly diminished at all.

Pulling her loose housegown closer about her thin shape, Harriet moved carefully towards the door. She felt lightheaded. The stairs when she reached them fell away at an alarming angle, but by holding tightly to the bannisters she managed to negotiate them. Feeling quite proud at having done so, she made her way into the deserted dining room, where Matthew's cabinet stood.

The decanter was half full. Best to make sure it remained that way when Ellen went to get some more. Though lately, Matthew had been eyeing it, frowning slightly. She'd never given him cause to suspect anything untoward. She was very careful about that – knew when to call a halt, when to hide herself from him if she thought it might show; always gargled with scented water and sucked mint toffees.

At the cabinet, she listened. The house was quiet. From the stairs to the basement came distant muffled voices – Mrs Downey talking to a tradesman. Ellen was out shopping. Jamie was sleeping. Sara should have been at school but she had a cold and had stayed at home. But she knew better than to come downstairs. And Matthew was at the office.

She lifted the heavy cut-glass stopper. No need to use too much, just enough to help her stop thinking . . . Jamie would never have a little brother for company now, poor Jamie. And poor little Matthew . . . the name she'd given the child so cruelly taken on the very brink of life.

Painstakingly she tipped the smallest of measures into her glass, replaced the stopper, replaced the decanter, then cuddled the glass to her bosom.

'Poor little Matthew,' she murmured, gazing into the tumbler. Tears flooded her eyes, blurring her sight. 'My poor little lost lamb . . .'

A movement behind her brought her twisting round so

sharply towards it that she nearly lost her balance. Sara stood in the doorway, dark curls framing her pretty face, deep blue eyes wide with surprise.

Harriet's voice grated sharp as a crow's. 'What're you doing here?'

The child looked startled. 'I heard someone. I thought it was Daddy.'

'Daddy's out!'

'I thought . . .'

'You know he's out. Why've you come down here?'

'I thought . . .'

'You thought you'd find out what I was doing. Spying on me. Why're you spying on me? Who asked you to spy on me?'

'N-no one, Mummy.'

'It's your father who's put you up to this. He's always watching me – watching me through you. Still trying to get his own back on me . . .'

'Daddy didn't . . .'

'Not that daddy, you fool! You evil little spy. It's him who put you up to it. From down there . . .'

Down there in Hell, still waiting for her. Her eyes roamed about the room. He might be watching her from any corner. Or through those deep blue eyes of his child, eyes so like his . . .

'He took my baby. My poor baby . . .' She was dissolving into tears, imploring him to leave her alone. 'It wasn't my fault – I never meant to push you. But you were so cruel to me.'

Sara came forward and held out her hands, hoping to

comfort. Seeing the move, Harriet recoiled, backing into the small occasional table behind her. She staggered as it crashed to the floor, the tumbler falling from her hand to shatter against the polished brass fender.

'Don't come near me! I know you hate me! Like your father.'

Sara didn't know what to do. Her mother was often excited, upset – highly strung, Daddy called it – but she'd never smashed things before. She wasn't sure whether to try and pacify her, or run from the room.

'Daddy doesn't hate you, Mummy,' she tried to soothe. She wished her father were here now. He'd know what to do.

A crafty gleam had come into her mother's lovely grey eyes. 'You don't know who your real father is.'

Sara stood looking blank. Of course she knew who her father was. She knew all about him. He ran a business; wanted to make it bigger so they could all be wealthy and have lots of nice things; wanted her to grow up to be a beautiful woman. He told her all those things when she sat on his knee. Of course she knew who he was.

Her mother had calmed a little, and now she steadied herself with an effort.

'If you knew who he was, you wouldn't be so cocksure of yourself. He raped me – put you inside me. That's what you are, the creature of rape. I never wanted you. And every time I look at you, I see him.'

Her eyes ranged the room. 'I know he's there. He killed my baby. Why can't he leave me alone? If he'd let me alone, it wouldn't have happened . . .'

'Nothing's happened, Mummy,' Sara attempted timidly, but she was confused. Who was Mummy talking about? Not her father? They loved each other. He was always tender and she was always so happy with him. Even when she wept, which was often, she'd cling to him – even after they'd had an argument.

She made another effort to reassure, but her mother's expression, so full of hatred, terrified her into silence.

'I never wanted you. I prayed and prayed you'd die at birth after your father died. Yes, he's dead, thank God. But you had to be full of life. I wish to God you had died too. All my poor little babies died. Poor little babies . . .' Tears strangled her voice to a whisper. 'I've only my Jamie left – and I can never have any more.'

Sara could only stare at her mother as Mrs Downey came puffing up from the kitchen to see what on earth was going on.

She watched her hurry forward to calm the weeping, trembling woman, wrapping her housegown, which had come loose, more closely about her, and, with an anxious glance at the fallen table and smashed tumbler, guiding her carefully past Sara.

'She'll be all right, your mummy,' she whispered as she passed, supporting the wilting form. 'She's had a bit of a seizure. I'll get her to bed and we'll get Dr Horder to have a look at her. I think he should.'

Sara watched them negotiate the flight of stairs, dis-appear at the turn of the bannisters above her, Mrs Downey's soothing voice going on all the way up. She heard the door close, the soothing tone cut to a muffled mumbling. She hadn't moved, couldn't move, wouldn't have known where to go if she had.

In two weeks she'd be seven. Seven years old. But her mother's words were now beginning to sink in with all the pain of one twice her age, making her heart feel unmeasurably ancient with truths discovered only a moment ago. The father she loved so dearly wasn't her father at all. *Her* father was dead, someone she didn't know, someone her mother had hated so much that that hate had been transferred to herself after his death. And the hurt it thrust upon her was hardly to be borne by someone only seven years old like her.

Yet how could she hate her mother? She loved her. She loved her father, only he wasn't . . .

Suddenly all the pain welled up from where it sat deep inside and she sank down in the doorway and cried and cried her aged heart out to be a child again.

# Part Two

# Chapter Eighteen

Now that September had arrived, the nights had begun drawing in. Sara stood at the window of the drawing room watching the rain bouncing off the pavement, making patterns. It was Saturday. She would be starting at the high school on Monday. She had won a scholarship outright, achieving the highest marks of 1905, according to her school report.

'I am so proud of you,' Matthew had said, his voice ringing with pride as he read the report. She felt no pleasure in her achievement, in truth felt no emotion at all. She had won the scholarship, would be leaving behind most of those she had known throughout her earlier days, but there was no sense of loss. She didn't feel sad or happy, pleased or sorry. She merely felt – immune.

'You can't even look pleased,' her mother had said. 'But then, you never have had any feelings. The older you get, the worse you get. Not a reaction, not a response. Nothing. You're unnatural.'

Perhaps she was right – she certainly hadn't been able to respond to Matthew's unbounded joy, though she knew she should be proud of her outstanding talents, as Matthew euphorically called them.

She had looked upon him as Matthew for a long time now, ever since that day . . . She'd been nearly seven then – was eleven now.

From that day, she had never again been able to think of him as a father. Stepfather was unwieldy to say. It was better to avoid calling him anything to his face, though if he noticed, he had never said.

The door behind her opened quietly. Ellen's small voice floated towards her. 'Dinner'll be ready in two ticks, Miss Sara.'

'Serve mine in my room, Ellen,' she said without turning round.

'Mr Craig said he'd like you to eat with him. Mrs Craig isn't coming down. She don't feel well.'

*Of course she doesn't,* Sara thought bitterly. *Because she's been up there all afternoon drinking that medicine of hers. That brandy.*

It was no secret these days. Matthew tried so hard to cover it up. It hurt to see him making excuses for her. It wrung Sara's heart, him pretending she ailed, never accepting any invitations to visit, never inviting people. He hardly went out except to go to the journal or, when he was forced, meet clients or attend a business function. 'Mrs Craig's health is poorly . . . Yes, I'll convey your good wishes for her speedy recovery.' Sara could imagine it being said. 'Recovering, but not strong enough to accept any invitation as yet. It's good of you to wish her well. Yes, she does suffer poor health these days.'

'So Mr Craig will be dining alone?' Sara spoke over her shoulder without turning round.

'Yes, miss.'

Sara frowned and lifted her face towards the ceiling. 'Very well, Ellen, I'll have my dinner with Mr Craig.'

'Very good, Miss Sara.'

The door closed as gently as it had opened, and she turned away from the window to regard the door with a blank stare.

They had a butler now – Ernest Seaforth, a smallish man, or was it that she was growing so tall that he just looked smallish? His shoulders were so narrow that his head seemed almost too big for the rest of him. But it was Ellen, dear Ellen, who made it her special task to tell Harriet of the approach of mealtimes just before Seaforth, in his official capacity, announced them. Ellen had taken it on herself to befriend Sara although Sara had never encouraged her. Unprepossessing, plain-faced and skinny, Ellen wore her thin sandy hair scraped back into some sort of bun beneath her cap, which made her look more childlike than her twenty-five years would have her be. But she was as near a friend as Sara felt she would ever have. She was not given to making friends as a rule, for which she blamed a deep-seated mistrust of people, although she knew of no cause for it, except an instinctive preference for her own company.

The little dinner gong in the hall gave a tinny buzz. To make doubly sure it had been heard, Seaforth came in to announce in a voice remarkably resonant for one of his stature that dinner was about to be served. Sara nodded and followed him across to the dining room.

It was a silly dining table. Long, designed to seat some

dozen to sixteen people, it hardly ever saw more than three. It was usually laid for that number – herself, Matthew and Jamie – her mother mostly keeping to her room. Jamie was eight now, and, no longer able to use his babyhood as an excuse to keep him by her, Harriet stayed up there alone.

He sat now, opposite Sara, his father between them at the head of the table. Why they couldn't get a smaller, more comfortable one, Sara could never fathom. Perhaps it gave the comforting illusion of a family larger than it really was. Matthew would have liked more children. He'd said as much to Sara herself in the past. But now it was too late. Mother was coming up to thirty-two, and for years she had kept to Dr Horder's advice not to risk any more pregnancies by the simple expedient of having her husband sleep in a room of his own, the one above hers. He was still the gentle, caring, attentive husband, but Sara's discerning eye noticed that that was as far as it went.

'So you start your new school on Monday,' he opened as the empty soup bowls were borne away by Ellen.

Sara didn't look up. 'Yes.'

'Looking forward to it?'

'I expect so.' She knew without looking at him that he frowned. Now would follow the questions – why did she only expect so? Did she realise it was a great opportunity? Faced with the problem of having to explain that she merely saw it as another school and she'd get on with it, she was grateful for once when Jamie intervened.

'I'm going up too,' he put in. 'Be in a junior class this term.'

Matthew laid his spoon down and sat back, smiling his

apology for having ignored him. 'You'll be a big lad now at school.'

'Wish I were bigger.'

'But you *are* big. You're taller than most boys of your age.'

'I mean bigger sideways. They call me streaky bacon at school.'

'That won't last. In a year or so you'll begin to fill out. Think yourself lucky not to be attending the sort of public school I did. An awful lot of bullying went on there under the name of strengthening one's character. One had to endure or go under. It was as simple as that. I'll make certain the one you go to is more pleasant – that is if you want to go.'

The thin, pallid face grew obdurate. 'I'll be glad to go to a public school; I'll be more important. It'll be better than being at *ordinary* school, coming home every day. I hate ordinary schools!'

'It is not ordinary.' Matthew grinned. 'It's a private one. A good one.' His grin broadened. 'I know: I pay enough for you to go there.'

Jamie pouted. 'It's not the same. I want to be *special*.'

'You will be one day.' Matthew laughed as the main course arrived, and didn't see Jamie poke out his tongue at his watching sister.

Last night the fog had been solid, thick yellow. This morning it was greyer, but still wall-like, reducing visibility to a yard or so.

Matthew walked cautiously along a seemingly endless

Victoria Park Road in the direction of Mare Street.
Passers-by loomed up suddenly to be swallowed up the
second they'd passed; the odd passing vehicle was heard
rather than seen – a deadened clipclop of hooves, a
blanketed rumble of wheels crunching on messy cobbles,
the occasional muffled rattle of a motor-car engine –
though now and again a ghostly shape would materialise
as the fog swirled to the movement.

Stepping off a curb to cross the park entrance was
disorientating. Feet feeling for the opposite curb, Matthew
hoped he hadn't inadvertently crossed over to become
quite lost on reaching Mare Street. It was a relief to pass
the fruit and vegetable stall on the corner of that main
road, the greyness taking on a bilious tint from the hissing
kerosene lamps. The optimistic stallholder crouched into
his jacket, muffled to the eyebrows, beating gloved hands
together as he hovered for customers. Matthew, glad to be
on the right track, turned left. Just half a mile to his office
from here. The fog-bound chug of a goods train on the
elevated railway to his right helped him keep his bearings.

It was good to be out of the cold. Leonard Hallet had
arrived half an hour before him to open up and the gas fire
was radiating golden heat through the office. His two other
staff were already at their desks, and Alfie Scott, a sallow
boy of thirteen, was brewing tea in a cubbyhole. Matthew
allowed tea to be made on cold inclement mornings. It
helped the staff to be more eager about their work, not like
some who had nothing until midday. A cup of tea at their
side first thing on a cold morning had a remarkable effect,
he thought.

'Busy, are we?' he asked as he took off his homburg and divested himself of scarf, overcoat and gloves, handing them to Hallet, who hung them on the stand for him. Hallet looked harassed. Hallet always looked harassed.

'Busy's not the word, Mr Craig. Snowed under is more like it. And it's only Monday morning. You've never seen so much post, Mr Craig. The staff's still sorting it and only halfway through.'

Matthew squeezed between his desk and the wall. These last three months lack of space in the office had become an increasing problem. He gazed at the mound of already-opened mail before him. 'Anything interesting?'

'Anything interesting!' echoed Hallet. 'Enough for a week's work and more. And it's only Monday.'

Matthew nodded and sat down as a cup of tea arrived at his side. At one desk Toby Billett, a married man of thirty, was separating subscriptions from contributions for Matthew to go through. At the other desk Eddie Wells, young and single, sorted invoices for Hallet, now Matthew's chief assistant, to deal with. Beyond the narrow passage was the printing room. Matthew could hear both presses clacking away, each manned by an operator, finishing off what had been left over from Saturday.

It was a busy time. Two weeks to Christmas, and this month's issue had had to be got out a week early. A couple of years ago this would have been no bother; indeed, they would have been scrabbling about for something to fill the journal. It was an entirely different story now.

In November the previous year the National Union of Women's Suffrage Societies had held its national convention in London. It had been the saving of the *Freewoman,* which had been teetering on the edge of closure when Matthew and Leonard had hurried to cover the convention. With his command of shorthand, Hallet had proved an invaluable reporter. Matthew, with camera and tripod, had taken pictures of a sort, vowing to employ a man skilled in the art of photography the moment he could afford it.

He was able to afford it a few months later, after reporting on another London meeting in Queen's Hall in support of the Women's Enfranchisement Bill, held in March. It was a very sedate, orderly meeting, attended by Members of Parliament in evening dress and their ladies in fine gowns, all behaving with decorum. Thanks to its coverage of the meeting, the next issue of the *Freewoman* sold enough copies to warrant a second print run, to Matthew's amazement and joy.

Since then he hadn't looked back. The women's suffrage movement had come out of its chilly isolation in northern England and invaded London with a vengeance. Matthew was made. In May he found himself covering a gathering of five hundred women at the House of Commons to hear the results of the second reading of the Women's Enfranchisement Bill. He was on hand to witness their frustration and then indignation as the time was whittled away on other things, and the bill talked out, hardly taken seriously.

His new photographer, Victor Long, got splendid coverage of the event, with stark pictures of indignation, outrage and anger, as police began moving women from the Strangers' Entrance; and then moved them on again as they tried to hold their meeting outside the House of Lords.

Matthew had a field day interviewing many of the women after the police finally allowed them to hold their meeting in the precincts of Westminster Abbey. He filled the *Freewoman* that month with accounts of their fury at the failure of the bill; at being laughed at in the Lobby by many Members of Parliament; at being hustled along in a most unladylike manner by the police. In a week, the *Freewoman*'s May issue had been sold out, and in the weeks following, the growing stack of subscriptions on his desk almost toppled over.

By summer Leonard Hallet was being sent up to Manchester to cover the meetings there. Matthew had no wish to set foot in that city ever again, and was content to leave it all in Leonard's capable hands. He now had a telephone installed, enabling Leonard to telephone news within minutes of anything special occurring. For Matthew it was the most marvellous gadget ever invented, even though it was costly.

In this way he got the news almost at the same time as the *Manchester Guardian* of Christabel Pankhurst and her close acquaintance Miss Annie Kenney being ejected from the Free Trade Hall amid scuffles in which Christabel twice struck a police inspector. And when Leonard secured a personal interview with Miss Kenny herself on how she was manhandled and flung out of the Free Trade Hall like a criminal, the journal sold like hot cakes.

Able to report so quickly on the two heroines being charged with disorderly behaviour and obstruction in October, their refusal to pay their fines resulting in three days' imprisonment instead, Matthew began to wonder if he shouldn't now think of enlarging his premises to cope with an ever-expanding circulation.

There was no looking back now. The imprisonment of the two women brought a crowd of two thousand to Stevenson Square on the evening of their release from Strangeways. It was Boggart Hole Clough all over again, although this time there would be no Constance Milne-Pitford. Matthew thought of her as he took down Leonard's report; wondered briefly where she was now and what she was doing. No doubt she had long since got over her zeal for women's enfranchisement and was now a wife, perhaps with a couple of children. Then he forgot her as he scribbled madly, trying to keep up with the torrent of news coming over the wire.

Leonard returned to London, and the following month they were able to cover the procession of four thousand wives of the unemployed of London's East End, marching from West Ham to Whitehall with a band blaring and hundreds of placards and banners demanding work for their menfolk and food for their children.

Just this week – after the December issue of the journal had gone out, unfortunately – there had been an uproar at the Albert Hall, again with a great deal of heckling from women sent there for that purpose amid more banners, and again ending with their being thrown out.

The general election in the New Year brought a Liberal government that flatly opposed giving women the vote. Indignant letters from outraged women flooded in, causing the circulation of the *Freewoman* to grow by leaps and bounds. In January Matthew went to his bank and secured a sizeable loan on the strength of it, to acquire a plot of land at the rear of his premises, a new modern linotype machine, and more staff to operate it and cope with the seemingly inexorable influx of mail and reportage.

Puffed up with success, he watched the print room grow brick by brick. Every now and again, though, as he watched the courses being laid, the puffed-up feeling would spring a leak. Was he overstepping himself? What if this interest in the Women's Social and Political Union, the WSPU, was a mere flash in the pan? If it collapsed, so would his journal. At such times Matthew found sleep impossible, tossing and turning for one half of the night, the other half fraught with dreams from which he would awake in a cold sweat of misgiving.

Spring and summer, however, saw the WSPU, bless it, proving an indefatigable force. There were more marches, and halls were filled to overflowing. The Union was now well established in London, attracting women rich and poor, eager to be heard, to have a voice, to have a vote. Women who were prepared to stand in the cold rain for their turn besieged the House of Commons and lobbied the MPs. New recruits flocked to join the London branch of the Union. Photographs of banners with 'Votes for Women'; of women storming ten Downing Street; of Miss Kenney leaping on to the Prime Minister's car and refusing to get down, turned up on front pages in all the papers, including the *Freewoman*.

Matthew was no fool. He knew well enough that his success was based solely on women *not* getting the vote;

that so long as the new Liberal government refused to
recognise them as potential voters, he would have material
for his journal; that the day women *were* given the vote,
would be the day the *Freewoman* would have to look to
its laurels. But at the moment it looked as though that
prospect was a good many years away yet.

On the strength of that premise, Matthew went completely mad and bought a motorcar with a chauffeur in
the hopes that Harriet might be persuaded to venture out
with him on those occasions she felt well enough in herself
to do so. He found her a personal maid, a quiet-natured
seventeen-year-old named Lilly, so she would have
nothing to distress her; for she was all too easily distressed
these days. All this was extra expense, of course, but with
the journal's continuing success, he could afford it, and
Harriet was worth it. They might not share the same bed
any more, nor even the same room, but he loved her dearly.
Poor darling, life could have been kinder to her.

From her window in Rutland Road, Annie saw Matthew
draw up. Beside him Harriet sat, her head bent, her face
hidden by a wide-brimmed hat held on by a veil. The
corners of Annie's lips curled downward. She'd done well
for herself, had Harriet, with her motorcar and fine clothes.
It was a pity she did not measure up to her improving status.
Everyone knew she liked her sip of brandy more than could
be called medicinal. And she hardly ever came visiting
these days. Annie wondered how Matthew stood for it.

She laid down her crocheting as Matthew leapt from the
vehicle, chequered dust-coat flapping in a stiff September

breeze. His face bore a strained look, she noticed, as he ran up the tiled path. His urgent rap on the knocker brought her to her feet, alarmed now.

'I'll get it, Lizzy!' Her housemaid paused on her way to answer, retracing her steps to the parlour she had been cleaning.

Matthew was in the hall almost as soon as Annie had opened the door. 'Annie – it's your father. He's been taken ill. Your mother telephoned my office. I came round straight away.'

Jack Wilson had been ailing for some time with heart trouble. His doctor had warned him against overworking, and since then he'd left much of his joinery business in his sons' hands. There had been a scare the year before, but the family, told later, had found him much better, sitting up in bed. This time, Matthew's appearance on her doorstep talking of telephone messages had Annie immediately in a fluster of apprehension.

'Is it his heart?'

'Your mother asks that you come straight away. I have the motor – we can pick up Clara on the way.'

Annie was already dragging her hat and coat from the hallstand, her voice echoing through the house for her housemaid.

'Lizzy!' The girl appeared, duster in hand, eyes wide in query. 'I want you to look after the children when they come home from school. Give them their food. Make sure they go to bed on time if I'm not back. When Mr Emmerson comes in, tell him where I am.'

'Where's that, Mrs Emmerson?'

'My mother's, of course.' Her reply was impatient. Hardly had Matthew closed the street door than she was beside the motor, even more alarmed by the sight of her sister's reddened eyes.

'What's happened, Harriet? How bad is it?'

'I don't really know.' Harriet's voice was feeble with tears. 'I only know Matthew came home and told me we've got to get round there as soon as we can. It's Dad's heart. They've called the doctor, but we don't know any more than that.'

'That's right,' Matthew told Annie as he helped her into the rear seat and laid a rug over her knees. 'We don't know any more than that, so let's not get too upset too soon.'

Clara's reactions were almost identical to her sister's, grabbing her outdoor clothes, instructing her maid on the needs of children and husband, running from the house in Ruth Road in a fluster of urgency.

Both sisters huddled in the rear seat, holding on to over-large hats not all that securely pinned in their hurry. In the front seat beside Matthew, Harriet was silently giving way to fresh tears.

'Don't begin weeping all over again,' he hissed at her. It never took much to make her cry, and once she'd begun, she could continue in bouts for any length of time. Matthew could feel his patience dissolving. It could dissolve all too easily these days where she was concerned. 'We don't yet know how serious it is. It may be nothing.'

'How can it be?' She fought her emotions with a tremendous effort. 'When Mum has to get to the post office to *telephone* you, how can it be?'

'People do use the telephone system these days – it's easier.'

'And quicker,' she finished off for him. 'If it wasn't serious she wouldn't have telephoned. She'd have sent someone round – like last time.'

'No point worrying until we get there,' he ordered brusquely. He was already turning into Mare Street, passing the premises of his journal. In two minutes they would be in Approach Road.

Sara didn't feel at all like eating. She sat silent at the dining table, toying with her food while Jamie wolfed his down as though he might never see another meal. How he could eat so much and never put on an ounce of fat or his pasty face look any healthier, beat her.

Jamie was nine now. He had celebrated his birthday the previous week, on the seventeenth of September, with a small party for some of his school friends, during which he'd eaten so much that he was sick afterwards. In a panic, his mother had sent for Dr Horder. Whatever Dr Horder thought about being called out for practically nothing, he didn't bat an eyelid, just patted her on the shoulder in a reassuring manner and went away to put in his bill. To see Mother with Jamie sometimes, people would think he was her only child. Perhaps in a way he was. Sara felt the old pang of resentment at the thought.

'Don't you care that Grandad's ill?' she said as he shovelled another forkful of minced beef and potato into his mouth.

He looked up at her, his eyes totally free of concern. He

had his mother's eyes, though his were blue, and where hers suited her vibrant colouring perfectly, his seemed to stare out from such a pale complexion as though there was in fact no face around them at all.

'Well?' Sara demanded.

Jamie shrugged. 'We're left here. There's nothing we can do about him, is there?'

'You could at least stop eating like a little pig.'

'If I don't eat, it won't make him any better.'

Sara threw her knife and fork down beside her uneaten food. 'You're so spoiled, you are. I wonder you're not crying after Mother, being left alone.'

He pulled a face. 'I think I'm grown-up enough not to do that. It's only that you're jealous because she thinks more of me than she does of you. It's me she pets, not you.'

'I don't need anyone to pet me,' Sara said coldly.

'He does.'

'Who?'

'Father. He pets you all the time. He never pets me.'

'You're a boy.'

'What difference does that make?'

Sara said nothing. The truth of that difference was that while she felt resentment of the favouritism bestowed on Jamie from the mother whose love she had always wanted, he suffered the selfsame resentment at Matthew's feelings towards her. The irony of it was that while Jamie could lap up the love their mother gave him, Sara felt alienated by love from the man she now knew as her stepfather. It was so unfair.

# Chapter Nineteen

Henry Craig relaxed his bulk back into the brown leather armchair and toyed with his brandy and soda in the hush of the club reading room.

'And what about your accountant? D'you consider him any good?'

Matthew regarded his father with a degree of affection. Since Henry had taken to coming up to London quite often these days, they would meet in the Britannic Club in Old Broad Street, where Matthew was a member, and spend a few hours chatting over a drink. They had grown closer these past few years despite his father's continuing reluctance to regard his son's marriage as a good match. They would usually have dinner, Matthew arranging for him to stay there overnight, drawing a line at inviting him back to the house. He no longer feared that his father would turn the offer down, but Harriet was not prepared – neatly, he evaded the true reason: her growing need for that sip of brandy to fortify herself – to meet guests. Much less his father.

Harriet was nervy these days, easily upset. Constantly in the care of Dr Horder, she had never really got over losing her son in childbirth. After all these years she still harped on it whenever things weren't going her way. 'I feel so deprived . . . I feel so guilty . . . I should have given you another son . . . What did I ever do wrong to deserve that?' and so on and so on. Undoubtedly, Harriet's health did not equip her to be a welcoming hostess.

Matthew dismissed the excuse from his mind, coming back to his father's question. 'My accountant is good enough for my purposes.'

'Good enough's not good enough, son,' Henry rumbled. 'If you want to go big with that journal of yours, you've got to have the *best*.'

'He's as good as I can afford at the moment.'

Henry Craig shook his head. 'You must do better than that. You need the best, not as good as. A good accountant is an asset to you as you expand. And another thing – if you can see your way clear at some future stage to buying that house of yours, do it! It never was any good paying rent. Doesn't get you anywhere. But you can't go wrong with a house in the bank. Once it's yours, you've got collateral – people will back you with houses in the bank. Take my advice. And something else . . .' He took a large swig of his brandy. 'That journal of yours. Wouldn't hurt to go public. Have a few shareholders financing it. Best way.'

Matthew's smile was faintly derisive. His father was full of advice, but there was never so much as a hint of offering any help should things go wrong. Even now, as he spoke so grandly of shareholders, and going public, there was no suggestion of himself investing in it for a head start. Matthew bore him no grudge, but he sometimes wished . . .

'I'll think about it.' Non-committal, he drained his brandy glass. 'Fancy another one?'

'No. Think I'm ready to retire. Early start back tomorrow. Sunday trains to the coast are the very devil. Can take hours.'

He rose and shook hands as Matthew got up, again reminding him to think over what he'd said, which Matthew promised he would.

In fact, there seemed to be little thinking to be done. Things couldn't have looked more rosy for him. The suffragettes, a word coined by the newspapers and now becoming standard to describe the militant women who aimed stones through MPs' windows and caused disruption at every one of their meetings, had admittedly made small headway, except to get themselves notorious for their violence. What these women did, however, made lesser women proud to be female, and it was these who bought the *Freewoman* and any other such journal they could lay their hands on.

Matthew was beginning seriously to consider moving into the City to be more accessible to news. He wallowed in visions of offices off Fleet Street, a team of reporters, a flock of office staff, his old premises retained solely for printing. There was no limit to what could be done – if one had the money. And who knew, as time went on, his father might be persuaded to invest. Meanwhile, another visit to the bank would do no harm. He was having no difficulty at all in paying back his earlier loan, proving he was a safe bet. He had every confidence that they would advance him enough for a more centrally situated office, perhaps in a year's time.

*

The earlier panic over Jack Wilson's heart had been another false alarm. The family had at that time once more found him sitting up in bed, to some extent recovered. With his usual bluff outlook on life, he'd laughed away their concern and days later was up on his feet, although most of his time was spent taking things easy in an armchair by an especially built fire to keep him warm, despite the October weather being unseasonably mild.

The summons six weeks later, however, was no false alarm. This time he did not laugh it off, or even smile. He lay inert and unseeing as they crept into his room in twos and threes so as not to create too great a strain on him. It didn't matter; Jack Wilson was beyond caring about strain. He was on the verge of not caring any more about this world.

Hastily brought into the room to try to communicate with him one last time before he left them forever, they gathered about him in a ring of hushed sorrow, Sara included now that she was twelve.

Beside him, her grandmother sat holding his hand. Beside her stood Aunt Clara, her round face creased in anguish. On the other side sat her mother, who had managed, Sara noticed, to get in first, leaving Aunt Annie to stand behind her. The circumstances were too grave for Annie to start making a fuss, which she would normally have done.

Sara stood nearer the foot of the bed, holding tightly on to Great-Aunt Sarah's hand. It was the first time she had witnessed death. She'd witnessed the results of it, of course, the weeping, the stoic words of comfort, the vicar in church echoing his beliefs in life everlasting. But this life was not ever-lasting, as Sara could see. She was old enough now to understand a lot more, and it tore at her heart to see the grandfather who used to throw her up in the air when she'd been smaller, and lumber around chasing her through his house, now so still but for the shallow breathing – so shallow that it hardly seemed enough to keep him alive, decreasing as the moments ticked by until it seemed only to be going out in small puffs with nothing at all coming in.

So quiet he lay that she didn't know he had gone until her grandmother gave a tiny, hardly audible, 'No.' Her uncles John and George moved hastily to comfort her while their wives stood back quietly to leave the way clear for the more immediate members of the family to show their grief with a kiss upon the cooling cheeks.

Her aunts had handkerchiefs clamped to their faces to smother the sounds of weeping, and even their husbands sniffed back tears for a man who'd been most respected and a friend to everyone.

Sara felt she too should be crying, if only as a mark of her own love, but she couldn't. She had loved her grandfather dearly. Still did. Yet tears refused to come. There was just an empty feeling: the same emptiness she'd felt so many times since the day her mother had turned on her with her cruel truths. Though this time the bitter feeling that usually went with it didn't accompany the emptiness, and she supposed that was because of love and not hurt.

Her mother was crying for all she was worth, her head

buried in Matthew's shoulder. Sara glanced at him. A thin rivulet had travelled down each cheek and into his moustache, though he didn't appear to be crying as such. He and Grandfather had grown close. Sara guessed he missed him. She turned away and looked again on the heavy features of her grandfather, now serene in death. She wanted so much to cry but though the tears reached her throat they refused to go any further. All it did was to make her throat ache.

'Come, child.' Great-Aunt Sarah took her shoulders and gently moved her away. 'This is no place for you.'

Unresisting, Sara let her guide her out of the room, the house already seeming empty. She wondered what her grandmother would do with no one but her staff here. Uncle George, the last to leave home, had married two years ago; he and his wife Irene now had a baby girl named Lucy.

Sara thought of her grandmother. 'She'll be so lonely in this big house,' she said, but her great-aunt smiled.

'I'll be coming to live with her,' she said quietly as they went downstairs to the parlour. Outside, November was all bleak.

The house echoed to sounds of unrestrained sobbing. Below stairs, the staff kept out of the way. In the old nursery, Sara, thirteen the week before, on the fourteenth of April, put a protective arm about a tearful James as they listened to the argument from her mother's bedroom below. Matthew, who seldom raised his voice, raised it now above the sound of weeping.

'He is not your *baby*! The boy's nine years old!'

Harriet's voice was pleading. 'But he's not strong. You only have to look at him to see that.'

'He's strong enough. Dr Horder can find nothing wrong with him. Admittedly he's thin, fair-skinned. In that he is like me. I am strong enough, and so is he. He'll have a wonderful time there.'

'You can't send him away! You can't!'

'If he's to be prepared for public school, we must. It isn't so far away. He'll be home at weekends. For his own sake he must have an education worthy of him.'

'But you hated public school. You told me yourself how you were treated there. You don't want that for Jamie, do you?'

'Not all public schools are like the one I went to. I shall choose carefully when the time comes. Meanwhile . . . You can't have him clinging to your skirts forever. You'll have him here with you until September.'

Her mother's voice was high-pitched with desperation. 'If you send him away, I'll have no one to love. No one.'

'You have me.' The tone moderated with an effort. 'You have Sara.'

'I don't want *her*! I want Jamie. Oh, please, Matthew.'

'Sara's almost a young lady. She'll be a friend to you.'

'*Friend!*' In her room, Sara cringed from the loathing in the tone. 'I don't want *her*. I've never wanted . . .'

Here it came, the hatred that after all these years Sara was still unable to truly understand. But Matthew cut the vituperation short.

'There's no point your going on this way, Harriet. James goes to Forest Hall in September. I've been delaying because you had such a traumatic time over your father's death. But it has been five months now, and James's education cannot be delayed much longer.'

The woman's voice had become petulant. 'Anyway, how can he go? You have to have his name down for years for decent prep schools like that.'

'It's been down since we moved here.'

'You never told me.' She sounded aghast, but Matthew's tone came as firm as ever.

'It was mentioned, but I never considered it an issue. I assumed you'd be glad for him to have the best education our money could buy when the time came. Surely you want him as decently educated as others of our standing?'

'But you never told me! How could you not tell me?'

'I've spoken about it often enough, but you've always shied away – clinging to him. Of course it'll be something of a wrench to you. It would be unnatural if it wasn't. I therefore thought it better not to refer to it too often until absolutely necessary. But it's now becoming absolutely necessary. I know it distresses you, Harriet. I know how strong is a mother's love, but you must be practical. We have to give James a chance to enjoy a first-class education.'

The argument was proving useless, her mother's wails sounding as loud as ever.

'You're breaking my heart. If you send him away, I'll die!'

'Don't be ridiculous, Harriet.' The irritation in Matthew's voice resounded in Sara's straining ears but her mother seemed deaf to it.

'I couldn't live without him. I shall die of a broken heart!'

'Now you're being bloody melodramatic'

His voice was loud with anger. In her room, Sara hugged Jamie to her to quiet his whimpering as Matthew continued.

'There's no point discussing this with you, Harriet. There's seldom much point discussing *anything* with you. When you're not drinking this stuff . . .' Sara heard the loud thump of a tumbler being slammed down, which she imagined he had snatched from her mother's hand. '. . . you're too distraught to be reasoned with. When you are drinking it, you have no idea what anyone is saying to you. You're in no fit state to make decisions of any sort. That's the reason I haven't consulted you before now, Harriet. But I am telling you. After the summer break, James will not be going back to that common or garden school around the corner. As of September he will be properly educated with boys of his own class, and with the journal doing so well, I for one shall not baulk at the fee.'

Her mother's cry rose, frantic and distraught. 'I won't have you do this to me, Matthew. I won't have it!'

'It's done. And there's an end to it. Now dry your eyes and try to accept the fact that James is no longer a baby. That he will begin to learn to grow up. And try to leave that stuff alone!'

Sara heard the door open, then slam. Matthew's swift footsteps pounded on the carpet runner of the passage below and on down the stairs to the hall. She heard him calling for Seaforth. Moments later came the distant slam of the front door. All that could be heard was her mother's muffled weeping, destined to go on forever by its sound.

It was left to her to soothe Jamie as he whimpered that he wasn't so sure he wanted to go away to school after all.

'Daddy did at your age,' she told him, compelling herself to refer to the name she had long ago lost pleasure in using as she tried to coax him to believe he would grow to like being away from home.

She knew that the main reason behind his father's decision was to prevent the boy being smothered by his mother. She wondered, though, if it wasn't perhaps nearer the truth that Jamie had taken much of Matthew's place in his mother's heart; that Matthew shared with her the bitter conviction of having been locked out. If that was so, he at least had the remedy of sending Jamie away. But what remedy did she have?

It had become unbearable at home. Now that Jamie had gone, Sara wished she too was at boarding school, but girls were not considered so important, unless perhaps in really upper-class families, and hers was far from upper-class, for all that Matthew's journal provided them with luxuries.

She dreaded coming home after school. Her mother hardly left her room these days, and Matthew spent his time at home brooding in his study or in the drawing room. Meals were taken in silence, with only him and herself at the table, he trying to be jolly, she not knowing these days what to say to him. At thirteen she had reached an age where she felt she had nothing in common with adults. And yet at times her mind already harboured adult thoughts.

It wasn't only her mind maturing, but her body too. The budding breasts of which she had become aware this summer had become more than buds. As her waist had slimmed, her hips had widened, and often she'd catch sight of Matthew's gentle brown eyes wandering over her.

If he saw her noticing, he would look away quickly. But it wasn't his regard, or the hastily averted eyes, so much as the way the fair skin of his cheeks would flush. It embarrassed her, yet at the same time made her feel, in a way, loved. Above all else, Sara wanted so to be loved, and yet . . . she felt uncomfortable under his glances.

To escape the baffling feeling, she spent much of her time with her grandmother and Great-Aunt Sarah, who was now an established part of the house in Approach Road. Sometimes her uncles John and George would be. there, the cabinet-making business having gone to them.

There was still a lot of trouble, she understood, following her grandfather's death. Something about a will being contested, and Aunt Annie saying that everyone should have had a share in the business. Sara had heard her mother talking along the same lines to Matthew, stamping her feet and getting excited as she did so easily, saying that what her father had left her wouldn't keep a mouse in shoe leather, which did sound silly. The squabbles of grown-ups were beyond Sara, but she did so miss Grandfather. His presence lingered, by the fire in the bay-windowed front parlour overlooking the road, on the stairs, along the narrow passage; all with him no longer being there. She knew just by looking at her that Grandmother missed him even more than she did.

*

Robert Emmerson, sitting with Annie in the solicitor's office for the umpteenth time this year, had heard enough this morning of her and the man arguing. Now he stepped in, reddening to his receding hairline.

'As far as I can see, we're doing nothing but pay out for your fees on this blessed will business. It's been going on a whole blessed year. Once and for all, is there any point in carrying on contesting it?'

Mr Greave leaned his long thin frame back in his leather swivel chair, swinging it a little to left and right, his narrow fingers linked together like one in prayer. 'We mustn't give up, Mr Emmerson, Mrs Emmerson. I know of cases like this that have gone on for years and at the end of it seen amazing results. Amazing results.'

'We need to see amazing results *now,* Mr Greave. We're not prepared to go on paying out our blessed hard-earned cash for ever.'

'Robert!' Annie rounded on him, her thin mouth – so much like her unknown grandmother's, seen only from a photographic portrait of poor quality on her mother's parlour wall – growing even thinner. 'It's not the money, it's the principle. How could Dad give it all to the youngest of his children and leave us older girls out?'

'We got a little something out of it,' Robert soothed, but Annie wasn't to be appeased by that.

'A hundred pounds! John and George must be laughing their heads off!'

Robert looked worried. 'There is your mother, Annie. She needs to be kept for the rest of her life on what he left.'

'Granted.' Annie's lips relaxed a little, then tightened again. 'I don't begrudge her. But I would have thought the business should have been put into her name. Then in time we'd all have had a share in it, when she . . . Well, you know. This way, it all goes to the boys and their wives after them, and their children. We don't get a look-in. That's why we should go on contesting Dad's will. That's why it's worth spending out, no matter how long it takes.' She turned abruptly to Mr Greave. 'And you can be sure that in the end we could win?'

The solicitor sat forward. 'As sure as anyone can be,' he hedged happily. *He* was assured whatever the outcome. No solicitor could be sued for a matter not coming to fruition. At the same time, he was being paid his fees, and if these silly, greedy, unfeeling people chose to spend their money on chasing moonbeams, it was not his place to tell them otherwise.

'I think the same as Annie does,' Harriet said obdurately from her dressing table. 'I think Dad's will should have been divided better.'

Matthew smiled. Harriet had always thought what others told her to think, happily deeming them to be her own thoughts. He loved her for it . . . had loved her. What she had possessed when he'd first met her – sweetness, daintiness, a tendency towards being led and an endearing fear of the great wide world – had made him want to shield and protect her. He had loved her for her adorable weaknesses.

Where had that love gone? She was still petite, beautiful.

Her beauty tugged at his heart. She could still be sweet at times, so in fear of the world at large. But something had gone. Perhaps it had never been there in the first place and he had only imagined it to be there. What it was that had gone he couldn't say. His feelings for her were the same as ever, wanting to shield her, guard her – these days against herself. It was now a different kind of love, an aching love with nothing to fulfil it. Something had been lost, long ago, and he was only now beginning to realise it was lost for good.

He had always hoped it would blossom again, as it had the first time after that ridiculous affair with that Milne-Pitford woman. He had finally established contact with Harriet. James had been the result. The loving contact had lingered until that last baby, when she had thrust him from her as though it was his fault. That was when it had all changed.

They lived separate lives now, separate but for his constant fight to cure her of her reliance on her 'medicine', as she termed that regular supply of brandy coming into the house. It was a battle he was losing, as he had lost the battle for her love.

But he was only human. Thirty-seven, still virile – he still dreamed in his sleep of making love. There *were* places a man could go to relieve himself. There were women . . . He knew a few colleagues who frequented those places, engaged the services of those women, came to no harm. But after that escapade in Manchester, never again would he be caught up that way. Not that he felt loyal to Harriet – she had ruined that – but he couldn't have faced the scandal should he be found out, as he had so nearly been found out all those years ago after the Manchester affair.

'And what would you have done with your father's business?' He posed the question quietly. It didn't do to fall into the trap of raising one's voice and thus turn her into a veritable uncapped fountain.

She looked bewildered. 'We could have all run it.'

'All of us?' Her naivety made him grin.

'You, Robert, Fred, and the boys, my brothers,' she enlarged.

'And share the profits between us, I suppose.'

'Yes.'

'And your mother? There wouldn't be a great deal left for her.'

'She's got the house. We could have looked after her.'

It was Annie speaking. He'd had enough of this foolishness.

'I prefer to run my journal, Harriet. And I expect Fred and Robert have no wish to give up their good jobs to tussle with a five-way share of one small business. Apart from John and George, none of us knows a thing about cabinet-making, and I for one am not prepared to start learning.'

Harriet got up unsteadily from her dressing table, balancing herself sufficiently to stamp her foot. 'Don't patronise me!'

'I'm merely stating a fact. It wouldn't work. Your brothers run it very well and your mother has a better share of the profit than if we all had a hand in it. It was, after all, your father's wish.'

'You think I'm being greedy.' Her eyes were growing

dangerously moist. 'I'm only saying what Annie said, that's all. I don't want Dad's money. You wouldn't allow me to have it if I did. If you can take Jamie away from me, you'd be capable of anything. You don't care how I feel. You don't care. No one cares. You all hate me!'

He left her quickly, closing the door on her sobs, and went downstairs into the drawing room. It was growing dark. The winter evenings were drawing in quicker than they realised, and Ellen hadn't yet drawn the curtains.

He could just discern a faint glow from the fire, which Ellen had banked up should the family wish to spend their evening there later. It hadn't yet begun to burn through and in the darkness he judged his way towards his armchair. It was even too much effort to reach up for the thin chain of the ornate crystal and brass gas lamp above him, which Harriet in her taste for the expensive had recently had installed. The cut-off gas pipes to the old curved lamps over the mantelpiece were still there, each like the stump of a severed limb.

Matthew sank down into his chair, but a tiny sound from a corner of the room brought him upright; he turned sharply in that direction.

'Who's there?' It was like a small animal, sighing.

Alert, he jumped up, and reaching blindly for the light, tugged quickly. The twin gas mantles popped one after the other. Through the bright crystal bowl, light spread across the room.

From a small cushioned footstool in the corner, Sara was looking up at him. She had been hunched over her arms and he thought she must have been crying. It was her sigh he had heard. He was beside her in a second, lifting her to her feet.

'What on earth is the matter, Sara?'

She pulled herself up to her full height, obviously embarrassed at being discovered. He noticed how tall she had grown in only a little while – nearly as tall as him, just a few inches in it, and already showing signs of becoming a shapely young woman. It was rather pleasant his being on a level with her rather than having to glance down as he did with Harriet. At this level and in this light, her eyes shone all the bluer. Such a dark, searching blue.

It was hard to credit that she was hardly yet fourteen. She looked much older, out of drab school uniform and in a white appliqué blouse and plaid skirt. Her dark hair curled down her back; in a few years it would be piled on top of her head. And in a few years, she'd be restricting those lovely natural curves with fashioned corset and whalebone.

He could feel the warmth of her skin beneath the sleeves of her blouse and thought of Harriet, how warm her arms used to feel. Oh, God, how he longed to hold Harriet and not have her stiffen against his embrace. He hadn't held her for years. Now he was holding her daughter. Not his daughter – *her* daughter.

'Sara.' A feeling had arisen in him that made him draw in a sharp breath. It was an abomination, disgraceful, what he was feeling. He fought to push it aside to make his voice sound normal.

'Sara, what's happened to upset you?'

For an answer, she fell gently towards him until her

head rested against his shoulder, her face turned away. He could feel her slim body trembling. Her voice croaked as though she were crying.

'It's Grandad. I remembered when we used to play. I miss him so much. I wish he was with us again.'

'Of course you do,' he soothed. Her dark hair under his smoothing fingers was so silky to the touch – as Harriet's had once been, but so much darker, heavier in texture, vibrant with the health of the young. He wanted to bury his face in it, but he didn't.

'You mustn't cry. The time has gone by, and you mustn't cry.'

'I'm not crying,' she whispered. 'I want to cry, though – so much. I felt so alone when I was at Grandma's today. Grandma and Great-Aunt Sarah were talking, and Uncle John and Uncle George came in, and they began talking to Grandma, and I felt . . . not wanted. Everyone was talking to each other and nobody spoke to me.'

'They have a lot on their minds at present,' he soothed. 'And it may be that you're feeling a little low yourself at the moment.'

'I feel miserable. I've had a pain in my stomach all day, a low, slow, drawing pain I've never had before, and I feel so miserable.'

'Oh dear God.' He sighed the words to himself and held her away from him. It wasn't his help she needed. It was a woman's. Things were happening to her that he could have no part in.

Her mother should speak to her, but her mother was in no fit state to speak to anyone; needed a shoulder to cling to rather than being able to provide one.

Who else was there who could explain the facts of life to this child, soon to become a woman? If his guess was right, tomorrow might be too late and this innocent girl, rigid with pain and distress, would be shocked into thinking some terrible, dire thing was happening to her.

There was Mrs Downey, she'd be the one to help. A motherly soul, their cook had been with them since they'd first come here, was like a member of the family. She preferred to keep her place, but she was a kindly sort. She would be able to explain things to this child. It must be made to appear that Harriet was sleeping off a headache. Matthew made up his mind.

'Listen, Sara, I want you to go downstairs. Tell Mrs Downey how you feel. Your mother isn't well at present. Don't argue . . .' He placed a finger to her lips as she began to protest. 'Go downstairs to Mrs Downey.'

The kiss he dropped on her cheek stirred him again and he stepped quickly away.

'Go on,' he ordered tersely.

# Chapter Twenty

Annie, at her wits' end, perched like a vulture on the edge of her chair in Mr Greave's dusty office, her thin breast heaving.

'We're paying you, Mr Greave, to handle this business. As far as I can see, it's been dragging on long enough. Eighteen months. We've got nowhere. Have we?'

For confirmation, she glanced at her husband, then at Clara and Clara's husband. Both men nodded obediently, but Clara remained deeply interested in the cream kid gloves she wore.

Clara, taking after her father, had put on considerable weight these last few years, but being so much shorter than he had been, looked plumper than she really was.

'I think it's time,' Annie went on, her tone sharp, 'we did more about it. Perhaps if you wrote to our mother explaining how we feel about things.'

'You must understand, Mrs Emmerson,' Mr Greave put in, unruffled by the woman's harangue. 'Contesting a will can take an inordinate length of time, depending upon circumstances. Legal wheels . . .'

'Blast legal wheels, Mr Greave! None of us has the money to sit and watch your legal wheels turning, your fees mounting, and nothing to show for it.'

Her lips compressed, her grey eyes revealed her feelings not only towards the solicitor, but towards Harriet, who had professed to not being well enough to attend this meeting, and Matthew, who had downright refused. At least he was honest enough to state reasons of disinterest, a fact she had to concede to, if without grace. It was all very well for him with his money and wealthy parents . . . Even if he didn't need to worry about Harriet getting a share of the will, he could have supported her family, seeing how he had married into it.

'We've come to a conclusion, Mr Greave,' she continued, having appointed herself spokeswoman over the menfolk, 'that you ought to write our mother a letter, setting out exactly what we had expected of that will.'

Mr Greave's suave face changed its expression to one of concern.

'Mrs Emmerson, with respect, I do not think you realise what a shock such a letter could be to one of your mother's years.'

'But she knows we're unhappy with the will.'

'Knowing you are unhappy and getting a solicitor's letter setting out in legal terms that you are unhappy are two different things.'

'I do agree there,' Robert muttered, and got a sharp look from his wife. Mr Greave continued without interruption.

'I take it your mother is upset by your feelings on this issue?'

'She is a bit upset,' Clara said quickly. She too was treated to a look from her sister. But she was made of stronger stuff than Annie's husband. 'I don't think we ought to start sending Mum solicitor's letters, Annie. I don't feel comfortable doing this. What with losing Dad, and then knowing we don't agree with the will, and now . . .'

'My argument's not with *her*,' Annie interrupted. 'It's with John and George, what they're getting out of it and us being given hardly anything to speak of. Mum can't even leave the business to us when she dies . . .' She ignored Clara's gasp of horror. 'Because it won't be hers to leave.'

'I don't know, Annie,' Robert was looking worried. 'Perhaps she's right. It is rather putting pressure on a woman bereaved?'

'It's only to make her realise that the boys oughtn't to be getting away with it. They're crowing, they are.'

Indignation began sweeping away her carefully studied vocabulary. 'Them and their families are assured for life. While we make do with what's left – bits and pieces thrown to dogs. They never even did do the right thing and offer us a chance of going in with the business. They could've done, you know.'

'But it'll still hurt Mum if we go on with this,' Clara ventured.

Annie turned on her, her expression livid, outraged that her motives were perhaps being called into question. 'Don't you see? It's to get her to put pressure on the pair of them. Surely even you can understand that, you stupid lump!'

'Here, I say!' Fred put a protective hand on Clara's. 'It's my wife you're talking to.'

'And my sister. We always had arguments as kids. I'll talk to her how I like.'

'You most certainly will not!' Fred's pale eyes glared from his rounded face. 'I'll thank you, Annie, to mind your p's and q's.'

Robert leaned forward. 'No call for that, old man.'

'I'm not having her call my wife a stupid lump, whether they argued as kids or not. They are not kids now, and I'll not put up with it.'

The solicitor thrust his hands towards his squabbling clients, his palms forward as though pushing against an invisible wall.

'Please, everyone. Let's not turn this into a bear garden.'

Annie ignored him, was on her feet. The two men also rose to glare at each other like a couple of fighting cocks, Clara's Fred pompously puffing out his cheeks, Robert with his narrow shoulders hunched, his narrow chest out. Clara, still seated, put a hand on her husband's arm.

'Fred, sit down. Sit down, Fred.'

'I'm not having Annie insult you . . .'

'Sit down, Fred!' For once Clara was asserting herself. 'I won't have you going on like this. I'll walk out of here, wash my hands of the whole thing. I'm not sure we should even be going on with this.'

But Fred had already sat down, his cheeks still puffing in and out like a steam engine coming to rest.'

Robert had also returned to his seat, but Annie was still on her feet, ready to do battle with anyone who questioned her rights.

'I come here, in the best of faith, to get us all no more

than what's due to us. And this is how I'm being served.'

Mr Greave, leaning over the table, pleaded as calmly as he could. 'I beg of you, Mrs Emmerson, please take your seat. There's no need for all this.'

But Annie was set on having the last word. 'Even so, Mr Greave, I think you should write to our mother. We are paying you to carry out our wishes, not to advise us. So kindly do what we're paying you for. It needn't be too legal like. It can still be, well, friendly. She'll understand that we have a point.'

But Mr Greave knew that no legal letter, couched in the terms of a family's demand for what they considered their just rights was ever friendly. He felt faintly sorry for the elderly widow; even in his position he could imagine her feelings when she learned of the callousness of some members of her family towards her.

Harriet sat in the drawing room listening to the discussion between her sister and her husband. When Annie conducted any argument, she always made it sound like a brawl, working herself up to a pitch before hardly a word had been spoken. Matthew's calming tones seemed only to rile her the more. He was shaking his head now, a pedagogue confronting a fractious child.

'I'm sorry, Annie, I have listened to you and understand how you feel, but I am still of the opinion that Harriet should not be part of this business.'

'But she's family. It's not the money. It's the principle.'

'For a principle you'd wound your mother that much, is that it?'

'No, of course not! But principles are principles.'

'Some are more ethical than others. This one, I believe, isn't. I'm sorry, Annie, but I think your intentions are purely from a point of self-interest.'

'Well, I must say!' Annie bridled, dangerously close to creating a scene, then went back on the attack. 'I've no intention of letting John and George get it all. Why should they?'

'Because they know the business, and none of us does. They were trained by their father and they'll keep it running efficiently, for your mother's sake, giving her a third share, which is right.'

'And what about us?' Annie had hardly listened to his argument. 'I think we should all have a share in our own father's business. I mean, it is our right – as his children.'

Matthew spread his hands disparagingly. 'We could go on with this argument till kingdom come and never solve it while you refuse to see any point of view but your own. My answer remains, Harriet wishes to have no part in this. We are both content to let things stand.'

'Perhaps Harriet wishes to speak for herself?'

As the words shot from Annie's mouth like bullets, Harriet wished only that she were out of this and back in her room where she could take a sip or two of her medicine to make her feel better. But Matthew was refusing to let himself be ruffled.

'Harriet is in no proper state to speak for herself. She is not as well as she might be, and I do not wish to see her harassed by all this. I speak for her.'

Annie's lips curled in a sneer. 'You speak for her. You're

supposed to be running a journal for women fighting to have their own voice. And all the time you won't let your own wife have hers. You know what you are, Matthew Craig? You're a hypocrite.'

'Be that as it may,' Matthew said evenly, 'there's nothing to be gained by your labouring your point. My answer is final. Harriet will not be part of this sordid plan to terrify your mother into giving up her rights.'

'Sordid plan? Sordid plan? I'm not staying here to listen to what we are only seeking as our just rights being called a sordid plan.'

'That is a bit strong-sounding, Matthew,' Robert put in, but Annie, who hadn't sat down throughout the visit despite a tray of tea having been brought in by Ellen, began pushing her hatpins more securely into a hat she had not even allowed herself time to take off in her eagerness to sort out the business.

'Come on, Robert. We're not staying here to be spoken to in that way. If that's how you're going to act, Matthew, we'll be leaving. And I'm not sure when we shall set foot in your house again.'

Sniffing indignantly, she gathered up her handbag and stalked to the drawing-room door, Robert following with a small shrug of his shoulders in Matthew's direction that seemed to say, 'We're only doing our best.'

Annie hardly paused as Matthew got to the door ahead of her to open it for them. 'No need to show us out.'

'But I must,' Matthew said, acidly polite. Seaforth was already in the hall. Like the perfect butler he was, hovering, hearing everything, knowing everything, yet

totally discreet, he went with his employer's relatives-in-
law to the door. Opening it for them, he inclined his head
respectfully as Annie swept past, Robert in her wake.

Sara was in the hall, too. Hovering, as Harriet saw it. As
the door closed on Annie she turned upon the intruder.

'Spying on me again, were you?'

'Harriet, my love . . .' Matthew hurried to her and took
her gently by the shoulders while Seaforth moved smoothly
towards the drawing room to retrieve the tea tray, giving no
glance towards them. No one noticed him return, going
downstairs to the pantry, unobtrusive, deaf to the domestic
scene, and that was how it should be.

'You're upset, Harriet. It's been a rotten day for you.'
Matthew made to persuade her towards the stairs, but
Harriet continued to glare at her daughter.

'Can't you see it?' she pleaded. 'She's always there,
listening. Always listening.'

'Annie has made you overwraught, my dear.'

'Of course I'm overwraught!' She tried to shrug away
from his hold. 'I sat listening to you two going on about
Dad's will as if I wasn't there. How would you feel, never
being included in anything? As if you were an idiot?'

He held firmly on to her. 'Then you should have spoken
up, Harriet.'

'You never gave me a chance, going on about what I
think. How do you know what I think? I might have had
something to say about it. I could have given my opinion.'

'What would you have said?'

She wilted. 'I don't know.' She felt sick, and somewhat

dizzy. She wanted to be in her room, in her nice quiet room, where she could take a little of her medicine and then have a nap. 'I need to lie down.'

'Yes, that will do you good,' he soothed readily.

Harriet nodded dumbly, letting him guide her now towards the stairs. She looked around for Sara with an idea of ordering her away, but Sara had already gone quietly up to her own room unnoticed.

Sara hardly spoke when Ellen came up to brush her hair before dinner. Ellen loved piling it on top of her head as if she were grown up. It always had to be taken down again, of course. It would never have done to keep it up that way, since Sara was only fourteen. It was a game, that was all, and Sara was usually happy to indulge Ellen in it, turning her fine head this way and that on her slender neck to get a better view of the result. This evening, however, she refused to let Ellen do any more than brush it until the heavy mass shone rich and dark. Throughout the process, the accepted hundred strokes, she never once smiled or allowed her gaze in the mirror to meet Ellen's.

Ellen knew that the master and mistress had had words again – Mrs Craig's shrill pettish voice had penetrated down to the kitchen. It always caused an atmosphere in the house. Even in here, her young mistress's bedroom, the air of disaccord had penetrated, and Ellen, a naturally chatty soul, felt she would have to be very careful about what she said.

At such times Mrs Downey would go out of her way to do 'something special' to cheer up her employers: a choice piece of gammon with pease pudding and glazed carrots for Mr Craig, a favourite with him – Ellen had come to associate the aroma of boiled gammon and pease pudding with domestic dissension. For Mrs Craig, a comforting bowl of soup or a piece of steamed halibut. Ellen would trot with it up to her room, knowing that within an hour she would be taking the lovely food back down to the kitchen, hardly touched. She'd notice, though, that the small bottle of 'medicine' would have gone down a deal.

Mrs Downey's ample chest would palpitate with pity at the sight of the untouched food, for Mrs Craig could be a very sweet person when she was well, and endeared herself to her staff. She never went at them as she went at her husband, even more so at young Miss Sara, but she never harangued the staff as some employers did.

At these times, Mr Craig would call for George Barriman to get the Talbot motorcar out. Mr Craig drove himself, hardly ever needing his chauffeur, who did odd jobs about the house instead; a sort of general handyman. Ellen thought it would have been much cheaper to engage only a handyman, whose wages would have been less, but Mr Craig didn't seem ever to worry about money, which he spent like water. He now had those new premises in the City, so she had heard, and there was talk of buying the lease of this very house.

Ellen remembered an awful argument a few months ago, to do with his wanting to get away from this area altogether, as posh as it was, to West London, to a smarter address. Mrs Craig had done a lot of protesting and crying, saying she didn't want to move away from all her family, that here she knew where she was. Whether that had done any good, Ellen didn't know, but there seemed to have been no more talk about it.

Her mind on these things, while Miss Sara sat silent and brooding, Ellen put all her energy into brushing hard at the dark, vibrant mass of hair, the way her young mistress liked it.

'Are you sure you don't want me to put it up for you, Miss Sara?' she ventured at one stage.

'Just brush it.' Terseness was a sure sign that all wasn't well and that Miss Sara was taking something very badly. Best to say little, but she had to know where Miss Sara would be eating this evening.

'Will you be having dinner downstairs?'

'Where is Mr Craig?'

'Gone out. Taking a drive. I expect he'll be back for dinner.'

'I had better have it with him then.'

'Very good, Miss Sara.' Ellen went on brushing vigorously, wishing she could be given permission to put the hair up. Then the terrible tension in the air might be broken.

Matthew wasn't at dinner. At his club, most likely, Sara thought, as she ate alone in the dining room. He often went there when Mother was in one of her self-pitying moods.

Sara sat toying with the gammon steak, made especially attractive in case Matthew returned. She had merely tasted her soup then pushed it away. Seaforth had removed it and laid the main course before her. But she had no appetite.

This too he would remove, then serve her a helping of the chilled cabinet pudding, another of Mrs Downey's specialities. She might manage its light texture. She would see.

At times like these she missed Jamie, even though she had never got on particularly well with him when he was there, since Mother made such a baby of him. Mother missed him too, dreadfully, as the whole household was made to realise. Jamie, however, had quite adjusted to being away, and was now in his second term.

When he did come home, he would throw his young weight about, with the staff, with her, even his father, if something didn't quite suit him. If he didn't get his way, he would go whining to his mother. She, doting on him, still wanting to keep him by her, would take his side against all comers, his father included.

Jamie's leaving again always upset her, and there would be an atmosphere in the house, with Harriet and Matthew arguing, followed by her refusing to speak to him. She never spoke at all to Sara, whether she was in a good mood or not, but Sara had become so used to that it didn't really worry her. Except perhaps when she was off guard enough to let it.

At this moment she felt very off guard, very lonely. If only she had a close friend. But she hadn't. Somehow it was so hard to make friends, and she could never say why. Some seemed to manage it well enough. Girls at school all made friends, were all so jolly, light-hearted, flippant. It jangled her nerves for some reason, And they noticed it – held her at arm's length – she knew they did.

'I don't care,' she said to her plate. But, oh, sometimes, she wished she had a friend, just one.

Sara had retired by the time Matthew returned. She was sitting up in bed reading when a light tapping at her door made her glance up.

'Who is it?'

'May I come in?' She recognised Matthew's voice.

'Of course.' She watched the door open slowly. He stood there in his fawn check driving suit, having left his dust-coat and cap downstairs.

'Are you all right, Sara?'

'Yes.' She put the book aside and sat up further in bed.

'I felt I should come and see how you were.' He came and sat with exaggerated care on the edge of her bed. 'You disappeared so quickly this afternoon. I felt that your mother, or perhaps I had upset you?'

Sara didn't reply. After a while he prompted, 'You can tell me.'

She compressed her lips and made a play of studying the cover of the book on the counterpane. 'She has never loved me,' she said at last.

She lifted her gaze to see him looking shocked, but he recovered enough to smile at her. 'How can you say that?'

'I've known it for a long time. Since I was seven, when she told me that she hated me more than anyone she knew.'

'She must have been angry, Sara. Parents say all sorts of unkind things, without thinking, when they are angry. She was probably sorry she had said it afterwards, but never told you.'

His smile broadened, as though he had solved some eternal enigma, but she didn't smile; met his without changing her expression.

'Oh no, she meant it. I think I've always known, but until then I hadn't dared to recognise it. I don't think I *really* understood then what she was saying, but what she said started something up inside me, and as I began to read the signs better, I came to know that she really didn't like me – doesn't like me – hates me.'

'No, Sara. Not hate.'

'Yes, Matthew. Hate.' Her use of his name caused him to frown.

'Matthew?' he queried, but she was not abashed.

'That's what I call you, to myself. I try not to call you anything when I speak to you. Perhaps you've never noticed – but I don't. You see, not being my real father . . .'

'You know that?' The way he said it, she realised that he genuinely had never thought that she knew. It had never been mentioned.

'Since I was seven,' she confessed. 'Since Mother told me, when she also said how much she hated me. I didn't know then that she had been married before and that she didn't love my father. She said she was glad he was dead. She said I reminded her of him, and that was why she hated me.'

Matthew didn't reply. He remained silent for so long that she felt obliged to say something.

'Was he so bad?' she asked. Matthew came to himself with a start.

'It's just that some marriages are not happy for one

reason or another. Your mother's marriage was one of those. He died just before you were born. They were married for only a year, so she never had time to find out if she would have grown to love him. You see, she is . . . She is not one to find it easy to love someone. There *are* people like that.'

'How did he die, my real father?'

'An accident. I gather he fell down the stairs and was killed.'

'And then my mother married you?'

'Yes. About a year afterwards.'

'She didn't mourn for long. She never loved my real father.'

'As I say, she never was able to display her love for anyone. Even with me it took her a long time to show her feelings.'

'I want so much for someone to love me.'

The words coming out of their own accord before she could stop them, she felt suddenly very sad, wanted to be held close by someone, as if they really loved her – if only to feel what it was like. There was only Matthew. She folded back the coverlet and put her bare legs on to the floor. Moving along the bed edge until she was beside him, she laid her head on his shoulder. He put an arm around her.

'I too,' he said and his voice sounded hoarse.

Sitting together in father–daughter embrace, Matthew listened as she began talking: how she wished she had a friend; about having no one at school eager to befriend her; about how the girls there would prattle on and on, hardly ever including her; about how she had never really felt herself to be one of them.

'I feel so much older than them. I sometimes wish I could leave and do something else. I'd like to work. I'd like to come and work with you on your journal. I'd feel wanted there. Needed.'

'Would you like that?' he whispered. His arm tightened about her shoulders. Against his cheek her loose flowing hair felt warm. Its youthful fragrance, reminiscent of peaches, filled his nostrils. He felt the movement of her head as she nodded to his question.

'Perhaps on Saturdays,' he whispered. His throat had closed up as though he were choking. Hardly knowing what he was doing, he gently brought his hand up and touched her cheek. His purpose had been to comfort her, but its smooth warmth brought an unexpected surge of intense longing for something more. He fought the sensation.

'On Saturdays,' he repeated with an effort, 'you could spend a few hours there. And perhaps . . . perhaps . . .'

'I'd like that,' she said. She hadn't drawn away from him, in her childish innocence unaware of the feelings she'd evoked in him.

'Sara . . .' Her name spilled from his lips like a sigh. 'I too need . . . affection – to be loved. Like you, I . . . I need . . .' Unable to help himself, he bent and brushed his lips against her cheek.

It was so warm, her skin. He hadn't realised he had closed his eyes. Opening them, he drew back, ashamed of what thoughts had really been behind that kiss, to see her looking up at him, her large, deep blue eyes, full not of fear but of wonder and trust. Shocked for even dreaming of abusing that trust, he guided her back into bed and replaced the coverlet over her. Leaning over her, he kissed her again, this time as a father should.

Her dark lashes slowly drooping, for some time he watched as she slept. How lovely she looked, a smile of contentment on her lips that he'd never seen before. His heart ached from the trust she had in him, yet why should she not trust him? He had taken on the role of father to her. How could he ever dare misuse that, even in thought? But he so needed love. Not carnal love, but gentle love, the love in the sharing of comfort, the mutual affection of one to the other.

Her breathing had regulated into a gentle in and out sigh. Getting up carefully so as not to awaken her, Matthew crept away, closing the door softly behind him. He did not feel ashamed now. There had been nothing of which to be ashamed. What had transpired had been but the expression of a tender mutual need of comfort so long denied to them both. This was what he told himself to assuage a tiny dark seed of wrongdoing buried so deep inside him that he almost believed it not there. He even vowed never again to put himself in the same situation, yet he knew he would visit her again – for the comfort he, both of them, had derived this night.

# Chapter Twenty-one

'How could they? My own children.'

Mary Wilson's voice was weak with shock at the letter she had received with the afternoon post.

In the parlour, dull from an overcast March afternoon, she sank down on to the leather sofa, the single sheet of stiff notepaper from Tompson, Greave & Sillitoe, Solicitors, still clutched convulsively in her hand, while Sarah and Harriet each supported an elbow as they sat with her.

The social visit by Harriet and Matthew had been made suddenly unpleasant by the arrival of the letter. They had each read it with shocked disbelief before handing it back to Mary, and now Matthew came to crouch in front of her, taking it from her again to return it to its envelope.

Without warning, the slight body began to sag. Their grip on her elbows tightened in response, but the small, lined face had gone oddly rigid and greyish, the eyes glazed and staring. She made an attempt to speak.

'They . . . could . . .'

The mumbling died away, and Matthew caught the shoulders as they fell towards him, the head lolling. He held on.

'I think she's ill! Let her lie flat!'

Harriet was already getting into a fluster. Seeing her mother in this unreal and frightening state, she was giving useless little cries of fear despite her aunt's urgent demand for her to pull herself together and help her mother lie down.

Sarah herself was very much in control of the situation, and took over without fuss.

'Get a cover!' she ordered her niece. 'From her bedroom upstairs. Anything will do. Call young Violet to run for the doctor, fast as she can. Matthew – a glass of water from the kitchen downstairs. Quickly!'

This last command was uttered sharply as Mary sighed and tried to sit up, but fell back like an old rag. She tried to speak, but the sounds that emerged seemed slurred and inarticulate. She was having difficulty in forming any words at all. It was then that her sister grasped the full horror of the situation.

'She's had a seizure. Oh, my God! A stroke!'

Harriet had clattered back down the narrow flight of stairs to the parlour, so laden with a voluminous eiderdown cover that she could hardly see where she was going. She burst back into the room, the cry already on her lips: 'Is she all right? What's wrong with her?'

Her aunt whisked the cover from her without replying, apart from a puff of exasperation at the unnecessary bulkiness of the article, and began wrapping it about the small form as Matthew returned with the water.

It was hopeless trying to administer a sip, for the lips were too stiff to receive it. The tiny amount of liquid merely ran sideways across her chin. Sarah bent close as Matthew retrieved the cup.

'Can you say something to me, Mary? Say your name!'

'Mmmmmmm . . .' came the drawn-out sound. 'Mary . . .' The eyes stared imploringly from pallid features. The mouth worked lopsidedly. Her sister laid a thin hand gently against the mouth.

'It doesn't matter, dear. You rest. We're getting the doctor.'

She turned to look at the other two, now standing uselessly by. Her face bleak, she whispered, 'I think it's definitely a stroke.' Her lips thinned and her eyes began to glitter with rage. 'It is them! Those ungrateful daughters of hers. Nagging at her. Worrying her with letters like this.'

She swept the letter up off the floor where it had fallen, and waved it under Harriet and Matthew's noses as though they too were guilty.

'Sending things like this. It's enough to give anyone a heart attack. She's never done them any harm. This is how they serve her, their own mother – for a few pennies. I shall never forgive them – never!'

Harriet was still in tears. 'I never took part in it.'

'I know you didn't, dear. Matthew, I feel proud of you both for staying aloof from this sordid . . . Has that girl gone for the doctor?'

'Yes, Aunt,' Harriet hiccupped. 'She went straight out of the door after I called her. Didn't even wait for her coat.'

'He should be on his way now. He's only up the next road.'

She turned back to Mary, who was waving her hand,

trying to attract their attention. The left hand lay inert at her side, a dead thing.

Sarah turned to her, her attitude changing to one of gentleness. At that moment the front door opened to admit the doctor. Puffing from his race along the road and up the flight of steps to the door, he came on into the parlour without ceremony, dropped his bag on the floor and yanked open its top to withdraw his stethoscope.

All three stood back as he made his examination, the housemaid, Violet, standing in the doorway watching silently, an anxious hand to her young mouth. Ignoring them all, he spoke gently to his patient, asking questions which she seemed incapable of answering.

'Is it a stroke, doctor?' Sarah taxed bluntly as he straightened.

He gave her a slow, penetrating look. 'Yes, I'm afraid Mrs Wilson has had a small stroke. A mild one, thank goodness. In time she'll recover some of her faculties, though no one can say to what extent. Her speech will return, I'm sure. It could have been worse. These things . . .'

'It's that letter,' Sarah burst in and began relaying its content, but he waved away her explanation.

'It need not necessarily be due to any one thing in particular, Mrs Morris. These things come quite out of the blue.'

'But the shock . . .'

'I'd lay no great store by that, were I you, Mrs Morris. It is possible, admittedly, that an upset may raise the blood pressure enough to . . .'

'I knew it! I said as much. It's them . . .'

'No blame ought to be laid at anyone's door. A moment of merriment could equally have brought this on. Or nothing at all. I have known victims to be merely beating a carpet or dusting when seized by . . .'

He gestured towards the prostrate woman, knowing that even if her speech was affected, she could hear adequately enough. Raising his tone for her benefit, he added, 'It is quite mild, I assure you. She has a left hemiplegia, but often recovery is as near complete to allow a patient to return to normal everyday life. Just keep her quiet and try to prevent any stress. As she recovers, let her carry on as if normal. There may be some depression for a while, of course . . .'

'Depression!' echoed Sarah, as the others drew in their breaths. 'If any depression has been caused, we know who has caused it.'

'Be that as it may,' the doctor went on, now aware of the events leading up to Mary's stroke from what Mrs Morris had related. 'What's needed now is complete rest, and for your sister to be afforded every assistance and understanding. I'm sure she'll recover and be as good as ever she was.'

But Mary Wilson was never again to be as good as ever she was. Though able to get about, hers became a shuffling gait; she needed the use of a stick, and the left hand was no good to her at all.

Harriet visited her mother more frequently now, the events of that terrible day somehow causing her not to resort to her medicine quite so often. Whenever she saw her, she felt tears prick her eyes and anger fill her heart against her sisters. Not so much against Clara, who was easy-going like Father had been, but against the waspish Annie who, even though she saw the damage she had caused, refused to shoulder blame, happy to quote the doctor's words of no one thing being responsible, relayed to her by Clara, who had received them from Matthew in his effort to reunite his wife's family.

'I'll never forgive Annie,' Harriet said furiously.

Annie had abandoned her legal battle. Thompson, Greave & Sillitoe's fee had been paid, and the papers filed away in their crypt until the yellowing correspondence would one day be dragged out and disposed of as so much waste paper.

But all the filing away and disposing of paper would never, as far as Matthew could see, fade the memory of that letter arriving at the house of a harmless elderly lady in Approach Road, or its results.

The journal was doing well, though not well enough. Moving into the City had drained Matthew's resources, which were stretched to the limit, repaying the bank loan, and paying the wages of a much larger staff both there and at the printing works in Cambridge Road. The machines were becoming outmoded with the newer and faster methods used by the large newspaper companies and a growing number of high-quality magazines. The *Freewoman* was beginning to look sadly old and Victorian. It would mean borrowing still more for new machinery. And following his father's advice, Matthew's venture into bringing in shareholders hadn't taken off as he had hoped, because he had not paused to think it out as carefully as he should.

The bit of advice he should have taken heed of – to get himself a better accountant – he had managed to ignore, and he was left wondering why he had overlooked something of such importance, the very thing that would have kept him on course. Too late, he realised his accountant had been an idiot, a smalltime dolt; his advice on setting the price of shares quite off the track. Few took up the offer. To attract more custom, again on his accountant's advice, the dividends had been made far too generous; Matthew, fool that he'd been, had followed the man's recommendations to the letter before realising his advice had been erroneous. In panic, he took on board his father's own accountant, in a firm down in Hampshire, which meant costly discussions over the telephone and irregular and time-consuming meetings, the price of experience all helping to drain dry the coffers.

But it wasn't only the journal that was draining him. Puffed up with earlier success, Matthew had bought the lease of the house the year before; and the bank, glad to lend him the money at five per cent while his repayments remained regular, was now clamouring to have its loans met in a more businesslike manner. What with repayments on the City premises, the need to buy more up-to-date equipment, and repayments on buying the lease of his house, Matthew found himself falling dangerously behind. By the May of 1909 he was at his wits' end how to cope with it all.

There was no use in trying to talk to Harriet. She had no

head for business and would panic at the least mention of financial worries. Nor did he dare confide in his brothers-in-law. What, and lose prestige in their eyes? His own brother, Richard, had no interest in him. He hadn't heard from Richard or his sister's family in over two years. That was how it was with his people, paddling their own canoes, minding their own business, and to hell with anyone else's problems.

There was only one ear he could confide in. Fifteen now, Sara was a beautiful, intelligent but serious young woman. About to study for her matriculation next spring, she would pass with flying colours and he was proud of her. He also knew that he loved her, with a gentle, caring love of which he told himself he did not feel ashamed. He would sit with her, tell her of his problems. She would give comfort if not answers.

Sara looked forward to Saturdays. It was like a breath of fresh air being away from school and doing something she had grown to love.

Eight-thirty each Saturday morning found her sitting primly behind a desk in the front office of Matthew's fine first-floor suite off Fleet Street. Matthew would drive her there in his new Vauxhall car. They would enter beneath the name, THE FREEWOMAN, embossed upon the stonework above the front entrance. It had once been an ordinary shop front, but Matthew had had considerable alterations done after he had acquired it and the first-floor offices. A smaller door next to it led up to offices above, belonging to some half dozen other businesses, but none as big as the *Freewoman*. Matthew was proud of his achievement, although lately Sara had thought he looked worried.

It was Friday, another school week over. Sara, gone to bed, sat with a book on her lap, the small oil lamp on her bedside table low. But she wasn't reading. She thought instead of tomorrow, Saturday, of being grown up for a day helping Matthew run his journal.

She wondered if he might come in to say goodnight. He did on occasion, would stay awhile, perhaps an hour, talking to her of his plans, his hopes and dreams. Mother never listened to him; had little interest in his ideas, he said, somewhat sadly, she thought. But Sara loved having him sharing them with her, having him near her, that special hour theirs alone, for the first time in her life feeling loved and needed. He was always so tender, so understanding.

Lately, though, she'd become aware of great changes in her body, and some inner voice seemed to be telling her that these visits of Matthew's were not quite the right thing for him to do. Yet she couldn't tell him so because she loved his visits – the only true comfort she'd ever known anyone to give her, and she adored him for it.

Her heart would leap to the soft tap on her door and she would whisper for him to come in, oddly excited by that need to whisper. As he sat at the foot of her bed, as he had done this past twelve-month, she would push back the coverlet, place her feet on the floor as she had that first time, and come to sit by him.

This was their secret, and that fact added to her sense of expectancy. Her mother, asleep in her own lonely room, knew nothing of the visits; the staff had gone to bed; the house would be silent. Matthew would talk and she listen, their bodies close, sustaining an unspoken need to be loved, sharing this special kind of oneness in each other.

She knew now that Matthew's need of affection was as great as her own. But sometimes she sensed something oddly disturbing about that need to be so close, though what it was she could not tell. At fifteen Sara had no knowledge of what passed between man and woman, yet this longing to be closer than they were already without knowing why confused her. She was happy, proud that he should want to be with her; felt protected and wanted, felt loved, yet her heart would feel so heavy as she gazed into that fair, handsome face, at times like an ache.

Whatever it was, it seemed to affect him too. Lately, as his lips touched her cheek after talking awhile, he would tremble quite suddenly, his arm about her shoulders tightening, and she would be sure he was going to seek her lips. She in turn wondered what it would feel like, his lips on hers, but always he would draw away and leap up hastily, almost pushing her backward on to the bed. Saying he had something to attend to in a most hoarse tone, he would hurry away, not stopping to tuck the coverlet around her as he used to, leaving her to wonder for half the night what she had done or said to upset him so. All she knew was it was happening more and more and that each time she felt more and more hurt, loving him so and wanting not to cause him annoyance.

It was at these times that the dread of rejection assailed her. Why did he become so abrupt? What was it that turned people – her mother, girls at school, now Matthew – against her? Though he would always return another night, it hurt when he pulled sharply away from her. If she knew what it was she might have been able to rectify it. But when she attempted to ask, he would brush aside her question, almost angrily, leaving her to lie awake trying to find some cause. But she never could.

Last year, 1908, they had spent their summer vacation in France: a few days in Paris, then on to Brittany for the remainder of the ten days. This year, to Jamie's exasperation, they were taking in Paris yet again. As if they'd not had enough of it.

Jamie hated Paris, hated wandering around museums and things. He trailed after them, his fair skin flushed by the stifling city-enclosed heat of late August, his face purposely drawn down in a picture of misery.

Harriet had constantly to warn him that he would get lost if he did not keep up with them but her warnings fell on stony ground. He was almost twelve years old. Even in a strange city he was sure he'd come to no harm if he did get lost. With his excellent command of French – surpassing his French master's every expectation at school – he was fully confident that he could enquire his way back to their hotel. He let his feelings be known in no uncertain terms, but his mother wasn't having any of it.

'I know it's boring for you, dear. But we have to keep together.'

Her parasol held daintily to shield her from the strong sunlight, she looked sweet and petite and very cool in white muslin, an enormous pleated hat of white silk perched precariously on top of her head. Jamie often wondered how ladies ever managed to keep such great big silly hats in place on top of their mounds of hair. Her grey eyes regarded him, her small oval face as stern as she could make it.

'It's only two more days, dear. Then we'll be on the train to Brittany. You liked Brittany last year.'

He couldn't wait to get to Brittany, that quaint little fishing village of Carnac they'd discovered last year with its swarthy yokels speaking funny French; to play on the fine sands and chase around the rocks with the local boys, his French far superior to their rustic accents; splashing about in a sea where one could wade out for dozens of yards without going out of one's depth. Sometimes, they almost had the small beach all to themselves, apart from a few local people. He longed to get there, longed for Paris to end.

'Oh, do come along, Jamie!'

'James!' This from his father as he lagged behind once more. 'Try to keep up, lad.'

'I'm tired.' The Arc de Triomphe seemed miles away, the trees in full leaf lining the length of the Champs Elysees doing little to combat the heat. 'It's hot. Can't we ride?'

'We've been riding. Now we're walking.'

His sister gave him a slow glance, reflecting their father's rebuke, pretending to be grown up, just because she was nearly as tall as him. In pale blue, her mass of dark hair tied back with a blue ribbon, with net gloves and white stockings, she looked elegant, he had to admit it. He poked his tongue out at her and she turned away, walking next to their father.

After the suffocating heat of Paris, Carnac was cool by comparison with Atlantic breezes wafting off the sea.

His mother sat under a sunshade, hardly doing anything but looking or reading. Father would put on a bathing costume and come in for an occasional dip. Sara would go for long walks on her own. Sometimes Father would go with her after asking Mother if she wanted to come. But she always shook her head, saying she had come here to rest, not to walk her legs off.

Jamie was glad. He didn't like walking either. It was so boring, gazing at headlands and picking flowers – weeds, really, as far as he could see. While Mother remained behind, so could he, which suited him, because often Father and Sara would be away for ages and ages. What they saw in it, or what they found to do, he didn't know, certainly didn't care.

Sara lay in the long grasses that rose like a fence all around her and gazed up at the sky, such a sky as she felt she could have swum in; warm and deep, it surrounded her.

Matthew sat beside her, his arms hugging his drawn-up knees, his fawn check jacket on the ground beside him, fawn-striped collarless shirt open at the neck, the hard celluloid collar in the jacket pocket for safekeeping.

Sara turned her eyes towards him. He looked completely relaxed, gradually cooling down after their long stroll under the hot Brittany sun. He was looking back at her and as their eyes met, he smiled, his lips beneath the fair moustache curving gently at the corners.

'You look so beautiful there,' he murmured. But he had

said this many times before and always just afterwards would become hard and tight-lipped, destroying the happiness his comment always brought. He said she was beautiful and she knew she was because he said it. Then he would take it all back by hurrying away from her without any explanation as to why. Now she did not return his smile, instantly on the defensive.

'You know that's not true! I'm not beautiful at all.'

For answer, he turned his attention to plucking a stem of seeding grass and, with a low, relaxed chuckle, proceeded to torment the tip of her nose with it.

Sara turned her face away from the tickling, trying to evade the tormenting seedhead, laughing now, her defences down. Everything was all right. This was a happy time. Matthew ceased trying to pursue her with the grass stem and she turned back to find him grown sombre, his handsome face above her composed, his brown eyes regarding her.

'You are beautiful, Sara. The loveliest creature I have ever seen, and . . . I love you. I've always loved you.'

She knew immediately what would happen; steeled herself for it. For a moment he stared down at her while she lay very still beneath the gaze, waiting for the warmth to leave his eyes. She saw him lean forward for a moment, his hand moving to hover over her as if to touch her, then he was on his feet, grabbing his coat up from the grass beside him.

'It's late. Your mother will be wondering where we are.'

The voice was harsh, the hand held out to help her up was cold and formal. Wordlessly she let herself be lifted to

her feet, watched him retrieve his collar, swiftly fasten it
around his neck, swing his coat over his shoulder.

'Why do you say I'm beautiful when you don't mean
it?' she asked as she matched his swift stride back the way
they had come.

'I do mean it, Sara.' He didn't slacken his pace.

'I don't believe you,' she cried, stopping abruptly. 'I
shall never believe you again.'

He stopped too and stood looking at her, his eyes so sad
she could have cried, but she wasn't prepared to let him
see her cry. She'd learned from years of feeling spurned
and belittled never to allow anyone to see her cry and show
herself belittled even more.

'Why do you think I say it then?'

'I don't know,' she said lamely.

'It's *because* I love you, Sara. A love I can't declare.
I know that confuses you but it's a love I shall never
acknowledge. I've no right to soil your innocence with
explanations. If I did, it would ruin what we do have
together. Now come on, Sara, we must go.'

She didn't move. 'Do you hate me, Matthew?' She saw
pain come into his eyes. His voice shook with emotion.

'How could I ever hate you – the only person I can turn
to in this unloving world I live in?'

'But you treat me so . . . so horridly sometimes.'

'It's because . . . Sara, don't ask me any more questions.
I can't answer them. You've asked me before. I couldn't
answer them then and I can't answer them now.'

'But you make me feel so . . .' She searched desperately
for a word. 'So unwanted. The way Mother makes me feel.

As though I've done something terribly wrong and you can
never never forgive me.'

'Oh, my sweet Sara, I could forgive you anything,
because I love you.'

'What have I done so wrong that you love me enough
to forgive me?'

'You're twisting my words, Sara. You are not old enough
yet to understand. Just be content that I do love you.'

'Then why?'

He had become harsh. 'No more, please. You must be
content with that. Now let's move on, or your mother might
suspect . . . She might wonder . . . Just come along now.'

He moved off at such a pace that Sara, her long legs
impeded by her lightweight but voluminous muslin skirt,
was forced to trail behind, her parasol up to keep off the
sun's rays also helping to slow her pace. And her mind
didn't know which way to turn. She only hoped that he
would forgive whatever she had done wrong and continue
coming to her room the way he used to. It was the only
comfort she had.

The very night they returned home from France, Jamie
was awoken from a disturbed sleep by a most awful pain
in his stomach. They often ate unusual foods on holiday
and Jamie guessed he must have had something on the way
home that hadn't agreed with him.

His first thought was to crawl out of bed and reach for
the pot that lay beneath in case he was suddenly sick. But
nothing was worse than being sick all on one's own. What
he really wanted was someone to be here to comfort him.

There was not a sound in the house. The servants had all gone to bed by now, and his mother and father were fast asleep too in their respective rooms. There was Sara. He could rouse her. He had no qualms about rousing her, in fact felt a wicked delight at the idea of doing just that. The trouble was that the pain was subsiding. Nor did he feel sick any more. But it would return sooner or later, worse than it had been, and he would be sick, he was sure of it.

Hoping in a way that this would be true, he crept out of bed and went to the door to call Sara. Quietly he opened it, but no further than just a crack, for the door to Sara's room was already open. A shadowy figure stood there – not Sara's – the shape of a man. Ghost-like, it hovered, gazing back into the room from which it seemed to have emerged.

Jamie froze. It was a ghost. He felt his blood run cold as, silently, the figure drifted towards him. Petrified, Jamie watched it move towards the head of the stairs leading down to the bedrooms below. It had to pass him. What if it saw him, raised its arms to freeze his blood so solid that he would die on the spot? Yet he could not close his door again lest it see the movement and finish him off in a most horrible manner.

A thin shaft of moonlight threading through the rear landing window briefly touched the gliding figure and it was then that Jamie saw its face. His first impulse was to leap out and yell, 'Thank heaven it's only you, Father!' But some instinct stayed him.

Fear receding before a different emotion, a reluctance to be seen watching, he stood peering through the crack of his door until his father slipped quietly down the stairs and disappeared. Listening intently, he heard his father's bedroom door open, then close with a faint click. There was no more sound, and Jamie moved back into his room and then into his bed. He did not feel sick any longer, but when it did return, he didn't go for help or comfort, but merely brought up the offending food into the chamber pot. Ellen could get rid of it in the morning.

'Why didn't you tell someone you were ill in the night?' Harriet cuddled her baby to her. 'You poor little darling, I'll get Dr Horder to look at you this very morning.'

Jamie suffered himself to be cuddled. 'I'm feeling much better. It went pretty quick once I was sick.'

'Even so, it could come back. I think we'll get Dr Horder to take a look at you just in case you're sickening for something worse.'

Dr Horder diagnosed a brief bilious attack and gave him some foul chalky-tasting medicine, two spoonfuls, thrice a day.

Jamie grimaced at the first dose. 'I don't see why I need take any more. All this fuss! I'm better now.' Rudely he pushed away a second spoonful. Ellen, who was trying to administer it, looked anxious.

'You don't want to be ill just before you're going back to school. You've only got another fortnight before term starts.'

'And I'm not spending it being dosed up with that muck! You can bloody well take it away!'

'Master Jamie!'

He didn't care. He'd learned to say worse than that at school. Real swearing. If you didn't use it you were a cissy. If you dared use really foul ones, like fuck and cunt, even though these had to be whispered, and even though you weren't sure what they actually meant, they sounded good and you rose rapidly in your fellows' estimation.

He had come to enjoy the feeling of superiority that his exclusive schooling brought him and felt quite justified in his usage of his father's staff; not, of course, Mr Seaforth and Mrs Downey, who in their way upheld their dignity against all employers, and woe betide young twelve-year-olds who tried to buck against them. But with lesser beings like Ellen, he could more or less say what he pleased. It made him feel good to shock her.

To add to his sense of superiority, he pushed the second spoonful away, spilling the chalky substance all over her apron.

'Master Jamie!' she exclaimed again, exasperated, but she didn't attempt to pursue the second spoonful.

There was no recurrence of that night's sickness, although he awoke at about the same hour two nights later for no apparent reason except with the feeling that he had heard something. Thinking of the ghostly figure of his father that other night, in a fever of curiosity he got out of bed and spent the next fifteen minutes peering through the tiniest opening of his door.

He was about to close it, his neck starting to ache from his post at the tiny opening and his bare feet grown cold, when the click of his sister's door alerted him.

As before, his father appeared, pausing to look back, closing the door softly, then moving stealthily off down the stairs. Jamie closed his door after he'd gone, mystified. What was his father doing? It was all very odd.

It was even more odd when, several nights after that, Jamie, now full of curiosity, and swept up by the strange double occurrence, forced himself to keep vigil. He was rewarded by the now familiar sight of his father emerging from Sara's room some time later. Jamie fell to wondering if Mother knew what was going on.

'Why does Father have to go into Sara's room in the middle of the night?'

Harriet looked up from helping him get his things together ready for his new term. There had been so much to buy: new clothes, new books, more sports equipment. The following day, Monday, he would be back at school, far away. She felt tearful. It was always a wrench saying goodbye to him, but bravely she held back the tears.

'I don't know, dear.' She stopped, frowning at him. 'I don't understand what you mean, Jamie dear.'

'Well . . .' Jamie was gathering up his new socks along with some older ones, and stuffing them into the corner of his suitcase. 'You know when I was sick? I went to see if Sara could come and help me feel better. I saw Father coming out of her room. I just wondered . . .'

Harriet stopped sorting shirts to interrupt. 'What time was this?'

'About half past twelve, I suppose.' Jamie was still haphazardly packing socks. 'And then it happened again a couple of nights later, around the same time. And then again, last night. I thought she mightn't be well or something. Like I was. But Sara can't keep on being ill, can she?'

Harriet stared at him but wasn't seeing him. Her mind had raced on, was becoming appalled by what it visualised. She felt suddenly weak, exhausted, full of fear.

'Finish your packing,' she said tersely, and left him, protesting, to the task.

In her room, her heart pounding, her breath coming in irregular gasps, Harriet let herself sink on to her dressing-table chair. Hardly able to stop herself shaking, she fumbled for her medicine in her bedside commode. This summer she had hardly needed recourse to it; had felt her life beginning to pull itself together. But this morning there was a great need of at least one small sip to fortify herself. The one sip, however, became two, then three. Before she realised, she had taken four glasses. Her vision blurred, but still her thoughts reeled.

No, it couldn't be what she was thinking. And yet. That she-devil knew she wasn't Matthew's child. Paying her out, that's what she was doing – enticing her own mother's husband . . . against her . . .

Yet how could she accuse him on the words of a small boy, an innocent little boy who might have been merely dreaming?

She took another sip of brandy and found a sudden need to drain this glass too.

# Chapter Twenty-two

'I don't know what to do!' In her mother's house, Harriet clung on to her, letting herself be held by that one good arm while her Aunt Sarah sat nearby, stunned by what Harriet had related.

'Crying's not going to solve anything,' she said sharply, with not much show of sympathy, though her expression spoke otherwise.

By comparison, Mary's voice held a new weakness since her stroke. 'Coming from a child's lips like that,' it quivered. 'I can't believe it.'

'That's what I mean. From a child's lips – James's. How can we be sure what he says is true? Don't forget, no one has given Matthew a chance yet to defend himself. I think he should be allowed to speak before we take the word of that young man.'

Sarah had never particularly liked James. It was a puzzle who he took after, unless it was Matthew's family. They had never mixed with the Wilsons, but kept themselves to themselves. Snobs, and ignorant to boot – that was her opinion – Matthew being an exception, of course.

'Jamie doesn't tell lies,' Harriet burst out. 'Especially

things like that. He wouldn't *know* about things of that sort
– at his age.'

'I know, dear,' soothed Mary. Her right arm tightened
about her daughter. In her lap, the left hand lay crabbed
and lifeless.

Sarah was not to be swayed by her niece's defence of
the boy. 'I'm appalled by what you've told us, Harriet. But
really you've no proper proof. Don't you think you should
speak to Matthew himself before jumping to conclusions
and getting yourself in a state?'

Harriet looked startled. 'I couldn't do that. If I was
wrong, I couldn't bear him thinking I'm accusing him of
something so . . . nasty. I trust Matthew. I've always trusted
him. I don't know what I'd have done without him to look
after me and support me and that.'

'That's your trouble, Harriet,' said Sarah, her tone still
hard. 'You've leaned on him from the very start – never
tried to stand on your own two feet. You have to find out
what's going on or you will never be sure and it'll always
be left hanging over your marriage. I personally don't
believe there's anything in it, but you *must know.*'

'Perhaps if she watched him?' Mary suggested waveringly. She took her hand from Harriet's shoulders and used
it to move her left hand to a more comfortable position,
grimacing at the pain such a dead limb could produce
when it could do nothing for itself.

Sarah regarded her sister with the pity she could not
give her timid niece. The years had proved Harriet a
disappointment and she now felt only impatience. Harriet's
daughter had far more courage. At fifteen she already

looked you straight in the eye as her mother never could, and it wasn't just her height. Sara had earned her approval in all things. And now this. Who should one believe? She couldn't for an instant take the word of a wilful child over that of Sara. A child herself, the girl could have had no notion that such unsavoury things went on in this world, much less be part of them. The idea was revolting. Even so, she resolved to get to the root of it. She herself would face her great-niece with this business and see what came out of it.

She never did face Sara with it. Events overtook them before she could. And to have attempted to do so afterwards would have been heartless and cruel.

Harriet felt quite unsteady, having taken too many sips of medicine to fortify herself for the coming confrontation. She knew she'd drunk too much. Had she not, she wouldn't have said the things she did.

She'd intended to follow her aunt's advice and watch Matthew to make certain of her facts before daring to charge him with assignations with her daughter. Instead, when he found her and tried to take the glass from her, saying that it was the bottle talking, she had flung its contents at him, screaming abuse at him like a harridan.

Now she sat limp and huddled, her eyes sore from crying, her head reeling from all the things she had said, half of them untrue, the other half silly supposition.

She had never seen such a look on his face as when he backed away. He'd said not a word in his defence to her wild accusations of betrayal – that he had probably been unfaithful to her for years; had probably even sought the services of prostitutes for his carnal obsession; that this was probably one of the reasons why he hadn't touched her for years.

It suited her to slide around the real truth of their rift: cringing from her wifely duties, she had no one but herself to blame if he had sought affection somewhere else. Yet in righteous fury she had screamed at him to get out, never come back, that she hated him, never wanted to see him again. As she collapsed weeping on her bed, exhausted by her own tirade, he had turned and left without a word.

She heard him running down the stairs. She had an urge to run after him, tell him that she was sorry, she hadn't meant to hurt him, that she did trust him. But her body wouldn't obey her. By the time it did and she'd sat up, the front door had slammed and he was gone.

Of course he would come back, she was sure of that. She sat on the edge of her bed, trying to think clearly. It wasn't easy with her head so muzzy. When he returned in a while, she would fall at his feet and beg forgiveness. She would tell him she trusted him, would trust him for ever more; that she understood how Sara, with her slimy underhanded ways, had tried to tempt him, but that she knew him to be a finer man than to be tempted by a slut of a girl she was ashamed to call her daughter. She would tell him how much she needed him and that she would try to change. She would confess that she'd been thoroughly stupid to listen to a child, and yes, she would be a proper wife to him. She thought all this and slowly relaxed, her tears drying as she waited for him to return.

He was probably walking off his anger, and rightly so. And he'd have forgiven her by the time he retraced his steps homeward. But in the meantime she felt so ill.

The half hour of genteel physical training suitable for young ladies within the high school's walled playing field had brought a healthy glow to Sara's cheeks. It accentuated her dark hair, now braided, and her clear blue eyes. A head taller than most of the other girls, she looked almost too old for school despite her school pinafore.

She stood breathing deeply from the healthy exercise, smiling her enjoyment of it as the school's headmistress appeared from the main building. The grave expression on Miss Haverfield's heavy features as she drew near banished Sara's smile and caused it to be replaced with a frown of consternation. What had she done wrong to bring the woman out here?

'Sara,' began Miss Haverfield, not unkindly. 'Please come with me.'

Sara followed bleakly. 'What have I done, Miss Haverfield?'

'Nothing, child. You have done nothing. Please follow me.'

Their footsteps echoing across the hall and along the corridors, Sara three paces behind, they proceeded to the headmistress's study at the front of the building. Miss Haverfield held the door open for her, and Sara went in. The hushed air inside the room was in sharp contrast to the echoing corridors.

Standing by the desk Sara recognised the short figure

and round face of the Reverend Crombie, vicar of their local church. He too looked sombre, and had obviously been waiting for her. He came forward.

'My dear child . . .' Advancing, he seemed to be much closer to her than she was to him in some unaccountable way. 'My dear child, how can I begin to tell you?' Sara stood looking at him in bewilderment. 'My child, I have some terrible news to impart . . .'

He stopped to glance at the headmistress. 'May she sit down?'

'By all means.' Miss Haverfield brought one of the several heavy, straight-backed, green leather-seated chairs that stood around the eau-de-Nil papered walls. Dutifully, Sara sat, already feeling dread pumping with sickening beats through her chest.

'What is it? Is it my mother?' She'd always felt something might happen to Mother. She didn't know why, only that Mother seemed vulnerable enough for something awful to happen to her one day.

Mr Crombie shook his head. 'It isn't your mother. You must try to be brave, my child.'

She knew then. In that brief second before the beloved name was uttered, she knew. The tidings coming faintly through a whirlpool-roaring of disbelief, her soul tore itself loose inside her – like something ripped out of her to leave a salty internal bleeding of tears through which details of the accident became jumbled together.

In a plea for what Mr Crombie was saying not to be true, her eyes met his. The man was smiling at her. A smile of sympathy. A smile meant to soothe but which was a travesty. A small round face filled with teeth. She couldn't take her eyes from those teeth, felt that when at any time in her future she thought of this moment she would recall only teeth, a white-fenced barrier between herself and reality – or unreality – as the details were unfolded for her.

Walking fast, not thinking where he was going, Harriet's accusations ringing in his ears, Matthew had turned into Mare Street. He had not heard the warning cry of the motorist.

This, Sara in part, deduced later.

What she did learn as the news was gently broken to her was that he had stepped off a kerb without looking, and had been bounced off the oncoming vehicle into the path of a brewer's dray. The great iron-shod hooves of one of the terrified Clydesdales had struck him, and the wheels of the heavy wagon, fully laden with barrels and unable to pull up sharply enough, had delivered the coup de grace. The Reverend was so sorry.

Sara came home to a house that held people but still felt empty. Many times over the years the house had known Matthew's absence, but part of him had always been there, awaiting his return. Now that presence was gone. All her mother's crying would not fill it; a hundred people clustered within its walls would not fill it; all the sunlight in the world pouring in at its windows would never again bring the feeling of his being there somewhere, even though Sara clung desperately to the impression that at any moment he might walk in at the door.

Jamie had been told. Sent home to mourn his father,

he stood about looking suitably lugubrious. Never having been close to his father, he watched his mother's grief-swollen face with a kind of passive resignation, longing only for all this to be over so that he could return to school.

Sara, sent home within hours of being told, found her mother inconsolable. She tried to do what she could to comfort, but her efforts went unacknowledged, and she even found herself pushed fiercely away. Trying to tell herself that it stemmed purely from grief, she knew that wasn't true: it had always been this way. And so she shrank into herself to nurse her own lonely grief.

She hadn't yet been able to cry. Tears might have diminished the pain inside her, building up so much that it must eventually burst through. But it didn't; it just kept on accumulating, being reabsorbed, only to accumulate again. It was as though her own eyes were barriers to the tears that should be shed, until all she could do was screw herself up bodily to relieve the pressure. How then could she ever take away any of her mother's sense of loss when her own was so profound that it was squeezing the life out of her?

She couldn't speak of Matthew. Not yet. How could it have happened so suddenly, so cruelly? If he had to depart this life, it should have been gently, with her there to comfort him. This violent ending – this wonderful light gone out with no chance of farewell – it was beyond endurance.

Sitting beside her mother on the sofa in the dim, curtain-drawn parlour, any word of comfort became a farce, inadequate, trite.

'I know what you are feeling.'

'No you don't!' The reply was harsh. 'I loved him so much.'

In her heart Sara heard the echo: *So did I – more than you will ever know.*

The small woman beside her had stiffened as though divining her thoughts, condemning her for them, cringing from that cautious half-embrace she had attempted to offer. Sara wasn't surprised. She had never cuddled her mother in her life, and was deprived of that privilege even now.

Instead she looked about the dimmed parlour, fixing on the large, heavily framed wedding photo hanging from the picture rail. Beneath its covering of black cloth she knew every detail of it: sepia, a studio photograph, Matthew seated, her mother standing beside and slightly behind him, one hand on his shoulder, small oval face serious, behind them an arbour of flowers. Another small oval-framed photo sat on the mantelpiece: Matthew on holiday, smiling, happy. That too was concealed, black-draped. Did he still smile beneath that piece of black cloth?

Sara turned her eyes away and saw Jamie sitting by the window, having resisted his mother's pleas to come and sit beside her. With him sat Aunt Clara, every now and again parting the drawn curtains to peep out on to the street below for sign of her Fred and Annie and Robert.

They had gone to sort out funeral arrangements on behalf of the helpless widow. They would be bringing Grandma and Great Aunt Sarah back with them, the house again full of people yet still as empty as ever.

She was thinking this when Harriet's frantic voice

startled all three, making Aunt Clara gasp, the curtains falling back from her hand.

'You!' came the cry. 'You didn't *love* him. You just wanted . . .'

A gush of tears engulfed the rest as Harriet's convulsive sobbing filled the room, only to be disrupted by yet another hysterical outburst.

'It was an accident . . . an accident, I tell you!'

'I know,' Sara endeavoured and this time her mother didn't shrink from the arm she put around the small, quivering shoulders.

'It wasn't my fault. I didn't mean it to happen that way.'

Clara came hurrying to her other side. 'Of course you didn't.'

The sobbing had become a convulsion of hiccupping. 'I only tried to keep him away from me . . . But he fell . . . Right to the bottom. I didn't mean to push him. But he kept on and on. He wouldn't leave me alone. I had to! I had to!'

Jamie was looking frightened. Clara had half risen, startled.

'What's she talking about?' she asked anxiously.

'I don't know,' Sara said, but it was dawning on her that this was about an entirely different person. Her mother's mind had gone back into the past, and she was confusing the death of one husband with another.

As gently as she could, she tried to help ease the mind back to the present.

'It's Matthew, Mum.' How raw the name sounded on her lips, her heart an aching weight against her ribs to have him here alive again. How it hurt to utter that beloved name. 'Matthew.'

Her mother had leaned away from her, staring at her with vacant eyes – no, not vacant, querying, confused, as though not properly recognising her.

'Matthew?' The convulsions stopped temporarily. 'No – he'd have protected me if he'd been here . . . He'd have stopped him. He didn't care I was eight months gone. Only wanted his pleasure. I tried to push him away but he fell all the way down from top to bottom. He didn't get up. I knew he was dead. I killed him. I didn't mean to. I only meant to push him away to make him leave me alone . . .'

She broke off abruptly. Her grey eyes, from staring only into the past, became in a moment aware of the present; and, seeing her daughter, grew full of hatred. As Sara made to touch her again, she flinched away like a startled animal.

'No! You're trying to drag me down there with him. I won't let you. You're nothing to me. You're nothing!'

'Mum.' Sara interrupted the babble. 'I'm Sara. I'm your daughter.'

'No you're not! You're his. You're just like him. Not mine.'

Fear clutched momentarily at Sara. 'But you are my mother?' Her plea was like a child trying to make some-thing come true that might not be. 'You did give birth to me? You did, didn't you?'

'I wish I hadn't.' The words hissed. 'Him – your vile father – put you inside me. Against my will. He didn't care how he hurt me. Just went on pushing and pushing with his filthy need whenever he wanted me. He forced you inside me. And then wanted more. Couldn't leave me alone, even when . . . No, you're not my child. You're his.'

Prompted to fresh sobbing by her memories, Harriet rocked herself while Sara stared at her, feeling some relief that she wasn't what people called a love-child – an odd reference when, even born in wedlock, she had not come into existence out of love. She knew that now without a doubt.

The sense of relief did not stay long, replaced by a wave of bitter understanding of her mother's unnatural revulsion of a daughter born out of pain and cruelty – her own father's cruelty – herself the result of it. Rejection – that was what she had inherited, her mother blaming her for the sins of her father. Why must she be the one to be rejected?

Not only Mother, Matthew too. That night before his death yawned now in her memory like a cold, bleak cavern. He had come to her as usual, and as usual had talked about the journal. Recalling their differences in Brittany – Matthew stalking on ahead that afternoon to avoid her company for the rest of the vacation – she had been so unhappy. But for two of his visits after the holiday there had been no tension, nothing said or done to disturb the content and tranquillity of sitting together for an hour talking – just talking. She had been so relieved to know it was all healed.

But that last evening it had begun all over again – the trembling of his hands, the tremor in his voice, and then Matthew's lips had touched hers for the first time ever, the sweet feel of them almost making her swoon. Then he was bearing her back on to the coverlet, and she was too overwhelmed to wonder what he was doing. Suddenly his weight against her had lessened and he had pushed himself away from her to stand with his hands clenched on either side of his cheeks. 'God forgive me!' She had heard his agonised cry.

His expression had been terrifying, looking down at her as one might regard a loathsome beetle or a filthy beggar. Beneath the fair moustache the lips that a moment before had been wonderful upon hers, had been twisted – with what? Hate? Repugnance? Again the pain and bitterness of being thrust away, of being shunned, unwanted, had torn through her heart.

Now Matthew, wonderful, gentle Matthew, was dead, and she could never ask what she had done to offend him. Her heart ached with the yearning to have him here now; with the devastation of her loss; with the emptiness he had left behind him; with the now and forever unanswered question.

'Please, Mummy,' she whispered like a child, just wanting love. 'Please let me try to make amends. Let me . . .'

'No! Don't come near me. You . . . whore!'

The last word tore itself from Harriet's lips as Sara leaned towards her, asking only for someone to take away the legacy of emptiness that Matthew had left behind. She wasn't prepared for the hand that swept out as if in self-defence, the way it must have done those many years ago fending off an animal of a husband.

The blow caught Sara full on the cheek. The force, surprising for such a small person, knocked her off balance, throwing her sideways as Harriet leapt up and ran past her and out of the door and up the narrow stairs to the landing above before anyone quite realised what had happened.

'Oh, my God! Stop her, someone! She'll kill herself!'

Ignoring the fallen girl, an alarmed Clara leapt up after Harriet as fast as her generous proportions allowed. Her heavy steps clumping hollowly up the stairs, she called Harriet's name frantically. Jamie just sat gawping, horror-struck, at Sara's fast crimsoning cheek upon which the fingerprints were beginning to stand out stark and white.

# Chapter Twenty-three

Even at the graveside, no tears came to wash free the grief. She could only stand beside it, breathing in the dank smell of wet earth while Reverent Crombie intoned the prayers for the dead.

'. . . Thou knowest, Lord, the secrets of our hearts . . .'

Her own heart hugged its secrets, concealed from the world. *Dear God, you alone know my secret.*

'. . . Forasmuch as it hath pleased almighty God in His great mercy to take unto Himself the soul of our dear brother . . .'

He was taking Matthew away, the special love they'd had, leaving a hole within her as gaping as that into which she stared. Why should she pray to Him?

'. . . earth to earth; ashes to ashes; dust to dust; in sure and certain hope of the resurrection of eternal life . . .'

*I shall see you again, dear Matthew. One day . . .*

Until then she would keep this empty place inside her which Matthew had once filled, where only he had dwelled. No one had ever loved her but him. Now he was gone and there was no one to love her ever again. She felt lost here, lost and small and insignificant.

Lifting her eyes, Sara gazed at those gathered here,

faces tight with the cold of the morning, and with sorrow. Jamie looked uncomfortable. *He shouldn't be here*, she thought, oddly detached; then switched her gaze to her mother. Face hidden behind a heavy black veil, she seemed near to collapse, held between the steadying hands of her brothers. From behind the veil came a steady disembodied moaning. Sara tore her gaze away in disgust and looked up at the overcast sky from which a light drizzle was falling.

Listening to the damp sighs, she thought of a love snatched away, felt the deep ache it had left in its wake. *I did love you, Matthew. I shall never love anyone else.* She wanted to cry so as to cement the vow, yet still the tears did not come. Would she ever cry again? She didn't think so. She made up her mind then that she never would, no matter what occurred to try to make her. She would give no one – no one – that satisfaction of seeing her cry . . . ever.

David Symonds regarded the wife of his old friend with a compassion few solicitors could afford to indulge in. One learned over the years that this was a business like any other and personal feelings should not be allowed to come into it. Some circumstances, however, made it difficult to be impersonal, and it was hard having to tell Harriet Craig exactly how she stood financially.

Long ago he'd warned Matthew about headlong over-spending following the joys of success, but Matthew had laughed. 'It's only money.'

How could one combat that sort of sentiment? And now he was sitting here before Matthew's stunned widow, telling her that the house, the journal, the printing works with its new and up-to-date machinery, everything, must be sold to repay Matthew's debts; that she had inherited virtually nothing from him; that his will was not worth the parchment it was written on. When the bank was paid back, there would be hardly enough to pay off the workforce, let alone the domestic staff. In a word, Harriet had been left penniless, without a roof over her head.

She sat slumped in a chair in her fine drawing room on which her husband had only recently spent a mint of money. In the marble-tiled fireplace a fire burned brightly against the November cold; reflected in her grey eyes that were now beseeching his help.

'All that money? All gone? Even mine?' She bit her lip as David nodded sadly. 'There must be some way of getting out of it?' It was a heartbreaking cry.

'I wish there were.'

'I've just lost my husband.' As if that alone was sufficient to melt the hearts of creditors. 'I've nothing left. We've got to find a way. The bank will just have to wait for its money. It's not as if they'll go broke waiting.'

David Symonds shook his head. 'Your husband's creditors must be allowed to take back what they are owed. It is, after all, their money. I'm so sorry, Mrs Craig. If I could do something, I would, believe me.'

He leaned forward, patted her hand. He still didn't know her very well. All the years he had known Matthew, he had only visited the house a couple of times on business when it wasn't possible for Matthew to come to the office. If not at the office, he and Matthew would meet in town, or at

Matthew's premises, David being given to understand that
Harriet wasn't a strong woman, and that her nerves did not
allow her to entertain easily. Whilst he was not fully able to
fathom how the wife of a businessman could allow herself
not to entertain her husband's friends and associates –
himself happily married to a robust woman whose very
hobby was socialising – he felt it to be Matthew's business
how his wife behaved.

He had to admit that, having met her on the odd
occasion, his impression had indeed been of a small, timid
person who followed her husband around, almost one step
behind him as though the ground would open beneath her
feet without him there, while her large, captivating grey
eyes set in an extremely pretty, oval-shaped face, gazed at
the world from beneath long dark lashes like a frightened
dog expecting at any moment to be attacked.

He sat now looking into those grey eyes, and said again,
'I really am truly sorry, Mrs Craig. There is absolutely
nothing I can do.'

Across the room, totally ignored, Sara sat very still.

She had not yet gone back to school. Although her
brother had gone rushing off to his at the first chance,
she'd hardly needed to plead to be allowed to stay at home
– her mother was oblivious to all else but her loss. She sat
watching the two people as though watching a play, hardly
able to believe what the solicitor had been saying.

Matthew had left such debts. She had never thought of
him as being financially imprudent; had felt safe with him
in all things. Yet even now she didn't feel bitter, only sad
and lost and missing him so. But she wouldn't think of that

at this moment. She would think instead of her mother and what they were going to do.

Forcing the longing for Matthew from her mind, Sara tried to think as the solicitor gave his condolences and made his exit.

Her first wild idea was out of the question. How could a girl, still months off her sixteenth birthday, think to manage a journal on the strength of a few Saturdays spent there? True, she knew a little stenography, and intended to study it until she had perfected it. She had proved herself a quick learner and could now type quite rapidly. She also knew a bit about editing and how to handle people. But that was when Matthew had been at her side to guide and bestow confidence. How could she handle people far older than herself without him? And what did she know about the financial side? When it came down to it, she knew nothing.

Another idea was forming in her mind, just as wild but with more promise. Matthew's father – surely he wouldn't let his son's family be thrown out on the street, which was what would surely happen? It was no use taking Mother into her confidence. She was too devastated to make any sense of her present, much less face up to her future. Sara would go alone. Maybe her youth would appeal to the more sympathetic instincts of Matthew's obscure and standoffish family. She didn't relish the task, but she would face it, for her mother's sake, for Jamie's sake.

The house wasn't half so imposing as Sara remembered. She could dimly recall it looming over her that one time she had been here. She had been, what, three years old?

That must have been when she had lived in Hackney Road – a fleeting image of a tiny kitchen and cramped rooms flashed into her mind. So this house she now approached would have seemed huge to her.

She remembered too feeling very subdued by the prison-like aspect of mullioned windows, an entrance hall hushed and spacious, doors that towered over her – a sensation of being very alone. Someone had been holding tightly to her hand, but all she really remembered was a feeling of overwhelming awe, of feeling so small.

She felt no awe now, grateful only to be out of the cold December afternoon as she was shown into a chilly, somewhat uninspiring hall by a portly butler a fraction shorter than herself. Her hat and coat taken, she was shown into a living room just half as large again as that at home. Rather than awe, she experienced a small twinge of annoyance on seeing the elderly couple waiting for her. Mr Craig stood like some aging bear, his back to the fireplace, his hands clasped firmly behind him in a way that indicated little intention of extending the hand of welcome.

Mrs Craig sat on the edge of a most uncomfortable-looking leather button-backed sofa. In mourning, as was Sara, she seemed swathed in it: black silk bombazine, high-necked and old-fashioned, festooned with jet beads and black lace; a large marcasite and amethyst mourning brooch clasped at the throat.

The pallid face narrow and stiff, the brown eyes hostile and bitter, she gazed past rather than regarded her visitor, as though she wasn't there. There was a strong resemblance between mother and son, but the generosity was missing.

No glimmer of welcome in that face either. Great-Aunt Sarah was right, these people were ignorant snobs. How had Matthew, dear, generous, gentle Matthew, come to spring from such people?

'How do you do?' Sara began, as politely as she could.

She was already beginning to feel nettled. Having written prior to embarking on this venture, she had received no reply but had assumed that the lack of one at least did not indicate a refusal.

Mr Craig nodded curtly but didn't move. His wife did not even acknowledge her, but continued to stare through her. She looked ill, the withered skin stretched parchment-like across her cheekbones. It was a fine-boned face. The woman must have been a beauty in her youth – no doubt it was from her that Matthew had derived his looks. Sara's heart became a small lonely thing inside her breast, thinking of those handsome looks gone forever, and she took in a deep breath to control it.

No one had invited her to sit down and she realised that her visit was expected to be as brief as possible. In that case, she would not inconvenience them by prolonging it. She lifted her head proudly.

'I assume you received my letter, Mr Craig, and I apologise for my intrusion . . .' The apology was veined with sarcasm. She was glad her high school education had managed to erase any hint of the London East End accent she'd grown up with.

'I shan't impose upon you any longer than need be,' she ended.

'I trust not.' Mrs Craig speaking unexpectedly, her

voice remote and rasping, took Sara by surprise. 'I marvel that one of such tender years thought it necessary to travel so far alone on a matter that needed only a letter.'

'You did receive my letter, Mrs Craig?'

'We did. But as it contained mention of a financial matter, there seemed little need for it to be followed up by your coming here . . .'

'Leave this to me, my dear.' Henry Craig's tone was low and gruff, imparting every intention of giving this audacious young woman short shrift. 'I wonder at your mother allowing you to travel all this way on your own, Miss Craig. But then, I have always thought she had few . . .'

'I said nothing to my mother about my coming,' Sara interrupted hotly but was ignored.

'If she imagines to appeal to our sympathies,' continued Mr Craig, 'sending a child to beg for her, she's mistaken. I shall not prolong this "visit", young lady. I'm well aware of the purpose behind it but I can tell you, here and now, that the ploy won't work. I've no intention of handing out charity to her. She is nothing to do with me. My only concern was my son's welfare. Now he has gone.'

He reached out and laid a large hand on his wife's shoulder as she drew in a tremulous breath, although her taut features did not change.

'I am sorry, my dear, these things have to be said.' His pale eyes returned to settle coldly upon Sara.

'The fact is, young lady, that I grieve not only my son's untimely death, but also the way he handled his affairs. Time and again I beseeched him to listen to me, but he would take no advice. He continued to squander his money and I strongly suspect that woman he married, your mother, had a hand in his foolishness with money – the woman we were so against his marrying saw our son only as an easy means to an end.'

'That's not true!'

'Kindly allow me to finish, young lady. As I see it, it's only too true. My son's mother and I have been devastated by his death, and we have been aggrieved by the debts he left. But if your mother expects me to pay them for her as your, may I say, impudent letter appears to imply, then she is barking up the wrong tree. With our dear son taken from us, your family has ceased to exist in my eyes. You have family of your own. I suggest you look to them for charity.'

Charity! What an ugly word it could be on some lips. Sara stood her ground. She hadn't advanced one inch from where she had entered the room, had not been invited to, and anger now seethed within her, not so much at this cold-hearted attitude as at being looked upon as a precocious child. She was fighting for her mother, as Matthew had once fought his parents for her. She was fighting for Jamie too.

'What about Matt . . . your son's child. I haven't come to beg for myself or my mother. But James is your grandchild. Your blood, Mr Craig. Are you prepared to see him go without too?'

The man took a step forward, glowering. 'Don't be impertinent. You inveigle your way into my home, assume upon our . . .'

'I'm being perfectly pertinent, Mr Craig,' she said

sharply. Her tone sounded far older than her years. The man blinked, then regained his composure, looking as though he loathed having to do so before an obviously inferior being, a child, and a female at that.

'Young lady, I see no reason why I should answer you. But I will enlighten you to this extent. Yes, we have considered James. As our grandchild, he will be provided for. He is to remain at his present school, his fees paid by myself. I gather he's a bright lad. We will arrange for his eventual entry to university, and a generous sum of money will be put in trust for when he comes of age. I can assure you, young lady, that he'll never go without. But if your mother thinks for an instant to benefit from our generosity in any way . . .'

'We don't need your *charity,* Mr Craig.' Sara lifted her head, bringing her height up another inch.

Why couldn't they have set out their intentions in their letter, thereby saving her this journey and the degradation of having to face them? How she hated them both. Her clear blue eyes, brittle and bitter, stared unwaveringly into the man's faded blue ones.

'We wouldn't for an instant dream of asking you for one penny. I know how shabbily you treated my mother, as though she were dirt beneath your feet. But I see now that we have nothing to be ashamed of. All I came for was to see that my brother – my half-brother, your grandchild – be given what is only his right. Now I have had that assurance from you, I feel better. We won't trouble you again.'

'My dear . . .' As Sara turned to go, Mrs Craig rose stiffly. Sara paused as the woman came towards her. She was already unfastening the mourning brooch, skeletal fingers protruding from the black lace knuckle-length gloves, fumbling. Reaching Sara, she pressed the brooch into her unexpecting hand.

'Take this, child. It will help pay your fare and a little beside.'

Sara started back as though the pin had jabbed into her flesh. 'I don't want your brooch!'

'Merely something to make amends . . .'

'There's nothing to make amends for,' Sara hissed. 'Making amends is too late. I won't tell my mother that I came here.' She raised her voice to reach the ears of an embarrassed Mr Henry Craig. 'She would feel so belittled, never having asked anything of you yourself.'

With that she swung away from them and strode out into the hall, the butler hardly given time to reach the door before her as she snatched her hat and coat from the waiting housemaid.

In Regent Street, Annie and Clara relaxed over light refreshments in a busy little teashop to recover their strength before continuing their shopping expedition.

One Saturday in the month was put aside for this, but this particular spree was special. They were looking for new dresses, ready for summer, to replace the black. Six months had passed since losing Matthew, long enough for a brother-in-law. They would still have to wear sombre colours, of course, making it more difficult, and so far neither had seen quite what they liked. But given another hour or so . . .

Amid the clatter of cutlery and the drone of conversation around them, Annie cut her toasted teacake into quarters with vicious strokes of her knife.

'I still think it's a imposition,' she said, picking up on the debate that had been going on intermittently most of that morning.

Clara watched her sister thrust a piece of teacake into her mouth as though wishing it nothing but harm. She nibbled her own guiltily. She was putting on far too much weight, and envied Annie her figure. Even if a little scrawny, it did lend itself to this year's tubular gowns. Clara, with her plump hips, was having problems. She abhorred the new sleek style, even if she did love the gigantic hats that accompanied it, and looked upon 1910 as being a most unpromising year for her as far as fashion went.

'I suppose it is a bit of an imposition,' she said, deliberating over the teacake. 'But I suppose they've got to live somewhere. I can't imagine what the poor things would do otherwise.'

'Poor things!' scoffed Annie, chewing avidly. 'Harriet hasn't done so badly for herself in the past.'

'I know, but that was the past. I feel sorry for them. What can she do, poor thing . . . Yes, Annie – poor thing. And Sara too. That child hasn't done anyone any harm. She looks so pale and far from well, honestly. I think she really loved her stepfather. You wouldn't wish them out on the street, would you, Annie?'

'Of course not,' Annie conceded. 'What I mean is, what are they going to live on? There's two of them, remember.

Neither of them bringing in any money. Harriet's got less now than she had when Will died. At least she had a place then, and the money he left. Now she expects Mum to keep her, and Mum like a fool, will.' Annie reached for her teacup to wash down the teacake.

Clara chewed on her lip. 'She'd do the same for us. But I did hear . . .'

Annie's cup hit the saucer hard. 'Don't you see? It'll be *our* money Mum'll be using to keep them. Using up what she gets from the profits of Dad's business.'

'Yes, but as I was going to say, I heard . . .'

'And when it's nearly all gone on keeping those two, there'll be precious little left for us when Mum dies.'

Clara's face dropped in horror. 'Don't talk like that about Mum.'

Annie's face remained obdurate. 'We have to face it, Clara. She's not getting any younger, and she had that stroke. She could have another one any time. Personally I can't see her making old bones.'

'How can you talk so callously?' Clara cried, but Annie swept on remorselessly.

'We've got to face facts, Clara. The fact is, Mum'll be using up something like half her weekly income on those two. It won't go back into savings as it should. When Mum goes, when it comes to sharing what's left – *three ways*, I might add, because Harriet will expect her share, and blow the fact that she'd have already had hers while Mum was alive – we'll be getting only a fraction of what we should get. Those are the facts, Clara, callous or not.'

Clara, still eager to finish what she had been trying to

say, gave a compliant nod. 'I do know what you mean, but I heard that Sara . . .'

'And another thing. I can't see how Mum's going to keep up with looking after them. You know Harriet still drinks, despite all that's happened. She does it in secret, but I know. Medicine indeed! That costs money. And then there's Jamie's schooling and Sara's going to college in September. Where's the money coming from, I ask you? Where's . . .'

If Clara had been standing, she would have stamped her foot. 'Will you let me finish what I'm trying to say? I've heard that Matthew's parents are going to pay for Jamie's education. And Sara won't be going on to college. She's decided not to.'

'But she won her scholarship. Got top marks in nearly everything.'

'I know. But she says she wants to go out to work instead.'

'Work!'

Clara had forgotten about her teacake. 'I think it's an utter waste of a clever brain. And there are suffragettes trying to make us more conscious of our talents and use them. She says she wants to help pay her way. But doesn't it seem a shame, her wasting all that education like that?'

'Well, I never!' Temporarily overcome by the enormity of her niece's sacrifice, Annie nevertheless quickly regained her former acidity. 'What can a girl of sixteen expect to earn? It'll be no more than a drop in the ocean to what Mum'll be asked to fork out.'

'It does prove she's trying,' Clara offered.

But Annie merely shrugged, popped the last of her teacake into her mouth, wiped her fingers delicately on her napkin, and said, 'Huh!'

Two letters had arrived for her the previous day. Sara gazed again at the results of her matriculation exam: she had got top marks in almost everything. She felt no pride in it, only a deep sadness that Matthew wasn't there to share that pride with her. Without him it meant nothing and she had no intention of taking up the place offered her.

Great-Aunt Sarah had praised her for her heroic sacrifice, but it had been no sacrifice at all. Even if they could have afforded the fees – certainly out of the question now – of the college for young ladies which the covering letter named, she couldn't have brought herself to go. She had too much on her mind to think of studying.

By the next week, their lovely home in Victoria Park Road would be theirs no longer. Oddly enough, Sara felt she couldn't have cared less, so forlorn did the place seem now. In a way, she was almost glad to see the back of it.

The bank had taken everything. Mr David Symonds had pleaded for them to be allowed six months' grace to seek other accommodation, and the bank had finally agreed. But with no money it had been impossible to find anything decent, and it had been Gran's generous gesture of open-ing her home to them that, in Sara's opinion, had only just saved her mother from being committed to a mental asylum. She'd never seen anyone go so rapidly downhill. Frightened by her mother's frail grip on reality, she had vowed to do all she possibly could to help pay for at least some of their keep. College was definitely not included in those ideas.

Laying the letter aside, she picked up the other that had arrived with it, and reread this one with satisfaction. It was to grant her an interview for the position of junior stenographer with a small City newspaper on a four-week trial. It stated that they did not normally engage young ladies, since the newspaper business was a harsh environment, but being very impressed by what she had written about herself and her previous experience on a journal, they would take a chance on her, purely as a form of experiment, and that she was to bear this very much in mind were she to be accepted.

Dated 14 April 1910, the letter made Sara smile. Today was the fourteenth – Thursday. Whoever had misdated it didn't deserve his job, that was certain, and if she couldn't do better than this, then she wasn't worthy of her sex. Experiment indeed! She would show them what a woman was capable of, and vowed to guard always against such mistakes that would let her down – should she get the job, of course.

Slowly she refolded the letter with its incorrect date, returned it to its envelope, then in an impetuous gesture of hope, pressed it to her lips. She knew implicitly that she'd get this job. Today, the fourteenth of April, was her birthday. It had to be a good omen.

# Chapter Twenty-four

The interview had been for the sixth of May, but with the death of King Edward, it was hurriedly postponed to the following Friday.

Sara's nervousness had been heightened by having to wait another week, and when it came to presenting herself at the offices of the *London Graphic*, she was a mass of nerves. To see her, however, no one would have suspected. What they saw as she passed through the noisy, cluttered newsroom behind her elderly interviewer was a tall, shapely young woman with a steady blue gaze and a certain carriage that drew all eyes – certainly the narrow hazel ones of the News Editor as he moved among the half dozen littered desks, checking copy to go to press.

The way she held herself, so erect, was enough to distract him for a few begrudging moments to follow her progress across the office in the wake of that old dodderer, Alf Berryman, who usually conducted most of the lesser interviews.

Becoming aware she was being watched, the young woman turned her head towards him and met his gaze for a fraction of a second before turning back to continue after Berryman's corpulent figure. In that fraction of a second, Jonathan Ward noted a smooth, unruffled, frigid expression, lips composed, chin firm; and deduced a woman self-assured and high-minded – not appealing in a female, much less so in one so young.

At twenty-five he wasn't yet married or even courting; had no intention of doing so for many years yet, if ever. He was married to his job. In love with it. Girls with their skittish demands and their emotional views, if they ever had any, were nothing but a liability.

He turned back to what he had been doing. By the time he looked up again, the young woman was seated at a desk in one of the small side offices. Berryman, seated opposite her, grinning all over his broad face, hadn't even thought to close the door – too bowled over by the obvious charms sitting there in front of him, stupid old fool.

He was going soft in the brain, Berryman. Probably wouldn't even think to test her capabilities, if any, before bumbling off to recommend her to Fred Mackenzie, the Chief Editor. It had been Berryman's suggestion in the first place to try out female staff, which came cheaper. Silly suggestion. Cheap or not, it would never work.

Ward's wide lips beneath a dark, narrow moustache twisted in a sardonic grin. It was time Berryman retired. Shrugging broad shoulders, he returned to checking copy, but could not help yielding to a temptation to one glance through the open door, to where the young woman was talking, Berryman's broad bald head tilting up and down to her every word all the while, like one of those nodding Buddhas.

*

'I start next week – general typing.' She felt no enthusiasm, was incapable of much feeling since Matthew's death. It was as though she merely floated on the surface of things, much as driftwood might on an oily sea. Her Great-Aunt Sarah regarded her quizzically.

'You don't seem terribly pleased over it. What're they paying you? Well short of what they'd be paying a man, I'll be bound.'

Sara laid her hat and gloves on the tiny table in the narrow hall. They had moved here to her grandmother's house in Approach Road over the weekend, with the minimum of fuss, there being little to bring with them since the house and its contents had gone to pay Matthew's debts.

She followed her great-aunt into the parlour over-looking the street. 'Six shillings a week. Something of a comedown, I suppose, after all I learned with Matth . . .' Sara swallowed, still unable to utter his name without her throat tightening up – enough almost to strangle her. 'After my being used to the journal,' she rephrased.

Grandmother was sitting on an upright chair, unable to cope with lower easy chairs since her stroke had made it hard to rise without assistance. She smiled tremulously at her granddaughter, her voice hoarse with pride. 'I think you have done remarkably, Sara, being even taken on – a woman. So brave. But with all those men, are you sure you know what you're doing, dear?'

'It's what I wanted.' Sara sat near the window and stared down into the sunlit street. She was exhausted. The newsroom had been like a madhouse, with everyone talking at once – not like the sedate offices of the *Freewoman*. And

that man watching her – it had made her uneasy in case
she made a fool of herself. Arrogant man, he hadn't even
acknowledged her when she looked straight at him. Why
should she have been first to smile, submissively? She'd
need to be on her toes at all times to prove herself, if only
to him. Then she wondered why she cared.

'Well, I'm glad they thought you good enough,' Great-
Aunt Sarah was saying in her sharp way. 'Perhaps it'll
make your mother feel a little better about it all – more
able to face the world again.'

'Where is she?'

'In her room, having a little sleep,' Mary said quietly.

'But it's mid-morning. I thought she would be down
here.'

Sarah gave a humph sound, but Mary's smooth, stroke-
warped face twisted even more in a maternal smile. 'Your
poor dear mother. It will take her years to get over her loss
– double loss – losing her husband and then everything he
had. She was never a strong girl.'

'She hasn't been . . .' Sara wanted to ask if her mother
had been drinking, but thought better of it.

It had become steadily worse these last months. Ellen
– who had stayed on a tiny wage long after the other staff
had been dismissed until finally she had to go, she too
needing to live – would come down from Mother's room,
her plain face as long as a horse's, to say, 'Madam's not
feeling herself,' meaning that Mother had probably drunk
half a bottle of brandy and was lying supine on her bed.
To try and manoeuvre her to a more comfortable position
was like handling a rag doll, her body worse than limp.

The smell of alcohol had come to associate itself in Sara's mind with all that was unhealthy, and these days made her nauseous even when not connected with her mother. She had come to dread coming home, especially after Ellen left, tearfully promising to keep in touch, and she had to manage Mother alone.

There were times when her mother, in a drunken stupor, would thrash out at her, arms weaving as she spat hatred; but at other times she would throw them about her neck, hardly knowing who she was, tears streaming down her face as she called Matthew's name, begging Sara to lie down beside her, keep her company until she fell asleep. Sara would steel herself to lie beside the drunken heap, after a while edging herself off the bed to creep away. Sometimes her mother would feel her move and cling convulsively to her in her sleep, preventing her from leaving until much later. Overwhelmed by the brandy fumes, Sara would fight to control her heaving stomach, counting the minutes until she could finally extricate herself.

At times like these, she would stand at the door looking back at her mother and wonder how such a lovely woman could have come to this. Love and pity would flow over her for the wreck life had made, and she would vow to do all she could to bring her mother back to her old self.

Now she looked bleakly at Great-Aunt Sarah, whose stiff face told all.

'I'll pay for whatever she's had put on your account out of my first week's wage,' was all she could say, and received a curt nod.

\*

Working on the *Graphic* was indeed not at all like working on the *Freewoman*. There, in secure and orderly surroundings, Sara had been under Matthew's gentle eye, with him ready to show, guide, back her up.

The eye of Jonathan Ward was neither gentle nor guiding. If he was not ignoring her, he was finding fault. Yet she couldn't understand why. She had always been bright, quick at picking things up. Matthew had found joy in complimenting her on how quickly she fell into anything that was explained to her, and it hadn't just been because he'd been her father – or rather her stepfather. It hadn't been because they'd been so close, two people in need of a loving relationship. She had really been quick to learn. She was still quick to learn.

Even so, her first six months were spent doing nothing more than running about the office, making tea and taking messages. Allowed to do a little filing at the end of that time, she did it without mistakes, neatly and efficiently. She would often become aware of Jonathan Ward – Mr Ward, as she was expected to call him, for all he was only a few years older than her – of his eyes following her as she moved about her duties. Should she turn suddenly to meet his look, he'd glance quickly away and pretend to be doing something else.

It wasn't shyness, that she had already deduced. Jonathan Ward was far from a shy person; was in fact very certain of himself, only too aware of his good looks in her estimation.

She had to admit he was very good-looking: a little taller than herself, relatively broad-shouldered, and narrow-waisted with slender hips that gave him an easy grace as he moved. Graceful movements, yet there was masculinity in his dark, lean visage, in the strong jaw and firm mouth that hinted at a purposefulness of will. A man to turn women's heads, she thought but as she suspected that he knew it, she wasn't prepared to have her head turned by him. Too good-looking for his own good, Great Aunt Sarah would have said. So she spent her time being as formal with him as she could, trying to be as polite as possible without demeaning herself when he found fault, obviously not disposed to having a woman on the *Graphic*, even in her humble capacity.

As time went on, she was occasionally expected to do copying on the great cumbersome typewriter, often from illegible notes the reporters flung at her, everything to be got out at top speed to catch some deadline. She made few mistakes, but when she did, fell under the stinging sarcasm of the News Editor. She came to hate that voice for all its attractive resonant quality; came also to a stubborn resolve to prove herself, to stand up to him no matter what.

She was sure that it was through this determination not to put a foot wrong that she came to the attention of Mr Mackenzie himself. A little short of a year after commencing on the *Graphic*, she found herself standing before the great man's desk in his large, heavily furnished office.

Fred Mackenzie presented a daunting figure. Large-featured, huge-nosed, jut-chinned, with the stature of an elephant and a voice that enveloped the whole office, he sat behind his spacious desk, glared at the slender girl standing there and bellowed, 'Always thought it was a mistake employing a woman. Sit down! I've something to say.'

Five minutes later, Sara emerged somewhat punch-drunk from the interview, Mackenzie's voice still ringing in her ears. Somehow she got herself back to her typewriter and sat down, staring at the ungainly machine. She smiled grimly at the thing. After the effort she'd put in – a year proving herself as good as the men around her . . .

She became aware of someone standing behind her, and swung round to face the slim but well-proportioned figure of Jonathan Ward. His hazel eyes probing, Sara met them challengingly, no longer overawed by him after her meeting with the great Fred Mackenzie.

'No thanks to you,' she said evenly, 'I've been promoted.'

'I knew you'd be,' he muttered. 'I've seen it coming for a long time.'

She stared in disbelief. 'You mean you knew? You approve?'

'No, I don't approve. I think women serve better in the home, not muscling in on a man's world. Like those daft suffragettes who think that getting noticed by causing riots'll get 'em what they want, even though they've called a truce.'

In the autumn of 1910, following Black Friday, the eighteenth of November, when there had been a bloody battle between the police and three hundred women, with more than a hundred and fifty women beaten up, in some cases sexually assaulted, a truce had been called. Now everyone was waiting to see what the government came up with.

Sara looked up at Jonathan with an arid stare, ready to defend her sex.

'Mr Mackenzie told me he has me in mind for something more than just playing little woman,' she said coldly. 'He mentioned sending me out on assignment to see how I do. And I shan't disappoint him.'

Jonathan nodded, exploring his back teeth with his tongue behind closed lips, an action betraying derision.

'Out there,' he said slowly, 'it's another world. A man's world. A newspaperman's world. It's not kind to pretentious young women.'

'I shall manage,' Sara said haughtily, busying herself tidying a stack of foolscap.

She felt rather than saw him grin. 'You're not a suffragette, you know. They've got each other to cling to when it comes to the dirty bits. You'll be on your own. Among men who don't pull their punches. Then, my dear, I can see this young lady dissolving in a flood of indignant female tears. That won't get you anywhere either.'

Sara stopped tidying and turned squarely to face him, head up, blue eyes dry as the Sahara, cold as Siberia.

'I've never cried in my life.'

'Never?' The grin hadn't changed.

'The father I loved with all my heart . . . I didn't cry at his graveside. I can't cry.'

There were no tears even now at the thought of that beloved, gentle man, lost to her forever. Her throat clenching up strangled any tear there might have been. 'I shall never cry as long as I live.'

For a moment, Jonathan looked as though he was about to make some acid retort, but instead he frowned, then walked away, leaving her staring narrowly after him, unbowed by Jonathan Ward's opinion of women.

In fact she suspected him of being secretly cowed by them. For all his pretended arrogance, watching him in his more unguarded moments, she was sure it was more pretence than anything.

There were times when, lost in thought over something he was writing, those tight cynical lips softening a little, he promoted in her a tiny ripple of tenderness, a sensation she immediately thrust away as she remembered Matthew, his love, his gentleness towards her, all women. Jonathan was never gentle, outwardly. Yet there were times . . .

It was December. She had been with the paper for eighteen months, and felt now that she belonged. In just over four months she would be eighteen, a young women in possession of herself, knowing from the way her male colleagues glanced at her that she could turn the head of every one of them if she so wished, but at the same time could take care of herself with a look should any of them overstep the boundary.

Mackenzie now treated her like some novelty prize; Jonathan still with a deal of scepticism, though she was sure he'd been instrumental in getting her promotion – perhaps if only to see how she would cope, even to watch her squirm. She had scotched his cynicism by coping very well these last six months, without a single noticeable wriggle for his satisfaction. Inside she squirmed a great deal, often thinking she must have been mad to want to tackle a man's world head on.

Last July she had again stood in Mackenzie's office, trying not to show how she quaked in her shoes, to hear him demand if she was ready to put her money where her mouth was.

'You've been harping enough about showing us what you can do.' His words thundering at her had made her blink, wondering how her most secret wish had got to his ears. 'So I'm giving you a chance to prove it. I'm sending you out on an assignment. Let's see how you cope.'

It was a challenge – not a show of faith in her as an asset to the paper, more a gauntlet thrown down for her to pick up. The gleam in Mackenzie's large faded blue eyes seemed to imply that he knew she would never dare to rise to it.

The same sentiment had been mirrored in Jonathan's narrow hazel eyes as he stood beside her later, making her suspect that he and Mackenzie had been in cahoots with each other. She had felt angry, and vowed never to let herself down as she went off on that very first assignment.

Fortunately it was a gentle one – they had spared her that much – covering a small charity garden fete given near St Pancras by a female group of Women's Enfranchise sympathisers. Perhaps Mackenzie and Jonathan had thought it was going too far to throw her in the deep end, though she'd felt no gratitude for that, only a fierce determination to win her spurs. She'd give them gauntlet!

And she had; bringing back a well-constructed, lively story that made Mackenzie smile, though she didn't know that, since he did it behind the closed door of his office. She only knew that he began regularly to send her to cover similar gentle and feminine stories. In this way, her taste for reporting had grown, and her ambitions along with it.

Jonathan often eyed her with a look she couldn't quite define. Admiration? Frustration? She couldn't tell from those eyes of his, though the lips, twisting slightly as his tongue explored his strong molars in that familiar cynical habit of his, betrayed his thoughts on the woman who dared to consider herself on a par with the men she worked with. Yet lately she had felt that he was planning something for her.

She found out just what he was planning five days after her eighteenth birthday. Her six months of successfully covering one story after another, proving that women weren't such a liability as men imagined, had encouraged her employers to take on two more women, one for mundane filing, the other for general running about after the male staff. Sara felt sorry for them; inwardly seethed that they should be looked upon as not bright enough for anything better; felt humiliated on their behalf; yet could not voice her feelings lest her own – for a female – exalted position be put at risk. She seethed even more when coming in at seven that Monday morning, she found a note on her desk.

'Sara. Liverpool Street station. Fast. Everyone here otherwise occupied. Take a cab. Ron Duffy too for photos. Someone's just reported trouble there. Knives used. Be quick. See what you can get.'

*

The note was in Jonathan's scrawled handwriting, though there was no sign of the man himself. Her first thought was of a joke on her. To throw her into the bear pit – a woman of tender years asked to jostle with seasoned male reporters – it had to be a joke. But she could not prove it, so she snatched up the note and found Duffy, a small, wiry man who took nothing as a joke, who grabbed for his camera and paraphernalia and ran out to find a taxi.

Sara's stomach was churning as they rattled towards Liverpool Street. It wasn't so much what she expected to find as the scramble of male reporters who would elbow her, a mere woman, out of the way in their eagerness to get photos, a story, be first back to their paper. She thought of suffragettes who'd been thus manhandled, the gentle sex having no protection. She could get a smack in the face as easily as they had, and there would be no one to support her, as Jonathan had once pointed out.

'I'll keep an eye on yer,' Duffy said, noting her white lips. He too had been a little shocked by Jonathan Ward's callous order.

Sara smiled her thanks, but felt small comfort. Once in the fray to get pictures, Duffy would forget her. He had his job to do.

It was the scene she'd expected. After she had explained herself to the police, ignoring their surprise, she and Duffy hurried down the iron steps to the noisy, smoke-blackened terminus with its stink of soot and oil, and across the stone concourse area towards the knot of gawping onlookers whom more police were persuading to keep their distance.

Elbowing her way through, she managed to reach the scene of the earlier affray, or rather a sea of reporters' backs. Coats tight across shoulders, they jostled for position, notebooks and pencils at the ready, cameras aimed, smoke from their flash-pans already rising in small white puffs above the throng, while police called for them to keep their distance from the two covered bodies, the Black Maria already having borne off the survivors of the fight.

Duffy was already up front – as a small man, he was able to wriggle his way through – and Sara began shouldering her way between two reporters.

''Ere, watchit!' One turned, saw her notebook and gave a loud laugh, assignment forgotten for the moment. 'Cripes, lady! Who d'yer think you are? George Bleedin' Bernard Shaw! Sod orf with yer!'

Sara ignored him, continued to edge forward. A painful dig in the ribs stopped her, making her gasp. A voice hissed in her ear: 'Bugger off, yer stupid bitch! No place fer you 'ere.'

Sara glared, then turned back to the two unevenly bulging sheets she could now see four feet from her. A hard thump caught her between the shoulder blades. ''Ere what I say? Or d'yer wanna get 'urt?'

What she would have retorted, she didn't know. In that second one worthy leaped forward to yank a sheet down enough to expose the face of one victim. Sara felt a shock wave strike through her at the sight of a pugilistic face gashed from receding hairline to heavy unshaven jaw, neck slit half across, blood surrounding the bullet head like a halo, the rest of the face, with its flattened nose, the colour of putty.

Her first instinct was to fight her way out, stomach heaving. Then she remembered why she was here. Duffy was already taking a picture as police pounced on the one who had yanked away the sheet. Duffy's camera turned on the ensuing struggle between police and reporter. A baton descending upon the man's shoulder as he battled with them did no damage, but a spectacular photograph was caught by Duffy.

Sara took it all in that second as calm was restored. She had her story; different, she hoped, to the rest of those around. Her hat had been knocked sideways, her foot trodden on, the dig and the punch she had received still hurt a little, but she didn't care.

'Who does he work for?' she demanded of a man next to her.

'*Daily Echo.*' The man, now uninterested in interfering women, swore angrily. 'Bloody coppers! No regard fer our rights.'

Sara called to her cameraman. 'Carry on here, Duffy!'

He looked up, bowler on the back of his head. 'Where you going?' But Sara was already on her way.

The taxi chugging towards the *Graphic* made her fume. The hansom cabs of old would have been far faster and more nimble, but they had gone in favour of the combustion engine.

The newsroom was in uproar, but blind and deaf to all but her story – 'Police Attack on Reporter' – she hurried to her desk in the corner. Eyes on the paper she fed into the clanking typing machine, not even pausing to take off her hat, she began typing furiously.

Jonathan stood at her shoulder, made her jump. 'You can't use that.'

She turned to do battle. 'Why not? It's a good story.'

'Maybe it is.' His voice held a grudging admiration. 'But you can't use it. Can't have a down on policemen doing their job.'

'But they beat him – one of our people. For nothing.'

'Defending themselves. No, my girl, you think again.'

Sara's lips tightened. 'But this is . . .'

'Sorry.' He was smiling. 'Scrap it. Anyway, we've a damned-sight-hotter story than that you are messing about with.'

Her blue eyes glared. An editor was free to publish or not to publish. Jonathan was deliberately blocking her – he had sent her out only to kill the story she'd brought back. Quite deliberately. She made to protest, but he cut her short.

'Haven't you even noticed what's going on here?'

No, she hadn't noticed. Now she did. From the relatively relaxed newsroom she'd left earlier – as far as any newsroom could ever be relaxed, the work from the night staff rolling through the rumbling printing presses downstairs – everyone was now rushing back and forth, bending over copy, frantically cutting, pasting, messenger boys running in from the wire room and out again. Even Mackenzie, usually in his office, had come up from the machine room to move about between the desks, impatient, urging everyone to greater speed. How could she not have noticed?

The story, coming moments before Sara's return, was still sending shock waves not only around this office but no doubt every newsroom in the country. She sat stunned as Jonathan relayed the news to her that the great new unsinkable *Titanic*, pride of the nation, departed a week previously from Southampton on her maiden voyage, had sunk. The cause was said to have been a collision with an iceberg off Newfoundland. It was not known how many lives were lost, but the huge liner was reported to have gone down within an hour – not many would have got off a ship that size in that time. In the face of what was a national disaster, what price Sara's bit of a story? All this Jonathan said in a gabble before turning away with Mr Mackenzie signalling urgently to him.

Sara had become aware of the silence of the building itself. At this time of day it was usually reverberating from end to end to the rumble of the printing presses churning out the morning edition down in the machine room. But all was still. The print run had been stopped halfway through. An expensive business unless absolutely imperative, the front page had been scrapped to accommodate this fresh and terrible news – and every newspaper in the country was stopping its presses for the same reason.

But why hadn't Jonathan told her immediately, instead of taunting her? Anyway, there would be room somewhere for her now piffling snippet of news. Disaster or no, the paper had to be filled with other news, trivial, banal; even if the front page was being frantically redrawn, reassembled, the wire-room lads bringing ever more detailed intelligence as it came through, morse-coded.

Angrily, she tore the sheet from the typewriter and threw it after his retreating figure. 'Here, scrap it! See if I care!'

His low chuckle floated back, but he didn't turn round, merely shouted for a lad trying to catch his breath to 'move himself!'

Sara turned back to her typewriter. She was sure now why he had sent her to cover that story. To teach her a lesson. To see how she would weather the vile language spat at her, the digs in the ribs, men delighting in hurting and humiliating a woman. It must be like that for suffragettes, at the mercy of men. They had to be admired, the way they fought, entirely voluntarily, against a world men had created for them.

That was it – voluntarily. Jonathan had ordered her into this; had hoped perhaps that she would cry so he could gloat and ask, *ready to give up*? Taking his male superiority out on her. Well, she'd give him no such satisfaction. She hadn't cried; hadn't turned away in horror; had stood up to the behaviour of her fellow reporters. From now on, she would go into the fray and dare them to do their worst. She had become a proper reporter, a good one, and to bloody hell with Jonathan Ward and his view of women. As far as she was concerned, he was the loser, not her.

The rest of her thoughts were swept away as she was pulled into the fervour of the morning's exciting, terrible news, Mr Mackenzie himself tossing a scribbled note for her to rush down to the waiting compositors to be fitted into their ever-lengthening sticks.

# Chapter Twenty-five

From the window of his lodgings Jonathan Ward stared down at the street below. A damp November morning. Nothing was stirring down there – everyone would still be in bed, families reading papers, kids fretting.

He hated Sundays – having to wake up alone after a Saturday night binge with colleagues, the whole day stretching in front of him, wondering what to do with himself as he waited for a muzzy headache to disperse.

There was no one to talk to, share his thoughts with. There was that girl he'd brought home last night, of course. Still in bed. But soon she would go – he wouldn't want her around anyway – leaving him alone again. At times like these, he wished he had someone – a real partner. Christ, he was good-looking enough to get the girls, but none of them had any depth, any brains. Those that had bored the shirt off you, going on about how much they knew. Women were a bloody trial. One was better off without them.

He moved from the window to the washbasin and poured cold water from the jug. It would revive him. Then what? Shove Emmy, Ella, or whatever her name was, out of his bed, tell her to get dressed and go. And then? Roam about his rooms, he supposed. Read through his stack of

Sunday newspapers. Study them. That would take up most of the morning, maybe a little longer, as it always did, spinning out the time. And after that?

He could take a bus and go home for the afternoon. That thought occurred to him briefly, then was immediately dismissed. He had a home. Two brothers at university. An older sister married, living up north with her business husband and two small toddlers. His father and mother lived their stately lives alone now, in Finchley. Father had wanted him to be a doctor like himself – in Harley Street – and had frowned on his chosen profession – Fleet Street. No, he wouldn't go home. Better be bored here than bored sick there.

The cold water cleared his head. He dried his hands and face on a rough towel. He'd have to start getting dressed, and prod that girl out of his bed. He couldn't even recall bringing her home, but was sure he'd fallen asleep the moment he'd hit the pillow.

He thought suddenly of Sara. Not that she could ever compare to the painted thing in his bedroom, but for some strange reason he found himself wondering what she would be doing at this moment.

He pictured her rising from bed, elegant body, near black hair dishevelled from contact with her pillow, those startling blue eyes blinking at the new day, dreary as it was. She'd stretch her limbs, languidly . . . Jonathan cut short the thought. God, he was going soft.

He threw the towel back on to the washstand and went across to the bed to rouse Ella, Emmy, or whatever her name was. He needed his rooms to himself today.

*

Saturday had been a beast of a day. Sunday looked to be no different. Harriet was having one of her bad times. She still had them from time to time. The cold November damp outside didn't help.

She wasn't drunk. She drank hardly at all now, money being so short, and she wasn't prepared to sponge off her benefactors. Even Sara had to grant her that, her face impassive whenever she came home from work and went up to see her.

'You should try to go downstairs a little more often.'

This was her daughter's answer to a broken heart. The girl had no feelings. *She* hadn't lost a husband – two husbands – with no one to show her any affection or care if she died of grief. Sara certainly didn't care. Cold, that was what she was. No emotion.

Even when Matthew had died – poor dear Matthew – Sara hadn't shed a tear. Not one iota of regret or remorse. But hide her soul though she might, there was no hiding what had been going on between her and Matthew; evil, underhanded creature that she was. She had been the cause of Matthew's death. Wicked, like her father. She'd never be able to forgive Sara for what she had done, yet now she must rely on her for money. The knowledge made Harriet cringe, hating to be forced to debase herself so in order to live.

If Jamie were here, he would have comforted her, but he was away at boarding school, paid for by his grandfather. Were he home and Sara away, life would be so much better. Harriet gave a tremulous sigh.

She knew she should get up. But downstairs she would

be taken for granted, unfeelingly assumed to be recovered. If she stayed up here, at least that fact would be noticed. Despairing of her, Mary and Sarah would often instruct Mrs Thompson, who cooked and cleaned for them, not to indulge Harriet by taking meals up to her. This would actually bring her more to their notice than if she had fought her misery and made the effort to appear. On the rare occasions that she made it downstairs, no one ever thanked her for doing so.

In the room she'd had as a child, Harriet lay on her bed, her face turned up to the ceiling. What had once been a much loved room had become a symbol of what she'd been reduced to, a constant reminder of all that had happened to her.

She had lost a husband she'd loved so much . . . Oh yes, loved, even though he had said she didn't, running out to leave her all alone and penniless, with only the clothes she stood in, forced to beg for this and that, to rely on Sara's wage for every little thing, subservient to the very daughter who had widowed her, and whom she detested. It was cruel.

A tear slithered from under her lashes. Without her medicine, she felt hungry. She would have to get up and go downstairs, sit with the others and pretend she was getting over her loss. But her loss would be with her to her dying day.

She thought of Will. So long ago now. Yet everything that had happened that terrible day was still so clear. Nightmares that had slowly diminished in her marriage to Matthew had returned since his death. It was her marriage to Matthew that now seemed dreamlike – the one to Will only too real.

She'd had a bad dream the night before, thinking him about to burst into her bedroom. She had come to her senses with a start in the very act of pushing him backwards down the stairs. It reminded her that she was getting older, must one day die, and she was petrified at what would happen to her when that time came. Would Will be waiting? Was that what Hell was: meeting someone or something you feared and loathed most in life, to spend eternity bound to that person or thing?

Harriet shuddered. She needed desperately to shut out the ghastly certainty. A sip of her medicine would help. But to have to ask Mum or Aunt Sarah to give her money to buy some – it was unthinkable. And pride wouldn't let her beg Sara to allow her an advance out of her wages. Instead she must lie here and suffer, alone. At times she was so terrified at being alone. This looked like being one of those times and she couldn't, dared not, stay up here alone, not today.

Slowly, Harriet got up, washed her face and with trembling hands tidied her hair as best she could, trying to ignore the grey streaks, then went carefully downstairs to present herself. If only Jamie were here.

James gazed down into the quad from the dormitory. It was Sunday. A few boys were wandering around, but most of those who hadn't gone home this weekend were somewhere inside the building out of the sharp January wind.

He hated weekends – wished he could be at his grand-parents' – that lovely rambling house where he even had his own bedroom for when he stayed. But he couldn't have gone there this weekend, having only just come back from spending Christmas and New Year with them.

He could have gone to see Mother, perhaps. It wasn't all that far away. But he hated her slobbering over him as though he was a little boy instead of sixteen this year. 'Are they treating you well enough at school, Jamie dear?' He wished she would learn to call him James. If his chums at school could hear, he'd be a laughing stock.

Not that he had many chums. They always seemed to shy away, leaving him to find new chums – jealous, probably, because the moment he began to tell them about how his grandparents doted on him and how he could get anything he wanted from them, they seemed to lose interest. The same thing happened when he asked anyone for a loan to tide him over. Boys were always borrowing from each other, but somehow no one obliged him.

He never told those at home how he'd hated school: the bullying in his first and second year, having to fag for the sixth formers. Now almost a sixth former himself, tall and gangling, he too could bully, demand errands. But he had no real friends to boast to. Lessons were different. He always did well, and his tutors were lavish in their praise. It was only at weekends that he felt lonely. He was glad when Monday came and he could shine.

Sara longed for Monday. At work she could be herself, forget who she had to be at home: the child dictated to by her mother's whims, living on her grandmother's charity, watching her manners in someone else's house – it was still someone else's house even after a year living there. She was aware of being a guest, and as such felt she had always to be on her best behaviour. Oh, how she longed for Monday, to be herself.

March 1913: only a month to go before she'd be nineteen. A journalist, one of only a handful in the country. Some newspapers were employing women, but mostly in mundane roles – typewriting, filing and general duties – all single ladies; once married they were dismissed. At least in one small way the suffragettes were reaping some harvest.

Sara had interviewed some of those suffragettes; had heard so many tales of their exploits: their daring bombing of church property, of railway stations, empty houses; the price they paid for it with their imprisonment, going on hunger strike and enduring forced feeding. At times she almost felt herself to be one of them, having to endure the snubs and taunts of men whose world she had invaded.

No longer assigned to little charity fetes, she had to jostle with other reporters, determined not to be pushed aside by them. All in all she felt she stood up well; she even enjoyed the fray, the proving of herself, for all the bruised arms and crushed hats she sometimes collected on the way to getting a story.

What did irk her was that she was never once rewarded with a byline of her own for all her pains. A woman, she wasn't considered even a tiddler in the small pond of the *Graphic,* her name being kept strictly off her stories. Sometimes, indignant after losing a battle to have her name shown and being told it wasn't good for the paper, she wondered if she might not be better appreciated in some other, more forward-looking newspaper; once or twice she was on the verge of handing in her notice and taking that chance. Yet something always stopped her. She wasn't sure what. Not lack of courage, she knew that, and she told herself that it had no bearing on Jonathan, though a small voice would come back that it had everything to do with him, that working on another paper without him around would somehow not be the same.

Thursday, seven in the morning: the newsroom was already buzzing, day staff taking over from night staff, alive with everyone building up to the next edition. Involved within minutes of arrival, Sara forgot that today was her nineteenth birthday, and so was taken by surprise when Jonathan came over and said casually, 'I take it you're not doing anything special this evening? Your birthday, isn't it?'

She shrugged, unoffended by what she saw as one of his vaguely taunting remarks. 'If you mean am I celebrating it, I never celebrate people's birthdays. Why should I want to bother with mine?'

Engaged in scanning a rival paper for something which might be competing with the *Graphic*, rustling through the broad sheets, he didn't look up. 'Thought some of us might take you out for dinner.'

'Some of us?' She stared, halfway through pulling together the two parts of a report she was typing up.

'Us – me – a few of us.'

'You?'

He straightened, hazel eyes regarding her quizzically. His steady, undaunted gaze could quell most people, even his superiors, but it did not quell Sara.

The regard she felt for him, part grudging attraction and part lurking respect, always with an ever-present sense of provocation, made her determined not to bow to his natural dominance, suspecting that he in turn respected her ability to stand up to him. She took in the brown, slightly wavy hair that refused to acknowledge restrictions of brilliantine to keep it combed flat, waywardly finding its own parting; the smooth, slightly sallow cheeks; the thin straight nose; the way the well-cut moustache gave a downward sardonic curve to the lips. Her own lips took a cynically curving upward path.

'You mean *you* want to go with us?'

The hazel eyes glowed. 'How many more questions? Just say yes.'

Stunned, she agreed, saw him nod tersely. 'Wear something deserving of a bottle of champagne. I'll pick you up in a taxicab at eight-thirty.'

No more was said. She pushed away the feeling that the invitation might not be genuine, that later he might call it off, saying his plans had changed. But as she left at the end of her day and he called after her, 'Eight-thirty, then,' she had to go along with it, or look foolish doubting him and not being ready.

She said little to anyone at home. In a biscuit-coloured evening dress that emphasised her dark hair, the narrow tube-shaped skirt and small cape suiting her tall, slim figure, she caught her mother's querying, accusing gaze as she passed the open bedroom door.

'You never said you were going out?'

She paused and looked at the small sad face regarding her from the dressing table. 'It's a birthday celebration.' Did she see her mother shudder?

'Yes,' came the soft, tremulous voice, as though the woman's mind was miles away. 'Nineteen years ago – can I ever forget the day you were born?'

'I thought you had.'

She hadn't meant it to sound so embittered. The expression in her mother's grey eyes seemed to be wandering on another plane.

'No, I never will.'

It was a most pleasant evening. Surprising, too. Taken to the Waldorf Restaurant off the Strand, a woman among four men – Jonathan, Wilfred Saunders, a sub-editor, Alf Peters, a reporter like herself, and Duffy – Sara found herself wined and dined and danced with.

Jonathan didn't dance, keeping somewhat aloof, as often he did, but as a surprise birthday cake was brought in halfway through the evening, the orchestra playing a celebratory tune, she thought she saw a tempering in that brittle gaze of his; felt her heart flip a little, surprised that it should.

He was a different person. Indeed, all evening there had been no sarcasm. There was even a certain gentleness to his smile that made him look far more handsome than in their workplace, with its ever-present haste and his ever-present cynicism, ever allowed her to see. The feeling he promoted in her now, she curbed swiftly, intuitively trying not to examine the reason.

Bringing her home in a taxicab, he was quiet and so was she. As the vehicle drew up, he smiled at her suddenly. 'I hope you've had a good time, Sara.'

Taken off guard, she began, 'I've had a wonderful time,' and at that moment became aware that he was leaning towards her.

Unsure how to respond, she thought his face, unguarded as it was tonight, was as near handsome as anyone's could be; but was aware too that apart from knowing him at work, she really knew nothing of him. He never spoke about himself, his life, his family if he had one. She saw in him the kind of person who needed to be private, and put it down to his being one of those born with a mistrusting nature, or maybe, as she herself had been, born into mistrust with much of it rubbing off. Whatever, she had realised a long time ago that they were of a kind, salt and salt; as such the one could never dissolve into the other but, as she saw it, would forever rub grain against grain.

Now, this evening, here was a different side of him. Sara's head reeled. Was he about to kiss her? Did she want that? Long ago, she'd made a vow. So strong had it been then. How strong was it now? Even as she made ready to receive the kiss she knew was on his lips, the vow made as Matthew's coffin sank to its resting place, descending like a shield of steel; made her stiffen, move back from him.

Her eyes focusing sharply, she saw his expression, the

look of someone whose face had been slapped. As though in a single movement, he leaned back and with a stiff smile, said slowly, 'I'll see you in the morning, Sara.'

'Yes, see you then,' she echoed, angry with herself, angry with him for not pursuing. 'Thank you for a very nice evening.'

'You're welcome,' came the formal reply as she let herself out.

It was as though that night had never been. Jonathan went back to his old self again, a little quieter maybe, avoiding her. She was her usual cold, efficient self; also quiet, subdued. He wouldn't know the ache she felt for what could have been. And yet she couldn't break those links she had forged for herself at Matthew's graveside, links too well made to break, even if she'd wanted to.

So went the year. There was no offer from Jonathan of a birthday dinner on her twentieth. No opportunity ever again to be as close to him as she had been, or almost been, that evening the previous year.

James was to go to Oxford next year. Henry Craig had been as good as his word, deciding on Saint Edmund's, the college his son had gone to. James's every need was indulged by his grandparents, whilst still not one penny ever came his mother's way.

That did not seem to touch her any more. On the rare occasions he came home between terms to see her, boasting openly to her about what he screwed out of them, she'd merely laugh with the delight of having him near her, would pounce on and coddle him as though he were still a small boy.

She still persisted in calling him Jamie – a name he now loathed. It was obvious to all but her that he couldn't wait to get back to school out of her clutches, his boredom plain to see.

'If it wasn't a duty,' he told Sara, his narrow, handsome face sullen, 'I'd never come home again. I hate it here.'

Sara nodded, regarding him without affection.

He had made a life for himself, although the spoiling he'd had as a child had left the young man wishing angrily for independence while still needing the indulgence of adults. His grandfather did indeed indulge him. Never saw him short of cash, he told Sara, adding that he often stayed with his grandparents between terms and did well out of it.

'Always good for a few bob,' he said with a beautiful smile and a deal of pride in his ability to wangle himself a bit extra on top of the already decent allowance they'd so generously granted him.

Sara saw how they would fall for his charms. James was charming. He looked so like his father. The similarity, however, ended there. He saw no ill in expecting the world to owe him a living, and could be sullen when it refused to do so. Matthew might have spent unwisely, and borrowed heavily from banks with the means to lend, but he had never begged a penny off anyone close to him. He had stood on his own two feet, despite a father who would have helped him, Sara was sure, had he gone cap in hand with promises to bend the knee.

Matthew had never bent the knee. Sara still experienced

that flood of loving admiration whenever these thoughts came to her. Even now she could still forgive him the loss of all they'd had. No one would ever take his place. No one would ever come up to what he'd been. It saddened her that James had not inherited that generous, loving, stalwart nature.

She couldn't like James, no matter how she tried. Perhaps it was because he was merely her half-brother, or perhaps his very resemblance to Matthew tore her heart so that she resented him for those looks that prompted such a rush of memories.

In the May of 1914 Mary died. After another, massive stroke that snatched away her senses so completely that she lay supine and staring, three days later, mercifully, she was taken from them.

Her daughters came to cry over her, see her decently buried, then to turn their eyes to the more immediate business of her will.

Harriet had no interest whatsoever in any will. At the graveside, supported on either side by her two brothers, she wept copiously into John's shoulder while George ineffectually patted her back. Their respective wives stood tearlessly by. Not being kin by blood, they felt no depth of emotion, and the deceased had after all been ripe in years, it seemed to those hardly into their middle ones.

Annie, viewing her sister's continuing heartbroken demonstrations long after everyone else had recovered – as most people usually did, confronted by the funeral lunch – curled her lip as she nibbled on a pressed tongue sandwich and whispered to Clara, 'She's making a big enough fuss, don't you think?'

Clara looked concerned, sipped at her tiny glass of sherry. 'She was closer to Mum than we were, I suppose.'

Annie's lip curled even more at the unwitting pun. 'You can well say that! A good four years closer to her. Had her share of Mum's will right enough in four years.' To which Clara nodded reluctantly.

To her husband, after they'd departed for home, Annie took time out to reopen the issue. She was taken aback when he turned on her, his mild and mediocre face thunderous.

'No, we're not going into all that again! I'm not dragging through solicitors' offices so you can get a bit more. The woman's dead. The will's drawn up. Signed, sealed, settled. Let's leave it at that!'

'I'm sorry,' Annie began, her tone haughty. 'I'm not prepared to leave it at that.'

'Yes, you are, Annie. That's my final word, take it or leave it.'

Annie glared, opened her mouth, then closed it again and let it stay closed, the look on Robert's face enough to tell her that in this he was wearing the trousers and had no intention of passing them over to her. Thereafter, not caring to see that look on his face return, Annie did not broach the subject again.

A few days later, Mary's will was read, and her wishes duly executed, uncontested.

Harriet sobbed quietly as her share was read out, remembering how the contents of Matthew's will had all gone to pay his debts. Her mother's will was sound, took no account of Harriet's keep these last few years, and if Annie had any views about it, she kept them to herself apart from a cautious sideways glance at Robert.

# Chapter Twenty-six

The previous year's dramas of suffragette outrages – even Emily Wilding Davidson throwing herself to her death beneath the king's horse at Epsom – faded before the unfolding of events this year. The press was full of the trouble in the Balkans with Austria-Hungary and Serbia at each other's throats, and the petty local affairs of silly women, as Jonathan put it, had been relegated to the inside pages, lesser columns.

'Damned sight more important things going on,' Jonathan observed, passing through the cluttered news-room. 'Not that most readers worry about anything if it's not on their own doorstep.'

'Well, what do you think is going to happen?' she asked.

'It's anyone's guess. But if we don't watch out, we're going to be led by the nose into a war, I can feel it in my blood.'

Jonathan was good at feeling things in his blood – wasn't usually wrong. It was what made him good at his job, what made her good at hers too – a sixth sense about things.

Sara looked at him with interest. 'How do you make that out?'

'You're bright enough to work it out.' His grin was lopsided as he delivered her the backhanded compliment. 'Think about it. If it does escalate, countries like Germany and Russia will start taking sides, and then . . . Germany has had an axe to grind for a long time, wants to feel her feet a bit. That's the way wars start.'

'That doesn't mean we'd be involved.' Sara saw his grin broaden.

'Maybe not. Hope not anyway.' He let his hand rest on her shoulder, a light pressure that made her heart begin unexpectedly to race. She was not prepared for her reaction as her shoulder stiffened almost of its own accord. The pressure lifted immediately and she saw his smile disappear.

'You're a cold fish, Sara,' he whispered as he moved off, leaving her to wonder why in heaven's name she must react so conversely to anything tender in him.

Sara had seen less of him lately. It wasn't her attitude that drove him away. He had been made Editor after Mr Mackenzie had retired in February, and he was now no longer so available, and though she refused to admit it, she missed his constant presence in the newsroom. Yet whenever he did appear, it always seemed to result in their coming to verbal blows, usually over her reports on her pet subject of suffragette activities.

'Can't you see anything else but that? There's a lot more going on out there apart from that.'

'You've got other reporters,' she blazed at him. 'Let them cover anything else going on.'

'You're here to cover a variety of news. If I'd wanted you as a gossip columnist I'd have let you do just that.'

Sara glared at him. She had long ago discovered that she had a journalist's instinct for news and could put a good story together. She had earned old Mackenzie's respect, yet it seemed that, no matter how good her reports, the moment she touched on suffragettes, her new editor would find something sarcastic to say about it.

'It's not gossip. It's about women giving up their freedom, their lives, for something they believe in. For women like me to be able to make their way in a world men have created for themselves at our expense.'

'I thought you did very well without their help.'

'Perhaps I do, but you would never understand the uphill struggle it is for a woman. The misery a woman has to endure just to make her way in your world. The humiliation, the insults . . .' She was seething now, then she saw that sardonic grin of his spread across his even features.

'I've always said women are too much victims of their emotions to make journalists,' he said slowly, almost vindictively, and somehow she felt that the sardonic grin he gave her hid some inner hurt; felt that she was the cause of that hurt in some way.

'You prove me right over and over again,' he continued, his tone soft yet stinging. 'You can't remain neutral, can you? A journalist has to be unbiased, write the truth. You break every rule. If you were a man, you'd understand.'

Wanting to protest, she knew he was right. A greater part of her was influenced by the heroic deeds and daring

campaigns of those forceful women. Did any of them allow
a man to put them down as she seemed to allow Jonathan
to do? Why did she let him do it; and why did he do it?
He never behaved this way to the other two women in the
office. Maybe they posed no threat to him, or maybe there
was something far closer between her and him than she
cared to think.

It didn't stop her feeling furious about his attitude
towards her own subject. But it was true: more and more
she had chosen to write about the suffragettes above other
news, extolling their endeavours to gain the right for
women to vote, commenting perhaps a little too freely
on the cruelty of the Cat and Mouse Act that allowed
the 'mice' to be released as hunger strikes brought them
dangerously near to death, only to have the 'cat' rearrest
them as they regained their health, knowing they would
again resort to hunger strikes and renewed force-feeding,
their health whittled away. The government's hope had
been to demoralise. Instead it served to intensify their
resolve. Sara could not help admiring their tenacity to their
cause.

She had written an enthusiastic account of the arrival
of the Women's Pilgrimage, as it was called, into London
– thousands of NUWSS members marching proudly after
six weeks on the road, waving their red, white and green
banners in an orderly march that permitted no interference
to their entry into Hyde Park – and was infuriated when
Jonathan had withdrawn her report.

The next day she'd confronted him with *The Times* and
an armful of other newspapers, each with a prominent

report on the march. She told him he had no place on the *Graphic* as an editor, and that he would cause its demise just because he couldn't bear to see her, personally, succeed. She had faced up to his dark frown, half expecting him to dismiss her. But he merely told her to calm down and stop behaving like a bloody silly woman.

'Perhaps you ought to examine your own motives before going off half-cocked.'

'What do you mean?' she flared.

He looked at her steadily. 'Do I have to spell it out? It's not just your need to uphold that cause. It's something else. I've thought about it a lot. Now you think about it, Sara.'

That last remark stunned her into silence. For the first time, she realised that her insistence on upholding the women wasn't so much because she admired them as a wish to put him down, to justify a need to combat those feelings she kept having for him. That he had peered into her heart and seen the truth – like a lover – made her feel strange. He had no right to see inside her.

It took her a long time to forgive him that. Then in March he sent her to cover a story at the National Gallery.

'Take a look at the results of one of your precious suffragette members' protest,' he remarked enigmatically.

She went off as ordered, came back subdued, wrote up her piece and presented it to him. Jonathan's satisfied smile said it all – he was deliberately obliging her to write up one of the WSPU's more senseless acts of protest to bring her back in line.

Wild women, the *Daily Mirror* called them, and

Jonathan echoed those sentiments in the face of Sara's stalwart protest that force-feeding was just as outrageous as slashing the Rokeby Venus painting by Velasquez, worth some £45,000, with a meat cleaver. But even she had to admit that the act had been quite senseless. Destroying empty houses with homemade explosive devices, or attacking a doctor from Holloway prison with a rhino whip had some point to it. Slashing a beautiful and irreplaceable work of art seemed quite pointless.

'Don't get carried away by them, Sara,' he said. 'You're worth more than that.'

The softness of his tone made her look up. The warm glow in his eyes prompted a corresponding warmth within her, as she used to feel when Matthew had looked at her. Confusion engulfed her. Was it Matthew's memory prompting this feeling of warm security, or was it Jonathan standing so close? *It can't be love*, cried something inside her. *It mustn't be. You made a vow . . .*

'Don't be so damned stupid,' she heard herself burst out, almost savagely, the retort stemming purely from her shaken resolve. Hating herself, she watched him walk off.

'You don't catch me like that, Jonathan Ward,' she whispered to herself, needing to combat the confusion of emotions churning inside her. If he thought she was going to melt before that false display of tenderness just now, he was sadly mistaken.

Her resolve *had* been shaken; she'd been humiliated by the lengths to which some women militants could go. But that didn't mean their cause was ill-founded. Jonathan saying they were all painted by the same brush was entirely wrong. She would prove it. She felt belligerent.

Belligerence led her to follow up, without pausing to report on a hastily delivered message coming through to her, on an uproar outside the Old Bailey after Annie Kenney, her health undermined by her previous imprisonment and hunger strike, was rearrested in May.

Sara arrived in a drizzle of morning rain to find two Black Marias drawn up, a dishevelled suffragette being frogmarched by two grim-faced policemen into one of the vans, and a knot of women still jostling and being jostled by more police. A crowd of bystanders of both sexes stood yelling abuse at the ridiculous female protesters with their hats and hair askew and their arms waving frantically.

'Bleedin' insult to proper women,' a truculent middle-aged housewife in flat cap and apron was yelling from the body of onlookers. Supported by cat calls from all sides, she gestured with arms flexed like huge hams. 'Gerron, you coppers, git 'em orf out of 'ere!'

The friend beside her scooped up a handful of gutter mud and flung it hard into the struggling throng. Sara, already on the perimeter of struggling police and militants, hoping to get a story from one of the protesters once the scuffles had died down, was the one to receive the clod of mud full on the shoulder of her beige suit.

It was her surprised cry of protest that made one police-man glance round.

'Oi! Another one of yer, eh?'

Sara found herself grabbed, her arm pushed painfully up her back.

'Let go of me!' she cried. 'I'm a reporter – *London Graphic.*'

'Don't come the old Adam wiv me, missus. Lady reporter, me arse!'

'I am. I have my credentials.' She struggled to free herself so as to reach into her handbag but found the policeman's grip tighten still more.

'No yer don't!' The man looked grim. Women were known to carry itching powder, sneezing powder, even wounding scissors in their bags and he wasn't going to be caught that way. 'You come along with me, young lady.'

Her imprisoned arm hurt under the pressure of being trundled away, and she struggled frantically. At his call, another policeman leapt to his aid. 'Lively one, this,' laughed the first.

Almost dragging her, they passed near to the crowd of onlookers. A cloth-capped man leapt from the crowd and, before the trio could dodge away, landed Sara a thump full in the face.

Thrown back by the force of the blow, her upper cheek gone instantly numb, she staggered from the grip of the police as they mildly remonstrated with her attacker.

'No call fer that, chum. Ladies, yer know, no matter what . . .'

But Sara was off, running down the street as fast as her hobble skirt would allow, the shouts of the two policemen following her. She didn't stop until she had turned the corner into Ludgate Hill. There she recovered her wits and her breath.

The police hadn't followed. Suddenly weak, her cheek beginning to swell and hurt like the devil, she leaned against a wall, wanting to cry, but she was in a public place. No one would see her cry, that was definite.

Passers-by looked curiously at her, this well-dressed woman, her appearance dishevelled, dilly-dallying and seeming not to know where she was going.

'Has someone been knocking you about, young lady?' A man had approached, and now he took her by the elbow. She almost flinched. It had been a man who had vindictively and scurrilously knocked her down. But this one was kindly, a middle-aged man, a city man in a topper and morning suit. 'Can I be of any help?'

Sara took a deep ragged breath. 'I need to get a cab.'

'You need hospital treatment more like.'

'No – just hail me a taxicab – please.'

'As you wish, but I really feel . . .' Seeing her expression, the gentleman said no more, but went to the kerbside and waved his stick in the air.

Within minutes, handkerchief held to her eye and cheek, wondering if she had thanked the man, she saw the dingy offices of the *London Graphic* loom beside her, the taxicab motor clacking to a stop.

How she managed to pay the cabbie and get herself into the building and up to Jonathan's office, she could hardly remember, but she found herself with her back to the door, seeing him half-risen in alarm from behind his desk.

'What in God's name!' He came round the desk and caught her as she fell into his arms. 'My God, you've got a shiner there.'

She made an attempt to extricate herself from his embrace. 'Don't be funny!'

Even in this dire circumstance, anger dominated any need to cry. She would not bow to tears; would not be left vulnerable to attack by anyone, especially Jonathan, witnessing them.

'What on earth happened to you?' he demanded, holding her.

Sara swallowed hard. To explain, to face up to his ridicule, his corrosive, 'I told you so,' was more than she felt she could face. But face it she must. She wasn't prepared to lie, but neither was she prepared to debase herself.

'A protest at the Old Bailey,' she gasped into the folds of his jacket as he guided her to the chair near this desk. 'A suffragette protest.'

This she uttered with a note of defiance, but all he said was, 'I see.'

Gently he sat her on the chair, then crouched before her as she let her head fall back with exhaustion and misery. Carefully he pushed back the lock of dark hair that had escaped her hat to cover partially the fast discolouring flesh on her cheek and around her right eye. She winced as a finger inadvertently touched the area.

'We'll have to get that seen to, Sara,' he said in the same quiet, gentle tone of concern.

The deepness of his voice seemed to pour itself over her. Unable to help herself, she lifted her head to look at him, the movement bringing a dull thudding of pain to her eye. She saw tenderness in his hazel eyes as he regarded her with something like fear.

'You must be careful, Sara. You had no right to go off without speaking to one of us first, letting us know what you were up to.'

'I acted instinctively.'

'Then next time, Sara, think. What if you'd been really badly hurt?'

'Don't you think this is bad enough?' she railed at him, again wincing at the pain her energetic reaction caused.

'It could have been worse. A broken bone. You in hospital. I could have lost a good reporter for weeks . . . No!' He caught himself up sharply, 'No – that's not what I meant.'

His expression was one of anguish, a strange one to her who had never seen such a look on his face before.

'Sara . . . my darling . . . if something were to happen to you, I don't know what I'd . . .'

She was in his arms, not knowing how she'd got there, somehow pulled off her chair, with him kneeling beside her, holding her. His face buried in the curve of her neck, she could feel the unexpectedly soft texture of his hair against her bruised cheek.

For a moment she listened to his words of love, wanted to respond, smooth her hand over that wonderful hair. Yet something froze within her. Matthew too had told her he loved her and then seconds later had backed away, his face contorted with loathing. She could not have borne for this man to draw away from her with the same look on his face. In a moment of panic she knew she had to take the initiative so as not to see that look. She must be the first to spurn and thus be saved.

'For heaven's sake, Jonathan. I'm not dying.'

He lifted his head.

'What?'

Embarrassment had tightened his lips. Sara steeled herself to face that look. She wanted to apologise but knew that apologies would only heighten the damage her stupid words had already done. There was nothing she could say or do, so she did the only thing open to her: she laughed. It didn't matter that it was a hiccup of a laugh, fraught with dismay, pain, anger at herself; it was a laugh to his ears.

Slowly, with deliberate care, he released his embrace and got up, helping her to her feet at the same time in one studied movement to lessen the humilation he was obviously feeling. He did not look at her.

Now she said it, the *coup de grâce* she had tried so hard not to deliver, and knew even as she did, that she was destroying forever what might have been built between them, yet like an idiot, she still said it.

'I'm sorry, Jonathan.'

'For what?' His voice was harsh, like sandpaper.

'I don't know. I just . . .' She wanted to bite off her tongue, wanted so much to heal the cut she'd inflicted, but what could she say? She moved away from him, fearing to look at him, and let herself out of the office.

'I'd get that eye seen to.' His voice followed her, its tone even, as though nothing had happened at all.

The episode smouldered inside Sara for weeks after. How dare he treat her as though she were a piece of his property, which was how she saw it, remembering. She found herself avoiding him whenever possible, which wasn't difficult, as he was quite obviously avoiding her. Oddly enough, this fact was vaguely irksome. Yet had he approached her on matters other than work, she felt she would not have known quite how to deal with him. It was such a confusion, such a muddle in her mind. For once she felt totally out of her depth.

The news in late June that Archduke Ferdinand and his wife, on a visit to Sarajevo in Bosnia, had been assassinated by Gavrilo Princip, a young Bosnian exile, finally took Sara's mind off her own affairs. Austria-Hungary accused Serbian officials of being in on the plot; Germany was ready to support Austria-Hungary against Serbia; France and Russia pledged to support Serbia in its rejection of Austro-Hungarian demands to bring those involved in the assassination to trial.

'Like kids fighting over a ball,' Sara remarked to Alf Peters as the morse-coded messages, telegraphed through the new automatic printing telegraphy system, were decoded.

She tried not to begrudge Peters, a reporter like herself, the cream of the jobs he was given. It wasn't his fault that as a man he'd be given preferential assignments over her, a mere woman, though it did rub whenever she considered it. But she liked Peters, his round, middle-aged face always showing a wry expression. Now the creases on his face spread in all directions.

'Quite some kind of ball,' he grinned with dry humour.

Sara nodded. Peters had hit the nail on the head. This particular ball could bounce in some rather nasty directions with Germany glaring at France while Russia had begun a general mobilisation on Germany's very borders. Things were hotting up.

By the end of July, news was pouring into the wire-room of the *London Graphic,* as into every newspaper wire-room. Serbia had refused, as a question of honour, to submit to Sir Edward Grey's proposal of arbitration by an international conference; and as a result found itself at war with Austria. With Russia persisting with her military preparations and France replying evasively to Germany's request to declare its neutrality, Germany had declared war on France as well as Russia.

The British went about their business as usual, blind, happy to enjoy the lovely summer weather, content to leave fate in the lap of the gods or the government. A few, excited, longing for a scrap, declared that this arrogant Germany needed to be taught a sound lesson. Others, more apprehensive, as some people would always be about anything dire, held their breath and said nothing.

'War's on its way all right,' Jonathan said to Sara as news came through of German troops crossing Belgium's borders as an easier route to Paris, despite the Belgian king refusing permission.

Sara glanced up from typing, surprised by Jonathan's voice in her ear. It was the first time he had spoken to her directly and of his own accord since the episode following the business at the Old Bailey. Now he paused to regard her thoughtfully.

'I'd like a word with you, Sara, if you've a moment.'

'What about?'

She didn't care for his use of her name after he had kept his distance for such a long time. Her tone was tetchy. She was tired. She had been in the newsroom since that morning, a boy sent to her home as evening drew on with a message that she'd be staying on to help cover whatever news filtered through on this war declared between Germany and France. It was now midnight and she was furiously typing to catch the early morning edition from a scribbled note, tossed on to her desk, that Britain was asking Germany to respect a treaty guaranteeing Belgium's neutrality.

'It's about that business between you and me in my office a few weeks ago,' Jonathan replied.

Her fingers poised over the wide-spaced typewriter keys, she looked testily up at him. Now was not the time.

'I don't think we need to discuss that.'

'I think we do,' he replied. 'Now more than ever. We have to get a few things straightened out while there's still time. Have you given any more thought to what I said that day?'

She looked back at the copy she'd been typing. 'I can't recall what it was you said,' she murmured, but her heart was racing and she hated the feeling.

'Surely . . .' He stopped, then began again in a more controlled voice. 'You must have given it some thought.'

'I think it would be best forgotten Jonathan, don't you?' she said without looking at him.

'I can't forget it.' He was hovering like a small boy waiting for a sweet, and it belittled him. She felt tense with shame that he should so demean himself. 'I can't forget it.

What I said that day was all true. 'I love you . . .'

'You can't love me!' She burst through his declaration. 'There's a war coming. I've no time.'

It was all she could think of to say. But her defences were already up – fear of entanglement, of being compromised. Why should she have such fear? But she knew why, all in that second. Once before she had been led to love, only to be rejected. It would never happen again. Another rejection would be too agonising to bear. This time she was wiser.

For a moment, Jonathan looked at her as though she had uttered some foul epithet. The next moment he had grabbed her by the arm, pulled her up from her desk and propelled her, protesting, towards his office that lay at the end of the passage from the newsroom.

Once inside, he sat her roughly in the chair beside his desk, then stood over her, his lean face dark with anger and determination.

'I meant what I said, Sara. I love you. I've never before loved any woman, but I love you. And I'm sure you love me.'

Never had he felt about anyone the way he felt about her, so oddly apprehensive. Though he would never, not if it killed him, let her see what turmoil of indecision she raised in his breast – he who had always been so decided about what he wanted in life. It was as though she stood on a mountain far above him, to be worshipped from a distance like some Greek goddess, while he was only too aware of his mortality.

But now he had said it, and now he stood over her where a man's place should be, awaiting her reply. Her deep blue eyes as she gazed up at him softened a fraction, just a fraction and just for a second, then they iced over, growing blank. And again she reigned above him.

'Jonathan – don't say things like that to me. I can't love you.'

'Why not? What is wrong with me?'

'There is nothing wrong with you. It's just that . . .'

'What?' he prompted as she hesitated. He needed so much to feel those wide lips warm on his. They looked cold but with a kiss must become warm, he was sure of that. Once he kissed her, of course, but her continued silence began to push that hope from him.

'Don't you feel anything for me?' he asked and cursed himself for what his own ears detected as a sad lack of masculine domination.

She shook her head, but the gesture struck him as being not so much negative as bewildered. He forced himself to speak gently, encouragingly. It was, perhaps, what she needed.

'We've known each other a long time, Sara. I know we don't always see eye to eye, but we can call ourselves friends. In that time my feelings for you have grown. Now I have declared them to you, surely you must have . . . must feel some degree of . . . affection towards me.'

He didn't dare to say love, but accentuated the word affection so that it could mean nothing other than love. He waited, then finally heard the words that made his heart suddenly soar.

'I do, Jonathan.' It was as though it came on a sigh, so quietly was it said.

'Then why . . .' he began, but in that second, she started up, cutting short his question.

'I'm sorry, Jonathan. It's not you. It's me. I just can't . . . I'm so sorry . . .'

Before he could stop her, she had bounded out of the chair, pushed him aside and run to the door. She flung it open and ran from the office.

Left standing gazing at the open door, the dark corridor beyond, along which came the hubbub of a newsroom suddenly going crazy, he knew that never again would he declare his heart to her – to any woman – as long as he lived. He had been a fool. And as a fool he saw himself as a clown in Sara's eyes. How could he ever face her again and not feel the clown?

'Damn you!' he muttered as he went and closed the door. 'You're a cold fish, Sara – a bloody cold fish. And it's the last time I shall ever humble myself before you.'

# Chapter Twenty-seven

James wasn't as happy at Oxford as he had thought he would be. It should have been the pinnacle of his ambition, but something was missing.

Clever, he'd gone up to university without any question a month after war broke out. It was now Michaelmas term of his second year and any gratitude he'd felt for what his grandparents had done for him was fast melting away, although he still took full advantage of their generosity.

There was no doubt about his being their favourite grandchild. The love they'd had for their dead son, his father, transferred to him, they had never seen him short for anything. During vacations he had the run of their home. His every whim catered for, his wallet full, or at least for a few weeks until he had gone through it like a termite through wood, he could lord it like a gentleman. So why wasn't he happy?

Mostly it was frustration at attending lectures and swatting for exams at the end of an academic year when he could have been out in the world already proving himself. He detested the whole stuffy insularity of university. It wasn't as if he had any interest in sports or an inclination to join discussion groups where no one saw him as anything special. Rag weeks were childish; the balls given on occasion were all very much of a muchness; lecturers were generally pompous, his fellow students generally boring, their talk incessantly of study, discussion groups, the next ball, girls. His lodgings were cold and uncomfortable, the lecture rooms, crowded, stifling and depressing, and he hated having to swat up during vacations.

To think that, with Grandfather's backing, he might already have been on his way to becoming head of some department. Instead, here he was, still regarded as a lesser mortal, still looked down upon by his college peers, still like a little boy at school.

He had approached the old man, as he secretly called him, hoping he might sympathise and take him away from Oxford to find him some decent position in his estates business, of which he was still a partner, though retired from active participation. But while Henry Craig indulged his grandson in most things, this he wasn't prepared to grant.

'You'll go further than I did, my boy,' he said sagaciously. 'I was, to some extent, a self-made man, on which account I am prepared to boast. It's my ambition to see you go to the top, and Oxford will see to that. Stick at it, my boy, and who knows – politician, statesman – the world's your oyster with an Oxford degree, James.'

James guessed that underlying his aging grandfather's plans for him were the ones the old man's son had thwarted, all that education flown out of the window on the wings of a foolhardy resolve to run a journal. The old boy couldn't see that James himself had no interest in education beyond the wealth and prestige it could bring. Meanwhile he must suffer, spending years being subservient to others, before realising that wealth and prestige.

The war was now in its second year, and most young men of his age had joined up and gone off to see the world. Thoughts of following them came to him often. Though he was young at eighteen, Oxford would stand him in good stead to becoming an officer. None of your squaddy starts for an Oxford man. He could be something in the army. Then there was the gallantry, the romance of adventure, being in uniform with young women swooning to hang upon his arm. He wasn't half bad looking – he'd cut a fine figure in officer's full dress.

'I've a good mind to join up,' he announced grandly on one of his rare visits to his mother, ignoring his great-aunt's disparaging glare across the Sunday tea table.

Sara eyed him with a look of not caring what he did. She'd become a beautiful young woman, he couldn't deny, but so hoity-toity for one not much more than a working girl.

His mother, however, gave out with a small squeak of terror.

'Jamie, don't talk like that! I've lost so many I love. First your father. Then your grandmother. If anything happened to you, Jamie . . .'

'Nothing's going to happen to me,' James mumbled, his mouth full. He wished she wouldn't use that stupid childish name. 'If I were to volunteer, I'd go straight in as an officer. University automatically makes me suitable material. I certainly don't intend being one of the riff-raff.'

Harriet wasn't listening, her lips trembling. 'I couldn't bear it if you should be killed. I should lose my mind.'

Her Aunt Sarah gave her a despairing look, half regretting the distinct lack of pity she felt. What a weak thing Harriet had turned out to be. Losing her mother had affected her more than the other members of the family, and for a time she had appeared to have lost all reason; had indeed become quite a burden.

Sarah, no longer strong herself, had felt considerably aged by the loss of Mary and for a long time after had found it difficult to cope with Harriet's violent swings of mood. At times she had even feared for Harriet's sanity, especially when she again turned to the bottle. It took all the go out of one of her years and at times she was left wondering just what she'd let herself in for.

Perhaps it was a mistake, but the house having gone to herself in Mary's will, she'd vowed that Harriet would always have a roof over her head for as long as she needed it. Mary's boys were content with that, having their own homes and families, the business their father had started continuing very well, even expanding under their guidance. Clara and Annie kept very quiet about things these days, but they did drop a hint that she could be making a rod for her own back. And perhaps they were right. She still wasn't sure.

It had been hard, though it was the better solution for Harriet and Sara to continue on in the house – the place was too large for her anyway. With three flights of stairs to climb, she seldom made the upper floors and now had her bedroom at the back on the ground floor. Not that she wasn't agile on the flat. She could still stroll in Victoria Park on a fine Sunday with the aid of a stick. But it was handy having them here – her great-niece's salary more than helping to pay for things that were needed. As well as Mrs Thompson to do the cooking, they could afford a girl for the housework, and a woman who had some nursing skills, hired occasionally to see to Harriet in her more contrary moments.

Even Sara had remarked in her direct way, reminding her of herself once upon a time, that her mother was becoming more confused as the years went on. But it fluctuated. There were moments when Harriet could be lucid, quite logical, but others when one really did think the woman must be destined for the lunatic asylum.

Today, however, though she was on the verge of tears over James's notion of going off to war, she was more or less herself.

'Please – don't do anything rash, Jamie,' she was begging abjectly. 'You have everything ahead of you at Oxford. Let someone else do the fighting.'

The news from the front was terrible. So many men were dying. The war, expected to end by Christmas, had been dragging on for eighteen months now, a bloody, deadly, to-and-fro tussle. A second Christmas had gone by and there was no sign of an end to the conflict.

'You're breaking my heart, surely you know that, Jamie?'

James gave a surreptitious glance at the clock on the mantelshelf. Perhaps in an hour he might extricate himself from these women, at least from his mother. His great-aunt looked peeved, his sister detached, as though both would be glad to see him take his leave.

'Don't worry about me,' he said testily. 'I can take care of myself. I know what I'm doing.'

But he had no idea what he was doing. He found that out soon after informing his tutors of his intention to 'do his bit', promising to resume his studies 'when it is all over'. Glowing under acclaims of, *Well done!* and, *Go to it!* he packed and went off to enlist.

Officer's college, however, proved to be as far from the freedom of university as a mole run from an eagle's eyrie. James had had his sights set on gaining the dizzy heights of a crown on his shoulder, returning to civilian life eventually to be known to all as Major James Matthew Henry Craig, but now found those sights having to be set a good deal lower. Constantly bawled out, vociferously insulted, made to feel the lowest of the low, worse than the meanest private while being incongruously addressed as sir, there was certainly no sign on his horizon of the dizzy heights he had anticipated. And as for the crown on his shoulder, his final reward was two pips, no more.

He was given only minimal training, good men being needed urgently at the front. At the end of April 1916, James, now Lieutenant James Craig, came to say goodbye to his mother, his grip packed for France.

Harriet was inconsolable, her eyes haunted by visions of dead and rotting bodies in the mudholes of Flanders. That night, after she had clung to her Jamie with a grip strong enough almost to rip off his uniform as he said his farewells, refusing to let go of him until his great-aunt had to prise her palsied fingers loose, Harriet had to be physically restrained by her doctor from throwing herself out of the top-floor passage window to the concrete in the back garden below.

From the open window, her shrieks of protest rang out: 'Let me die! I've nothing to live for! I want to die!'

The doctor's advice was urgent but unwise. 'You've your daughter. Think of her – how would she feel, left on her own without you?'

Back came the savage scream: 'Her? I wish she was dead! I wish she'd died the day she was born.'

Looking on, Sara's heart seemed to flicker out inside her, a black lump that she'd been foolish enough to think had a little spark still left in it, enough to light her way through life.

The black lump a weight in her breast, she turned her back on her mother. It was time to go her own way. And though she felt sorry to leave Great-Aunt Sarah, who obviously treasured her, perhaps needed her, she didn't think she would bother to see her mother again.

For the first time in her life Sara felt free, able to breathe, be herself instead of forever walking on eggshells. Several times that week she went over that last scene, regretting the way in which she had walked out on her mother. Then she would recall the times over the years that she had been hurt by her, often for no obvious reason, often quite deliberately and with such hatred as to be almost unbelievable. Then her pricking conscience would smooth itself out as she gazed about her new flat, feeling immeasurably free.

Over the years she had saved little by little, being nowhere near as well paid as male reporters of the same standing. With her modest nest egg she found a small but nicely furnished two-room flat just off Holborn, only a stone's throw from her office. Here she would be happy.

But if troubles were said never to come singly, heartaches most certainly came in pairs, for hardly had she adjusted to having dropped her bombshell on her mother than Jonathan dropped a bombshell on her.

Coming up behind her while she was busy at her desk to ask her how she was settling into her new home, he then remarked casually that on Friday she would be twenty-two. 'Quite a woman now.'

Dumbfounded, she could only stare at him, so seldom did he come anywhere near her other than on a matter of work, and then with an uncomfortable atmosphere, present since that episode all of two years ago. She was even more surprised when he gave her an easy grin and suggested out of the blue that he might help her celebrate her birthday.

'May be the last chance I'll ever have,' he had said meaningfully.

The ominous ring in that remark made her draw in a quick breath.

'What are you saying?' But she knew what he was saying. His narrow hazel eyes glinted.

'They're calling up all sorts these days.'

'They've not . . .'

'Not yet. But it is only a matter of time, I expect.'

'You're a newspaper editor. You're valuable. They can't . . .

'Oh, they can. Though I might not wait for that. It depends.'

It was lightly said, with a shrug of the shoulders, and she couldn't be sure whether it was meant just for effect, to amuse or anger her. On what did it depend?

'Well?' he prompted as she continued to stare up at him, unable to respond. 'Are you going to let me help celebrate your birthday?'

'I don't . . .' she began, confused, but he suddenly and unexpectedly put a finger to her lips. The thrill of the light touch, brief as it was, rippled through her, but even as she felt herself melt, she pulled herself together and said as calmly as she could, 'Well, if it pleases you.'

'It will please me very much,' he said slowly, and with a slow smile, walked away, leaving her to seethe with conflicting emotions and uncertainties for the rest of the day, refusing to bow to the desire to go and confirm it with him all over again.

There was only the two of them. 'My treat,' he said as he helped her into the taxi. 'Eat, drink and be merry, for tomorrow . . .' He broke off with a laugh, but she felt a prophetic shudder pass through her, and asked him not to say such things, at which he only laughed again.

The Café Royale was as opulent as ever it had been in peacetime. There were still evening top hats among the military scarlet and blue and bottle-green, the drab khaki of lesser ranks of course banished to pubs and cheap eating places. But for the abundance of uniforms, there might never have been a war going on, it was all so gay and carefree.

The brightness of the huge candelabras above the diners made the sheen of her lilac ankle-length dress glow softly, and brought auburn glints to the darkness of her hair, recently restyled in the new fashion, cut shorter at the sides, the rest caught into a soft chignon.

Amid the chatter, she and Jonathan enjoyed the best of the Café Royale's offerings, which felt sinful when they knew ships were being blockaded to such an extent that shortages were rife, and rationing ineffectual.

She mentioned it as a small but beautifully decorated birthday cake was brought to the table on Jonathan's orders. The way he looked at her made her glow for all she tried not to. She was unable to abandon herself to enjoyment of the moment, partly from reawakened wariness at the love glowing there in his eyes, partly because she heard again those words: 'Eat, drink and be merry, for tomorrow we die,' seeing them reflected behind his regard, the sense of foreboding so strong that it took all her effort to shrug it off. She experienced such churned-up emotions that enjoying her cake, after it had been ceremoniously cut and served for her by a liveried waiter, was virtually impossible.

Despite it all, conversation did manage to flow between them for the first time in ages. Aware that he could be stolen away at any time by those conducting this war, she felt a need to take in both hands what was here while it lasted.

For once the compelling urge to deny the shiver of expectancy she felt as she looked across the table at him did not present itself. He had never looked so handsome. All else was forgotten; she might never have had a past. No thoughts of Matthew came to haunt her, that old love was dead and buried all so long ago. Sara could see only Jonathan, feel only the glow inside her. The glow lasted all the way through the meal, and continued all the way home, until the taxi drew up outside her flat.

He had obviously defined her mood. As she made to leave, he leaned forward and lightly kissed her cheek. Taken off guard, she forgot to draw back and, heartened by what he saw as a willingness to be kissed more intimately, he drew her to him, his mouth on hers.

Through the kiss, she heard him say, 'Marry me,' the champagne and brandy they had drunk in celebration of her birthday faintly sweet on his breath.

It was the words that broke the spell. Pulling back, she looked at him from arm's length.

'What?' It was as sharply said as if she had been insulted. She hadn't meant it to sound that sharp.

Jonathan's face went bleak. His words came weighted, challenging.

'I said, marry me.'

'I can't do that.' How could she have said that when it was all she wanted in the world at this moment?

'Why not?' The sharpness of the question made her start.

'You've never proposed to me before.'

'I'm proposing now.' He made an attempt to draw her back to him, but her body had grown taut, the defences she no longer understood already up, fear already raising its ugly head – fear and guilt. All these years she had known him she had never once seen him unsure, but here he was, gauche, clumsy, his words far too rapid.

'I love you, Sara. You've known that for years. But you're always so frigid . . . I'm wary to get too near you lest I frighten you off. I know you love me. I know it. Why do you hide it? Sara, I know you're not happy. If you marry me, I promise I'll make you happy.'

It was like listening to a melodrama being played out on a stage. It all sounded so unreal.

'I can't, Jonathan.'

She needed time. It was true she did love him, yet what if . . . The old barrier formed before her eyes. What if she gave her soul to this man, as she'd once done to Matthew, only to see it ripped apart as once before it had been ripped apart, leaving her naked and ashamed? That fear would never go, no matter how long he gave her. That invisible barrier, that old fear, that ache of love dismissed, the look of revulsion on someone's face . . . No, she couldn't suffer that again.

'I can't. You don't understand.'

His hazel eyes had darkened. 'What don't I understand? Drop me a clue, Sara, as to what I'm supposed to understand. I'm not given to pleading, even on a thing like this. I never thought I'd be asking any woman to marry me. Now I *am* asking you to be my wife. Tell me, what is it I am expected not to understand about that?'

'What about my job?'

It sounded so silly. But it was the only means of escape – a way out of the real reason behind her refusal.

'What about your *job*?' The question held a note of incredulity.

'Married women can't work on newspapers. I shall be dismissed.'

'You'll be married to me. You won't need to work.'

'It's my life . . .' In the front the cab driver was beginning to look impatient at this delay to receiving his fare, the engine already switched off.

'Your *life?* Jonathan's lean face darkened with incomprehension.

'It's . . .'

'*I* shall be your life, Sara.'

'Is that what you'll be – my life? What about me?' Something inside her was crying, *Matthew was your life. He destroyed it, left you to go on loving him, vowing no other man would take his place. What of that vow now?*

'I've a career . . .'

'Damn your career! Just be a woman, for God's sake! Just be mine – my wife . . .'

She was angry, glad to be angry. 'How dare you! How dare you take away my choice to be myself – what you as a man take for granted!'

It was a lie, this anger. It was an excuse. Did she really want to be angry, to have this being inside her taking everything away from her just as her heart needed to go out to someone?

*Oh, Matthew, let me go*, cried that anger. *What allegiance do you still expect of me after all this time? I so loved you but it was so long ago.* Anger was the only means of justifying that thing binding her to an old dead vow. How could she explain it to Jonathan when she couldn't explain it to herself?

She saw him slump a little. The next second he was himself again, his reaction typical, full of cynicism, his words searing into her brain.

'I'm sorry, Sara. Sorry I bothered you. No, you go on with your career, my dear – see if it brings you happiness. I hope it does, for your sake. But there'll come a time . . . What is it, we reap what we sow? Something like that.' He gave a hard little laugh. 'You should buy yourself a cat, Sara – to keep you warm in your old age.'

Before she knew what was happening, he had leaned across her and opened the taxicab door. The next thing she knew, she was standing on the pavement, watching the cab drive off with Jonathan sitting back in his seat. He didn't look round.

On Monday, Sara went into his office to find him not there. Someone – she was so stunned, she couldn't recall who it was, but she thought it was Duffy – said that he had enlisted that morning and wouldn't be back. The last three words rang like a dire prophesy. She heard them as if from a great distance, forced a shrug for the benefit of those with whom she worked, and went to her desk to resume her morning tasks. He hadn't even said goodbye.

# Chapter Twenty-eight

Mackenzie had been brought out of retirement. Taking up his place behind the desk Jonathan had used for so short a time, he looked upon Sara with a speculative eye.

Those the war had left behind to carry on were either approaching his sixty-five years, were sickly or mere youths. Sara, although a woman, filled the gap and, for the first time ever, was proving of extreme value in the absence of good men.

At last Sara knew her own worth. Gone were the sidelong smirks from male staff, the pretence of putting up with her in their midst, her ideas looked upon as interference in the decisions of men; at best being ignored, at worst, being treated as an interloper into their domain.

With so many men conscripted, and the death toll mounting daily (though the government request to keep down the numbers reported had been honoured to some extent by all newspapers – for the good of morale), women were needed in every workplace. This necessity was still largely expressed in the same vein as the idea that a woman was needed at home by her man, which was the way Sara saw Mackenzie's acceptance of her worth: patronising, his welcome too exaggerated. It irked. But there were now women in every sort of job: at munitions factories doing the work of men; working as ticket collectors on trams and buses and as guards on railway stations; driving lorries and ambulances; sweeping the streets. Many were even becoming journalists and reporters like herself. One London paper had a woman sub-editor. And they were still able to look after their children and homes when their work was done – something no man had ever been capable of.

For her part, Sara threw herself into her work, if only to fill the emptiness of Jonathan's leaving. It felt like losing Matthew all over again. Yet in a way it was not. This time there was not the sense of finality, only the *fear* of finality; a formless fear, unreal yet real – she didn't know what to call it except that it was there – all the time. And love . . . she was sure it was love, but now it was too late for anything to be done about it.

Yet could something be done? There was a need to compensate for the guilt building inside her that she had sent him away. If she could be nearer to those who had gone off to fight, maybe to share some of the burden Jonathan had taken up, the guilt might lessen a little.

On the strength of this, Sara went to Mackenzie, looked into those tired, rheumy eyes, and requested – no, insisted – she be allowed to cover the stories of those wounded being brought home from France. In some part this would help assuage the guilt.

'I could bring you the human angle,' she argued. 'A woman's view of what they're going through and how they are bearing up.'

'Not a sight for a woman,' Mackenzie said wearily.

He didn't want to be hassled. He had been enjoying his retirement, what there had been of it, even though he'd missed the comradeship, the special bond with his colleagues in newspapers. When the Managing Director had begged practically on his knees for him to fill the gap, what could he say? He liked being back in the swim, but it was telling on him, particularly the long hours, which any younger man would hardly have noticed. Added to that was the knowledge that he had been retired as too old to continue, then, like an old horse, had been put back into harness because the young colt had kicked over the traces.

'Nurses see sights like that every day,' Sara said obdurately.

Mackenzie sighed. 'They're trained for it. You're not.'

'Why should you worry? You'll get a better story out of me than from the old men we have working for us, or these brash youngsters.' She used the 'us' with conviction. Her years on the *Graphic* had made her feel as though it was almost hers.

Mackenzie was well aware of the pitiful state of his staff. He gave in as Sara continued to badger him; gave in because he had no fight left in him.

He had come to respect this headstrong young woman. He would still shake his head at her, however, when she came crying back, shocked by sights no lady should see, nurse or otherwise. But then he had never once seen her cry. This fact was known throughout the *Graphic*. Its female journalist never cried no matter how angry, no matter how frustrated, how put upon – she never did.

Perhaps this might be the one time she would, after

her first time looking upon severed arms and legs, shell-blasted bodies, mutilated faces and sightless eyes – the fruits of war. It might do her good, make her more humble. He hoped so. But there was no denying it – she was a damned good reporter.

Why had she done it? Why had she been so stubbornly insistent on coming here? For what purpose other than to cleanse herself or maybe torture herself? She was a penitent. She had been the cause of Jonathan's leaving. If harm came to him, the blame would be on her. But what she was doing did nothing to vindicate the penitent.

She stood at London Docks breathing in the smell of oil, bilge water and a heavy, sickly-sweet stench she couldn't define.

She watched the great, grey ship unload its gaunt, grey, human cargo: long lines of ragged forms, grey-faced, mud-stained, bloodstained, unwashed, blanket-shrouded, eye-bandaged; a hand shaking still from shell shock on the shoulder of the man in front, to be led shuffling hesitantly down the gangway by a nurse or an aid worker or a comrade who still had his sight.

Stretcher-bearers carefully manipulated their burdens out from the ship's bowels on to firm soil; bundles immobile beneath blankets, red to hide blood, manhandled into waiting ambulances followed by trim blue-and-white-clad nurses. Veterans of the front limped past on crutches, a khaki trouser leg pinned at knee height, or at hip height. Others followed with one or other sleeve empty, many with bandages bound about foreheads, an eye, an ear;

now and again a swathe of bandages hiding and holding together shattered facial bones. The odd lucky one with a few fingers missing would still have some semblance of order to his life.

On the dockside, lady charity workers stood ready, faces stiff to express nothing, certainly not pity. They doled out their chocolate and comfort, led the walking wounded away, or took the hand held up limply from a stretcher in the need to feel the clean stability of a female's touch after an aeon with entrenched comrades in arms.

Sara thought of Jonathan, these men bringing a stark message of what lay out there for him. Her eyes as arid as ever but wide with the knowledge of what she had sent him to, she longed uselessly for yesterday to be lived again when, wiser, she could have given him a kindly word, her silly childish vow put behind her, and taken him in Matthew's place. But yesterday could not be regained, and she must stare at the horror her dry wide eyes conjured up. Oh, dear God, please let me cry! But tears were a forgotten luxury. So long ago vowed never to be shed, they refused to come at her bidding, as though punishing her for her unnatural suppression of them, an unwashed suffering, bereft of their soothing panacea.

Long years of holding back had left her as invisibly maimed as these poor wretches were visibly, her soul alone left to weep unseen. Tears had been for her mother, never for her.

Sara turned away, walked towards the nearest presentable soldier and, as gently as she could, began to probe – how did he feel now he was out of it? But what was gentle when the man's eyes turning to hers were hollow with visions, abject with relief to be back in Blighty, for a fraction of a second resenting her intrusion?

She got her story. She got several. Brought them back to present to Mackenzie.

Many of the men had held her hand, gripping convulsively as they spoke haltingly, hoarsely, the words staccato.

Others had turned away, told her to bugger off, to mind her own bloody business. One man burst into tears and gave her no words, but the tears told the story.

A soldier who said his name was Jack Crabtree, and who spoke with a Lancashire accent, had looked at her and the horror in his eyes had faded as though wiped away. He had even smiled up from his stretcher.

'By goom, but you're a beauty, miss – a sight for sore eyes right enoof. Would you give a brave soldier a kiss?'

She had laughed at the feeble joke, had allowed the kiss, had bent close to the grey face. The bandaged shoulder and arm wafted a faint odour and she knew then what the sickly-sweet smell was that she had first noticed in the air mixed with oil and bilge water. It was the smell of stale blood and gas gangrene.

Sickness flooding over her, she had moved away hurriedly to hide her hideous reaction to a man who had been dying even as she kissed him.

But she had been humbled enough to know she would be there again when the next Blighty ship docked, whether Mackenzie liked it or not. And it wouldn't all be to get stories.

Dared she hope Jonathan might one day be among these

men coming home, walking down that gangway? It would mean he would be out of it, safe from the ultimate price – lying dead upon the field of battle. Yet even some of these men were destined to die, many more to be maimed for life if they lived, forever useless, dependent upon others. Was that what she wished for him? No, she couldn't wish him among any of these just to satisfy her own self-indulgent peace of mind. That was not love, that was selfishness.

But there was something she now knew she must ask of Mackenzie. The problem was, would he grant it? She was resolved to badger him until he did.

The telephone on her desk tinkled. Putting down the report she was checking on the hazards confronting women working in munitions factories, Sara unhooked the receiver, stretching her neck to peer around the filing cabinet at her colleagues in the noisy newsroom.

She still sat in the same corner allocated to her when she had first been given a desk, half-hidden by the same two filing cabinets that had never been moved, almost as though partially out of sight she was also out of mind, enough not to cause the minds of her male colleagues to wander off their work. There had been a time when she had fretted over it. Now she merely thought of it as beneath contempt. If any of them needed a word with her about work, or merely a little sly fraternisation, which some did occasionally, they knew where to find her.

'Miss Craig here,' she said into the earpiece.

The female telephonist, who had taken over from a male one, sounded a little breathless.

'Miss Craig. Someone called Mrs Morris. She says she's your great-aunt. She wants to speak to you. She says it's urgent, important.'

'Very well, Miss Harris, put her on.' Sara's voice was sharp with sudden concern, her first thought being her mother.

'Sara!' came her name hardly had Great-Aunt been handed over. 'You must come home! It's James. He's been reported missing, believed taken prisoner, and your mother's in a terrible state. I can't do anything with her. She wants you.'

'Wants me?' No longer sharp, her tone was now cold.

'That's all she keeps asking for – for you.'

'All right. I'll come as soon as I can.'

'Can't you come now? She is in a state. I've had to leave her to find this phone. There's only Mrs Thompson there with her.'

'I'll come now,' she said, and with her great-aunt thanking her profusely, quite out of character, she replaced the earpiece back on its hook.

Her nerves had begun fluttering. Even so, she felt cynical. After all these years, her mother wanted her. When had she ever been wanted? James was the one her mother had turned to, ironically the one who had never returned the love she'd showered on him, yearning only to get away, while she, until recently, had stayed on, knowing how little she had ever been wanted. Now, with Jamie missing, Mother wanted her!

Even in this crisis, her half-brother provoked no affection in her; concern, perhaps, but no aching fear for his safety. What did frighten her was the possible parallel of his fate with Jonathan's. What if the same had happened to Jonathan – or worse?

All these months, and not a word. Not even to his colleagues. It was as though he'd washed his hands of them all. And who knew where he might be? He could be safe in England, or could have been sent abroad immediately for all any of them knew. This was what was happening now – with hardly any prior training, men were being sent out to fight, needed only to fill the numbers lost. It was horrific.

Perhaps she could have found out. But the manner of his going had brought the pride up in her. She would not beg in seeking him. She might have contacted his parents – their address was in his file from when he first joined the newspaper as a junior reporter ten years before. Yet she couldn't bring herself to do so. She didn't know them and they didn't know her. And she refused to reveal her private feelings to strangers – in a way it seemed akin to begging, and she did not beg; never had begged. Yet deep in her heart she knew she was wrong.

There was nothing for her to do but hope that a letter might eventually arrive saying all was well. She tried to console herself with that, but it was hard. Then had come the bad dreams, beginning after that first time she'd stood at London Docks: of men being carried down from a great ship, and one of the dead laid at her feet turning out to be Jonathan. The precious tears, so long withheld, would run hot down her cheeks. Yet as she awoke, it was to find that she was not crying, the tears only in the dream. The dreams varied, of course, but always drifted towards the same ending: Jonathan lying dead at her feet, her crying bitterly, only to awake dry-eyed.

'Please, bring him home safe,' she prayed in the taxicab taking her towards Approach Road. The prayer was not for James but for Jonathan. She had not once thought to pray for James.

She paid the cabbie and hurried down the diamond-patterned slate-tiled front path with its brick edging, and ran up the short flight of stone steps to the front door as quickly as her narrow skirt allowed. Below her, at the foot of the basement steps, Mrs Thompson, a person who could get more words into one minute than most managed in five, gazed up at her.

'We've 'ad a terrible time with your mum, poor woman. The doctor should be 'ere any minute – to give 'er some medicine to quieten 'er. This terrible news 'as fair sent 'er off 'er 'ead. I'm so sorry about your brother. Terrible. What a performance we've 'ad.'

There was no time to reply as the housemaid opened the door hardly had she reached it. She must have been watching out for her.

'Where is my mother?' Sara enquired, stepping into the narrow hall as the basement door closed below, Mrs Thompson also going indoors.

The girl's mouth opened to reply but Sarah Morris was already leaning over the bannisters, having somehow managed to get herself up that one flight of stairs to Harriet. Her small, lined face peered down into the dimness below.

'Your mother's up here in her room. Hurry!'

She had expected to find her mother perhaps face down

on her bed weeping, or pacing the floor wringing her hands. She was not prepared for what she did see.

A small wild animal, her mother looked like. She was crouching by the window of the front bedroom, a kitchen knife clutched in her hand, the beige wall behind her stained with vermilion streaks, the beige flowered curtains ripped, the stiff, heavily starched lace curtains splashed by blood.

'My God – what's she done to herself?'

'She just went mad. I couldn't stop her.'

Great-Aunt Sarah's voice was high from the situation she had been forced to face. 'She ran down to the kitchen. Before either of us could stop her, she grabbed the kitchen knife off Mrs Thompson and began stabbing at herself. We tried to get it off her. Mrs Thompson got her hand cut. I gashed my arm.'

For the first time, Sara noticed the fresh bandage wrapped about her great-aunt's arm.

Her mother was still crouching as though at bay, her expression that of a hunted animal.

'Mum . . . put it down.' Sara made a small attempt to move towards her but received a terrified snarl in return. The knife wavered threateningly towards more self-inflicted wounds.

Sara straightened up, helpless. 'How could she do such a thing? What are we going to do? She's bleeding.'

'Not as bad as it looks,' Sarah Morris said unsteadily. 'I don't think she's done herself too much harm. But she won't let us near her to clean her up. If I try, like you just tried, she threatens to cut herself again.'

Sara stood transfixed at the sight her mother presented. There were cuts on the face, not deep, more scratches than anything, but still seeping blood that without treatment gave a frightening aspect. More long shallow cuts on her left arm dribbled blood and her blue flowered summer dress was stained and ripped by ineffectual slashing. But it was the look in her eyes that frightened Sara the most – wild and staring, as though her wits had gone completely.

'She's been standing there by the window ever since I telephoned you,' her Great-Aunt supplied shakily. 'She said she wanted you, so Mrs Thompson stayed here while I found a telephone. I sent Ethel for the doctor. He's arranging an ambulance now, and some people to come to get her away. I can't cope, Sara. I've had enough. We're waiting for him now.'

Even as she spoke, the doorbell jangled. Ethel, the housemaid, ran for the door, and they heard the doctor's enquiring voice as she let him in.

Harriet had heard him too. Her eyes switched in the direction of the door. *She knows enough to know what is happening*, Sara thought, hopefully. Her wits hadn't gone that completely.

'Don't let him in!' The hiss broke from Harriet's lips. Her eyes sought Sara's. 'Come here,' she hissed. 'Next to me. Push him away if he comes near me. He tried to kill my Jamie. But I won't let him. Come here, I said!'

Sara took a deep breath. It was like pacifying a child as she went towards her. But it wasn't a child, it was a mad-woman wielding a naked knife, finely sharpened, ready for cutting meat. Would that blade rip through her own flesh in a moment or two? She forced herself to continue walking. When she came within arm's reach, her mother's free hand darted out, caught her wrist, and with surprising strength dragged her forward.

'You'll protect me. Won't you?' Still that grating hiss, totally unrecognisable as her mother's voice.

'Yes, Mum, of course I will,' Sara said as evenly as she could. The blood on her mother's hand felt sticky on her wrist.

'He wants to kill my Jamie. My poor little Jamie. But he won't kill you. Not his own daughter. Not his flesh. I won't let him take me or my Jamie down to Hell. Oh, my poor little Jamie . . .'

There seemed a moment when the wildness melted, and awareness of time and place returned. 'Missing . . . Sara, don't let him be dead. Don't let them kill my poor Jamie, my little boy . . .'

The wail died away. They could hear the doctor's tread on the stairs, and several others. Beneath the tousle of greying hair that still showed fading strands of auburn, the grey eyes grew suddenly alarmed, then angry. The face turned up to Sara's contorted.

'What're you doing here? Get away from me. I don't want you here!'

'You said you wanted me, Mother.'

'Yes.' Anger in its turn died. Was there a hint of sanity in those eyes? But no, more the crafty sanity of the insane, the mind thinking, but on another plane, in another time.

'That's right – I wanted you. Can't push him downstairs again on my own. Not strong enough any more. You do it.

Mustn't let him take me away with him. He says he will. He tells me in my dreams. Because, you see, I killed him – your father. He's been waiting for me ever since. I always thought it was an accident, but it wasn't, was it? You see, I was glad he was dead. I told no one I was glad, so I must have wanted to kill him. If you stay here, he won't . . .'

She broke off as the doctor came into the room, a nurse with him as well as another man to give any assistance needed. Harriet's grey eyes had opened wide as the doctor came forward with slow confidence, one hand out, his deep voice soothing, requesting the knife.

'No-o . . .' Her voice rose upward on the vowel. 'Sara – he wants to kill me. You mustn't let him.'

She seemed to have forgotten she still held a knife. It clattered to the floor as she let go of Sara to place both hands over her face in self-protection.

They were able to overcome her gently enough and bear her to the bed, the doctor already easing a phial between her lips, the nurse gently binding her arms with a roll of bandage so that she could not flail about. But she seemed suddenly weakened even before the potion took hold; again appeared not to know what was happening, staring about as though in a strange place as they gently helped her, wilting, down the stairs to where an ambulance was already drawn up outside.

Sarah Morris followed them down, awkward with her arthritic knees, but Sara couldn't move. Her smart suit besmeared by blood from her mother's cuts, she stood rooted to the spot. Tears were welling up, great, heaving sighs of them. Angrily she forced them down.

If she was going to weep, it would not be for her mother, a woman who had made her what she was: cold, withdrawn, a woman who could turn away the man she loved – yes, she knew that now, with absolute certainty – *loved,* yet too frightened, too conditioned by a loveless existence and one love that had been a lie – she knew that now, too – to reveal the emotions churning inside her.

She would not weep for a woman who hadn't given one thought to her all these years that did not carry a weight of loathing. She'd done nothing to warrant it except to be the daughter of a man her mother had loathed. No, she wouldn't cry for her mother. She couldn't hate her, but she wouldn't cry for her either.

Through the open window, her mother's cries were wafting, weakened by what she had been administered, but enough to bring faces to windows and street doors to witness the sight of a madwoman being taken away to an asylum, now bound and doped.

# Chapter Twenty-nine

'I mean no offence, Sara dear, but I can look after myself still.'

Sarah Morris smiled with staid serenity into the anxious blue eyes of her great-niece in the parlour of what was now her large and empty home, since Harriet would never enter it again.

They had just returned from a visit to her, though they might as well not have bothered for all the notice Harriet had taken of them. Most of the time she was engaged in talking to Jamie – Jamie aged something between two and eight years old, depending upon how she saw him at that moment. It wrung Sara's heart to watch her, even though there was some relief in that she seemed content most of the time with her little Jamie, oblivious to much else.

James had been officially listed a prisoner of war, somewhere in Germany; hopefully the letters Great-Aunt Sarah had written to him would reach him, given time. But Harriet seemed not to comprehend any of this, merely sighed and smiled at the little boy she remembered. Nor did she weep so often these days. It was as though her memory had obliterated all the ugly things, the unkind and hurtful things of her life. She no longer spoke to her first husband, but to Matthew, usually to tell him how baby Jamie was doing. It was heartbreaking to watch.

It was like entering another world unconnected to the one outside, where nurses moved untouched by strange noises, not quite human, from unseen parts of the asylum, and shrouded figures moved absently along corridors, through wards, up stairways.

Harriet was usually to be found sitting by the window in the small room the family had clubbed together to provide, appalled by the condition she had been reduced to. She would be conversing with the pane in which she no doubt saw her own reflection as that of her little boy, her Jamie, her hands moving continuously in conversation with him or with Matthew about him.

It was a relief to return to the real world when the visitors' bell rang hollowly through the green-tiled wards and corridors of the asylum; a relief to come back to Approach Road and to sanity.

In the weak afternoon sunshine of late October, slanting in through the window of her parlour, Sarah Morris's small shrunken figure was as stick-straight as ever as she shook her head at her great-niece's suggestion of moving in to look after her.

'I may be getting on in years but I've all my faculties. Up here,' she tapped her temple, 'as well as bodily. And apart from a little arthritis here and there, I can look after myself well enough.'

'But the house is so big now. The whole of the upstairs is empty with you unable to go up there easily.'

'I'm well looked after by Mrs Thompson and Ethel.

Ethel keeps it all nice and clean and tidy up there. And I don't think I care for lodgers – strangers, I mean. I'm not hard up for money now, and I don't intend to be a burden to anyone. Least of all you, Sara.'

Her voice died away as she gazed around the parlour at all the treasured things belonging to her and her sister, most of them Victorian: fussy ornaments under glass domes; pictures; framed sepia photos of dead relations ranged regimentally along the sideboard among the lighter, newer snaps of her great-nephews and -nieces – Clara and Annie's children on the beach at Southend or Margate. Her grey eyes followed the flower-patterned wallpaper; the tassled embroidered runner across the marble mantelpiece, the tassles and embroidery done with her own hands, once so skilled but now bent and deformed by arthritis; the heavy lace at the window and flowered draw curtains. Her smile revealed her quiet pleasure in it all, her acceptance of years numbered now, perhaps in just single figures.

'Besides,' she added slowly, meaningfully, 'I wouldn't want to spoil what you've got in mind. I've no intention of standing in the way of that.'

'In the way of what?' Her great-aunt often had a way of speaking in riddles.

Sarah Morris's smile grew shrewd. 'You forget, I'm very good at knowing people's minds. My sister, Mary, your Gran, used to say I had second sight. That made me laugh. I merely manage to see what a lot of people miss because they're too busy with themselves to see other people. When I look at you, my dear, I do see a little beyond my nose. Those blue eyes of yours are yearning for someone. Not for your stepfather. For someone else.'

'My stepfather?'

'He was more than that to you, wasn't he? It wasn't his dominance over you. No one could dominate you unless you wished it. You gave your heart willingly enough, didn't you? And you're still feeling you have to continue with it even now he's gone.'

She nodded as Sara made to protest. 'I've eyes in my head, Sara, and a brain sharp enough to interpret what I see.'

Sara's face flared scarlet. 'I'm sure you must be confused . . .'

'It was made known, Sara. James in his innocence told your mother of seeing Matthew coming from your room at night. Your mother came to us quite distraught and not knowing what to believe.'

'I didn't know.' Her cheeks had grown raging hot with the shame of exposure after years of thinking her secret safe, hers and Matthew's, but her great-aunt seemed not concerned by it.

'It's old history now, dear. Best forgotten. There's another now. Is it that young man on your paper who took you out once? I know, you have something you need to do but you're afraid of asking permission – not so much of others but of yourself. You had better ask yourself if your feelings for that young man are strong enough to take you through fire and water. Strong enough for you to forget about Matthew.'

Sara stared at her. All these years of knowing Jonathan,

she had never mentioned his name to anyone outside the *Graphic,* yet her great-aunt seemed to know all about it.

'Who are you talking about?' She tested and saw that shrewd smile again.

'There is a young man, isn't there? And you love him very much, but he's gone away, hasn't he? Did he go off to the war? And you've lost touch with him? And you want to find out where he is. I think you should.'

Mollified, Sara had an overwhelming need to confide, to unburden herself. Great-Aunt Sarah was the only one she could tell, and not just because there was no one else – if a hundred people were gathered around her, her great-aunt would be the one she'd choose to open her heart to.

In an instant she was pouring out her secrets, the love she'd held in for so long flooding out: Jonathan's outwardly cynical proposal which she now realised had been the only way he'd had of expressing it, covering his own secret sense of unprotectedness; her stupid and misguided rejection, sending him away from her – it all came out.

At some point while she spoke, it seemed easier to come and lay her head in her great-aunt's lap, maybe to obviate the chance of eye contact and thus self-awareness, and with the woman's small crabbed, vein-laced hand smoothing her dark hair, the words came spontaneously.

Her story finally ceased, her great-aunt said quietly, 'I think you've overcome your indecisions, haven't you, dear?'

Sara knew she had. Since that first day at the quayside with the unloading of the wounded, she had teetered on the boon she'd intended to ask of Mackenzie. One assignment after the other had followed: covering the German zeppelin raids on the City that had brought the war to the very doorstep of civilians; the hard and exacting war work carried out by women in their men's absence; the stoicism of those bereaved by the unprecedented loss of life all along the Western Front; the way women were coping with food shortages and haphazard rationing – all of that should have given her hardly time to think of anything but the job in hand. Yet still, after four months, that one unasked request nagged her. And now it nagged no longer.

'I know what I have to do now,' she said quietly, and felt the pressure of Great-Aunt Sarah's clawed fingers upon her head adding their own approval and reassurance.

Forgetting to nibble on her third Bath Oliver biscuit, Clara frowned at her niece in disbelief.

'You must be out of your mind. You're not serious, surely? How can you even think of such a thing?'

'Of course she's not serious, you duffer! It's just a silly whim.'

Annie, frowning in her turn, hadn't touched the plate of assorted biscuits Sara had put out for her two aunts.

On occasion they would pop in after a bout of shopping, Sara's neat little flat being convenient to Holborn and other areas of nice respectable London stores, taking the chance, of course, that she'd be at home. This Saturday afternoon had been one of those occasions.

'What would your mother say if she knew what you're up to?' Annie was saying. 'Not as she knows anything much these days, poor Harriet. It was the shock of James that sent her off her head. If she knew you wanted to go carting off to France too, she'd have a fit.'

*She'd probably put her hands together*, Sara thought with momentary bitterness. *She always wanted me dead anyway.* She had said as much.

Aloud she said stubbornly, 'I am serious, Aunt Annie. I have to go out there.'

'But why, in heaven's name?' cried Clara.

'Why not?'

She wasn't prepared to tell them why. Only Great-Aunt Sarah knew why, and that was only from what her own sharp old brain had told her, for nothing specific had been said. Anyway, hoping to find Jonathan in that huge area of conflict, among all those men, could prove utterly futile in the end. Perhaps it was all just a silly notion, but she knew she had to try.

Sara had finally swallowed her pride, had written to his parents and found out where he was: with the Third British Army somewhere in France between Arras and Ypres. It was a logical step, as far as she was concerned, to follow him.

She would be following in the footsteps of many other women, going out there as Voluntary Aid Detachments, Mostly titled or wealthy ladies able to afford to, for they were expected to finance themselves. Anxious to do their share helping the troops, they would procure a private ambulance and take it across, driving it near to the front line to ferry the wounded from dressing stations and field hospital tents back to clearing stations behind the lines. Frowned on by General Haig, who thought this unnecessary risk to civilians should be discouraged, they went nevertheless. Brave, selfless women who in peacetime had perhaps been weak, self-centred women of wealthy husbands, or widows of means safely cossetted by servants and a paid companion, they now saw sights no gentlewoman should ever look upon, yet they didn't shrink from what they saw as their duty.

Sara intended to do much the same, but to bring back first-hand stories from men who had fought and been wounded; stories of their courage and bravery for the benefit and morale of the loved ones left behind. Only good news, of course. Certainly nothing to undermine the fortitude of those back home. She was under strict instructions on that score.

It had taken endless argument to get Mackenzie to agree to let her go. Now, in February 1917, after four months of cajoling and entreaty, he'd finally given in. She would become a foreign correspondent of sorts for the *London Graphic* – much against his better judgment, he stated, and although she had proved herself time and again to be a competent reporter and journalist, he had added a proviso.

'You go no further than Calais or Boulogne. I'm not having it said that I let you risk your neck being sent too near the front line. It could alter overnight and then you'd be cut off. Where will I be if I have to report that sort of thing to the directors? That I was responsible for sending a woman into danger? Get your stories from hospitals away from the front line. I can understand nurses and VADs going out. Doing a grand job for our lads. But you . . . I'd

send a man if we had any half as good as you. We badly
need stories. But a woman . . .'

How could she tell him the truth behind her valiant offer?
How could she share her insane hope of finding Jonathan
somewhere out there in that no-man's-land? How she even
imagined she'd find him among all those thousands of men
was beyond her own comprehension, but she had to try.
She refused to let herself think of failure.

Now she raised her chin stubbornly as Aunt Annie
continued on her worthy tirade.

'I'll tell you why not,' Annie was saying, bringing Sara
out of her reverie to the challenge she had almost forgotten
she'd issued.

'I'll tell you why not, Sara. It's because two wrongs
never do make a right. Your brother volunteering like he
did – that was very wrong. He didn't give a fig for how his
mother felt. I heard how she was so devastated when he
said he was going off, and I felt for her, I really did. Now
you're doing the selfsame thing. No one in their right mind
should volunteer, knowing they could be killed out there.'

*Jonathan volunteered*, Sara thought grimly, *and I drove
him to it. I can only try to make amends. It's what I have
to do.*

'Neither of you has stopped to think how your family
feels,' Annie was going on. 'Too young to care. Too caught
up and full of your own wisdom, such as it is. Us older
ones have lived enough years to know what wisdom is.
James never did have much of that about him, but you . . .
Your Uncle George has been taken away from his family
to fight. It's only because the business must be kept going

by *someone* that your Uncle John is exempted from going. Both me and your Aunt Clara have had our sons taken from us. They're out there fighting in France, and Lord knows if they'll ever come back . . .'

'Annie – don't!' Clara stopped in the act of taking yet another Bath Oliver. She had long since given up trying to stay as slender as her sister, surrendering herself to her inherited chubbiness. If only, she often sighed, she were a few inches taller it wouldn't be quite so horribly noticeable.

'It's bad enough,' she burst out, 'having my boys taken away from me, without you talking about them never coming back. I know they'll come back. I have to make myself believe they'll come back.'

'Of course they will,' Annie said tersely. 'Don't go on so.'

Dismissing her sister from her mind, she turned back to her niece, taking up her point again.

'You need your head examined, Sara, you really do. Your duty's to those at home, not to men you don't even know. Going off sacrificing yourself, and for what? That paper of yours, that's what. It's that paper of yours has talked you into this caper. I feel almost like going and having a word with them. With your mother in that mental asylum, you're all alone in the world. Who's to guard over you?'

Sara almost laughed. 'I am nearly twenty-three, Aunt Annie. I live on my own. I earn my own money. I pay my own rent. I can take care of myself.'

That was how her great-aunt had survived for years, taking care of herself, her own mistress. It was on her great-aunt that Sara modelled herself, and was proud to do so. But now she longed to belong to someone else, and to hell and damnation with pride.

Annie sniffed. 'That's a matter of opinion. This ridiculous mission you're planning proves you can't. I for one think you're completely mad. You'll end up like your mother if you're not careful – in a lunatic asylum.'

# Chapter Thirty

Aunt Annie was right. It had been a mad idea, she realised that now. It was now high summer – she had been in France nearly six months, telegraphing report after report back to Mackenzie – and she was no nearer to finding the man she sought. Having got herself as near to the area Jonathan's parents had given her, the chaos of war made it like looking for a needle in a haystack, as a journalist she had not realised the enormity of what lay before her.

By the end of August, a hundred thousand men had already been lost, the wounded a continuous stream passing through the hospitals and clearing stations where she made her reports. In peacetime the corn would be ripe and dusty brown by now, spattered by bright red poppies. Corn and poppies had long since been blasted away; the only red, she gathered, tucked too well back behind the lines to see for herself, would be the red of blood, all else churned to a mud brown.

All summer it hadn't stopped raining. Fields and woods had been shell blasted to oceans of mud, the men brought into the clearing stations caked in it, proclaiming the fearful conditions in which they fought. Mud, blood, the stench of wounds, bodies unwashed from weeks in trenches – all filled her nostrils as she moved among the men interviewing those who would be interviewed, taking down messages for loved ones back home – nearly always the same message: 'Got a Blighty one. Tell 'em I'll be seeing them soon. Thank God!'

A prayer of thanks for timely deliverance. An arm, leg, or both legs gone, the speaker perhaps confined forever to a wheelchair, his thoughts were not on how he'd survive with no job for him – realisation of that would come later – but that he was going home, out of this bloody hell forever.

Cleaned up, patched up, half-dead or half-alive, lice-ridden, stinking of trench-foot, that distorted prayer of thanks would still be offered up for being out of it, for being still alive.

There were others, many, who cursed being alive, prayed even now for death: the blinded; the maimed, already visualising the fate that awaited them at home; the shell-shocked, who hardly knew where they were, much less had the faculty to offer up a prayer of deliverance.

Sara's heart ached for them all; turned over in fear of Jonathan's fate. A new British attack had begun several days before in an attempt to break the German right flank at Ypres. Was he in the thick of that? But there was no way of knowing.

The worst of the fighting was going on around a ruined village called Passchendaele. Sara could hear the heavy thud of artillery even from here, a place just east of St Omer, where she had managed to get herself on a VAD transport van to a small clearing station.

She did her best to keep out of the way of the snarls of

overtaxed surgeons and the irritable tuts of harassed nurses, but the VADs were kind and appreciated her assistance with the mundane jobs she felt compelled to help with, seeing the conditions under which they had to work. It also gave her more chance to talk to the wounded. Whether she had developed a knack or naturally drew them to confide in her, she didn't know. All she knew was that, as it had been at London Docks, the abject trust some of the men had in her to carry their stories back home humbled her. Perhaps it was this that allowed her to listen with more sympathy than she ever suspected she possessed.

In all this, how could she dare think only of herself, of this base quest for one man? Yet she couldn't help herself, hate herself though she did. Above all else there was always the question on her lips, coming between other general questions:

'Have you come across a Captain Jonathan Ward? He's somewhere in this area, I'm sure.'

How easily he could have been here in her place, coming as a war correspondent instead of fighting. Mackenzie would have willingly sent him out.

Instead he had joined up blindly with no idea of what he was going into. Few had. She'd had no real idea of the confusion these men felt about what was happening to them until that first experience on the quayside at London Docks. Even being on a newspaper, the numbers of slain coming in daily, they had only been that – just numbers, by which to be horrified in the comfort of her daily life. Even the women and children in black, the endless sight of drawn curtains, had not truly brought it home to her. Now, it was all too stark: these broken men she spoke to, this smell around her, this chaos through which she moved. Real, too, were the desperate grins of some, the hopeless jokes, the whispered assurances that they would be all right now.

'It's only part of one leg, you see. They can never take me back to fight with only part of one leg, now can they?'

She held the hand of the fair-haired Welsh boy, the stump crudely bandaged. Nineteen, he told her. Had volunteered eighteen months ago, lying about his age.

A lot of them had lied about their age. A lot of them would never grow older: lay in the ground, their seventeen, eighteen or nineteen years decaying away to become part of the world's billions-of-years-old soil. Ashes to ashes, dust to dust . . .

Sara thought momentarily of Matthew, saw again the graveside, felt the return of a pang of an old vow, childishly made. She thought of Jonathan, who, without knowing what he did, had destroyed that vow, had made her his, though he didn't know it. Would he ever know it now?

She forced herself not to think of that, to think only of this present moment. She smiled down at the boy.

'Have you a family?'

'Me mam an' dad, miss.' The accent was Welsh. 'A couple of sisters as well.'

'That's nice.'

'Me mam'll look after me. Me dad's chesty, see. He's a miner, you see. So she knows how to look after the sick well enough.'

'I'm glad.'

'Not as half as glad as I am, miss.'

A touch on her shoulder, a cultured voice, turned her attention from the lad.

'Would you lend a hand here, my dear? I simply cannot make this poor man understand that I have to move him somewhere else.'

The woman was one whom she'd come to know well these past weeks. Lady Thurber-Smith was a woman in her early forties whose husband had something to do with the Admiralty, or so Sara gathered. In normal times she would no doubt have been at home to guests, elegant in a tea gown, hair elaborately dressed, face serene as her butler brought in a silver tray for her to pour tea graciously from a silver pot.

Here she wore a harsh dun-coloured drill tunic, her hair desperately scraped back into a tight bun, her face drawn and tired, her eyes alight with that unnatural alertness of the over-stressed.

'The surgeon needs this bed, but the poor man is being quite wild and will not let me get him up. There is no one else about to help me with him.'

Sara laid a hand on the shoulder of the lad by way of apology, and hurried with the woman to a makeshift bed, a plank of wood covered by a groundsheet, a filthy pillow and a grey blanket, now in a turmoil where the man had thrashed around, resisting attempts to quieten him.

'It is this shell shock thing. He ought to be given something to quieten him, but there is nothing we can do for these cases but hope they learn eventually to control themselves.'

Sara took one look at the twisting head, the twitching arms, the phenomenon denounced by many as cowardice, and felt her sympathies go out to this victim.

She knew something of the cruelty of being misjudged – saw again a child whose mother had stormed at her in a fury of loathing, accusing her of evil deeds; that same child forced to cope alone later when her mother grew drunkenly hysterical; the trembling feeling inside when it was over; the need to cry but feeling too shaken to do so; never knowing quite where to turn, feeling it must be her fault. She hoped she knew a little of what he was going through; could perhaps give him the calming words she had so often longed for but had never received, except for those Matthew had given her. And that too had proved not what it seemed.

Quickly she crouched beside the patient – not a boy, a man, maybe with a wife and children back home, yet his face was like the face of a child in terror, his brown eyes dark and wildly staring, his mouth working, twisting, his cheek muscles flinching.

Taking one of the palsied hands in hers, resisting its efforts to jerk away, she gently and continuously caressed the back of it until she felt it relax, all the while talking to him, not demanding he calm down, but with casual conversation as though she had just met him in the street.

'I expect your family will be glad to see you home, won't they?'

She hoped as she spoke that he had a family and she hadn't made a tactless blunder. It could be so easily done. But at least he would be going home. Thurber-Smith, as she'd asked to be called, had said the man's wounds weren't too serious, an arm smashed by shrapnel – enough at least to get him home and patched up.

As she talked, the eyes became less staring, the face ceased its twisting. After a few minutes, he began to respond. His voice hoarse, his words broken and stuttering, he began talking jerkily of shells bursting around his head, of lying in the mud unable to move. His arm wouldn't do what he wanted it to do, he said. They had come for him, picked him up and brought him here on a stretcher because his legs wouldn't move either, though they had found nothing wrong with his legs. They'd gone away disgusted that he wouldn't walk for himself. The voice rose suddenly.

'But I c-couldn't! I really couldn't. I th-thought I'd lost 'em.'

The journalist in her had already begun to make mental notes of what she would write on this incident. Now she laid a quiet hand over the mouth that was beginning to work again.

'It doesn't really matter now. You can move them now, so it's all right. It was only temporary, like when a leg goes to sleep.'

'I suppose so.' He calmed. 'It was just the noise.'

'I know. But it's quiet now. Listen.'

He listened, then nodded. 'I f-feel better now.'

'Of course you do.'

'I'll be better, won't I?'

'I think so. It'll be so much easier once you're home.'

'I will g-go home, won't I?'

'Yes, of course you will.'

Unable to help herself, now that he was calmer, she asked her inevitable question, full of self as she was.

'Have you come upon anyone by the name of Captain Jonathan Ward?'

'Ward?' There was no stutter now, but she was interested only in the ring of certainty in the tone.

'Captain Ward. He made me follow him. We went out from our trench. Walking pace. Couldn't run. Mud weighed us down. Packs too. There was this house – farmhouse. Our artillery had been bombarding it. They started up again. Over our heads. Shouldn't have done, with us going over the top. Should have stopped when we made our push . . .'

His breathing was beginning to grow rapid. 'It was the n-noise. Never worried me before. I couldn't make my legs move. Captain Ward said I'd be all right, he'd keep in front of me, shield me. He got me up over the top with him. The machine guns started up and . . . I don't know w-what happened. I w-was underneath him . . . I was under . . .'

He began stammering again, but Sara couldn't wait. She was so near and so afraid. Taking his shoulders, she shook him, the worst thing she could have done to a man in his state, but sense had taken leave of her. All she knew was that she had to know. After all these months of despairing, she was so near. So near. And so terrified.

'Captain Ward. Where is he? What happened to him?'

'I th-think he's dead. He didn't move . . . Oh, Christ . . . I w-want to go home. Don't m-make me go back . . .'

'Did you see if he was picked up?' she demanded.

'Where would they have taken him? How long ago was it? Do you know where at the front it was? Exactly where?'

'Don't know. The village – Passchendaele. Flattened. Just b-bits of stone . . . Sticking up. We c-could see it. Told to take it . . . I couldn't move . . . It was all the n-noise.'

Her questions were terrifying him. He was beginning to rant and an alarmed nurse hurried to pull her away, reprimanding her for the harm she was doing, but Sara fought the clutching hands.

'Captain Ward – did they leave him behind? Tell me – please!'

'I d-d-don't know! I c-couldn't t-take the noise.'

'This is no good, young lady!' The nurse's voice was incensed. 'If you can't help us, then kindly . . .'

But Sara was already racing off between the makeshift beds beneath the damp stretched canvas of the hospital tent, skirting around the stretchers, the men with bandaged limbs sitting on stools or standing apathetically about for their turn to be seen by overworked surgeons and nurses.

Outside, the rain had dropped to a drizzle, but had it still been pouring she would not have noticed. She made towards a small group of women standing beside two vehicles, one vehicle with a white bedsheet spread across its roof, anchored to its frame and painted with a red cross, the other looking like an ordinary civilian van that in England might have delivered bread or groceries. One girl was climbing up into the so-called ambulance with its red cross, hoisting her ankle-length drill skirt to give her more movement. Sara ran up to her.

'Where are you going?' she demanded of her.

The girl paused, looking down at her. She had a pleasant, merry face, a little begrimed now. 'Are you volunteering then?'

'Yes, if I know where you are going.'

'Does it matter? It's all the same out there.'

'Can you go towards Ypres?'

'I can go in that direction. Is there someone you want to see?'

'I have to get to some village called Passchendaele,' Sara evaded.

The girl smiled. 'There's a lot of fighting going on there. You can't get near. They bring them in on stretchers as they find them and we load them aboard some way back from the front line. We're only allowed to go within a mile's distance. Even then General Haig isn't keen on us . . .'

'If you can make for Passchendaele,' Sara cut in desperately, 'I could scout around.'

'You *are* looking for someone.' The girl grinned, then nodded. 'Hop aboard.'

The van had seen better days, having received a bit of a bashing over rutted roads and across fields.

'Hope her springs don't give out on me,' said the girl who had given her name as Beatrice Heatherfield as they bumped along the few miles, the sound of gunfire growing louder, the air beginning to fill with the faint acrid tang of cordite. Sara felt her stomach going over with fear and a strange excitement, but mostly fear.

They pulled up some way behind the British lines, as was expected of them. Sara could see the shell bursts, the sound of their explosions arriving just afterwards across the distance. It all seemed so unreal, rather like watching pictures on a cinema screen. She thought of a film she'd seen – was it only the previous year? *The Birth of A Nation*, that was it. The battles of those times were so long ago as not to matter any more, and anyway, were only on celluloid, make-believe for an audience.

Here, each shell burst, each crump of gunfire, meant some life lost, flesh torn by shrapnel; each clatter of a machine gun meant a bullet in a soldier's body. There was a strange smell like burnt earth, even this far away, it was enough to sting her nostrils.

The van drew to a halt. It was raining again. The August mid-morning could have been a January dusk, the sky was so overladen with drifting smoke and heavy rain clouds. The stretcher-bearers and orderlies, their gas capes shedding water in cascades, were already bringing their charges forward. The mud clung to Sara's boots, making walking difficult and slippery, and causing a sucking sound with every step she took. From beneath the sou'wester Beatrice had handed her from the van, her hair hung from its bun like rat tails; water streamed from the mackintosh Beatrice had also given her.

Automatically she began to help the orderlies lift the half-dozen stretchers allocated to her van on board while the walking wounded waited their turn in the rain to clamber up. The same procedure was taking place with a second van already there and two official khaki-painted ambulances.

Helping as best she could, Sara took the opportunity to ask where the village of her quest was.

'A mile or two that way,' said a medical orderly, pointing south across the flat, colourless land, bereft of trees or distinguishing landmarks of any kind. 'You might almost see it from here if it weren't for the weather. But you can't go there.'

'Could an ambulance go?' she asked, breathlessly man-handling a stretcher up to the floor level of this inadequate private vehicle.

'Not this ambulance. Only military ones.'

'Can I get a lift in one?'

'You most certainly cannot. No, you ladies wait here and we bring the blokes to you. It's better that way. There's not much you can do out there.'

'But I'm looking for someone. I was told he was . . . he was hurt.' She couldn't bring herself to say killed.

The man looked sad and wise, seeing behind her expression. The look went through her, filling her with certainty about Jonathan's fate. Sara felt her heart shrink with despair at that certainty.

'If it was yesterday, miss,' the man was saying through the blur of hopelessness, 'any wounded we found is gone. Others . . . They're laid out for burial a bit further back, if we find 'em, that is. If it was before yesterday, they'll be buried by now, I should think.'

'Would you have names?' There was a sickening thumping in her throat. She saw the orderly spread his hands sympathetically.

Beatrice called to her. 'Give us a lift with this one, Sara?'

Automatically she complied, got the stretcher aboard,

hardly aware of doing it, her mind spinning, her heart pounding painfully, her breathing unnaturally fast. It was as though she were swooning, yet she remained on her feet.

'Tell me,' she cried, clutching the orderly's arm as he passed her again. 'Tell me how I can find out.'

The man pointed to a small tent nearby. 'They'll have lists. You can ask them. But it's incomplete. Always is, because . . .'

Without waiting, Sara hurried towards the tent, ignoring the pleas of the woman she had ridden there with to help get the walking wounded up into the van.

Inside the tent, wiping the rain from her face with the back of her hand, she fought to calm herself.

As the officer looked up, the two men on either side of him, one a corporal, the other a sergeant, eyeing her, surprised by her sudden appearance, she burst out: 'Do you have a Captain Ward on your list? A Captain Jonathan Ward?'

The officer recovered, his enquiry dispassionate. 'Dead or alive?'

She shook her head. 'I don't know. I just have to find him.'

'There are two lists. One for dead. One for wounded.' The officer looked tired, his tone that of a man who seemed to have given up on normality.

'Can you look in both of them?' Sara asked, trembling at the idea of that ultimate list.

'It's a tall order, ma'am. D'you know how many we've . . .'

'I don't care! Just look! Please! Try yesterday's list.' It was the only thing she could think of, and that a forlorn hope.

Whatever the expression on her face, the officer stared for only a second longer, then bent down and brought a battered attaché case out from under the folding table at which he sat. This he undid and drew out several thick, rolled wads of paper. Dividing them into three, he gave one batch to the sergeant, another to the corporal, taking some himself.

'Name?' He spat out the command.

Sara smothered a stupified feeling as she answered. The bundles of paper – each sheet of each roll, a couple of feet in length, had to hold several hundred names – brought home more vividly than any sight she had yet seen, just how many in this one area of conflict on the one day had been killed and wounded.

'We'll go through the dead first. Mind, they're not all here. Some might have been . . .' He stopped short of saying blown to pieces, said instead, '. . . not found yet. Or captured. Those we'll hear of in time.'

*Please*, she prayed. *If he's not wounded, let him be captured. But not dead, please God, not dead.*

Yet these were not the only lists, she knew. All along the line would be tents such as this, each holding an attaché case full of names. How could so many men be laid low, in a single day, and all the days of this war so far – how could it be?

The fingers of the men in front of her ran swiftly down the names; when they came to the end of each sheet, they were licked for turning to the next. Sara waited. How long had she stood there? Time had no meaning. It could be all for nothing. The fast-moving fingers could easily miss the name. The sheet with Jonathan's could be the very last one. Or the list bearing his name might not be here at all, but in some other tent. If so, how many tents must she visit, and could she go or be allowed to go through them all? It was an impossibility. She had come here on a fool's errand, from the very start. She knew that now.

'Jonathan Ward, Captain.' The triumphant shout so startled her that she hardly heard the rest, his regiment, his number. All that rang in her head was the name. All she could hear was the last words: 'Might still be at the field hospital.'

He was alive! Thank God! 'How badly injured is he?' she heard herself say, as though she were asking the time of day.

'Couldn't say. The field hospital for this area is back there, to the rear, straight as you go.'

Whether she thanked them for their efforts, she couldn't remember afterwards. How she got back to the VAD ambulance she couldn't remember either. She saw Beatrice climbing up into the driving seat, the wounded all aboard. Beatrice paused, seeing her running towards her. Her young face was no longer pleasant, but peevish.

'Come back now all the work's done?'

It was then she saw Sara's face and her tone changed. 'What is it? Is it the man you were looking for?'

'They said he might still be at the field hospital.'

Beatrice brightened with relief. 'That's where we're

taking this lot. I've to come back here for another load. I can leave you there.'

That was where she found him. Or was at least informed by one of the nursing sisters that he was somewhere, she wasn't sure where. Her face was grave as she looked up from scanning her register after Sara had explained her purpose there.

'I'm sorry. It says he had broken ribs. A rib pierced the lung, and . . .'

The world had begun to spin. Sara felt herself sway, and clung on to the sister's arm for support as she was guided to a chair and lowered gently on to it.

All this, only to find him dead. All this, never to see him again. All this . . . all her life . . . She knew now how much she had loved him, now that she had lost him.

A wet towel was being pressed to her forehead, its cold shock bringing her to herself. Smelling salts under her nose made her gasp, jerking her head up. Her blue eyes met the searching grey ones of the sister.

'What do I do?' she implored, her voice small, a child seeking love, any love, knowing there was none. 'Where can I go?'

'You can go and sit by him. It's a matter of waiting to see if he survives the operation. But I must warn you . . .'

It was enough. Sara's eyes opened wide. 'He's alive?'

The woman's smile was sad, she saw that too. And the words – *if he survives* – brought first a moment of panic, then a sense of urgency, but more a feeling of fate, that she must be there to whisper her love before the end came. It was imperative that he knew.

'Yes, I understand,' she whispered.

She was taken to where his truckle bed lay in a corner by the tent flap. *Where they can bear his body away quickly,* came the thought as she stared down at the grey face, the face that had once been mobile with cynical humour; the face that had annoyed her on so many occasions, now so still with death upon it. To see him again, but like this, tore through her entire being.

Given a low rickety stool, she sat down. How long she sat there she couldn't tell. It seemed an eternity. Someone brought her a mug of hot strong tea with hardly any milk and very little sugar. She took a sip because it was required of her. It was bitter and she put it aside. And all the time, the grey face did not change, nor did the eyes open.

'Look at me, Jonathan, just once. Just once more,' she whispered. She wanted to kiss those eyes, to wake them, but was afraid the kiss would in some manner fix them forever closed. It seemed hours that she sat watching him, watching for some flicker of his eyelids, some twitch of his lips. People moved about the huge tent, men in faded dressing gowns, nurses inspecting patients, helpers taking away slops in buckets, replacing them. The light began to fade. A lady volunteer worker came round lighting oil lamps that cast a sickly glow over the rows of beds. Now and again a harassed cry issued from one of the beds, short, sharp, terrified; or a moan as a patient turned over in a fever of restlessness. The lamps' wicks plopped and spluttered.

Did she see Jonathan's eyelids flutter or was it just a trick of flickering light? It must be the latter, for there was no more movement after that one moment of hope. Yet she had been so sure . . .

Outside it had grown dark. A nurse came with the surgeon. They moved her away to make a brief examination. The surgeon straightened up and looked directly at Sara.

'Are you a relative?'

'No.' There was a strange expression on the man's face. She was sure, then, that it was over. 'I'm . . . his fiancée.'

The surgeon nodded. The strange look was kind, almost a smile, but was it a smile of sympathy?

'Looks more encouraging than we'd dared hope,' he said slowly. The smile had begun to broaden. 'He might even wake up in a little while and say hullo to you.'

Sara sat a long time after they had left, the surgeon's words of hope in her ears still.

It was very quiet. In a way the small restless movements of other patients accentuated that quietness. Somewhere, a long way off it seemed, someone was playing a mouth organ. Single notes, lonely, plaintive, echoing notes, hanging on the air, the tune recognisable: 'Keep the Home Fires Burning'. A sad, haunting melody, written to lift up the soul, but more likely to sadden it with longing when played on a mouth organ by someone lost in this wilderness.

Perhaps it was the song, perhaps the peace on the still face beside her, but inside her breast came a movement, a slow surging upwards. This man she loved. This man she would tell her love to and there would be no going back.

The surge inside her had become more intense. She had felt this before, many times, but always it would die, evaporate, leaving her as dry as a desert. It reached her throat, as often it had before, but now came on, steadily, steadily. This man was her life, would always be her life.

Her eyes were prickling and, with a deep, slow spasm of indrawn breath, the tears of life welled over Sara's lower lids and fell gently down her cheeks.